ISLE OF THE FORGOTTEN

THE DARKNESS SERIES
BOOK TWO

KATHRYN BREAUX

Isle

of the

Forgotten

Title: Isle of the Forgotten

Series Name: The Darkness Series

Author: Kathryn Breaux

Ebook ISBN: 979-8-9912957-5-8 || Paperback ISBN: 979-8-9912957-3-4 || Hardback ISBN: 979-8-9912957-4-1

Developmental Editing by The Blue Couch Edits

Copy/Line Editing by Emily Andriko-Peace

Proofreading by Kenlee Flowers

Cover & Dust Jacket Design by Selkkie Designs – www.selkkiedesigns.com

Map illustration by Worldwyrm Maps

CONTENT NOTES

This book is intended for mature audiences and contains sensitive content that may be upsetting to some. You must be over 18 to read Isle of the Forgotten.

For more information, please visit www.kathrynbreauxwrites.com for more information and a list of warnings.

To those who once let the darkness win.

To those who are still fighting.

And to those who are ready to bite back.

CAMMON
Northern
Training
Camp
CITA
DARAMVEER
SHADO
N
S
E
W

RIS
MOUNTAINS
ISLE
BRINKYM
ANDORWOOD

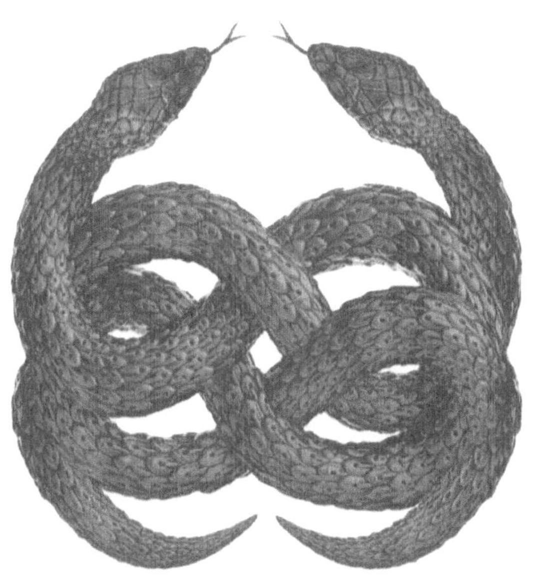

CHAPTER 1

A beautifully vicious voice taunts me, day and night.

The voice whispers of threats. Of temptations to give in.

I'm tired—tired of running and tired of hiding. But I'm stuck in my worst nightmare, and there is no way out without *him*. I'm waiting desperately for him to find me.

Kalix wants me, and she's patient in the darkness—listening and waiting for her turn to take over. Time passes differently here —wherever here is—and every second I remain stuck in this misery, I feel myself slipping. Wanting the bitter taste of madness to stain the very depths of my soul.

Anything that distracts me from what lurks in the obscurity of my personal hell.

I think I'm dreaming—I must be—but this feels too real.

Silas hasn't called my name, but I wait and listen—just like Kalix—for my chance to escape.

Except, I'm running out of time.

With each passing moment, it gets harder to ignore her offers. I hear screams in the distance, just as desperate as mine to be freed, but I can't make out who they belong to.

I'm slipping.

I'm fading into the darkness of my own mind, and I'm lost—so very *lost*. Barely a whisper leaves my dry throat, and I crumble.

Silas.

Help.

The trees hum in my presence, as if they are on my side, helping me remain hidden from the Great Wiitch. She has stalked me since I escaped her grasp, which feels like weeks ago. The breeze calls to me but never whispers the word I so desperately need to hear—my name from the lips of the person I love.

My kingdom burns around me again, an awful reminder of what my future will look like if I can't stop this. If we can't stop Carobon.

I crouch behind a tree to take a moment's break, my lungs burning from the falling ash and the lack of rest I've allowed myself. My legs are covered in scratches from the sharp brush, and hot blood drips down my legs. Creatures move around me—nearly invisible, except for the faintest glimmer of light when they approach, like a subtle distortion of reality. A slithering sound disrupts the silence every now and then, chilling me to the bone.

If I stay still for too long, Kalix or the invisible creatures will find me, so I propel my aching body forward. My feet ache against the uneven feel of the sharp rocks as I move over the rough earth, desperate to find anything to conceal me for a second's break. A murder of crows follows me nearly everywhere, and the beating of their wings fills the space like battle drums.

"Briar, my darling," an angelic voice whispers, traveling over the breeze. "I won't hurt you, my child."

I cover my ears, refusing to listen to her lies.

"Why do you fear the one who can bring you greatness?"

With each passing day, resisting the call to join her gets harder. She promises that my suffering will end, but I have to be strong. I have to get home without giving in to temptation.

But I'm struggling. My chest feels like it's fractured, my eyes are bloodshot, and I can feel myself fading.

The breeze calls once more, a gurgled whisper in the darkness pushing me to continue—to move forward—even though each step feels as if it's my last. A patch of trees moves in the wind, and I squint my eyes, my eyelids slowly blinking away the grit.

It can't be.

I'm dreaming, and this is just a cruel illusion she has cast once more.

Everything here is a cruel daydream.

A figure stands in the tightly overgrown trees. No cloak hangs over its body. No freakishly long arms hang by its side. It's tall and moves with a familiar, strong grace. The figure before me appears almost translucent, like it's not quite here. Each pounding step echoes in my ears as the figure races closer, its body growing larger as the distance between us closes. I take a step back, afraid of what or who charges my way, when the breeze halts—the calm before the storm. A strong gust of icy wind snaps my hair in all directions, blinding me for a moment, and my gut twists, like roots beneath a large tree.

Unable to move, I slam my eyes closed when I hear it.

The voice.

His voice.

"Briar."

A tall figure emerges from the darkness before me, like a hurricane of madness. I blink through the constant stinging that pains my dry eyes and try to focus. The ash filling the gloomy sky makes it nearly impossible to see far in the distance. I wipe my eyes and cover my ears, trying to ignore the call I'm hearing. It's not real, anyway. Kalix has done this countless times—projecting things that aren't real.

The voice continues, and each scream sounds more desperate than the last.

The wind continues to swirl, causing the ash to blind me again. The figure grows closer, and instead of fear, a calmness floods my system that I can't explain.

Maybe this is my body finally accepting defeat.

"Briar."

The desperate sound hits my ears once more, and I lift my head higher in an attempt to see what's coming. My mouth parts, and through the ash and pain, I see a strong male body rushing toward me, like a storm moving across the black sea. The rough ground doesn't slow him, and he charges toward me with a warrior's grace.

Oh Gods.

Silas's strong body moves toward me, unlike how I left him —broken and mangled. He rushes forward—unharmed and determined—as if he's been searching for me. A black fire smolders behind his piercing green eyes, capable of turning a city to ruin.

"Briar!" he screams, trying to gain my attention again through the darkness.

I wipe at my eyes, unable to believe what I'm seeing, and tears pour from my eyes like falling rain.

It's a trick.

It's Kalix messing with me once more. I attempt to stand to run in the opposite direction, and my legs give out under me. The ground rips at my knees—like claws tearing at my flesh—and fear encases me like a panicked fog.

Another shout fills the air with desperation, and I listen to the voice.

I feel his presence pull at me like a flare in the blackened night, and my soul blazes with a desperate yearning to reach his. I push with everything that I have left and stand on shaky legs, feeling the blood trickle down my legs. I grasp the tree behind me, the rough bark scratching my palms, and prop my shoulder against it, grateful for its sturdiness.

"I'm… here." My voice is hoarse and barely audible through the ripping winds.

"I'm here."

The shouts from Silas attract unwanted attention, and I notice black roots—similar to those that adorn my hands—begin to stir beneath the brush. Kalix edges closer with every second I linger, and fear bubbles in my body like boiling water.

Silas pauses, his piercing green eyes scanning the grey surroundings as I lift my arm. My muscles scream against the motion, but I bite my lip—almost immediately tasting blood from my cracked lips.

Black and crimson clouds begin to roll over the sky, and a hurricane of crows swoop down looking for me. Their black wings slap against the air, deafening all other sound around me for a moment. A shadowy haze fills the sky, dimming all light around me and letting darkness threaten to take over.

I lift my arm higher, attempting to take a step away from the tree shielding me from plain sight.

My leg trembles under my weight, but I grind my teeth and take another step.

There is only one person I need—only one person I have to find.

Another sob leaves my lips as I watch Silas look for me. A

panic I've never seen takes over his expression, and a tear rolls down my cheek.

"I'm here."

He pauses briefly, closing his eyes as if focusing all his energy on me. A powerful breeze swirls around him, and I watch, still unsure if this is real. His chest heaves quickly, and I see his hands trembling as they try to relax at his sides. He lowers his chin, then suddenly opens his eyes, revealing the brightest green I've ever seen. I almost gasp, but step closer. His intense stare slowly sweeps across the wasteland, leaving my jaw slack.

Silas's eyes meet mine.

A flood of emotion sweeps across his handsome face. He dips his head and charges toward me, continuing to shout my name— as if awakening every dark creature in this realm is of no concern to him. With the fury I feel radiating from his body, I understand that I shouldn't be worried, either. But in this nightmare of a world, I am.

Very worried.

His body moves swiftly across the ashy ground. His arms pump against his body, and he shifts in small bouts closer to me— like he's only got a little magic left before completely fizzling out. My hands begin to tremble.

He's here.

He found me.

I step forward, feeling almost too heavy to move. A distant feminine scream pulls me back to reality, and I nearly run back to the tree to hide, just like I've been doing for what feels like weeks.

I have seconds to reach Silas before the Great Wiitch finds us both, and although my heart pounds against my ribs, I make up my mind to take another step. My unsteady legs somehow propel me forward, and adrenaline hits my stomach like bricks.

Silas.

Our connection tugs at me to continue forward, because if I

stop, I know I'll be caught. I take off at a dead sprint in his direction.

Kalix's wicked voice booms through the damp air. "He's found you, Briar. Your tether between worlds." She laughs wildly. "What happens next time when he can't find you? What will you do?"

Kalix pauses, letting the words sink into my horrified body.

That won't happen.

This won't happen again.

"My poor girl; he *will* fail you. He will leave one day. You'll see. You think you are found, but you will always be lost—so fucking lost—just as I am."

My steps quicken, ignoring her words, and I move my sore arms to push myself faster. My hair moves behind me, flying through the air, and tears coat my face. He's here and nearly within my reach.

Kalix's laugh travels through my body like the icy touch of a cold finger. With every cackle, she draws closer. The crows begin to dive bomb me, and I shout, attempting to avoid their claws.

A few more steps. I can do this.

I hear Silas shout again, encouraging me. "Keep going."

You are Briar Blackbyrne. I repeat to myself. *Push.*

A sob breaks from my throat, and although the pain threatens to take me to my knees, I keep going, knowing the pain will be worse if I stop.

"Eyes only on me," he screams.

The hiss from a distant creature fills the chaotic air, and my stomach rolls. The commotion has awoken everything visible—and not—in this realm, and our time is running out.

"That's it," he screams, breathless. "Ignore that."

Another sob breaks from my lips.

"Get to me," Silas pleads.

A few steps left, and my lungs nearly give out. His presence grows in the darkness, and my trembling hands fall to my side as my legs give out. I feel myself slipping, unable to keep going, but he catches me.

Silas and I crash together.

His scent overtakes those of burning ash and the decaying surroundings I've grown used to all these weeks. His warmth wraps around my body, and I weep. He's here. I'm not alone. Relief floods my veins, but it doesn't slow my racing heart.

I close my eyes, unaware and uncaring of the surrounding ruins anymore.

"I found you." Silas's voice dances in my ears. "Gods, I finally fucking found you."

I listen, and the world around me begins to quiet; the burning smell fades, and Kalix's miserable laughter subsides.

"Keep your eyes closed," he whispers, wrapping his hand around my head, pressing me against his chest.

The simmering crackle of the once-burning kingdom is replaced by the whooshing sound that hits my ears.

Silas's arms stay wrapped around me. The warmth of his body floods into me like the heat of the sun—something I haven't felt in what feels like weeks.

"Hang on," he breathes into my ear, his strong chest heaving from exertion. "Never let go."

I squeeze him—tighter and more desperate than ever before.

My nails dig into his clothing, and I fear that even this isn't enough to hang on. I can't lose him again; he can't slip away. Panic rushes in my veins, like water from a dam that has just given way.

We dissolve into mist. The weight of my body—the world—seemingly becomes nothing, and I lose all sense of where we are. Where we've been. The torture I've been enduring makes me realize that the only thing that matters is Silas.

But I know a few things for certain, and they weigh heavily on my heart and soul.

Silas is with me.

He found me in the darkest of places. He awakens me from the darkness that lives deep within my soul. With him, I'm safe.

I also know that it wasn't a nightmare; it was real—a world existing within ours, unseen by most and feared by all.

I awaken in a small, dim cabin in the ship's hold, with the sun peeking through the small porthole, casting a flickering light that dances around the walls. The darkness has passed, but the motion of the boat on the waves immediately makes me feel sick. My head throbs against the warm sheets of the cot, and my dry mouth suggests that I've been unconscious for days.

But where am I?

Why can't I remember anything?

A figure sits in a chair propped against the far wall, their silhouette blurred along the edges. My vision is blurry, as I expected it to be after days of sleep. After I wipe the sleep from my eyes, the figure comes into focus.

Rose.

She sits silently reading a book, not realizing I've woken up.

Her head snaps at my small movements as she quickly rises from her chair, nearly tipping it backward as she snaps her book shut. "Oh, Gods. You're awake."

Her voice flowing through the room is music to my ears.

I must be hallucinating.

Rose and Lang should be on their way to Brinkym with Oak's father, safe and far from what's to come—including the danger I seem to bring everyone. I lift my shaky arm and rub my temples, and my memory flares.

Rohhit. The pier.

We had to flee Daramveer.

Eden.

The memories come crashing into me harder than the waves outside, and I am seconds away from being sick. Everything comes together in a chaotic blow to my chest.

"You're here?" My mouth hangs open as I gawk at her. "How are you here?"

More memories flood my aching head, and a throbbing sensation distorts my already unsteady vision.

She rushes to my side, smiling, and gently runs her fingers through my tangled hair. "We were leaving town when we ran into your friends. They told us that you had disappeared and shared the plan while Oak and his father said their goodbyes."

She kisses my forehead, her touch so similar to my mother's that if I close my eyes and settle back into the cot, I can pretend it's actually her for a moment.

"I told you I'd never leave you." Her eyes soften. "Plus, Arieste would haunt me if I let you do this alone, and I don't want that happening." Rose wipes a falling tear from my cheek. "I will serve you and help you rebuild Daramveer, whatever it takes."

My heart soars at the sight of her face, yet a lingering darkness weighs heavily on my chest. My thoughts feel fuzzy, as if I'm walking through a haze.

What happened?

I turn my head to glance out of the round window, watching the waves crash against the ship's side, the wide world ahead of us.

I'm safe.

For now.

"Wait. Lang can't be here." I snap back into the harsh reality of where I am. "This would be too hard on him."

"Don't worry," Rose chuckles. "I sent his old ass to Brinkym with Oak's father. He didn't object, either." She keeps rubbing my head, trying to calm my nerves. "Lang knows he would slow us down."

"Thank Gods," I sigh out, relaxing into her touch.

"He and Oak's father have become quick friends. The King of Brinkym is very excited to have a new chef in the castle with his experience."

I smirk.

She squeezes my hand, her smile thawing my cold heart.

Rose pauses for a moment before continuing. "This will be the longest I've ever been away from him. He's been like a father to me all these years, but he will be safe." She nods, almost as if convinving herself. "Oak's father will make sure of that."

I sit up further, a memory flashing into my mind: the boat.

"Silas—is he okay?" I try to lift myself off the cot, but fail to do so, my muscles too weak to hold me up. "His arm. It was horrible, so burned and mangled." I flinch at the images flashing through my mind. "Where is he?"

She pats my hand, rising from the seat beside me to help me sit up, slowly. "He's fine. He is standing outside the door, impatiently waiting for me to invite him in. I can practically hear him pacing." Rose nods toward the heavy wood door. "Nosey one, that boy is."

I glance toward the closed door.

"I had to threaten him to keep him out of here," Rose says, smiling as she rubs my head again. "He woke up two days ago, and he's been desperate to see you. Barely sleeping or leaving your side most days."

"Sounds about right," I say, affectionately.

She smirks. "You have some kind of hold over him, Briar,"

she says, continuing to smirk as she glances over her shoulder. "Alright, boy."

The door immediately creaks.

"You can come in now."

The door opens as Silas walks in. His dark hair is a mess, his shirt wrinkled, and dark facial hair peppers his face, casting a shadow to line his jaw.

Even with his arm heavily bandaged and tucked into a sling, he stands tall and strong—as if the events have unfazed him. However, I know better. I can see the faint signs of worry settling deep in this demeanor.

"This is the first time I've ever waited for an invitation to enter your bedroom, I suppose." He smiles, his face hard, but those beautiful eyes pierce into mine.

Rose huffs at that comment.

"This one is tough, but she's a good guard dog." He smiles, touching Rose's shoulder.

Rose chuckles and moves toward the door, smiling like a proud mother taking her leave. "He will fill you in on everything. I'm going to check on the horse."

She leaves, shutting the door behind her. The crashing sound of waves echoes throughout the room as we sit silently for a moment.

My eyebrows raise, "Horse? Myah and Xena. You got them?"

"Yes… and no." Silas lowers his head, pausing momentarily. "Oak was only able to get one… Myah is here with us."

My body goes rigid.

"Xena was left behind."

Dread washes over me like a wave. "Oh Gods," I whisper. I cup his face, gazing into his eyes, which are filled with sadness. "We will get her back, Silas. I promise."

In an instant, his eyes darken, filled with a desperate rage. "Oh, I'm sure of that."

I lean forward on the edge of the cot, sleep still heavy on my mind. "What happened?"

He brushes my hair away from my eyes, and his lips form a thin line. "You've been asleep for six days."

Reality and my nightmares blur in my memories, and as hard as I push in my own mind, I can't make sense of either.

"You don't remember, do you?"

"You almost lost your arm." I glance down at his sling. "I remember getting you on the ship."

He nods, and sadness settles behind his eyes. "You saved me, but in return, I almost lost you."

I lower my head, and at this moment, the world around us is calm and quiet. There are no storms, no danger, just us. Together. My heart aches, knowing these moments are limited. I stare at my hands, noting that the veins are still dark and haven't faded as I had hoped. I glance up through my lashes to find him staring at me, a burning intensity in his bright eyes.

"Kalix," I whisper. "It was all her."

He nods, glancing at the black marks tattooed on my hands and up my wrists, the tips of my fingers nearly black.

The memories become clearer as they flood my mind, hitting me like blows to the face.

The ash.

The ruin.

"My nightmare… I waited for you. I couldn't wake up." A quiet sob leaves my throat. "It felt like weeks passed, and I never heard you call to me."

I rub my throbbing head, the memories almost too much to bear.

"Silas, she was after me. She *is* after me. She's going to take over. I can feel her creeping closer each day." Panic swirls, and bile rises in my throat. I start to squirm, as if I'm still coated in the gray ash that constantly falls from the sky in that realm.

Silas takes my hand. "Once Maines healed me, I came to—I ran to you. You wouldn't wake up, but I could somehow feel you. I could hear your thoughts, as if your prayers were meant only for me." He squeezes my hands, trying to stabilize me for what he's about to say next. "I stayed here with you, desperately trying to wake you, calling to you." He lowers his head. "I couldn't eat or sleep for days, until my body could no longer handle it." Silas's hands tremble slightly against mine, squeezing harder. "I drifted somewhere when I slept, closer to you. It was similar to the dreams I had before I met you. I let myself go, and that's when I found you."

Bits and pieces come back to me.

Silas's panicked face as he ran in my direction. The ruin—the darkness—but it's blurred, like my memories of the nightmare fade with every second I'm awake. I glance up at his face. His dark hair falls in all directions, and his piercing green eyes stand out against the purple under them. Even in this moment, his ineffable beauty is hard to ignore.

"It doesn't make sense," I say, squeezing his hands just as tightly as he's squeezing mine. "I don't think it was a dream, Silas."

I shuffle my legs under the warm blankets, and a zap of pain jolts through me.

"Ouch," I hiss.

Silas jerks his attention to my legs, slowly pulling away the thick fabric that covers them. Nearly healed scratches run down both of my legs, coating them with blood—now dark brown instead of red—as if days have passed.

"I don't think it was a dream either, Briar."

I notice his chest heaving as he covers me once more, his concerned eyes gazing into mine. He dives into his own thoughts, and I can only imagine what is swirling through his mind at this moment. He's trying to process everything, just as I am, but I wish he would talk to me.

He whispers, "You need to rest."

I jerk my gaze to meet his. "Rest? No, you need to tell me what's going on."

He sighs. "I don't remember much, either. It's like it happened years ago, and the time that passed is messing with my memory."

I lower my head once more. "That's how I feel."

He lifts my chin with his finger, forcing my gaze to find his.

"Hey," he says, sharply. "You are safe right now. We are safe, and that's all that matters." Silas kisses my forehead before settling onto the bed next to me. "You with me is all that matters."

I rest my head against his broad shoulder. "Apparently, my running off to save everyone gave you three all kinds of ideas in Daramveer."

He huffs a soft laugh, his body finally relaxing against mine. "Maines found out that Carobon was trying to be resurrected. Something I now know you could have told us, but didn't." He nudges me. "If you weren't so impatient and keen to keep secrets, you'd have known all of this before you snuck out toward your death wish."

I grimace, trying to keep the memories from drowning me in this moment.

"Any other secrets you'd like to tell me about?"

I shake my head, the lie making it painful to look at him, and I swear he knows I'm lying.

"Don't keep things from me, Briar." Silas's voice is deep as he pleads with me. *"Please."*

I lean forward, planting a soft kiss upon his lips.

He flashes a worried smile. "You know, Carobon doesn't want you dead anytime soon, Briar. He wants another chance to prove his strength against Kalix and all Shadow Wielders." He sits straight up, turning his body toward mine as he continues, "He wants another chance for the Lumor Wielders to rule over all. I have strong suspicions that he fully possesses Rohhit, and that they are heading to Eddris. They are going to raise an army, just like what happened all those years ago during the Great Battle."

"We knew this would happen," I say.

He pauses, grabbing my hand before continuing. "We're going to endure another epic war. We must fight him, but we can't allow Kalix to take complete control of your body. We've got to figure out how to harness the Great Wiitch's strength without putting you in jeopardy." Silas stares deep into my eyes. "I can't lose you again."

"You won't," I whisper, trying to convince myself as much as him.

He glances down at my hands, noticing the black lines that remain, and his eyes meet mine. "Those aren't going to fade this time, are they?"

"No." I flex my hands. "I think they are here to stay."

I'll tell him the promise I made Kalix in the water another day.

"You stayed on the dock. You placed yourself in danger to hold off Carobon. Why didn't you come with us?" I ask, accusation in my tone, along with concern and frustration.

He breaks eye contact, like the question makes his thoughts travel somewhere dark—somewhere he doesn't want to go. "I knew he would kill us if we all let our guards down to shift. And, I knew you left something behind that meant more to you than anything." I tilt my head, waiting for him to continue. "The letters. I thought maybe I could grab them for you."

My mouth slightly parts in shock. "You risked your life for that?"

He gazes into my eyes, revealing something I've never seen from him before—something tender and vulnerable. "I'd risk my life—repeatedly—for the things you hold dear, Briar."

My heart soars, and neither of us speaks for a moment, just letting the silence of the cabin surround us in a comforting embrace.

My mind reels for those poor people in Eddris facing the destruction heading their way. Silas continues, "Oak's father is going to keep us updated on the moves they are making, since Brinkym is our only connection to the mainland at this point."

I nod, speechless in this moment.

We have no real plans, no armies, and no supporters—especially with me as queen. Everyone ran from me, fearing me because of the stunt I pulled. I let my father get to me, and regret hangs heavily on my shoulders. Not only will I have to rebuild Daramveer, but if we don't stop this, we will need to rebuild the entire realm. I feel like I might be sick again, and I breathe sharply through my nose, trying to keep it at bay.

"It's going to be okay." Silas kisses my forehead, brushing a strand of hair from my pale face. "We will figure this out. Together." His kisses shift from my forehead to my mouth, and I can't help but feel uncertain about trusting his words entirely. It's hard not to feel hopeless in this moment, and I know he understands.

"You promise?"

He responds, gazing into my eyes as he says, "I promise."

"Where are Maines and Oak?" I ask, changing the subject.

Silas chuckles. "They are on the deck. Oak has really taken a liking to the ship life—he's practically the captain now. However, Captain Darcy seems to think otherwise."

I huff a laugh, rolling my eyes.

"Maines is annoyed with him, naturally, but I've never seen her smile so much. She filled me in on everything only a moment ago."

"Great." I laugh, shaking my head. "Another reason for him to boss us around."

I turn my gaze out of the ship's small window, noting the vast sea before us and black clouds forming on the horizon.

His gaze joins mine as we watch the waves crash against the ship. "We will be there in a few weeks."

I snap my attention back to Silas. "Wait, where are we sailing to?" I realize I never thought to care where we were going.

He grabs my hand.

"Well, you need an army, right? A following of supporters and people to help us win this battle. We need soldiers who aren't afraid of death or destruction and are crazy enough not to fear Wiitches, Wielders, or Gods."

My eyes widen as I process what he's saying—where we're heading—but before I can speak, Silas does once more:

"Andorwood."

CHAPTER 2

2 weeks later...

B*riar!*

I jolt from sleep as my name fades from the darkness into reality, the familiar voice now one I hear most days. I catch myself saying silent prayers, thanking the Gods that we are safe—away from Daramveer and Carobon—but dread looms over me still. My nightmares are becoming more real, and knowing where we sail doesn't help the growing pit in my stomach.

Andorwood.

The nightmares have ceased on most nights, which is reassuring. However, every time I close my eyes, the dread of their return haunts me more than the nightmares themselves. Neither Silas nor I have discussed much about what happened when he woke me. We can't recall much, so attempting to talk about it has proven futile. We still need a plan for saving Rohhit, but every time we meet to brainstorm, it always ends badly—usually because my ideas are unrealistic, at least by Silas's standards.

Being awake these days is more challenging than the nightmares of my past. The dark veins still cover most of my hands, and the tips of my fingers are still nearly black—serving as a constant reminder of who lurks deep within me.

My vision comes into focus as I wipe the sleep from my eyes. Silas leans against the doorframe of the small cabin with his arms folded and a smile painted across his handsome face. "You're awake. I've only been calling your name for five minutes," he says casually, stepping into the small room. "Try all you like, but I'm not letting you sleep through this."

We've been on the ship for a few weeks, and the constant waves pounding against it makes my stomach churn daily. The only thing keeping me going is knowing that soon my feet will be on solid ground, even if that solid ground is Andorwood.

"Come on, get up." Silas waves his hands. "Maines and Oak are waiting for you on the deck."

"Fine," I say, smiling.

"No, really. Hurry," Silas says. "Oak is drunk."

His gaze lingers on me for a moment. He knows my thoughts and fears are haunting me, yet he's trying to maintain a sense of normalcy—as normal as it can be for now. We all understand that we are just days away from everything changing forever.

I roll out of the small cot, my feet hitting the cold, wooden planks that creak under my weight. I haven't told my friends how badly I'm struggling, although I know they notice—especially Silas. The past few weeks took a toll on me physically and mentally as I've learned to keep her at bay. Kalix still lives within me, desperate to break free, but my tricks for keeping her buried within seem to be working for now. She's at rest, but I know the promise I made will come back to haunt me.

"I'll be there in just a second," I say, forcing a fake smile in his direction.

Silas bounds across the room toward me faster than I have time to blink. "Happy birthday, my love." He kisses my forehead, pulling back to flash me a wide smile, his eyes lighting up in my presence. Before he turns to exit our tiny room, he leans in and says, "You can do this, Briar. I'm here for you. Whatever you need."

The smile I return is genuine this time, because his words strike true.

Today is my twenty-seventh birthday.

I dress quickly, applying a dark pink to my lips and cheeks before brushing my tangled raven hair. I don't want to keep them waiting too long. I glance in the small cabin mirror and notice my autumn-colored eyes contrasting sharply with the purple circles beneath them.

My birthday.

I thought my brother would be with me today, and memories of him quickly swarm my thoughts. He always made this day special for me with a ridiculous cake, sometimes unwanted praises of my passing years, and always ended with a surprise present that he had handmade. Or he did, until he left.

The weight of what happened in my kingdom and to my family presses heavily on my chest. Every time I'm alone, I can't help but reflect on my life's most recent events: Carobon, Rohhit, and leaving Daramveer in a desperate attempt to flee. We move further from my kingdom with each passing second, and my stomach twists at the thought of what I left behind and what I'll be returning to.

I've spent many nights pondering what I will do upon my return to Daramveer, and it always involves ensuring that Eden will never betray me again. I glance down at my dark-stained fingers. The shadows within me respond quickly when I pay attention to the mark bestowed by Kalix. The veins swirl around my palms, and I allow a few shadows to come forward for a bit of release. Although the familiarity of my magic is comforting, I can't shake the sense that something is amiss—like a pain within me is building.

I brush off the persistent discomfort and smooth my new clothes, chosen by Maines for this special occasion.

Maines and Oak have been enthusiastic about my birthday for far too long, likely planning something that will once again require me to wear a smile. I wish I could share in their excitement. Most days, I remain in my small cabin, reading the limited books we have on the ship, or visiting Myah to drown out my thoughts.

Silas refuses to leave my side, but I don't mind. We've spent countless nights talking until dawn about Andorwood and planning for what's ahead, yet we never discuss the night he saved me from Kalix. I worry that Silas is still hiding part of his life, much like I have for all these years. But, the days tick by until he must face the harsh reality of being on Andorwood soil, and though Silas has told me much about Andorwood, I can't help but think there are many things he's chosen to keep buried.

When we arrive, we will likely be greeted by his father, Malachi Nastronde—a ruthless man who tormented Silas for years. Although Silas has come to terms with his father's actions, I'm not sure I can trust myself to be as forgiving.

Breaking out of my thoughts, I cross the threshold of my cabin and head toward the ship's main deck. A few members of the crew bow as I pass, and I flash a smile and wave in their direction. Everyone has been so lovely and accommodating during our time on the ship. The narrow hallways felt cramped at first, but now they feel normal—they feel like home.

The sound of laughter hits my ears as I approach the steep staircase leading to the top deck. The narrow wooden stairs creak beneath my weight as I ascend. Oak and Maines are likely teasing each other about something trivial, and in this moment, I'm reminded how grateful I am to have them by my side.

As I near the top of the stairs, the wind begins to whip my long hair into my face. The fresh air tickles my nose, proving to be a nice break from the musty cabin air I've been accustomed to.

I peek over the top of the hatch and see a small table in the middle of the deck where Oak, Maines, and Silas are sitting and sipping dark wine, which explains their uncontrollable giggling. The table is decorated as well as it can be, with matching plates, a few silk napkins, a box I don't recognize, and candles struggling to stay lit in the strong sea breeze. The spring air cools my reddened cheeks, but it's carrying the first hints of warm days to come. My birthday always falls around the first warm day of spring.

I watch them for a moment as they talk amongst themselves— safe, and in this moment, happy. Silas laughs at something Oak says, his muscular neck tipping backward as his deep laughter floats into the night air. Maines joins in, and her amusement moves around the deck like music. My friends—my family—are before me, waiting for me. If they can relax now, maybe I should try as well.

Silas pauses, and his head snaps in my direction, and I awkwardly wave. I'm caught snooping and grin, this time a genuine smile.

Smiling isn't so hard, Briar.

You can do this.

"There she is." Silas stands, his chair moving back with force.

Maines and Oak follow suit. "Happy birthday!" they both shout, laughing.

Oak's glass tips slightly, spilling some of the red liquid. "Fuck," he shouts, flumbling the glass.

I smile and continue up the last steps, joining them on the deck.

"We thought you were going to miss your own party," Maines laughs, wrapping her arms around my neck for a warm embrace.

"I know you all would never let that happen," I joke.

"Come. Sit with us. We are celebrating tonight," Oak urges, ushering us back toward the cozy table setting. "And drinking."

Their eyes remain fixed on mine as I sit down, smoothing my blouse dotted with wrinkles. Maines smiles broadly, attempting to make me feel more at ease.

"What is everyone staring at? Can you all please act normal?" I cringe at their eyes upon me. "It's just another day, after all."

"Nothing," Maines cuts in, and smiles. "We are just happy to see you here with us. You spend too much time below deck. Some fresh air will do you good tonight."

"She's right," Oak chimes in. "You spend more time with Myah than with us. I think Silas is starting to get jealous."

Silas flashes Oak a warning gaze, mouthing, "Careful."

"Oh, relax, you grump," Oak laughs.

Silas tips back in his chair, stretching his large arms over his head as he takes a breath. His powerful muscles dance in the moonlight, and even Maines watches him.

"We've all been through a lot recently," Silas says, shrugging nonchalantly. "Let's cut Briar some slack on how she spends her days. I can assure you," Silas winks in my direction, "that I am not jealous."

"Whatever you say," Oak responds.

Silas slides a cup of dark liquid my way. "Shall we get back to this celebration instead of poking fun at Briar, please?"

"Cheers, everyone, and thank you for doing this for me." I lift the glass toward the sky. "You sure know how to make a girl feel special on her birthday," I laugh, and we clink our glasses together in unison.

"Cheers." Silas's eyes meet mine. No worry is evident, just a gentle happiness finally peeking through.

We grow quiet for a moment, the waves the only sound around us. The past few days have felt strange between us as our nerves heighten the closer we get to our destination. Darcy, the captain of the ship, announced this morning that we have just one more full day of sailing before we arrive. Silas seems more on edge, but I know he's putting on a brave face tonight for my birthday.

"We will be arriving tomorrow," Oak says, as he cuts the silence.

Maines's smile fades. "That's what I heard, too."

"Silas, what should we expect upon arriving?" Oak asks.

A sinister smile spreads across Silas's face. "Should I keep it a secret or would you prefer I stress you out now, Oak?"

"A fight? Daggers at our throats? Creatures ready to attack?"

Silas chuckles and places his hand on my knee under the table, gently squeezing it. "Tomorrow will be interesting, to say the least. I don't think they will try to kill us upon arrival, but I've been wrong before."

Maines takes a long drink and drops the glass on the table with a thud. "Who is going to greet us?"

Silas sighs. "That's one thing I'm not certain about. This ship will look familiar to them, so the men at the port will probably recognize me and send word to my father. That is a plus. Outside ships aren't welcome in Andorwood." He narrows his eyes toward the sea, as if imagining our arrival. "For example, if Oak were sailing in on a ship from Brinkym, they would likely kill him on sight."

Oak grimaces.

A dry laugh escapes Silas's throat. "I'm kidding."

Oak adjusts his seat, shooting Silas a sarcastic grin. "Very funny, Mr. Nastronde."

"So, your father could be on the pier when we dock?" I ask, wondering how much I really want to know.

Silas turns his face to meet mine once more, the candlelight dancing off his scar. "It's possible," he takes a drink, "although it would be out of character for him to be there. Whoever greets us will take us to the castle." Silas brushes at a piece of hair that has fallen out of place. "It won't be safe for us to linger around the port as it's near the town center, and that's not where I want to be at dusk."

"Why?" I ask.

Silas doesn't respond.

Glancing toward Oak and Maines, who are now in their own hushed conversation, I take a sip of wine, basking in the sensation of the warm liquid sliding down my throat. Silas squeezes my knee once more.

He leans toward me. "It's going to be okay," he assures me, placing his hand against my cheek. "They are going to take you seriously and listen to you—to us."

"I appreciate your kind words, but you can't know that for certain."

"I know."

"Rumors travel, just like we have, and I fear what they've heard about Daramveer could cost us everything. And it would be my fault."

He leans closer, pressing his forehead against mine. "Then, I will personally handle anyone who doubts you, questions you, or tries to harm you. You might feel like you're in unfamiliar territory, but I can assure you, I am not."

I lower my gaze. "Do they fear you?"

"Yes."

My gaze remains low as I let the world around me sink in.

"Right now, you need to believe in yourself—just like we do."

He lifts my chin with a single finger, forcing me to meet his eyes. "Don't doubt your shadows; you need to embrace them."

I lean into him, not wanting Oak or Maines to hear me. "I want to run from my shadows, Silas, but I don't feel safe, even now. In the light she hunts me, but in the darkness she haunts me."

He grabs my jaw, hard. "Bury her. You know how to control her. She hasn't fully taken over after all these years, which is a testament to your strength." He relaxes his hand and kisses my forehead. "Keep holding on for a little longer, and we will figure this out."

Silas's finger traces my jaw, pulling me to him until our lips meet. In this moment, my worries vanish, and I let him kiss me deeply. His soft lips take their time, as if he wishes to freeze this moment forever, too. My eyes roll back as I savor this brief moment of intimacy before all hell inevitably breaks loose tomorrow.

He pulls back, and I wipe his lips with my thumb as he playfully bites it. "More of that later. Whatever you want from me tonight, my love." He winks with a smirk, and my cheeks flush, a thrill running through me as his hand slides up my thigh.

Maines laughs from across the table. "Oak, what are you going to get me for my birthday?"

"Oh, Maines, darling, you won't be able to handle what I will give you," he responds, his voice stern, but with a joking lilt.

"For some reason, I don't doubt that, Hombern," she chuckles, shoving his broad shoulder as he flashes a wide grin.

For the first time in a long while, tonight feels normal. Tonight feels happy. I glance over the ship's edge, the dark sea surrounding us—as if the darkness is trying to suffocate me. I quickly shake off that thought as Rose appears from the narrow staircase leading below.

"Happy birthday, my shadow," she says, her calming voice helping to ease my nerves.

Rose has been busy on the ship; she and Captain Darcy have grown closer, and she's taken a role in the kitchen. According to her, cooking is the only thing that keeps her sane most days. Now, she carries a small dish of pastries with a candle sticking out of the center of the plate.

"Make a wish," she whispers as she places the plate on the table.

I close my eyes and take a deep breath of the salty air.

A wish.

Silas's words replay in my mind—*bury Kalix.*

When I open my eyes to find that the candle has already been blown out by the breeze, as if I wasn't allowed to make that wish, I see everyone's eyes on me again. Friendly smiles spread across their faces as they study me, and I know they are checking to see my current mood.

"Let's do presents," Maines says, taking another drink of her wine. "We all know what Silas is getting you for your birthday, but we wanted to get you something to open, too."

I glance toward the box, which is now sitting on the floor. "When did you all have time to get me a present?"

"Don't worry about what we do in our spare time," Oak winks.

"Gods help us if it's something from this old ship," I mumble.

"Watch it." He huffs in offense. "This ship is beautiful and mine; don't speak ill of her," Oak says, clearly irritated. Silas laughs.

Maines picks up the box and sets it in my lap.

The weight of whatever is inside presses against my thighs, sending butterflies dancing in my stomach from anticipation. I carefully lift the top of the box to reveal tan, crinkled paper covering something near the bottom. I glance at Maines, whose smile could brighten the darkest night.

Focusing back on the box, I remove the paper to see a golden point peeking through, and my heart leaps.

My mother's crown.

The familiar black crystals resemble vines swirling around the points, and the bright gold glimmers in the night sky. I take a deep breath as I remove it from the box, and tears start to well up in my eyes. "Where..." I stammer. "*How* did you all get this?"

Maines nods at Silas. "Well, I can't take all the credit. It was his idea, and Oak retrieved it."

I glance between the four of them.

"I'll be honest, I didn't have a choice," Oak slurs, taking a sip of his drink. "Silas would have killed me if I messed this up,"

Silas laughs into the rim of his drink.

"I can't thank you all enough," I say, fighting back the emotion welling in my throat. I snap my head in Silas's direction. "What made you think of this?"

"You are a queen now, traveling to Andorwood. Not that you need anything to prove yourself, but I thought… Well, we thought this would come in handy—really make a statement." Silas smiles widely and continues, "Plus, it's your mother's. I told you I'd do anything to protect the things you love."

My hands tremble as I touch each crystal, feeling the smooth, firm stones against my fingertips.

Memories of my mother swirl in my mind, and for just a moment, I swear I hear someone softly calling my name.

She loved this crown. My mother wore it even on the most casual occasions. Every painting in the castle depicted her wearing it; she always told me it would be mine one day. I always dreamed of the moment I would wear it, but now it feels heavier —almost sour—like the weight of the entire kingdom will rest on my head.

"Thank you. Thank you all so much." I can't stop the tears streaming down my cheeks. "This means more than you will ever know." I smile through the tears, and Silas takes my hand.

"And," Maines chimes in, "you're going to look like a total badass wearing that in front of these unruly men."

We all share a moment of laughter.

"Well, I'm going to disappear for the night," Rose says, patting my shoulder. "You crazy kids behave yourselves. Especially you, Hombern." Oak raises his glass toward Rose as she continues, "We have important things to do tomorrow."

I stand, my chair sliding backward, and embrace her tightly. She is the closest thing I have to a mother, and when she's around, I feel as if my mother is here, too.

"Thank you," I whisper.

She offers a gentle smile and moves to the narrow staircase, heading below deck.

While the others engage in a new conversation, I take a moment for myself and walk to the ship's edge. Though we are close to Andorwood, all I see is darkness ahead. The black night resembles a wall of shadows, pulling me back to the pier in Daramveer—the chaos, fear, and ancient power haunt me. What are we going to do? How can we save Daramveer and our realms…

Rohhit.

I grip the wooden rail as my knees buckle, and the overwhelming sensation of sinking takes over. My knuckles turn white from my hold, and the ship begins to swirl around me. *It's not happening. We are safe right now.* I breathe through my nose, a technique Rose taught me, and count to ten.

One.

Two.

As my chest begins to rise and fall more steadily, I feel my nerves start to ease. By the time I reach ten, I'm able to stand upright and take in a full breath.

The sinking feeling fades, and I find myself standing on solid legs once more. Braver this time, I glance back at the darkness and narrow my eyes, attempting to peer past it rather than directly into its depths.

I am Briar Blackbyrne, Queen of Daramveer, and I am not afraid.

The waves crash against the ship's side, and I can't help but wonder if I'll ever stop hearing this sound. It's been so constant for weeks now, and all I want at this moment is to be on solid ground—even if that means standing on the soil of Andorwood. In the distance, I swear I hear my name being called again—like someone shouting down a long tunnel. But this time, I know it's not Silas. I'd recognize his velvety voice anywhere, now. This voice is hushed and filled with a deep, desperate sorrow that sends a chill straight to my soul.

"I was worried that the gift would upset you too much," Maines says, walking up beside me. "I was hesitant to let them give it to you."

Her voice startles me, and I slowly shift my gaze toward her, pulling it away from the all-consuming darkness. She offers me a gentle smile and takes my hand.

"No, I love it. It's exactly what I needed." I smile and grasp her hand back. "It's hard to think about her, but I know she would be proud of me—of us—for doing this."

We gaze into the darkness together, uncertain of what's to come, but knowing that if we do this together, we will be alright.

"You know, Briar. I had an idea for a gift from me, but I'd never do it without your permission." She continues to stare forward. "Everything happened so quickly once the trials started... Your brother..."

I jerk my head in her direction.

"I feel like you never got the closure you needed, and if you were interested…" She trails off, as if the words are still tender.

"A ritual," I manage to say.

She meets my gaze. "Only if you want to. I know you need more closure; it's bothering you." Her hand squeezes against mine. "I see it every day, Briar. You are struggling, and maybe this could help."

My eyes narrow as I look at her. "You want to cast an illusion of Barlowe, don't you?"

Maines breaks her stare and looks out over the sea before us. "I think it could help for some closure. But, I'd never do it without you wanting it first." She breathes, letting the words strike a chord. "He was taken so quickly both times, and you never got to say your goodbyes. If we did this…"

"Stop," I snap.

Maines grimaces.

"It wouldn't be real, so what is the point?"

"No, it wouldn't." She pauses, lowering her head. "But, it would seem real. I've done this countless times for people at the House of Hedro, and it truly helps them move on from the trauma holding them back."

I feel myself begin to sink, the overwhelming feeling hitting me harder than the crashing waves below us.

One.

Two.

Three.

I count to ten and breathe, letting the sea breeze rush over me to calm my pounding heart.

"No," I reply. "I'm not ready, nor do I know if I will ever be."

Maines looks at me, and opens her mouth to speak, but hesitates.

"Please don't bring it up again," I whisper. "Unless I ask for it."

"I'm sorry, Briar." She lowers her head. "I only wanted to help. If you change your mind, I'm here for you. You know that."

"I know you mean well, Maines." I attempt to smile. "I'm forever grateful for the offer, but no."

I sling my arm around her neck. My Maines. My best friend. Perhaps my past self would have stormed off and felt upset, but I've changed, and I know she was coming from a place of love.

"What do you think tomorrow will be like?" Maines asks, changing the subject.

"I honestly have no idea. Interesting to say the least."

"I'm nervous," she confesses.

I glance in her direction and offer her a reassuring smile. "It's going to be okay. Silas is with us."

The wind rips around us, and I pull her tighter as the cold air moves across the deck of the ship, like a storm is on the horizon. I can't help but focus on the dancing nerves that swirl in my system, because what I didn't confess to her is that I'm nervous too, and the growing pit in my stomach has been growing for days.

"Are you two going to stand over there all night?" Oak shouts from the table, another glass of wine in his hand.

Silas sits beside him, a smile spread across his face, as he clinks his glass with Oak's.

"We'd better go, before he drags us over there," Maines says, chuckling as she heads toward the table.

Oak shouts again, louder than necessary. "I'll drag your ass over here."

She laughs, glancing in my direction. "Told you."

CHAPTER 3

The night air whips my hair around, and I take another deep breath as I hear it again—my name, softly carried by the wind. I look toward the table where my friends are talking among themselves. No one is looking at me, let alone speaking directly to me.

"Hello?" I whisper into the darkness, but no one answers. Only the slapping of the waves echoes around me.

A chill runs up my spine as I step away from the ship's edge, absolutely uninterested in figuring it out at the moment.

"Briar, come relax," Oak shouts, as I move their way. "Have a drink."

"You better hurry, or Oak may drink it all," Maines chimes in.

I make my way back to the table, my footsteps silent against the roaring waves. Although my hearing is often limited on the ship's deck, I can't shake the feeling that I need to listen.

I place both hands on the table and lean in, staring directly at Oak. "How much have you had to drink?"

"A few." A wide grin spreads across his face. "But not enough."

"Oh, I beg to differ," Maines snaps.

"Okay, maybe five glasses," Oak laughs.

"Try eight," Maines adds.

Silas coughs, propping his ankle on his knee. "Light weight."

"Fine," Oak huffs. "I've had enough that I might finally let Maines tie me up tonight. She's been begging to."

Silas and I snap our gaze to Maines before exploding with laughter.

"Okay, Mr. Hombern." She turns red, and her jaw drops. "I believe you've officially had and said enough tonight."

"Nah," Oak says, offering his wrists to her with a wink.

"That's what happens when you start drinking long before the party starts." Maines grabs his cup, and points. "Look at Silas. He isn't a drunk fool."

"Come on," he argues, reaching across her for his cup. "He's always this stiff."

Maines stands and places her hands on her hips. "I think it's time we retire for the night. We have a big day tomorrow, and I don't think you will want to spill your guts on the pier in front of the wonderful people of Andorwood."

Oak grabs the bottle and tips it back.

"Let's do this, darling," he says, wiping his mouth with pride. "It's time to be roped."

Maines snatches the bottle and slams it down on the table with a thud, glaring at him.

"If you two don't hear from me tomorrow," Oak wobbles and a laugh booms from his throat, "please come untie me."

Rage radiates off Maines as she pulls him away.

"Pray for him." Maines tugs at his waist. "Because if you don't hear from him tomorrow, it's because I've fucking killed him."

Silas laughs as she stomps toward the stairs, Oak stumbling close behind, both of them waving their goodbyes.

"Oak Hombern is something," Silas says, still laughing. "I've never met anyone quite like him."

"He's been this way since we were children. Well, not a drunk fool, but he sees the fun side of life."

"It's important to have friends like that," Silas says.

"As children, he always made me laugh until my stomach hurt. I'm happy to say that still happens now as adults," I respond, smiling as I reminisce.

My mind goes back to a summer when Oak and his father visited. We spent our days outrunning guards, reading books, and I often made Oak perform any ritual related to his Lumor ability. Even at a young age, I was fascinated with the magic of light and wished I could wield some myself. Ritual after ritual, Oak would show me how he could illuminate the world around us. He has a way of brightening the darkest nights, even outside his magic.

"Tonight was fun," Silas says. "It felt normal. I know that isn't something we've had much of, but when this is over, I'm excited to experience the joys that this life can bring us." Silas leans back in his chair, taking another drink, and I just look at him for a long moment, enjoying the view.

I grab his hand and rise, pulling him to do the same. His strong body towers over mine as I stand on my toes to reach his mouth. I gently slide my tongue across his lips, teasing him, before I whisper in his ear, "I want my other birthday present now." I slide my hand across his abdomen and down to the seam of his pants. "Some distraction would do me well, don't you think?"

Silas jolts from the touch, his gaze filled with heat.

"Finally." Silas smirks. "I've been waiting all day for this."

His eyes darken as I lead him down the stairs toward our small cabin. His hands begin exploring my body from behind, trailing up and down my spine and sending shockwaves straight to my core in anticipation.

Before I can make it across the threshold, Silas spins me, and his lips find mine. His kiss becomes feral as he guides me backward toward our bed. I turn us before he can sit me down, causing him to fall onto the cot with a thud, his eyes growing large in surprise.

"Now, now, Mr. Nastronde, I believe you said you would do whatever I wanted."

"I did," he agrees.

"So, I'm in charge."

His gaze turns wild. "Go on."

"Lay back," I demand.

He hesitates but obeys.

"Good boy," I mock.

Silas stretches his arms wide above his head before tucking them under his messy hair. A devilish grin spreads across his face as he waits for me to continue.

"You may only move when I say you can."

He nods.

"I need your words," I say, sharply. "So, use them."

"I'll only move when you say I can."

"Perfect."

I move toward the bed and place my hands on his muscled thighs, slightly massaging them, before moving my hands up his body. I remove his shirt, revealing his toned stomach with the many faded scars in no organized fashion. Starting at his neck, I begin to kiss him, soft and gentle. I make my way down his chest, then stomach. A deep moan leaves his lips as I move lower, just barely above the waistband of his pants, before I pause.

Raising my head, I gaze at his handsome face, his eyes drunk with lust and a hint of wine. I begin to slide down his pants, never breaking my stare, and start kissing once more. Lower and lower with each delicate peck, I flick my tongue against his warm, tanned skin. His hands move and tighten in my hair as I near his cock with my mouth. I lift in a flash, and his hands drop to the side.

"Are you moving?" My shadows begin to dance around my body as invisible hands snake up his, slowly massaging their way to pin them down.

"Briar, let me fucking touch you."

I return to my ministrations, teasing him with my lips.

"Seeing you utterly defenseless brings me joy," I breathe. "I want you to beg, Prince."

He growls low. "It would take me mere seconds to pin you down, Briar."

"Not yet."

His head lifts from the bed as he props himself on his elbows. "You. Are. Wicked."

"Silas," I warn, asking him to lie back.

His head falls backward onto the sheets once more, and I begin to move my mouth, my lips grazing over his tip. I flick my tongue in a rhythm that has him squirming under my hold.

"That delicious fucking mouth will be the end of me," he groans, voice low and needy.

"Is that all?" I ask, moving my tongue from his length. "That doesn't sound like a plea to me."

His gaze meets mine, and his hands attempt to move against my hold, desperate to touch me. His stare is filled with hunger, only for me and what I'm teasing him with. My heart races in my chest, and my body fills with excited anticipation.

"I *need* you, Briar."

"More," I snap.

"If I don't have you right now," he pauses and groans, "I will... fucking die."

I lower my gaze, returning my mouth so close to his tip that I know he can feel my breath.

"Then let me be the one to bring you back to life."

Silas Nastronde, the Prince of Darkness, is helpless under my touch. It brings me great pleasure knowing that I am among the very few who might be stronger than he is. I lick slowly from the thick base of his length to the tip, before wrapping my lips around his entire cock. A low moan leaves his mouth, desperate for more, as I pump up and down as far as my mouth and throat allow. I move my hand in tandem with the rhythm of my mouth, gripping hard.

He's enjoying this, and so am I, his moans echoing around us as I lower down again. After a few minutes, I release him, wiping my mouth slightly, and he barks in protest.

I step back a few paces, my shadows still pinning him down, and stare at him. Silas looks stunning while totally under my command. I slowly begin to unbutton my shirt until it falls to the ground in a graceful descent. His eyes grow wild, staring at my bare breasts.

"Get over here," Silas demands, but is still unable to move. "Now."

"Such an impatient man," I reply, smirking.

"I'm not fucking joking."

I begin to unbutton my pants. He wiggles under the hold of my shadows, desperate to free a hand to touch me. Just like my blouse, I let my pants fall to the ground, having purposefully skipped undergarments earlier tonight for this very moment. I stand and bask in his gaze for a moment before I begin to lower my own hand, tracing every inch of my chest and moving toward my hips.

I take my time before I reach my own wetness and tip my head back at the touch, my body desperate for friction.

"Fucking Gods," he whispers.

I plunge two fingers into my own body, causing a whimper to leave my lips as he watches.

"Do you want to touch me, Silas?" I ask, on a moan.

"Yes," he rasps.

"Do you want to fuck me, Silas?"

"My love," he groans, the impatience obvious in his tone. "I want to fucking ruin you right now."

I grab my aching breasts, staring at him.

Silas trembles as he watches me, desperate to reach me. "I want to devour you, your soul, and make you forget your own fucking name. I'm going to make sure mine will be the only godsdamn name you ever scream again."

I snap my fingers, releasing my shadows. "Then ruin me."

Before I can blink, he shifts from the bed and pins me against the far wall. Both hands slam against the wall on either side of my head as he leans in close, nipping at my bottom lip.

"You will regret teasing me in the best fucking way."

"Is that a threat?" I bite his bottom lip.

"You should know by now that I don't make empty threats."

He lifts me against the wall, fingers digging into my sides, his cock already poised at my entrance. A devilish smirk spreads across his face.

"Only promises."

Silas's lips crash against mine as he slams into me with a hard thrust.

A moan leaves my mouth, and my nails dig into his back as he pumps in and out of me. From the show I put on moments ago, I'm already close to exploding, and from his feral movements, I know he will torture me until the end.

"Harder," I moan against the nape of his neck.

Silas slams his hips against mine, and the wooden wall digs into my back, but he doesn't slow. "You are so wet and fucking perfect."

His deep thrusts become more rapid, and I squeeze my legs around his waist as tightly as I can. My entire body shakes, and I bite his neck, which is my undoing. A white, dazzling heat spreads across my whole body, and I'm blinded for a moment. Silas pulls his gaze down to watch where we're connected as a new hunger drives his expression wild. He continues to pump into me, like tonight is all we have.

"You are mine," he groans into the nape of my neck. "You are fucking *mine*."

With what we will experience tomorrow, I'm thankful for the ferocity. I continue to ride the incredible high, unable to stop myself from unraveling against his strong body. I moan his name as he covers my mouth with his hand. Another orgasm slams into my chest as he continues to thrust his hips against mine so hard my thighs tremble. A blast of pleasure sends tingles through my entire body, and I dig my nails into his shoulders as my head tips back against the wall.

The sensation forces a pleasured sob from my throat, and Silas leans forward.

"Quiet." His hand wraps around my throat, tightening. "Unless you want the entire ship to hear all the fun we are having."

Silas travels his hand from my throat to my jaw as he presses his thumb into my mouth.

"But, go ahead if you'd like." His gaze bores into mine. "Let them know who you belong to."

My moan becomes a muffled desperation of pleasure as I bite down, hard.

The pleasure swirls in my throbbing body, like the rising waves against the ship, and my chest heaves. Silas keeps a firm hold on my legs wrapped around his waist as he continues to thrust in and out of me.

He watches me, his eyes filled with lust.

"Look at you."

Thrust.

"How undone you become."

Thrust.

"Just for me."

Seconds later, Silas releases a rough moan as he slows, emptying himself deep inside me.

I melt against his strong body, leaning away from the wall, and he catches me, propping one arm on the wall behind me while he catches his breath. His chest heaves against mine, but his hold doesn't waver. My legs stay wrapped around him as he carries me back to our small bed. Silas sets me down gently and falls to the bed beside me, still breathing heavily.

We breathe silently in unison for another moment before he props up on his elbows, gazing at my naked body once more.

"You can do this, Briar," he says.

"Do what?" I question.

"Win."

I blink and don't respond.

"You don't realize how strong you are, but I do."

I trace my fingers over his scarred chest. Silas tips his head back, but continues speaking.

"I see it every single day. You have a way of commanding the room without even trying. Just look at what you did to me." He winks. "You're the only person I'd let nearly bring me to my knees."

I huff a near-quiet laugh.

"You can do this. But tomorrow is going to be challenging," he sighs.

I meet his gaze. "I'm nervous."

"And I would be lying if I said I wasn't as well."

I look into his piercing green eyes. "No matter what you say, I'm worried I can't do this. If I fail…" I trail off.

"You won't fail." Silas's strong hand clasps around my jaw. "You are tough, yet kind. You care deeply about doing what's right and creating peace in our lands. Your passion will keep you going. We will find a way to separate you from Kalix. And Rohhit from Carobon."

Rohhit's name sounds sour on his lips, and I flinch.

"Even his name bothers you?" Silas's eyes turn to stone.

"Everything about what happened to him bothers me."

"I see," he says, and I know it troubles him.

My deep feelings for Rohhit—even though they aren't romantic—bother him.

Silas nods, returning from his thoughts. "We will save him, but you have to keep going. Keep trying."

"I will do whatever needs to be done to stop this."

"I know you will. And to be honest, that terrifies me," he says, his lips pressing against mine. "But, I'm not going to let you do this alone." He leans back, lowering his head onto the bed. "You have to let us help you."

I nod.

"Silas, I still don't know what connects us, but you make me feel safe, and I hope that never fades." I rest my head against his chest as he holds me.

"I'm not going to let that fade."

"You promise?" I ask in a whisper, feeling sleep heavy in my words.

"Promise, my love," he replies.

His breaths deepen before I can speak again, and I know he's drifted off to sleep. I study his face for a moment, memorizing his profile—just in case. I move a strand of hair from his peaceful face before rolling over and allowing sleep to grace me just the same.

The rumble of thunder wakes me after what seems like just moments after drifting to sleep. I sneak out of bed and head toward the small cabin window, making sure to be quiet so I can let Silas rest. Sleep has never come easily to me, and even though the nightmares aren't haunting me, the habit remains like a persistent headache.

Glancing over the waves, I see a wall of darkness. My heart races, and sweat begins to dampen my palms as I remember Silas on the pier defending us against Rohhit—Carobon. The wall builds before my eyes, and lightning crackles through the black clouds. My breath hitches, and I feel like I'm back in Daramveer, so close to death. Another rumble of thunder crashes, rattling the window, as Silas stirs in the bed next to my empty spot. My entire body freezes, and the panic within me starts to bubble.

One.

Two.

Three.

The panic doesn't subside. I move against the far wall, pressing my back into the wood which scratches my skin, and drop to the floor, covering my ears.

It's not real. It's not happening again.

The boat rocks back and forth, and the waves crashing against the wooden boards echo throughout the room, and no matter how hard I try to steady myself, I can't. The lightning continues to clap outside, casting bright flashes all around like bombs going off.

He's here.

Carobon has found us.

A scream leaves my mouth as I wrap my arms around myself tighter.

Silas springs from bed, startled awake by my scream. "Hey," he says soothingly, rushing to my side. "It's just a storm. Look at me."

The tears continue to stream down my face. I can't calm down.

"Briar, look at me." He cups my jaw. "Breathe. I'm here." Silas wraps his arms around my trembling body. "You are okay. I'm okay. We're safe."

Another crackle of lightning illuminates the cabin as Silas observes the severity of the storm. The shadowy water swirls around the boat in a chaotic dance, as if the surrounding darkness is trying to capsize us. The black clouds overhead resemble a giant beast attempting to drag us to the depths of the darkest realms, and fear overrides my system.

"We need to get dressed right now. I will head to the deck to see what's going on."

I remain frozen, the fear controlling me.

"Briar," Silas calls again.

Tears fall like the rain outside.

"Briar," he snaps. "I need you to listen."

Just like always, his voice brings me back. I jolt back into my right mind and begin to grab my clothes as the boat rocks from side to side, causing us both to fall off balance.

"As soon as you finish dressing, meet me on the deck. Okay?"

I nod and continue shuffling around the room, grabbing what clothes I can. He moves toward me and kisses my forehead. I holster my two axes; the gold weapons shimmer in the dimly lit cabin, helping me see. Thunder claps around the room, and we can now hear the shuffling of many feet—likely the ship's crew—springing into action.

Silas rushes out of the room, glancing over his shoulder one last time, before disappearing. I grab a bag and begin stuffing a few things inside, including my mother's crown.

A wave hits the boat, causing me to lose my footing as I crash to the ground.

Maines bounds through the threshold in a panic.

"Gods, are you alright? We need to get to the deck." Terror floods her expression. "Oak just rushed up there to help the crew. He's half drunk." She glances around the room. "Where's Silas?"

"He's up there as well. The storm, Maines. It... It's so similar."

She nods. "I know. I thought so, too. It's not, though—we are far from Rohhit right now. It's just a storm, but it's a bad one."

I shudder.

"We heard people saying the storm had pushed us off course and toward a cliff. We're close to Andorwood, but not close enough."

Panic rises once more in my core, "Rose and Myah. We have to get Myah off the ship if we must abandon it. We can't leave her. She'll drown."

Maines nods in agreement. "Okay, first we need to see what's going on. I promise we won't leave her. Silas won't let that happen, either."

She's right. If there is someone who loves this horse more than I do, it's Silas. We follow the same route that Silas took to the top deck. We bound into the hallway, the staff pushing against our bodies in a rush to get to the deck. Shouts and curses come from all around as people panic and fight to keep their balance against the rocking ship.

As we ascend the narrow staircase, Maines grips my arm tightly. The ship's crew hurries around the deck, seizing any ropes they can find to secure the masts. The chaos is disorienting, but I breathe through my nose, trying to quell the fear surging within me. Rain splatters our faces as we struggle to make out a few figures. Silas, Oak, and Captain Darcy are on the quarterdeck, shouting at the crew below and pointing behind us toward the cliff approaching at a rapid pace.

Sprinting to the deck beside them, Silas grabs my arm, steadying me. "Rose went to find you. You weren't up here, and I got worried." A crashing wave sends us stumbling backward. "They needed me here to grab the helms. We are going to have to abandon the ship, Briar. The storm is too strong to control anymore."

I glance at Maines with a concerned look. "You can shift people out of here and onto the cliff's edge. You need to start moving now. Many of these Wielders won't be able to make the shift on their own."

"What do you mean by us?" Maines responds. "You can help, too.

"I need to go to Rose and Myah. She went looking for me," I snap back in protest. "I'm not going to leave her down there."

"You are insane if you think I'm letting you go down there," Silas says. "This ship is going to sink, and if you are down there when that happens…"

The wind continues to howl as the ship moves closer to the rocky shore with each passing second. The movement of the masts against the wind sounds like beasts groaning in the night. I watch the sails whip in the raging wind, and there are no signs of this storm passing soon or gently.

"We don't have time for this, Silas. You need to start helping now." I push back. "I can handle this. You know I'm strong. Let me assist her while you help the others. You know this area. They need you—they need your direction—and you know it."

He stands completely frozen for a moment and sighs. "Go save her. But know if something happens to you, I won't be able to live with myself for allowing this." He kisses me before returning to the captain and Oak to devise a plan.

"Maines," I shout through the storm, "Stay with them and keep an eye on Oak. He listens to you. Start helping get people off the ship. I'll be back as soon as I can."

"Where are we going to go?" Maines cautions.

"Trust Silas." I move toward the narrow staircase. "I'll find you when I can."

She nods, yet her brows tighten in silent protest.

Rushing from the quarterdeck, the boat continues to sway. I barely maintain my balance on the slick deck. Flying down the narrow stairwell, I crash into the walls as the waves tip the boat. Frantic shouts echo from the deck above while I continue down the hallway toward Myah's stable. Myah's high-pitched neighing pierces my ears, and I fear her stomping may penetrate the wooden floors as I enter the room.

"Briar, what are you doing down here?" Rose shouts.

"You need to go right now. They are starting to evacuate the ship. The plan is to head for the nearby cliffs."

Myah continues to neigh, her tramping becoming more frantic as the waves slap larger against the ship.

"Shhhh, Myah. It's alright," I try to calm her. "Rose, please take this bag and go to the others. They're helping to get people off the ship and onto solid ground."

Her stomping continues as I notice a halter and lead rope close by. I rush to grab it as Myah rears up, nearly kicking me, and I dodge her massive hooves.

"You can get her up on your own?" Rose questions.

"I can do this, Rose. Go find Silas. Now. He's waiting."

She grabs the bag filled with my mother's crown and exits the stable in a flash.

"Be safe," she calls, disappearing.

Her determined footsteps fade in the storm, and I say a silent prayer that she's quick.

The raging wind bangs against the small window, like a creature of darkness desperately trying to break in. Putting on the halter, I rub Myah's head for a second, hoping to calm her before we begin our ascent.

"We can do this, Myah. You need to trust me." I stare into her beautiful eyes, but no calmness meets my gaze. "Let's go."

I place my head against her strong cheek. Her worried eyes meet mine, and we share a moment of silence before a strike of lightning pulls us back.

I tug on the lead as we make our way down the hallway. The shouts above have subsided, and I can only pray that most of the people above have moved somewhere safer. Considering the horse's weight, I quickly realize that we won't be able to do the same. A clap of lightning echoes through the air, and Myah rears behind me with barely enough room to spare. The lead rope rips through my hand, taking my skin with it.

A loud crash distracts me, and I know we only have a few moments left to reach the deck and escape the ship. I hurry down the hallway, Myah close behind, as we ascend the stairs. The fear of being trampled weighs heavily on my mind with her at my back, so I remain constantly aware of Myah's condition.

The top deck is deserted except for a fallen mast that now blocks most of the wooden area. I look around in every direction but only see darkness surrounding me and a soaring wall—not of shadows, but of rock—to my right. That suffocating feeling returns, making my stomach churn. I can feel my head starting to spin as the towering cliff closes in on us.

Keep it together. Count to ten.

Except now, I don't think we have that time left. Something to the left catches my eye, and I swear I see a ship in the distance from the flicker of a few small candles. I turn back to Myah, who's anxiously awaiting my lead.

"Myah, we are going to have to jump."

She continues to stomp and neigh frantically as I lead her toward the edge.

"Can you do this, Myah? Can you jump?"

She rears and pulls against the rope in response as I try to move her toward the churning water, avoiding the edge where I need her to go. The black water below surges like a wide, open mouth, and I feel a shiver run down my spine. Its darkness threatens to swallow us whole if we enter, but either way, we are going in. As the seconds run out, I back us from the edge toward the middle, where the mast has fallen.

"If you won't jump on your own, then we will have to go together."

I grasp her long mane and swing my leg over her strong back, settling in as securely as possible. Her white body gleams in the darkness, like a beacon in the night.

"You ready?" I pat her neck.

She neighs in response, a high-pitched echo moving around us, telling me all I need to know. She is as terrified as I am.

I take a long, deep breath, looking at the edge before us. With a solid kick, my feet press into her sides, and she bounds forward.

Another loud crack rattles in the night, and I glance behind me to see the second mast splinter, falling our way. Myah's hooves echo on the deck as she nears the edge of the boat. With only a moment left, we leap over the edge. Time seems to pause, and the screams of the storm become muffled. We crash into the darkness below, and I gulp a mouthful of water. Panic floods me, and I cough, desperately trying to catch my breath.

The ripping black water surges above my head, but I hold a firm grip on the rope. For a moment, I'm unsure which way to turn. I break the surface of the water, glancing in all directions. The current tore me from Myah, but I pull on the leather straps still in my hands.

Myah treads water near me as I shout, "This way."

The crashing waves blind me, stinging my eyes, but I swim away from the sinking ship through the choppy water, pushing my body as hard as I can toward the rocky shore.

In the distance, the smaller ship approaches, with another one waiting nearby. A crash shakes the cliff to our right, and our ship shatters like glass against the rocky surface, the final mast tumbling into the water, barely missing us.

In the distance, I hear the shouts of people as the boat approaches, but the tumultuous waves begin to pull me down. My mind travels back to the second trial—the Serpyndens. My swimming becomes frantic as I'm desperate to leave the dark water.

"Myah!" I shout behind me. "This way, girl."

The horse keeps swimming, struggling as her head bobs up and down with the blinding waves. As the boat nears, my nerves tighten as the size of the ship grows like the black waves. I desperately scream toward the boat, and right now, I don't care if the enemy has found me. I need to get Myah out of this water quickly. I can deal with whatever's ahead once she's safe.

The ship slows as it approaches.

"There she is," Silas screams. "Fuck. She has Myah, too."

He disappears over the edge of the ship. Instant relief floods me, knowing they are safe.

The lightning starts to diminish as the rain ceases above. My vision sharpens, and I spot Maines waving frantically from the ship's deck. As the waves begin to calm, I guide Myah toward a rocky bank, no longer in fear of the jagged edges shredding us. She needs to rest almost as urgently as I do.

I cling to one of the flat rocks and push Myah to follow, ensuring I get her on solid ground first. Her strong legs find a shallow patch as she begins to push herself onto the pebbly bank. Myah immediately drops her head, taking a moment to rest, while I crawl up the rocks beside her, breathless. I lie on my back with my hand still clenched to the lead rope, and my heart feels like it's seconds from exploding.

Silas shifts next to us on the rocky shore, but I don't move. My chest rises and falls rapidly, and my lungs burn like a blazing fire.

"Are you okay?" He scoops me into his arms.

"I'm…fine." I cough, the taste of salt still in my mouth.

"You did it." He kisses me. "You fucking did it."

I relax in his arms. "I couldn't let you lose them both."

He smiles, presses my body harder against his chest, and glances at the horse. Water pours off her body, but she lifts her head, as if telling him she's okay, too.

Exhaustion weighs heavily on me. "How are we going to get Myah on the ship?" I nudge him toward the horse.

"I think we can shift her safely with a few of us. I have a few men standing by in case we need them." He scans our surroundings. "Top commanders from Andorwood."

My eyes shoot up to meet his, and I cough. "Andorwood?"

My chest caves in as I still try to regain my breath.

"Yes," he responds. "Whose ship do you think this is? I told you people aren't very welcoming in Andorwood." He hugs me tighter, refusing to let me go. "Someone surveying the storm spotted us coming toward the cliffs and sent a ship out. Lucky for us, my army just saved our lives."

Silas isn't wearing his old clothes. He leans over me, dressed in black armor darker than the night around us, showing off his perfectly muscled physique. The armor has ornate snakes on the chest. The Prince of Darkness is back in his familiar setting.

"The others are on this ship and the one in the distance—we got everyone off safely."

He whistles into the night air, and a moment later, a few men shift to the rocky bank within seconds. Myah snorts at their abrupt arrival.

Three men stand before us, and their stature takes me aback. They are massive and quite an intimidating group, but it's nothing I can't handle. I find myself immediately wanting to know more about each of the men before me after reminding myself that I fought against men just as large in the trials.

Silas watches me, waiting for my reaction as he sets me down onto the bank from his arms.

"Briar, these are my top commanders in Andorwood. This is Larkin, who oversees our ocean fleet."

Curiosity hits me from his name, and I narrow my gaze as I study his chiseled face—light colored hair, dark eyes, lean, and very tall. Larkin doesn't meet my gaze, but instead keeps an eye on the raging ocean. Silas quickly moves on to the next man standing near Larkin.

"Hux Ackerley, who oversees all land operations."

I glance at the Shadow Wielder. His large, bright blue eyes shine in the night, and a twinge of nerves twists in my stomach. I square my shoulders, not showing an ounce of weakness in their presence.

Silas continues, "And this is Warrick Pierce. He oversees Larkin and Hux and is my right-hand man."

Warrick dips his head in respect.

Silas continues, "You can formally meet them later, and I promise they will each be a huge pain in your ass at some point."

Warrick's dark eyes find mine, and a kindness sits behind them that eases my growing anxiety almost instantly.

"Nice to meet you, Briar," Warrick says. "We've all been impatiently waiting to meet you."

They all bow in my direction in unison, and I cut my gaze toward Larkin once more, who yet again won't meet my stare.

"They are going to get Myah on the ship safely," Silas says, sternly. "Aren't you?"

The men nod at Silas, keeping their gaze focused on the task at hand.

I cough again. "It's nice to meet you all." I glance behind me. "I'm sorry about your ship."

"It wouldn't be the first time Silas sank one of my ships," Larkin mumbles under his breath.

Hux nudges his shoulder, and Silas shoots them both a warning look.

Warrick steps forward. He is the largest of the three, standing as tall as Silas and nearly as broad—though a few years older. His hair is as white as snow, and his eyes are almost as black as the churning sea surrounding us—a Lumor Wielder.

"Sir," his strong voice echoes above the waves, "where is Xena?"

Silas's expression turns harsh, giving Warrick the hint not to continue the conversation. "We will discuss that later."

Silas turns toward me, still dripping wet and freezing.

"You." Silas points at me, his gaze stern, and his tone holds a command that makes my skin crawl. "You are coming with me. We are going to get you dry, and there is someone else I'd like you to meet."

"Oh, lucky Briar." Warrick huffs a laugh and smiles. "You get to meet perhaps the biggest pain in all our asses."

Silas chuckles. "You would know."

The other men remain silent, and I watch them all closely, studying their interactions. They are disciplined, but I can tell they are friends on and off the battlefield, having gone through many challenges together. I narrow my gaze, examining each of them, and wonder what it's been like to be here with Silas all this time.

Silas nods in the men's direction, a silent order on the next steps from here, and grabs my hand.

We move through the air like mist before landing in a small, dim cabin on the other ship. Tiny candles line the wooden walls, and the bed in the far corner is covered with onyx silk sheets. There is a desk in the middle of the room covered with papers and maps. It's cozy and much nicer than the ship we just spent weeks on.

"I hope you know letting you do that on your own nearly

killed me, but people's lives were saved because we acted so quickly. You came with orders tonight in a crisis. You had a plan." Silas steps back to look me in the eyes. "You acted like a queen tonight, Briar."

My expression tightens. "I did what had to be done. I knew I could save her while you protected the others."

He reaches for me again, placing his hand behind my neck and pulling me close. "You are going to make an incredible ruler, Briar." His lips find mine, gentle and soft, and I return the kiss. As he pulls away, a shiver runs through my body. "Let's get you dry and changed."

My arms feel like stone as I lift them over my head. Silas removes my shirt, the soaking wet material sticking to my body. I drop my arms, too exhausted to help. He then moves to my pants, slowly pulling them down. They hit the floor with a wet thud, and a pool of water quickly dampens the rug.

Before standing, he plants soft kisses along my hips, traveling up slowly before towering over me once more. My core tingles from his touch, but exhaustion overrides my senses. I lean into his warm chest, standing bare before him. He wraps a blanket around my shivering body before lifting me in his arms and carrying me to a nearby chair. The soft, warm fabric feels like floating on a warm summer cloud.

He steps away, grabs a stunning black gown from a small dresser next to the bed, and extends his hand toward me. His hungry gaze lingers on my bare body, and he peels his eyes away, stopping himself.

"I was seconds away from diving into that water to find you," he says.

"I'm okay," I assure him.

"We are exhausted and nearing Andorwood. Don't worry about the ship. Like Larkin said, it wasn't the first time I wrecked, and I honestly believe it won't be the last."

"How many ships have you destroyed?"

He pauses, obviously in thought. "Three, I think. But one wasn't my fault, I swear."

"Gods," I mumble. "Reckless?"

"Younger me was a fun time."

"Fun," I mockingly say back. "I'm sure other words were used to describe you."

Silas smiles. "You'd be correct."

The water still trails down my body, and a shiver runs up my spine.

"Get dressed," he says. "Someone is anxious to meet you."

I stand once more, placing the delicate fabric over my head. The dress hugs my curves and pools on the floor like fresh rain. A slight shimmer dances across the fabric, mimicking a galaxy of stars.

"Breathtaking," Silas whispers. "And perfect for Andorwood. We tend to gravitate toward dramatic clothing here. And from what I've seen you wear in Daramveer, you'll fit right in."

I smooth the dress around my hips when a knock on the door startles me, snapping my head in his direction. Nerves tingle in my stomach, and I quickly run my fingers through my messy, still-wet hair.

"Silas," I whisper. "You never said who wanted to meet me?"

A devilish grin spreads across his face as he strides toward the heavy cabin door. He peeks out, then waves for someone to enter. The dim lighting makes it difficult to distinguish who is approaching from the hallway. Silas closes the door as the woman comes into view.

She looks familiar, sharing the same facial structures as Silas, though there's no scar above her left eye. Her pitch-black hair cascades past her shoulders, and she stands about my height. From her perfectly plump face, I can tell she is a bit younger, but not by much.

She wears the same black armor as Silas and the men I met earlier, and curiosity swarms me. She walks toward me with purpose and confidence, but I remain rooted in place, devoid of emotion.

Silas steps behind her, allowing the woman to stand before me. She places both hands behind her back and angles her head, studying me intently, as if she has waited for this moment for a very long time.

Silas smiles. "Briar, I would like you to meet someone."

The woman smiles ear to ear with the exact same sarcastic smirk that he has, and that's when I know.

"Briar, this is Fenmore Nastronde—top Commander of the Andorwood army, and my younger sister."

CHAPTER 4

Fenmore grabs my shoulders, squealing, and pulls me into her. I flinch against her warm embrace, my sore body protesting the touch.

"Oh, shit. I'm so sorry. Did I hurt you?" She pulls back, her brows knitted in concern as she scans my body, as if checking for injuries.

I notice a stunning necklace hanging low on her chest. The dark green jewel dances in the candlelight, and I can't help but be entranced by its beauty. The jewel seems to pulse, and I fight the urge to reach out and touch it. She notices my gaze and wraps her hand around the necklace, smiling.

"It was a gift from my mother," she says. "She has one just like it."

"It's absolutely beautiful. I've never seen anything quite like it." I smile back at her, still trying to get a read on her.

"Thank you," she replies, tucking the stone into her blouse. "It's so wonderful to meet you, Briar. I feel like I already know you, since Silas was always talking about you."

Fenmore smiles again, and it's a replica of Silas's.

Silas flashes an uncomfortable glance at his sister for being so forward, and I nod, signaling that it's fine. They look similar, yet different in a way. I can't help but wonder if Fenmore takes after their mother or father.

I glance around her body and gaze directly at Silas.

"Talking about me, are you?" I joke.

"Fenmore knows more about me than I know myself, I'm afraid." His eyes soften. "She knows about the dreams."

I glance back at Fenmore, who's smiling almost wider than her face allows, and she pumps her brows twice, making me laugh.

"It's nice to meet you, Fenmore." I bow to the Princess of Andorwood.

Who I had no idea existed until now.

"Oh goodness, never bow to me." She waves her hands. "You are a queen, and news about the goings on in Daramveer has spread fast." She continues to stand in front of me, smiling, as if there isn't a care in the world. "Please, call me Fen."

Silas steps forward. "Fen is in charge of the men you met earlier; however, she pretends otherwise. Fen can talk herself into or out of almost anything. You should have seen her as a child."

"The last thing I want to do is take care of a group of assholes who don't want to listen to me." She winks in my direction. "Silas gave me that job so he doesn't have to do it."

Silas rolls his eyes. "Don't listen to her. They are all afraid of her."

I glance toward her shoulder, where a prominent scar snakes out from under her clothing. She catches my look and says, "Another unfortunate thing Silas and I share."

She glances down toward the scar, and her lips tighten as memories seem to flood her mind like an unwelcome intruder.

She clears her throat, pulling herself out of her thoughts. "Although his are a bit more noticeable."

"I think I'm handsome," Silas jokes, scratching his temple.

"Oh, we all know you feel that way, brother," she snaps back, rolling her eyes at his cocky response.

I chuckle, watching their exchange.

An ache burns in my chest, thinking of the silly moments I had with my brother growing up, and reality hits me once more that those days will never happen again. Silas grabs my hand, somehow understanding precisely what I'm thinking, like always. Maybe I do need the closure Maines wants to give me.

I shake the thought from my head. "Are we close to docking in Andorwood?"

"Yup," Fen says, nodding. "We should be there in another hour or so. Don't worry; your feet will be on solid ground soon. That's when the real fun begins." She drags her hands through her hair before sighing. "I'm going to check in with Warrick. Someone has to keep these men in line." She moves toward the door before turning back. "Briar, I look forward to getting to know you more."

She exits the room gracefully, and leaves me alone with Silas again.

"She's…vibrant, isn't she?" he asks, with a chuckle.

"She's confident. It must be a Nastronde trait," I say back.

"She's strong, like you. We've been extremely close since we were young. She's been the best person to go through this fucked-up life with." Silas sits on the large chair, extending his arms behind his head. "I know you two will be thick as thieves in no time. Or, I hope."

"You two are alike," I say.

He raises his brows. "You can't honestly say I'm that chipper."

I laugh, joining him on the chair. "No, you aren't exactly the chipper type."

"Fen is always positive, but she has scars—scars deeper than mine, and not all visible." He touches the scar on his brow. "I'd do anything for her, and she would do the same for me."

My chest aches.

"I know that's how you felt about Barlowe. I wish I could have met him."

My chin drops to stare into his eyes. "It's nice to see this side of you, Silas."

"Is it?"

His gaze drops, and I squeeze his hand. "It's okay to care for people. It doesn't make you weak."

His gaze shifts back to mine as he lifts my chin. "But that's where you are wrong, my love. It can make you weak." His gaze turns hard. "Having people you openly care for can be used against you. I've spent years blocking out emotions, building walls to conceal my weaknesses. Fenmore is the reason I went to Daramveer. She told me to find you. I owe her everything."

"Will seeing your father change everything?" I ask. "Will this Silas disappear?"

I think back to the boat, the few fun nights we had that were calm and normal, and a pit grows in my stomach, knowing that won't last.

"Things will be different once we dock. I have an image to uphold, but please know it's not me. Things won't change between us. You are mine, and I'm yours. They will see that."

"Should I believe that?" I ask.

"Yes," he replies. "Now, let's go find Maines and Oak. We will be docking soon, and I want us to be together." He stands, leading me toward the door.

Before we cross the threshold, he turns to kiss me, and I taste the dishonesty on his lips.

The ship's deck is crowded—more so than we are used to. I catch the look on Maines's face as we approach, and she appears cautious—a heaviness hanging from her. She and Oak stand with Warrick and Fenmore, closest to the boat's bow, watching the shoreline become more prominent with each lapping wave. Silas holds tight to my hand as we move toward them, ignoring the looks we get with each thundering step. Fen smiles as we join them. She points to a speck on the horizon that grows larger each second.

"That's Andorwood," Fen says loudly, over the crashing waves.

I notice Warrick move closer to her, and she immediately creates a casual distance by leaning over the ship's railing with a flirty smile, as if teasing him. I examine his strong face. Warrick's cheekbones are prominent, yet his face is full, and it strikes me how large he truly is, especially next to Silas. I scan the area for the other two men under Fenmore—Hux and Larkin—but don't see them.

"Where are the others?" I ask, not particularly to anyone.

Warrick peels his gaze from Fenmore and responds, "As Hux oversees our land operations, he is likely somewhere near the quarterdeck, desperate to get off this ship. He's known to get very seasick."

Fen laughs to herself.

"And Larkin," Warrick points high above us toward the crow's nest, "is there. Per usual."

I glance up to see the tall man with near white hair standing in a small lookout tower high above the deck.

"Would you like to go up there?" Silas asks, leaning in. "The view is quite amazing."

I turn to him, a grin curling my lips. "Are you sure we won't be bothering him?"

Warrick laughs at my response and says with an almost feline smile, "All Silas does is bother us."

I cast a quick glance at Maines, and she returns a weary smile—letting me know she will be fine—before she moves closer to Oak. I watch Fen observe them for a moment.

Before I have time for another thought, Silas grabs my hand and shifts us to the lookout. We land with a soft thud, and the distance between us and the ground makes my head spin. My stomach flips, and I grab onto the railing as quickly as possible before Silas steadies me.

"You can't possibly be afraid of heights," Silas chuckles.

"I'm afraid of falling to my death." I clench my eyes shut briefly before opening them once more to the blinding light around us.

Larkin remains unfazed, still studying the horizon, mumbling to himself.

"We thought you looked lonely, Larkin." Silas turns to face him on the small platform, one that is very close to being cramped. "Figured we would bother you for a second for this view."

"I'm making sure we dock in one piece after the storm that just blew through," Larkin responds. "I wouldn't want us to sink a second ship in less than a day."

He grins this time, but only at Silas. A smile brighter than the sun catches my attention, and I take the opportunity to introduce myself, even though his hostility hangs in the air around me. Either I've done something to offend him, or he's an asshole.

"It's nice to meet you officially, Larkin." I extend my hand, but it is met with emptiness.

I look at his face; it's sun-kissed, with a few freckles scattered across his nose. His white hair sits just above his ears—it's well-groomed—and sways gently in the breeze.

A memory flashes into my mind. Larkin—that name. I've heard it before, and the person I heard it from makes this meeting very interesting, so I smile broadly.

Larkin dips his head in my direction, refusing to make eye contact. "You too."

My brows furrow at the exchange, but I keep my hand extended for him to take, not backing down from the diss.

Yeah, an asshole.

Silas notices the unfriendliness and clears his throat as my hand hangs in the empty air.

"Larkin," Silas warns, and tilts his head. "Don't be rude."

Larkin bites the inside of his cheek, turning toward me. His stern face doesn't show kindness or remorse as he shakes my hand firmly. "Apologies, Silas."

I grip his hand, almost too hard, and grin sarcastically. His deep eyes lock onto mine, and a flash of shame causes the darkness in his eyes to flicker before disappearing as quickly as it had happened.

I still feel snubbed and somewhat embarrassed, so I pull my hand away from his and tilt my head.

What did I do to him?

I hesitantly brush it off and look over the railing of the crow's nest. The vast world around us is captivating, and the way the blue sky meets the dark water on the horizon makes it seem as if the world goes on forever. There's no end in sight—just sky and water. A thought flickers in my mind that I could sail away forever with Silas. We could hide on the seas for the rest of our lives and pretend none of this is happening. But that thought quickly fades.

Silas places a hand on the small of my back while Larkin

moves to the opposite side of the tower, giving us space, or perhaps to get away from me. I'm not sure.

"Beautiful, isn't it?" Silas breathes, his mouth by my ear.

"It just seems to go on forever. I've never seen this much of the world at once," I respond, completely in awe of the beauty around me.

Turning to the side, I see a piece of land nearby, and I can faintly make out the Kingdom of Andorwood. Even though we are arriving with the sun still gracing us with its light, the kingdom is dark and quiet. A tall, brooding structure sits farthest away; its jagged black towers pierce through the dense clouds, casting long, eerie shadows over the desolate town below.

The island itself seems to absorb the sun's glow as we sail closer. Andorwood appears as isolated as the tales have said, as if it has been forgotten by time itself. The flickering lights on shore are the only indication of life on the island, and a disturbing feeling runs up my spine. Magic oozes from the landmass, and I can't tell if it's from the people or something larger at play. But, I know it fills me with unease.

"Home, sweet home," Silas says, breaking my intense stare.

CHAPTER 5

My mouth parts as I take in the dark kingdom in front of us. "Everything is about to change."

He jerks his chin in a nod. "Everything."

The ship's wooden hull groans as we approach the shore. Our surroundings quickly fill with the sounds of the ship coming to a stop. The crew below begins to hustle, ensuring each deck area is prepared for our arrival. I grab Silas's hand while Larkin heads off to assist the others below, shifting into a bright light of mist. A loud splash catches my attention as the ship's anchor drops with a sharp clang, followed by the sound of it settling on the bottom. The thick air holds an unsettling stillness as we prepare for what's next.

Silas inhales deeply, holding his breath momentarily—as if to steady his pounding heart. "We should head down."

I lean in, pressing my lips against his, wanting that connection before the chaos begins. Silas kisses me back, deep and slow. We linger in this moment before I pull away. My heart races, and anticipation settles into my veins, causing my shadows to bubble, as if preparing to defend.

"Silas…" I gaze into his troubled eyes. "I am yours, and you are mine."

"I am yours, and you are mine." He breaks his stare, looking toward the kingdom—as if staring into the eyes of the civillians. "They will know that."

My feet hit the solid ground for the first time in what feels like years, and a soft groan leaves my lips. Though I stand firm, a rocking sensation moves through my body, and will likely remain in the weeks to come. Maines, Oak, and Silas stand by my side as we stay on the pier, while Rose remains on the ship with Captain Darcy and Myah. She'll come to the castle once we call for her—once we ensure it's safe.

No one is around.

Even though the vast sea crashes at our backs, the breeze seemingly dies around us. Warrick, Fen, and the others remain on the boat—likely giving the crew last-minute orders—and I find myself wishing Fen were with us to guide the way. Silas has been gone for months, and the unknown of what lies ahead causes my insides to throb, like small bursts of electricity in my veins.

"Where is everyone?" Oak asks, with a shaky breath.

"Don't." Silas cautions, motioning for us to stop. "Speak."

My hands tremble slightly, but I remain upright, my shoulders squared and my chin high. Looking horrified won't make a great first impression, since I'm here to win these people over, so I harden my face and walk confidently next to the others.

We take a moment to look around. The town before us is quiet, evoking an abandoned feel that hangs over the dark kingdom. With no one in sight, the unsettling feeling becomes unbearable. Even though my demeanor may give the impression that I'm not afraid, my insides vibrate with anxiety. I'm expecting someone to emerge from the alley at any second and drag me into the darkness.

The townhouses are constructed from weathered stones and dark timber, allowing them to blend into the surrounding darkness. The architecture is haunting, yet still stunning and elegant. I continue to scan my surroundings, and my jaw slacks when I notice the tall castle in the distance, turrets encased in clouds.

The tall houses share similar points to the castle, like the entire town was built cohesively. A crest of two small golden serpents marks each home on the wide, wooden doors. I'm not sure if it is a warning or an invitation, but they match the snakes that sit upon Silas's armor.

The homes vary in size, likely depending on status, but the weathered black stones shine in the sun's dim light. Dark green vines snake up each home, some flowing directly into the windows—as if the outside world is desperate for shelter from the kingdom around it. Large windows sit at the front of the homes, reflecting the sea that surrounds them.

Like Daramveer, a dense forest envelops the rear of the kingdom, and the iron gate does not separate the castle from the town —it keeps the kingdom apart from the forest. I can't help but wonder what they are trying to conceal in the shadowy forest of Andorwood, or who?

I look toward the large cliffs we narrowly escaped only hours before, noting a dark house overlooking the kingdom, which isn't separated from the forest by a gate. I turn to Silas to ask, when a gust of wind blocks my vision for a moment, nearly knocking me off balance. I hear Maines curse under her breath, and I grab Silas's hand to steady myself.

When my eyes open, a crowd of people stands before us—as

if they all shifted at once. A gasp escapes my lips in sudden shock. My eyes dart from person to person, and I widen my stance, prepared to fight if necessary. The gold axes hum against my back, and I clench my fists, ready to reach for them. From what I know about Andorwood, these people won't be pleased that Silas has brought company.

It also doesn't help that my reputation has already spread this far.

Silas steps forward, making quite the entrance for himself as his shadows ripple around him like a shield. His dark hair flows as the magical breeze he's created from pure power and emotion grows around us.

The Prince of Andorwood has returned.

The ground vibrates around him, welcoming him home at last, as he lowers his chin, challenging the people surrounding us. They collectively take a step back as they realize who stands before them.

No one moves, and not a single breath escapes.

The world silences.

The breeze stops, and Silas steps forward once more.

"Wielders of Andorwood!" Silas shouts.

His deep voice booms like thunder, and another tremor moves throughout the kingdom.

The crowd stares for a moment—no movement, no breathing—before erupting into a roaring boom of cheers. My ears ring from the startling celebration—shouts, growls, and metal clang together over the noise of the cheers. My jaw drops, and I scan the crowd before us. The return of their prince didn't lead to an epic battle on the dock of Andorwood. On the contrary, his people are thrilled about his return.

I snap my gaze to Silas, who is now looking directly at me. He wants to gauge my reaction, and from the awestruck look on my face, he knows we didn't anticipate this. I glance at Maines and Oak, feeling comforted to see their expressions mirror mine.

Fenmore and Warrick approach, joining us on the dock.

"Show off," Fen whispers in my ear, standing beside me. "Not what you were expecting?" She angles her head.

"I'm not sure," I respond.

"Don't let this fool you." She leans closer. "There are people in this crowd that aren't what they seem."

I peel my gaze from the crowd and look at her.

"Keep your guard up," she whispers. "They are here because they are fearful."

I tilt my head, looking at her questioningly. "Of Silas?"

"And my father."

Unable to respond, I turn to look over the crowd, none of them taking their eyes off Silas. Deep down, I can feel my darkness bubbling up in defensive mode. I swallow hard, choking back the feeling of losing control.

Those standing before me aren't monstrous; instead, they are a sea of striking individuals. Dark and light hair intertwine while shadows and electricity dance in the sky, as if their powers are interconnected. I know this reaction stems from their prince's return, but I can't help but think—*why are they so fearful?*

What would this welcome be like had someone inadvertently stumbled onto the pier? They're a trained kingdom, an army capable of moving in unison to sweep away the masses if provoked.

"My father isn't here," Fen speaks again, still whispering. "He'll be waiting for us to arrive at the castle."

The cheers fade, and the crowd parts to let us pass.

Silas takes my hand, prompting a few huffs from those around us. Maines and Oak step forward, hand in hand, staying as close to us as possible. Fenmore paves the way through town with

Warrick bringing up the rear. They surround us, for who knows what these people might try to do to outsiders.

"Keep close," Warrick's rough voice echoes.

Fen keeps a quick footing about her, weaving through the few people left standing in the streets who are curious about our arrival. Whispers echo through the alleys as we pass, and I can't help but hear what they say about me.

She'll destroy us all.

Go back to Daramveer, you possessed bitch.

Anger and shame run through me like a chilled breeze. Silas grips my hand tighter, quickening his steps but otherwise not reacting.

"Don't listen to them. Right now, we need to get you inside the castle grounds," Silas warns. "Nightfall is coming. I can deal with them later."

"There isn't even a gate to keep them from entering the grounds," I reply. "How do you know I'll be safe there?"

"They know better," Silas replies, his voice deepening to a growl.

We continue down the streets of Andorwood, Maines and Oak staying close. The sun dips low behind the clouds, casting a muted glow around us, and as its warmth begins to disappear, causing a cold chill to run up my spine. Silas notices my shiver and moves closer as we near the castle.

"Briar," Maines starts, coming up behind me. "What the fuck was that welcome?"

I cut my eyes toward her and raise my shoulders. "I'm not sure yet."

I peer at Silas, but his stern gaze is trained forward, as if he's trying to see through the castle walls to see where Malachi is. Candlelight flickers in the castle windows, and I swear I see shadows passing by each window as we approach.

"Are you alright?" I ask, moving into his body.

"I'll explain soon," Silas replies sharply, pulling me against him. "Keep quiet. Just a moment longer."

The town's cobblestone streets end as we reach the castle grounds. The castle looms above us like a dark fortress of shadows, and its sheer size leaves me speechless. The vast size of both the castle and the mountains behind it are intimidating.

As I scan the area, I notice that there are no guards stationed outside the castle to protect those inside. My brows furrow.

At least my father had guards around the castle grounds.

I turn back to see Maines and Oak having a hushed conversation, likely about the same thought I just had. We move quickly across the large courtyard, each step soundless in the dimming light.

"Silas," I say hesitantly, squeezing his hand. "Where are the guards? Who protects the cas—" I trail off, an unfamiliar tingle of nerves moving through me.

The grass rustles as a cold breeze blows by, racing past me. I turn to find Oak, Maines, and Warrick moving forward with ease, not noticing the change in the air.

The chilled breeze whips past us again, and I tighten my grip on Silas's hand. He returns the squeeze and quickens his pace, pulling me forward, as if he also notices the shift around us. Unease fills my stomach, and my hair stands on end as I shudder, the darkness within me perking up.

"Something isn't right," I whisper to Silas.

He slowly pans his gaze to mine, feeling the shift, and his eyes widen.

A low growl sounds behind me, and my hair moves in the gentle breeze. I flinch so hard that I fear my neck will snap.

"Fuck," I curse, louder than intended from the scare.

"Don't acknowledge it." Silas tugs my hand away from the sounds. "Keep moving and get inside the castle. Now."

Goosebumps cover my entire body, and I quicken my pace,

still feeling the hot breath of something upon me, like I'm being hunted by something I can't see.

"Fenmore," Silas shouts. "Inside. Right now."

She turns instantly, grabbing my arm to pull me away from Silas. I try to object, but the growing unease pushes me to distance myself from Silas to get inside the castle walls.

I allow a few steps to separate us, and I watch Silas seethe at the darkness around us. He shifts into a shadowy mist. Confusion curls my brow as I hear the noise again, except this time it's faint, as if it's following something—or someone. I freeze, paralyzed by my fear. My mind snaps back, bringing a faint memory of a similar creature to the surface.

"Get inside," Warrick's voice booms.

Warrick moves close behind, pushing Oak and Maines into the towering castle seconds later. The ancient black walls of the castle crowd around us as we enter a small hallway just off the courtyard.

"Where is Silas?" I demand.

"Likely saving your life," Fen says casually, grabbing my hand to force me forward.

"What the fuck was that thing?" Maines cuts in.

"Andorwood guards. Annoying fucking things," Warrick grumbles. "I can only assume they sensed what dwells inside Briar."

"And they were going to attack?" Maines asks.

"They aren't supposed to harm us, being who we are. Only outsiders," Warrick explains. "But to them, you seem... dangerous."

Maines grimaces.

Warrick cuts his gaze to mine. "Especially her."

I keep my stare harsh, but focused.

"She is dangerous," Oak says, abruptly. "You don't want to piss her off."

Fen huffs a laugh and angles her head toward Oak. "Well, aren't you honest?"

He smiles, and she responds with a gentle curl of her lips, her eyes shimmering in the soft flicker of the torches.

Maines watches their interaction closely, and I study her. Her brows furrow as she observes Oak smile toward Fen. Jealousy burns in her eyes, and I'm tempted to touch her arm to bring her back to reality. Oak turns his gaze toward Maines and slides his hand into hers, squeezing gently.

Fen's eyes cut to their hands wrapping around one another, and she smiles once more, turning her back to them.

I glance back down the long hallway, hoping to see Silas approaching, but instead I'm met with darkness. Fen's voice pulls my attention forward, interrupting my thoughts.

"Come on." Fen continues moving through the hallway. "Silas will be a while." She urges us forward and waves her hand. "I'll show you to your rooms. Dinner will be ready soon."

CHAPTER 6

The inside of the castle is gloomy, the atmosphere making it feel like we've entered another world. The thick air that flows through the hallways carries the scent of musk and rich incense, which intensifies as we move deeper into the castle. The floors are made of flawless, dark stone that is so cold to the touch that it sends chills coursing through my body. The walls are lined with weathered stone, and I assume we are deep within the castle at this point, because it feels damp. Light green moss grows in the corners, and torches dance along the narrow corridors, casting additional shadows in all directions.

We round the corner, and the hallway opens wider, allowing us to walk shoulder to shoulder. Maines, Oak, and I walk forward in silence, waiting for the moment when we can speak in private, while Warrick and Fenmore lead the way.

"Almost there," Fen says, interrupting the silence to point in front of her.

Warrick leans in and playfully whispers something in Fen's ear, and she brushes him away with a huff. He slides his hand to the small of her back, trailing his thumb in small circles, and she takes a step closer to him after their lighthearted spat. His body towers over hers as she leans into him, and I can't help but wonder what Silas thinks about his Commanders being in an obvious relationship.

Rooms begin to line the walls; each thick wooden door has a serpent on it that winds in a different direction, open mouth pointing to the ornate door handle. The snakes look so realistic, as if poised to strike the second you touch the handle, ready to sink their sharp teeth into your hand.

A thought crosses my mind: Silas has never discussed the meaning of serpents within Andorwood. But then again, Silas hasn't revealed much to me, it seems. My stomach churns with anger, and the urge to talk to him intensifies with every step.

"Here we are." Fen claps her hands together. "Briar, your room is here to the left." She throws her head in the direction of the door. "Don't worry, Silas's is next to yours."

A golden snake with ruby eyes is engraved on the door that she indicated as mine.

I peer around her and Warrick to see a larger wooden door right where she said Silas's is. Black jewels sit where the snake's eyes should be, and the serpents are bright gold, standing out against the darkness. Curiosity moves through me.

What does his room look like?

"I can't believe it. I'll get to see the Prince of Andorwood's childhood bedroom," Oak jokes, cutting into the silence and offering us a quick chuckle. "Seriously, it's a bucket list moment."

Laughing, Fen points across the hallway and says, "Oak, this room will be your accommodation for your pleasant stay in Andorwood."

We all look, and Oak's door is similar, but the snake's eyes are adorned with a royal blue jewel.

"Nicest room in the castle, I'm sure," he quips.

We all ignore him this time and wait for Fen to continue. "Maines, your room is here."

Pointing a few doors down, Maines is the furthest from ours. Her door is jeweled with a dark violet and looks smaller than the others.

Her reaction is cold, but she dips her head. "Thank you."

Fen grins, shifting her gaze back to mine. "Dinner is in an hour. You should all freshen up. Father has prepared quite a show for tonight's entertainment. You'll find all the clothing you need in the wardrobes."

"Thank you," I say.

"We also had a few people shift any belongings we could find on the ship for you," Warrick says. "You all should be comfortable."

"When you're ready, head down this hallway and down the grand stairs; the Great Hall will be on your right. We will wait for you to arrive and enter together," Fen says, stepping to take her leave down the dark hallway.

"Where is your room, Fen?" I can't help but ask.

She smiles, but Warrick answers before she can. "We stay down the hall and to the left, near Larkin's room." He smiles. "We're close, so don't hesitate to let us know if you need anything."

"You two have a room together?" Maines asks.

Warrick laughs. "When she allows me to stay with her."

Fen gives him a nudge and rolls her eyes. "He's so melodramatic."

He pinches her side, and a playful laugh leaves her lips.

"I can assure you I am not the dramatic one here," Warrick responds, flashing a glance to Fenmore.

"Like I said," Fen continues. "We will see you all very soon."

"Don't be late," Warrick adds, and his tone is a warning to us, returning the conversation to the night ahead.

Warrick and Fen make their way down the hallway toward the Great Hall. He wraps his arm around her shoulders, and I hear a chuckle leave her throat, brightening the dim hallway around them. As they round the corner, they vanish, leaving Oak, Maines, and me alone for the first time since our arrival.

"What the fuck is going on?" Maines snaps, after making sure we are alone.

"That was quite the arrival, I'd say," Oak chimes in.

They both look at me, waiting for me to add anything to their conversation, but I remain silent, unable to find the right words.

"Did Silas tell you they would cheer for his arrival? I thought they would kill us on the spot from the things I've heard of this place," Oak continues.

"I agree," Maines adds. "I've heard terrible things since I was a child, like that only forgotten monsters come to this island, but that clearly isn't true."

My head is spinning.

I need to talk to Silas. Immediately.

"Silas told us there were good and horrible people here. Maybe it is all a rumor." Oak rubs his head. "And then we get here, and he bails? What is up with that?"

I feel anxiety bubbling inside my veins. "Fen told me not to let the cheers fool us. Something is going on, and we will find out. I trust Silas to explain more when he can," I defend. "Right now, we need to go to our rooms and prepare for dinner."

"What is up with her, by the way?" Maines crosses her arms.

"Who?" I question. "Fen?"

"Yes, her. She doesn't like me, and it's very apparent," Maines huffs.

"You're overthinking this, Maines. We've been with her for a day." I move toward my door, the snake's eyes gleaming in the hallway. "Give her a chance."

I reach for my door handle hesitantly, still half expecting the snake to rear up and bite me. I hold my breath and close my eyes before I grab the handle, releasing my breath quickly as the door opens easily and without a snake bite.

"I'll see you two soon," I say over my shoulder.

I hear Oak tell Maines that he will walk her to her bedroom as I shut the door.

My back scratches against the heavy wooden door as I lean against it, inhaling deeply for the first time. I need a moment to think.

The sun has set, and the moon quickly rises outside. The darkened kingdom looks back at me from the tall, narrow windows that line the entire back wall of the room. Rich, deep crimson curtains hang to the floor, reminding me of my Daramveer bedroom. However, this castle is much nicer.

I move through the room, observing my surroundings. The furniture is sparse, yet each piece is crafted from dark walnut and adorned with engravings that hint at its age. My eyes fall on the bed against the far wall—one with a large canopy draped in rich red velvet. The silk sheets are also a deep crimson, and a chandelier hangs from the ceiling, resembling falling stars.

I realize the eyes on the snake indicate the color within, and I am instantly curious about the other bedrooms.

I sit on the side of the bed and melt into the softness of the sheets as I try to process today.

What is going on?

Think, Briar. Think.

But, nothing comes to mind.

My mind is a mess of thoughts as I try to process our arrival and Silas's actions since we've been here. We have things we must accomplish, and I cannot afford to be distracted. We must find a way to prevent this war from starting, saving both Rohhit and me in the process. I look down at my hands, the black fingertips and darkening veins never letting me forget.

My eyes begin to close against my will, and my body relaxes.

I feel myself drifting into sleep, exhaustion overtaking me, even with memories that are almost too much to bear. My body feels as if it is floating. The heavy sensation of sleep presses down on me when I suddenly hear someone familiar screaming my name.

Briar.

I sit up abruptly in bed, my heart racing, and glance around. Nothing but the crackling fire responds.

I know that voice, but I'm not ready to admit it to myself just yet.

I walk to the heavy door and crack it open, peering into the dim hallway. To my surprise, it's empty, with only the shuffling of feet in the distance reaching my ears. The candlelight in the hallway casts an unnerving shadow against the stone, and I swear something is watching me, waiting for me to step into the darkness. Quickly closing the door, I brush off the unsettling feeling and rub my tired eyes.

I walk to the large walnut wardrobe and pull on the doors.

Gowns in all shades of red and deep burgundy hang before me like the morning sun. This is an interesting color choice for me, as I typically gravitate to blacks, but red will be a fun change. I'm willing to give this a chance since it reminds me of the dress Rose brought to me from Eddris. The gown I currently wear is peppered with dirt from the walk here, so slipping into something fresh will make me feel better.

After a brief perusal, I pull out a scarlet gown entirely made of silk. Thin straps rest on my shoulders, leading into the billowing, low-draped neckline that hangs perfectly over my breasts. The fabric alone makes this dress breathtaking; no jewels or embroidery are needed.

I kick off my old clothes and slip into the red dress; it fits my curves perfectly. It's beautiful, but there's something about it that I can't identify, which leaves me feeling uneasy. I try to brush it off as a familiar shimmer catches my eye from the bottom of the wardrobe. My mother's crown rests atop a small box, almost hidden beneath the dense sea of dresses. I grab the crown, admiring its beauty for a moment, before I place it on my head and close my eyes.

You can do this.

I glance in the mirror and smooth my hair, adding the final touches before heading to the door.

I gaze out the large window at the town, uncertain if the shock of being here will ever fade. I'm in Andorwood, the kingdom of criminals and the forgotten. And I, Briar Black-byrne, am here to win them over. Honestly, my brother would have loved to see this. Instead of my heart fracturing at the thought of him, a smile graces my lips. Barlowe would, in fact, have done anything to see this, and I find myself shedding a quick laugh.

The quiet town beneath me is eerie yet captivating. I'm eager to learn about this kingdom and its hidden history. Something old resides here, and I'm confident I'm in the right place to find answers.

A knock on the door snaps me from my thoughts.

I move across my bedroom, my dress trailing behind me, and jerk open the door. Silas stands there, dressed in all black with a heaviness on his face that I've never seen before. Like his armor, his clothing is perfectly tailored.

"Hey," he whispers.

"Where have you been?" I snap, lunging forward into his body.

He wraps his hands around me and inhales deeply. Even though his body is strong, I can feel the weakness that stems from the worry we are all feeling.

"You... You look stunning," he breathes in awe, as he steps back to take me in. "Are you alright?"

"It's you I'm concerned about." I cup his face. "You have a lot of explaining to do." I pull on this hand, but he remains steady on the threshold.

I furrow my brow, never breaking my stare, and tug against his strong body once more.

"Silas, come in."

"We need to head to the Great Hall. My father is waiting." Silas's head falls.

"But, I need to speak with you." I furrow my brows, annoyance running through me. "Now."

"Briar," he whispers. "Please do not make me make that choice right now."

I glare at Silas, unable to control my tone as I snark, "What? This entire arrival has been odd, and you've not even been here with us." Anger dashes through my body. "I'm just asking you to speak with me."

"I'm sorry, but we don't have time. We will talk later tonight." He gazes into my eyes, a gentle worry behind them. "You will only have me and my attention. I promise you that."

I remain unmoving for a second, our hands still wrapped together, and calm my anger.

One.

Two.

Three.

His eyes flash with something unfamiliar, and I realize that he's scared. It's terror that sits in his green eyes.

My stomach drops, and I let it go, not wanting to push him right now.

"Okay," I breathe. "Later, you will explain everything. You promise?" I run my hand up to his elbow and pull him toward me.

He lets me, giving me complete control in this moment. I pull his forehead against mine and inhale deeply. My Silas. Mine.

"Yes," he replies.

"Whatever is going on, we will figure out what to do together." I kiss him softly. His posture relaxes for a second, allowing me to move to his body, lost together in this moment.

I pull away, wrapping my arms around his neck.

"Let's go," I whisper into his ear.

He nods.

We move down the hallway, knocking on Oak's and Maines's doors. To no surprise, we find them together in Maines's room.

Like mine, her room is adorned with rich velvets and silks, but of a dark violet hue, with ivy weaving through her space—as if inviting the forest inside. My jaw drops at the beauty before me.

"You should see mine," Oak says, noticing my stare. "It's lined with bookshelves. It's like they knew exactly what room to put me in."

"You won't stay in your room at all," I say.

He laughs, shooting a glance in Maine's direction. "Alone? Absolutely not."

Silas steps in. "We can go through our rooms later; we need to head to dinner."

"Nice to see you too, buddy. An explanation would be nice," Maines sasses, brushing past him in a flowing gown of deep purple. "But, I'll let it slide since you look stressed as fuck."

Silas doesn't respond, but turns on his heels to head back into the dim hallway.

We head down the grand staircase toward the Great Hall. Hux, Larkin, Warrick, and Fen wait outside the large double doors adorned with jewels and serpents. They, too, wear clothes as fine as ours, and nod as we approach. The men are dressed similarly to Silas and Oak, while Fen wears a dark green gown that hugs her beautiful curves, leaving nothing to the imagination. Her curled black hair falls to her side as she moves toward us with a deadly grace.

"You ready?" Fen moves in front of her brother, brushing the shoulders of his tailored suit.

"Fuck no," Silas replies.

"Too bad," she says.

I glance toward Larkin, whose stare could burn straight through me, and quickly turn my head—that's a conversation for a less stressful moment. Focusing back on the double doors, Warrick knocks, and I suck in a breath as they open.

It's time to meet the King of Andorwood.

CHAPTER 7

The wide doors open into the Great Hall, and I do everything I can to keep my jaw from dropping. The black marble floors are adorned with silver and gold lines, resembling a metallic river. The ceilings are high and arched, with dark wooden beams steadying the tallest windows I've ever seen. The stars in the night sky blend with the room, and I feel like I'm standing in the dark clouds for a moment.

Silas stands next to me with Maines and Oak on my opposite side. Fen and the others confidently move into the room, proving they've done this many times before. I glance at my oldest friends, both sending a *holy shit* look in return. My eyes cut to Silas, but his gaze remains focused ahead, a bead of sweat forming on his brow.

He grabs my hand, giving it a hard squeeze, before entering the room. He leads me toward a long, wooden table in the middle of the room, always with his body in front—as if protecting me from something I can't see. The table is situated under a dark chandelier with high-backed chairs surrounding it. The large room is punctuated with intimate sitting areas along the far walls, each lined with small couches and tables for post-dinner drinks. Place cards line the table, indicating our exact placement for the evening.

Scanning the seating chart, I'm near the head of the table next to Silas, with Larkin on my other side. Across the table sits a name I'm not familiar with, and next to that sits Fen. Oak takes a seat next to her, followed by Warrick. Maines sits on the opposite side of Larkin, followed by a large empty table after her.

"Where is Hux?" I lean into Silas.

"He's near the cliffs. Someone has to keep watch while we endure this evening's torture," he whispers, moving his chair closer to the table. "He rarely attends these things."

"Lucky him," I whisper back.

The head of the table, followed by the seat immediately to its left, remains empty. I can only assume for Silas's parents. My stomach churns with anticipation, and every sound has me on edge.

Fenmore and Oak have a hushed conversation sitting next to one another, and Warrick and Larkin talk across the table. I lean around Larkin to find Maines sitting alone, glaring at Oak, speaking quietly with Fenmore.

"Maines," I hiss.

She snaps her head in my direction, and her cheeks turn a light pink. She knows she was caught glaring. "Yeah?" Maines replies.

"Are you alright?" I stretch my neck further in her direction, earning a huff from Larkin.

"I'm fine," she snaps.

Larkin turns to me and nearly bites my head off. "I'm sitting here."

My brows raise. "Oh, are you one for politeness now?"

My response catches him off guard, and he shifts in his seat. "You don't know anything about me."

"Now," I whisper. "That isn't all true."

He nearly snarls.

"What is your problem with me?" I snap.

Silas hears our exchange and places his hand on my leg under the table.

"Be nice, Spiridon," Warrick snaps at Larkin from across the table. "You are being ruder than normal."

My body tenses at the surname, and I glance at Warrick, who gives me a reassuring smile, confirming he has my back at this moment. I return a grin and settle into my seat, feeling victorious at flustering Larkin. Two can play this game, and I'll win.

Larkin places his open palms on the table and opens his mouth to speak, when two doors in the far corner—*I didn't notice them before*—open slowly, causing a creak to echo around the room.

A tall woman enters the room first. Her black, flowing hair peppered with gray cascades to her waist. She wears a dark green gown—the same shade as Fen's—which flows gracefully with her. Her shoes click resoundingly against the smooth floor as she strides purposefully toward us. Piercing eyes that mirror Silas's meet mine momentarily, and that's when I realize his mother, Aerona Nastronde, has just entered the room.

She's stunning, clearly aging gracefully. She smiles at Fen, taking a moment to remain standing to meet the stares of everyone around her, thin lines forming around her eyes as she does so. A bright jade amulet hangs from her neck, catching my attention. It's beautiful and seems to suck in all the light that dares twinkle around it. I glance beside her at Fen, noting it's the same necklace that adorns her neck, with similar features in the stone that are hard to miss. Fen definitely inherits her looks from her mother, although I can't help but notice the slight differences between Silas and his family.

"Good evening," Aerona says, her voice floating around us.

I only stare as the others nod in her direction, smiling without speaking, except Silas. His face remains hard and focused on the double doors that seem to pulse in the darkness. Warrick quickly stands, brushing his hand over Fenmore's shoulders, and walks to pull out the large wooden chair for Aerona to take a seat. She offers him a soft smile, and a nod as he pushes her against the table. Fenmore watches with a look of pride in her eyes and winks as he sits back down beside Oak.

Everyone continues speaking in hushed tones, all a bit too casual for how I feel inside. Silas's hand stays on my leg, and for a moment, I feel it tremble slightly. I move my hand down to squeeze his tightly, just to let him know I'm here. Aerona leans over, gently kissing Fen on the cheek, and whispers something in her ear. Fen tilts her head back with a laugh, and I watch their exchange.

The queen leans around Fenmore and says something to Warrick, who nods with a dazzling smile that creases his dark eyes. I keep watching them, glancing back toward Silas now and then, but nothing has changed. His brow tightens, and he only seems to focus on the doors, as if he's on high alert, unable to pull himself into reality.

His mother flashes a look across the table, noticing my stare. "Briar Blackbyrne."

The entire table pauses.

I sit taller in my chair. "It's nice to meet you, Aerona," I say, dipping my chin in respect.

"You as well," her regal voice responds.

"Thank you for hosting us." I shift in my chair. "Your home is stunning."

She narrows her gaze. "You are polite."

I angle my head and notice the tension pulse around the room like a heartbeat as the others stop breathing to observe our exchange.

"You expected otherwise?"

"Your reputation has followed you across the sea." Her gaze looks me up and down. "I wasn't sure what to expect, if we are being honest."

I smile. "I always prefer honesty."

"Your eyes are quite stunning." She tilts her head as her gaze bores into mine. "Beauty, confidence, and eliciting fear—the three deadly qualities a woman can possess." She pauses. "Among other things."

I pause momentarily, letting the words wash over me like an ice bath.

"Those are three things I care nothing for," I snap back.

"You should."

I angle my head in curiosity. "And why is that?"

She smiles. "Power."

"Believe it or not," I huff a laugh, and the table tenses around us, "I'm not interested in that."

"Well, what is it that you care for then, Briar?" Aerona angles her head. "My son?"

I glance in his direction, and he stiffens, anticipating my response. I let the silence fill the air for a moment, thickening it with tension, before turning my gaze back to Aerona.

"I care about peace. I care about the people of Daramveer, Eddris, Cammon, and Brinkym," I say, placing my visibly stained hands on the table.

Her eyes shift to my hands. The black veins are ever-present against my sun-kissed skin.

I lean forward. "I care about the people of Andorwood, which means everyone at this table. And yes," I pause, letting every ounce of the deserved tension build, "I love your son. Deeply."

A hard breath leaves Silas's lungs, and his grip around my knee tightens.

Aerona cuts her gaze to Silas before quickly reverting her attention back to me.

"You two would be extremely powerful together," a soft smile curls her lips. "Dare I say, lethal."

My brow raises. "It seems, apparently, that it's only power you care for."

Larkin clears his throat at my abruptness while Warrick nearly stands. The others seem shocked by the words I'm brave enough to speak, but I remain unfazed and stern.

She grins, glancing down to pick at her nails. "It would be no good for us to be on each other's bad sides." She straightens in her chair. "I fear the world may implode."

I nod. "I believe that is something we both can agree on."

"I look forward to getting to know you better, Queen," she says, relaxing back in her chair.

Everyone's eyes are on us as our conversation falls silent.

Silas's grip loosens, and I feel his gaze burning into my side. I don't look at him at first, but focus on Aerona, who has returned to speaking quietly with Fen. Silas and I haven't said those words yet. Declaring them in front of an audience may have been a mistake.

Against my better judgment, I look at him. It's as if his presence is pulling me in. Our eyes meet, and his piercing green eyes bore into mine. He slowly blinks, as if still processing everything since arriving, and I open my mouth to speak, but stop as my gaze is pulled to the large double doors.

The room goes cold, and our breaths quickly fill the air with a white fog. The doors we entered open with force, and four women rush in dressed in black silk that doesn't leave much to the imagination. They carry long gray, silver, and black fabrics behind them that flow from their arms and across the floor like black rivers.

"Tonight's entertainment," Fen states, leaning over the table toward me. "An Andorwood tradition."

I look back at the dancers as they line up before the table, preparing for the music to begin. A dark melody fills the room, signaling them to begin. As quickly as they rushed in, the fabric wraps around them like a second skin, and they begin to move. The fabric moves to the music like their limber bodies, whipping through the air in all directions. The bass builds in my chest like a thundering heartbeat, and the sounds of their footsteps fill the air alongside the melancholy tones.

They part for a moment, moving behind each of our chairs, causing the fabric to brush across our faces at times, and I fight the urge to swat it away.

Oak, Maines, and the others watch in awe as the beautiful women dance in unison around us.

One woman, in her late thirties, keeps her gaze fixed on Silas. Her white hair shines in the dark room like a blinding light. The haunting music moves her body around, but her stare never breaks from him, and my stomach begins to twist with jealousy.

Who is that?

The music intensifies. The blaring bass reverberates through the room, guiding their fluid bodies as each twists and grinds in its own way. With every boom, their bodies change direction, their arms and hands moving in sync to create angular gestures. It's beautiful, yet I feel my rage surfacing as I watch another woman look at Silas with such an expression.

I take a second to look at him while the others are lost in the dance. Silas looks down, still haunted by whatever lives here, and clearly unaffected by the women around us—as if he doesn't even see them or feel the stare from the woman so desperate to get his attention.

And that's when I notice a new shadow rippling behind Silas's large frame, like a creature of the night.

Malachi Nastronde sits at the head of the table.

I do my best, but I can't hide my surprise at his sudden arrival. He's older than I expected. Deep lines mar his face, and an all-white beard covers most of his jaw. Gray streaks run through his black hair, and his bright jade eyes gleam in the dim light of the Great Hall.

Malachi stares at me, but the others don't seem to notice him. Silas remains lost in thought while the others watch the dancers move through the room.

"Briar, Queen of Daramveer."

His deep voice coils into my mind despite his lips remaining still. I attempt to look away, but it's as if my gaze is fixed on his.

"The others neither see nor hear me. Only you, Briar," he nearly hisses. "How lucky."

A horrified feeling courses through my veins, leaving me fixated on Malachi's face. Silas pulls his gaze up and notices my frozen state. Even from my periphery, a wave of dread washes over him as his face drains of color.

He knows exactly who I see.

"You've traveled far to be here."

I blink, unable to move or react.

"You think you will win this kingdom over?"

His hands rest on the table, and I notice the slightest move-ment. Black vines start to slither from his sleeves toward me. The thin vines snap on the wooden table, drowning out the muffled beats of the music. One quickly moves my way, attempting to wrap around my wrist, and my stomach rolls.

Terror floods me.

His piercing gaze settles into my soul, and I study them—they aren't eyes like Silas's or Fen's. They are different—darker—and something I've never seen before. I burrow down, attempting to focus on my magic, begging my shadows to come forward. I need them to shift me out of this castle immediately. I need to get the fuck away from this man.

"Briar," Silas says beside me. "Don't listen to what the shadows say."

A tear settles heavily on my lower lid as I remain stuck.

"Look at me."

Still in a trance, my eyes sluggishly blink. Malachi furrows his brow, watching me slowly return to life against his hold.

"Briar," Silas says once more, louder, causing the others to look our way. "Eyes on me."

Fen and Aerona ignore us, choosing not to involve themselves with what's happening. They already know.

"*Please*," Silas reverts to a gentle voice.

I blink harder this time, and Malachi begins to fade into black smoke. His eyes burn into Silas as he watches his son pull me back into my body and out of his invisible claws that wrap around my mind.

He vanishes as a tear rolls down my cheek.

I gasp, and my back hits the tall chair behind me.

"Briar?" Maines calls from down the table. "You look like you've seen a ghost."

My chest heaves, and I shiver, thankful that the vines are gone and no longer snaking toward me. Silas turns my entire chair as if it were weightless and wraps his arms around me momentarily.

"I am so fucking sorry." He presses his head against mine, barely whispering, "I'll explain everything soon."

Tears begin to form in the corners of my eyes again, but I refuse to let Aerona see me cry another tear.

"W—Why," I barely muster out, "didn't you warn me?"

Silas notices my state, and regret hangs in his eyes, like bringing me here was possibly the worst mistake he could have ever made.

The far back doors of the Great Hall pulse as someone approaches, the darkness of the shadows concealed by the night.

"It appears that the party has started without me."

Everyone halts once more as Malachi Nastronde floats into the room like a black storm. I look around, praying that the others see him, and from their reactions, I know he is really before us this time. A king glides toward us, his long black cloak hanging around his body, making him appear like a nightmare. Shadows pool around his feet, as if they are carrying him to the table, and the room around us seems to hold its breath as he approaches.

Malachi Nastronde sits at the head of the table, ignoring the other guests. Aerona tries to stand, but Malachi waves her off with a dismissive gesture. She quickly takes her seat and lowers her chin, as if she somehow offended him.

Out of the corner of my eye, I see Silas's jaw clench so hard that I fear his teeth might shatter. I slowly turn my gaze toward Malachi and quiet the fear running wild in my veins, shifting my chair back against the table.

The darkness inside me throbs in his presence, and I take a deep breath.

The King of Andorwood stares directly at me. "Now, where were we, Miss Blackbyrne?"

CHAPTER 8

Everyone goes deathly quiet as a wide grin forms across Malachi's face.

"Did I startle you all? I apologize for my abrupt arrival. I rushed in, knowing I was late. Something had me quite held up this evening," he continues, directing a menacing smile toward us, pausing on me for a moment.

He claps, stopping the dancers and the music. The dancer who had her eyes transfixed on Silas now stares at Malachi with wide eyes.

"You all are dismissed." He lifts his hands, and a gust of shadows pushes the doors open abruptly.

Eager to flee from his presence, they hurry out of the room.

Silas glares at him, and I glance down when I feel his grip tightening around my leg.

Aerona speaks first. "I'm glad you could make it, honey. We didn't start dinner without you, only the entertainment."

He dismisses her, more aggressively this time.

Malachi clears his throat. "It's an exciting time in Andorwood. We rarely have guests of this kind of *status*." He emphasizes the last word, as if it were sour on his tongue. "Oak

Hombern, all the way from Brinkym. The son of Soren and Hera Hombern. I met your parents a long while ago. How are they?"

"They are well. Thanks for asking," Oak responds. "Andorwood is just lovely."

Malachi's lips curl. "Sarcasm. Just like your father. I should have anticipated that."

"I guess it runs in the family."

Malachi flashes an unamused grin. "Humor like that can get you killed with bad timing."

"Hasn't happened yet," Oak quips.

Malachi, growing impatient at the joking, growls out, "Yet."

"It's nice to meet you, Your Majesty," Maines interjects, attempting to ease the rising tension toward Oak. "We do appreciate you being open to our presence here."

"Ah, yes. Maines Madden. I heard of the passing of your father and brother recently," Malachi says with a shrug. "I can't say I was upset at the news."

Maines's eyebrows raise, and Oak furrows his, ready to fight should Maines react poorly to the statement.

"Their passings were inevitable. I knew their actions would have consequences one day," Maines says, sharply. "There are few people who will miss them."

Oak makes a fist on the table, and I hear Fen whisper to him, "Calm down. Right now."

He takes her advice and settles back into his chair.

Malachi moves down the table with his eyes. "Who else do we have here? Larkin, Warrick, and Fen—good evening and welcome back."

They dip their heads in silent acknowledgment.

Sweat starts to bead on my brow, and I realize who's left for him to address. I take a breath—counting to ten—already attempting to calm my racing heart.

"Silas," the King of Andorwood says, in a deathly calm voice, "welcome home, my son."

Silas tenses. "Hello, Malachi."

The world seems to pause, and an unsettling silence moves through the room.

"Thank you for ruining yet another Andorwood ship," his father mocks. "Seems to be a pattern with your foolish antics."

"We saved dozens of people in the process." Silas leans forward. "A ship can be rebuilt; lives cannot."

"So noble of you, Silas."

Shadows begin to flicker off of Silas's back as his anger grows, but Malachi brushes him off and finally returns his gaze to me again.

"Briar Blackbyrne, the Queen of Daramveer in Andorwood. I believe I've seen it all, now." He looks around, wanting the others to join in with his amusement. "Your father is probably rolling in the grave you put him in."

The others watch intensely, as if the room might explode at any moment. Their stares are scorching, like the sun's rays against my back, but I ignore his dig and maintain my cool façade, refusing to give him the reaction he wants.

"Daramveer has fallen. My people have fled, and the Great Wiitches pose a terrible threat to us all."

Malachi leans back, crossing his ankle over his leg, as if bored.

"I'm here to save our realm from destruction."

His brow rises. "And who travels with you?"

I glance behind me, ready to speak about Maines, Oak, and Rose—who is still safely on the ship with Captain Darcy. I open my mouth to speak, and Malachi raises a hand.

"No." He glances at my hands. "Not them."

I narrow my eyes at him, allowing my shadows to ripple around me for a second, refusing to back down from this man.

Silas slowly turns his head, horrified at my challenge toward his father, but I push further, darkening the room around us.

"Briar, breathe," Silas pleads.

I cut my eyes to his, but don't speak.

"Why spoil the fun we're about to have, son?" Malachi raises his hands as he says, condescendingly, "Now, let her make her own choices."

"Do not speak to him that way," I snap.

Malachi laughs. "I will do what I want with my son. I have his entire life, and I won't stop now because you are here."

I glance at Silas, preparing for the anger radiating off of him to blind me, but to my surprise, he sits back in his chair.

"Now, answer me," Malachi demands. "Who travels with you?"

My blood begins to boil.

"You know who lives within me. I'm not here to play games." The black veins on my hands begin to throb. "And I think it would be unwise for you to ignore the fact that we're going to war soon. Your entire kingdom is at risk, and here you are, taunting us."

"Taunting you?" He angles his head. "I'm having a conversation."

I huff a sarcastic laugh.

"Malachi, you know why I'm here," Silas chimes in. "We need the help of the Andorwood army. We need to build a following. With their help, we can stop the enemy from burning this realm to the ground."

Malachi moves back in his chair, relaxing his shoulders. "Andorwood will never help her. She will destroy us all." He picks at his nails. "Just look at what she's done to her own kingdom."

I open my mouth to speak, but a voice from down the table echoes instead.

"How dare you?" Maines snaps from her seat. "She is the queen—an equal to you, in case you forgot—so, I would show her some respect."

Malachi laughs. "You are all such fools. I suggest you not get comfortable in Andorwood."

"Why is that?" Maines barks back.

"I'll have the ship ready for your departure in two days."

"You won't even give us a chance?" I interject, coolly. "Meet with me privately. Let's discuss this like leaders. Your actions are making you seem like a child."

Anxiety twists in my guts, and I fear my luck is running out.

"A child? I'm protecting my people from you. Look at you." His gaze burns through me. "The dress you wear is as crimson as the blood on your filthy, stained hands," Malachi claps back.

Silas slams his fists onto the table and stands with force.

"Enough!"

The table shakes with force, and shadows gather on his back like a towering tidal wave. A breeze flows through the room, casting a chill over all of us, and I swear for a moment his eyes glow green.

"I refuse to sit here and listen to you speak to her that way," he steethes. "You are the only fool here, Malachi, and if you won't join us, then we'll watch Andorwood burn to the ground along with the rest of this world." Silas's eyes darken, and the room pulses with his anger. "Have the fucking ship prepared. We will leave."

He cuts his furious eyes to mine and grabs my hand, pulling me to stand with him.

Oak and Maines stand with us, leaving Warrick, Fen, and Larkin seated at the table, unmoving. Silas turns his back, and we move across the hard, smooth stone. With each step toward the door, I feel our chance slipping away.

I feel our future is turning to ruin, just like the nightmares that have haunted me.

"She will destroy you, son." Malachi stands at our departure. "You are bound to her, and she will be your downfall. Briar will drag you to the darkest realm," he yells.

Silas throws an uncaring look over his shoulder, and rips open the wide doors.

"Then let her destroy me. Let her fucking ruin me. I'd happily allow Briar to be the reason I crumble," Silas fumes. "Because life without her, I fear, would be darker than any fate I can imagine."

My eyes stay locked on his, and I watch jade flames blaze in his irises, an unimaginable anger directed toward his father.

The four of us exit the Great Hall, and Malachi's words hang heavy on my shoulders.

"Fucking idiot," Silas mumbles under his breath as he charges toward our rooms, up the massive staircase.

"Are we really leaving?" Maines calls from behind us. "Without even trying?"

"After that, I'd be surprised if he spoke to us again at all," Oak replies.

Silas's grip remains tight on my hand, like he can't bear to be distanced from me, or he's fearful I'll somehow slip away. Neither of us replies to Maines and Oak's questions as we round the final corner before our rooms. I can feel the fury leaking off Silas's body, and between steps, I trace my thumb against his hand in a desperate attempt to calm him. I'm not sure how, but his thoughts and emotions swirl inside my own mind like an irate sea.

Hate.

That's all I can feel.

Silas strides to his door, waving his hand before the golden snake's. The black jeweled eyes turn in his presence, and the door unlocks with a loud click.

"Get inside," he demands.

Oak pushes past Silas, eagerness propelling him forward, and enters the onyx-filled room. "Don't have to tell me twice."

The large bedroom before us exudes dark elegance, evoking both ominous and regal vibes—a space perfectly curated for the Prince of Darkness.

At the center of the room stands a grand four-poster bed draped in luxurious black silk sheets. Various decorative elements —including an antique mirror and ornate, Gothic sconces— enhance the beautifully grim atmosphere. A towering fireplace dominates the far wall with dark antique furniture arranged around it.

"This was your room as a child?" Oak asks, looking around the dark room.

"Yes." Silas rubs his temples. "Until I moved out, this was my bedroom."

"It's...inviting." Oak makes a pained face. "Explains a lot."

I remain near the door with the threatening words from earlier still racing through my mind.

"Briar, come sit," Maines urges, indicating a chair around the crackling fire.

I stare blankly for a moment before stuttering out, "I...I want to change."

The red dress is blinding in this dark bedroom, and when I look down, I no longer see a stunning gown of crimson.

I see blood.

I see Barlowe lying in the courtyard, covered in blood. I see Oak's broken leg bleeding before my father. I see Silas with an arrow that nearly pierced his heart. I see his mangled arm on the ship. I see Rose's bloodied body, about to take her final breaths. And I hear Malachi's taunting words.

I'm covered in blood.

I'm drenched in their blood.

I look down at my hands and no longer see the dark veins tattooing my pale skin. Instead, I see streaks of crimson in their place. I see dripping blood falling from my hands to the floor, like every tear of the fallen is pouring out of me. I hear the drops of blood hitting the hard ground like exploding cries, and it begins to consume me. The blood slowly covers my arms, trailing up my body like bloodied snakes. Their mouths open, ready to devour me with their razor-sharp fangs, and I can't breathe.

I deserve it.

I deserve the pain.

My heart races, and my stance becomes as chaotic as the veins shooting up my arms. I claw at my own skin, trying to rid myself of the bright red blood, and my heart drops as my mother's crown slips from my head, crashing against the hard floor.

"Get this off of me," I cry, my voice breaking as I squirm, trying to escape my own body.

They all jump up and rush toward me. The overwhelming feelings bubble up in my throat, and my chest heaves as tingles of fear, shock, and anxiety move through me like lightning bolts.

"I'll grab you something from my room." Maines rushes to the door with Oak following closely.

Silas takes my hand and pulls me toward the bathroom. I move from clawing at my skin to the gown, desperate to wash off the blood, ripping through the red silk fabric.

"I'm covered in blood," I pant out, panic lacing my words. "It's everywhere, Silas."

"No, you aren't. Just breathe," he says softly, attempting to steady my breathing. "It's only a gown." Silas grips the fabric, ripping it from my body as quickly as he can.

The torn fabric falls to the ground like crimson rain, and my stomach rolls.

"Don't listen to Malachi's words. What happened is not your fault."

Tears streak down my cheeks.

"Barlowe, my mother, the resurrection stone, leaving Daramveer in Eden's hands... It's all ruined; it's all my fault." Tears stream down my face. "Everyone is gone because of me. Everything is fucking *crumbling* because of me."

I can't control myself, and my movements become as frantic as my thoughts.

The crushing feeling of the past months floods into my mind like a tidal wave. I wipe the falling tears from my cheeks and pull my hands away to see more blood.

Blood.

So much blood.

Silas grabs me, wrapping both arms tightly around my body. "Please, just take a breath. Let me help."

His words swirl in my mind, but they don't calm the panic. Instead, another emotion begins to bubble up in my chest, and I cut my gaze to his. Silas's face is warped with concern, and I realize what else is driving me right now.

Anger.

The dam within me breaks, sending my emotions crashing out like charging horses on a battlefield.

"You," I snap, pushing him away.

Silas stumbles backward from my unexpected force.

"You haven't explained anything. You have been distant and scared." I point my finger in his face. "How do you expect we win this war if you can't let me in or stand up to your fucking father?"

"Briar, stop." Silas steps closer, trying to reach for my hand. "You're upset."

"No." I jerk my hand back. "I have every right to ask questions and to be upset. You don't get to tell me when to stop." Tears fall from my eyes as I look at him, my gaze hardening. "You don't get to tell me how to feel."

Silas tries to pull me into an embrace once more, but I recoil —desperate for space and distance. For the first time in so long, I need him away from me. It's as if I can smell the deceit radiating off him.

I narrow my eyes. "Get out."

Silas freezes and grows pale.

"Go," my voice rumbles.

"Do not push me away right now. Please."

I point toward the door. "Since we arrived, all you've done is push me away."

"That isn't true."

I narrow my gaze, letting the anger out into the room around us, my shadows pulsing in the flickering candlelight.

"Briar," Silas repeats. "That isn't true."

"You didn't warn me about your father."

"I thought I was protecting you."

He tries to take a step forward, and I push against his chest, shoving him backward.

"Get the fuck away from me."

His shoulders fall, and for a moment, I swear I hear his chest crack.

"My love."

"Get. The. Fuck. Out. Silas."

He lowers his eyes, as if he can't bring himself to look at me.

"I'll have Maines bring you some new clothes." He steps away, reaching for the door, and glances over his shoulder. "Briar, I'll explain everything. I know I owe you that. Just…let me know when you're ready. *Please.*"

I glare at him.

"I'm so fucking sorry," he whispers, then shifts, shadows swirling around him as he melts into the mist.

The silent room feels deafening. I avoid the crimson dress pooled on the floor next to me and gaze into the mirror.

Count to ten, Briar. Breathe.

One.

Two.

Three.

I stumble forward, gripping the porcelain sink as tight as my knuckles allow.

Regret fills my veins from my outburst, but not my words. Silas needed to hear that. He's been distant and quiet since he arrived. Before I can forgive him, he has a lot of explaining to do, and I need to calm down before that can happen. I splash some water on my face and gaze back into the mirror. My autumn eyes are gone, now black. Veins darken on my cheeks, and with each passing second—the closer they get to my throat—the more I fear Kalix will claw her way out.

I stumble backward, slamming my eyes closed.

A familiar, haunting voice whispers in my mind, *"Who is here to protect you now, Briar?"*

I swallow down the anxiety—my shadows pounding in my mind—desperate to choke her down.

"Fuck off," I scream into the mirror. "Leave me alone."

A feeling of hopelessness washes over me, and I collapse to the ground. A numbness takes over my body, and I struggle to take in a deep breath.

"Briar?" A knock on the door sounds. "Are you alright?"

Maines cracks the door.

"Don't come in," I beg, feeling the haunting shift still staining my eyes. "Do not look at me."

Maines sees my state and rushes into the room anyway, crashing to the floor next to me. Nothing about the darkness surrounding me scares her. All she sees is her friend in desperate need of help.

She's holding new clothes and rapidly wraps what she can around my body. "What's going on?"

"It's too much." I don't look at her. "I can't do this, Maines. I screamed at Silas." I lower my head into my hands. "I'm furious with him. And I'm so fucking mad at myself for not being stronger."

She strokes the back of my head. "You are strong."

I collapse into her hold and weep.

"We aren't leaving, and we aren't giving up. And to be honest, you have every right to be mad at Silas. He's been completely absent since we got to this island." Maines brushes the hair from my face. "Maybe a good verbal lashing will snap him out of his own head."

I take a deep breath before I lift my head, afraid to show her my eyes, but all Maines does is smile. Our eyes meet, and I find a softness behind her ice-blue eyes.

"Beautiful and perfectly hazel," she whispers, tucking a piece of hair behind my ear.

She turns to give me a moment of privacy while I get dressed. I pull on some snug black pants paired with a flowing grey top. A calmness settles over me, and I take another breath.

"Thank you."

She turns and grins.

"We all need to be on the same page and understand what's happening here," I say. "If we're going to win them over, it will take all of us."

She nods. "You are right, but we have a problem."

"What?" I caution, as I tie my boots in place.

"Silas is gone." She winces.

"What do you mean, gone?"

She grimaces. "He left the castle."

"I would have, too." I roll my head back, heading for the door. "It's my fucking fault."

I pull open the large door to find his bedroom empty except for Oak, who is sitting by the fire and flipping through a book.

"What did he say, Oak?" I ask, rushing into the bedroom.

Oak looks up, his glasses low on his nose, and closes the book. "Not much. Only that he was going to go think until you were ready to speak."

I sigh.

"Do you know where he went?" Oak asks, placing his glasses in his chest pocket. "He was upset, more so than normal."

"No." I motion for them to follow me and head for the jeweled snake door. "But, I know who will."

CHAPTER 9

"Don't tell me we are going to see Fen," Maines complains from behind me, as we walk down the quiet hallway.

Candlelight dances off of her sharp cheekbones, but even in the dim lighting, I can tell she's annoyed.

"What is your problem with her?" I question.

She shrugs. "She hasn't been inviting to me. That's all."

"She's letting you stay in her house," Oak chimes in. "I'd say that's about as inviting as you can get."

"Oh, of course. Stand up for her over me." Maines pushes ahead of him, and he rushes to catch up.

"Whoa. I'm not standing up for anyone, Maines, and you know that." He takes her hand. "Just give her some time. This whole situation might feel strange for her, too. I mean, the Queen of Daramveer is dating her brother, and now we're in her kingdom trying to persuade an army—*her* army—to fight alongside us."

Oak is right.

This probably seems strange to everyone around.

"Fine," Maines snaps. "But I'm not going to be friendly until she is."

Oak smiles, nudging her shoulder. "I expect nothing less, darling."

We continue down the long hallway while I scan our surroundings. I memorized the doors as quickly as possible on our way to dinner earlier. Each door held a jewel that matched our outfits. If my memory serves me correctly, the person I want to speak with was wearing a dark shade of auburn.

"I think the room should be… here." I urge everyone to stop in front of the ornate door.

Auburn eyes look back at me from the jeweled snake, and I take a deep breath before knocking, telling myself that the snake will not bite me if I extend my hand forward.

My fist thuds against the door as I drive my hand into the heavy wood.

Silence is the reply.

I knock again, harder this time, in case the person behind the door is asleep or avoiding the intrusion at this hour.

I hear feet shuffling behind the thick wood. I glance behind me at Oak and Maines, who both are staring at me with an intense curiosity.

The large door barely opens, revealing nothing but darkness. As it opens wider, Larkin appears, and a look of surprise flashes across his face.

"What?" Larkin mumbles.

Asshole.

"I'm sorry to bother you." I make a pained face. "But I need to know where Silas is."

"Quite a fight you two had, I heard."

"He told you?" I question.

"I don't know the details—"

"Oh, I'm sure," I interrupt, sarcasm lacing my tone.

"—because I didn't ask." His brows rise as he continues. "He came to tell me where he was headed, and I put the pieces together from there."

"Fantastic," I huff, annoyed that I have to ask him for help.

"Why are you here?" Larkin asks.

"What?" The abruptness catches me off guard.

"You know where he is," he snaps. "So, why did you come to my room?"

I look back at Maines and Oak and think for a moment.

Our arrival—the house on the cliff. He mentioned moving out at some point.

"He's at the small house that sits upon the cliff. I'll call it a hunch, but I assume he's there." I angle my head and look at Larkin. "Right?"

He slowly nods. "That is where Silas resides when he is not at the castle."

"So?" I add.

"So what?" Larkin's voice grows more impatient by the second.

"Do you think he's there?" I push. "You are the last one that spoke to him."

"Yes," he sighs. "I would assume that is where he went."

Another thing that Silas didn't mention—a completely different house where he lives. I caught him staring at it as the ship was docking, and from the longing look on his face, I knew that house meant something to him.

"I want you two to shift there and check on him," I add, looking at Maines and Oak.

"What?" Maines snaps. "No."

"You aren't coming with us?" Oak angles his head.

"Not yet. I want you to go and talk to him. What I said was horrible, and even though he said so, I don't think he's ready to see me just yet." I smile, assuring them that it's fine to leave me. "Go tell him I'm okay, and I will meet you all really soon."

"I'm not sure…" Maines starts, but I cut her off.

"I'm fine. Please go talk to him."

"Well… if you say so." Oak looks unsure. "He's going to be pissed at us for leaving you here alone."

"Well, good. Maybe he'll be mad at you two and not me by the time I get there."

Oak and Maines swap anxious looks.

Maines steps forward. "Promise me you won't be long. I'll be left out once those two get together."

I snort. "Promise. Please check on him. He listens to you."

Maines nods, and they grab hands to shift, leaving me standing there with Larkin, who doesn't look thrilled about this entire plan. I take a deep breath, letting the silent tension build around me. Steadying myself, I think of the things I need to say.

I turn to him.

"Can we talk?"

He tenses his brow. "No."

"Larkin."

"What about?"

"Are you going to make me stand in the hallway, or may I come inside?"

He rolls his eyes, folding his arms before stepping aside, allowing me to cross the threshold.

The dark auburn room is elegant, yet worn. Candlelight dances across the walls, casting a sunset-like glow throughout the space. It's beautiful, but something about it carries a sadness, as if the objects—including Larkin—conceal a grim secret. The air is thick with the scent of aged wood, and dozens of books line the far wall.

I make my way to the small sitting area and plop down in a cushioned chair.

I use the silence to study his face.

Larkin reminds me of Oak. He has the same dusty white hair that falls messily in all directions, along with some that shades his lower jaw. However, he's older—probably my brother's age—and his eyes aren't as kind as Oak's.

His eyes are darker—like the events of his life have tainted them.

"Again I'll ask," Larkin says, sitting down in a leather chair across from me, crossing his legs, "why are you here?"

"Because I know you."

Shock flashes across his expression. "Nope. You don't."

I smile, letting the tension build as I begin to pick at my nails.

"Well, I don't know you, but I know who you are. You know my brother, Barlowe. Or, I should say, you knew."

The words sting coming out.

Larkin leans forward, placing his elbows on his knees. "And how would you know that?"

"He talked about you." I relax my shoulders. "Years ago, when he first arrived at the training camp. A powerful Lumor Wielder from Eddris who always talked about traveling to Andor-wood." I pause, leaning forward to match his demeanor. "Larkin. Spiridon."

He runs his fingers over his facial hair, sizing me up.

I raise my brow. "I wasn't sure that was your full name until I heard Warrick say it in the Great Hall."

He studies me for a moment and sits back in the chair, as if not wanting to confirm or deny anything I'm saying. The dim light bounces off his stony face, and I watch him ponder my forwardness and how he wants to respond.

"Yes, that is my full name," Larkin responds harshly. "And remind me to tell Warrick to watch who he shares information with in the future."

"I thought so." I smile, feeling victorious, and sit back in my chair following his lead. "But, I'm trying to figure out why you acted like you didn't know who I was."

"I don't think I directly acted that way," he says. "I just wasn't very interested in meeting you."

"Rude."

"No," he immediately replies. "I'm honest, the no bullshit type."

"Or an asshole," I mumble under my breath, causing him to glare in my direction.

Fuck.

I'm losing this conversation.

I shift in my seat. "I'm sure Barlowe talked about me. Right?"

He doesn't respond, but I watch his hands begin to fidget in his lap.

"Were you close?" I ask.

Larkin breaks eye contact with me and looks toward the dark window, as if even his thoughts are desperate to get away from this conversation.

"How long were you at the training camp with him?"

Again, no reply, he remains lost in thought, the tremble in his hands increasing with each passing second. I notice his jaw tense as the rising tension around us becomes unbearable, even making me uncomfortable in my own skin.

I lean forward, growing more frustrated by the second, "Did you hear of his passing?"

Larkin stands, nearly knocking the chair over behind him. His chest heaves, and his eyes flip between panicked and angry as he looks at me.

"I think you should leave."

"What?" My mouth falls open. "Why?"

"Because it's late, and you need to go check on Silas."

"That man is fine," I protest. "I wanted to speak with you."

He places his hands in his pockets. "I never asked to speak with you."

"Gods," I exclaim, standing after him. "You are so fucking rude."

He barks a laugh and shrugs. "I'm sorry you find my honesty offensive."

"No, you aren't."

He steps toward the door. "You are right."

I glare at him, doing a horrible job at hiding the annoyance that boils out of me.

"There's so much I don't know about my brother once he left. I was hoping you could help me understand some things I've been questioning."

"Why would you think I could help you?" he snaps.

"Because you were the only friend Barlowe ever spoke about."

"Friend?" He huffs. "I barely knew your brother, okay? So, I wouldn't be able to help with anything, anyway."

Larkin walks to the door, forcefully pulling it open wide for my departure. The darkness of the hallway billows through the door, and I storm forward, never breaking my stare. I push past him and step back into the hallway, still shocked by his rudeness.

I turn around, determined to say my piece. "I don't think that's true, Larkin."

"Think what you'd like, then. It's not my job to convince you otherwise."

My mouth falls open, and Larkin only stares at me, his dark gaze burning into mine.

"What aren't you telling me?" I push.

Larkin glares at me one last time. No gentleness or kindness lies behind his dark gaze, and I cross my arms, expecting them to soften at any moment.

He flashes a sarcastic smile at me before slamming the door so hard my teeth rattle in its wake.

I remain frozen in the dark hallway, unable to pull myself away from the door, and I hear the lock click into place.

Fucking. Asshole.

I lift my hand but fight the urge to slam my fist against the wood and demand he let me back in. Instead, I turn on my heels and stride down the dark hallway toward Silas's room. I won't be going back to mine anytime soon. The thought of blood staining the walls isn't what I need now.

I arrive at Silas's door, the Prince of Darkness's childhood bedroom, and I can't help but let my thoughts take over.

If I had told myself a year ago that I would be standing here, I would have laughed.

I reach for the jeweled door and open it, stepping into his room. The dim lighting casts shadows throughout the empty space. Each flicker of the candles jolts my senses, making me feel like I'm doing something wrong. Like I'm not welcome here.

I move to the sitting area and stand before the crackling fire. I close my eyes and inhale deeply, trying to calm myself. Our arrival has already been a disaster, and I don't see the rest of the trip going well at this rate.

A faint sound from in front of me makes my eyes snap open.

A familiar, haunting creature stands tall in the fireplace. The same thin body wrapped in a black cloak floats before me. Its hollow, soulless eyes pierce into mine, and I jump back, fearing I will never get used to its abrupt arrivals.

"I'm getting tired of you scaring the fuck out of me," I snap at the creature.

It remains frozen, lingering.

Always studying me.

"Hopefully, you are here to help me?" I ask. "Because if not, I'm seriously not in the mood to be haunted right now."

If anyone were to walk in, I would look completely insane, arguing with a creature made of pure darkness.

"So?" I ask again, pushing aside any fear I have toward it. "What do you want?"

The creature moves out of the fire, its black cloak dragging on the ground.

"*Care...ful,*" its low, hissing voice says, moving through the room like a fog.

"Sorry," I say. "I'm in a piss-poor mood."

It moves toward the door, leaving ash in its wake. It pauses and cranes its long neck in my direction, clearly waiting for something.

"Are you telling me to follow you?" I question.

The creature moves through the door and vanishes into the dark hallway.

"*Come,*" it growls.

I'm going to fucking regret this.

I rush to the door and fling it open, stepping into the hallway. I catch a glimpse of the black cloak vanishing around the corner ahead of me. I sprint into the obscurity, the winding corridor seeming to stretch on endlessly. I barely keep pace with the floating creature as each step draws us deeper into the dark castle.

The flickering candlelight dims, as if the castle longs to be enveloped in darkness. Faint trickles of water echo around the stone walls, and a musty scent tingles my nose.

I round the last corner and come to a halt.

A blank stone wall stretches silently before me. There is no door or window—only the impenetrable surface looming over-head. The creature is gone, and I feel like a fool for having chased it into the depths of the castle. A lone sconce hangs on the wall, and I approach it cautiously, pressing my hand against the rough stone. The air around me grows heavy and oppressive, and the silence around me feels unnatural—as if the wall is holding its breath.

The stone sends vibrations through my body, causing me to jerk my hand back. The black veins on my hands tingle as I slowly raise my eyes to examine the wall. I cautiously lift my hand, anticipating another zap, but this time, the wall seems to shift against my touch. Something is telling me to turn around, but the darkness within me whispers, *open.*

"I've lost it. I'm about to talk to a fucking wall," I say aloud, knowing no one can hear.

I glance over my shoulder, and the awareness of being completely alone in the darkness sends a cold chill up my spine.

"Open," I whisper, pressing both hands against the hard wall.

My veins dance in response, the black vines growing toward my elbows, and a shadow slithers from my palms between the stone cracks.

Yet, nothing happens, and I'm left standing with both hands on the cold wall, like an idiot.

"Yes. I've lost it."

I turn, defeat guiding me away from the wall, resigned to return to Silas's room. I round the corner when I sense something pulling me from behind. I spin on my feet with my fists raised, prepared to fight the invisible creatures that haunt Andorwood.

Instead, the wall changes.

The rough stone begins to shimmer, and some deep urge pushes me toward the wall. I squint my eyes in disbelief. Everything within me screams to turn away, not to move forward, but my curiosity gets the better of me. Always.

This can't be happening.

I approach the cold stone wall, hesitating to touch it because of the sheer fear coursing through my body. I hear something down the hallway toward the central part of the castle. The same unnatural feeling I experienced in the castle courtyard washes over me, and my eyes widen. The invisible Andorwood guards must be lurking around the castle, doing a final sweep. If they find me while I'm alone without the protection of the Nastrondes, who knows what will happen?

Panic rises in my chest as I glance around.

"*Run*," something ancient and familiar whispers in my ear. "*Follow your instincts.*"

I rush toward the shimmering wall and extend my hand—hoping it will stop me from slamming my face into the stone—and the vibrations electrify my entire body. The air is cold, yet I press on, allowing the magic to engulf me. The wall begins to consume me, and I slam my eyes shut, whispering a silent prayer that I haven't walked directly to my demise. The world halts, the air tightens, and I feel as if I'm being compressed into nothing.

I try to scream, but there is no air available to leave my lungs. I claw at my throat, feeling like I'm suffocating.

The vibrations cease, but I keep my eyes closed. The air is filled with dust, and the smell of aged paper and worn leather surrounds me. I'm deep within the castle of Andorwood, a fortress cloaked in shadows and total mystery, and I truly don't know how I got here. The air has returned to my lungs, but the panic doesn't falter.

You can do this. You are Briar Blackbyrne.

I wish I could convince myself I was brave, because right now I want to pass out from fear. My heart races, my palms begin to sweat, and a lingering terror fills each of my cells.

I slowly open my eyes, and my jaw drops.

Where the fuck am I?

CHAPTER 10

The space ahead of me is vast, yet feels suffocating. The sconces on the wall ignite at my presence—burning away the cobwebs hanging from them—and I jump. Dozens of towering bookshelves rise to the ceiling, standing before me like mountains of history. Stories long forgotten by time fill the shelves, and each book looks to have been softened from years of neglect.

I step further into the room, struggling to adjust my eyes to the flickering candlelight attempting to illuminate the deep, dark shadows that linger in every corner. The room is silent, as if it's been frozen for centuries. I grab a candle from a nearby reading table and reach to light it from a sconce on the wall. The candle's flame wooshes to life, and I take a deep breath, steadying myself. There are books and scrolls scattered everywhere. How could anyone ever read everything in this room?

To my left, a longer hallway leads into complete darkness—to nowhere but despair. To my right, the room boasts large, towering bookshelves. I scan the room once more, taking in my surroundings, and my eye catches sight of a few small snakes moving about, minding their own business. I cringe.

With the center of the main room filled with light, I make my way to a wooden table cluttered with books, stepping over a few snakes on the way, thinking that being in the light—and avoiding the tunnel of darkness and despair—may be the safest route. I scan the table of books and notice most of the spines have faded over time, so choosing which book to grab first feels like a gamble. The persistent urge to look over my shoulder with each passing second weighs on me, but I force my eyes to stay straight.

There is no wind in this room; however, I notice a slight breeze from the left—like the room around me is taking small breaths.

A stunning dark amber leather-bound book with ornate vines woven into the cover captures my attention. I run my hand along the smooth binding. The black tattoo coating most of my hands tingles, my darkness urging me to open the old pages.

Does Silas know about this room?

My hands tremble as I begin to open the ancient book.

In the distance, something large crashes. My entire body jolts, the snakes quickly slither away, and the book in my hands falls to the floor. The rugged leather slaps the ground, and an echo reverberates around me—as if responding to the sound seconds before. Another crash in the distance snaps my gaze into the darkness before me. The disorienting shadows that line the bookshelves seem to pulse, and my heart races.

A low growl snakes from the darkness, and I feel the blood drain from my face.

I keep my feet planted on the cold ground and stare into the darkness, paralyzed by my fear. The shadows become darker by the second, and the panic rises in my chest, causing it to heave.

Oh, Gods.

I can't move or think for a moment, because whatever is before me has petrified all my senses and ability to reason. Somehow, the darkness between the two large bookshelves seems to stretch—opening wide to suck me in, never to return. This is a different darkness—something ancient and long forgotten. The room around me takes another breath, and a gust of wind causes my hair to whip my face from all directions, blinding me momentarily.

The dark creatures of Andorwood.

I backpedal, completely terrified of what's in front of me and what lurks in the dark hallways of the castle. At this moment, I'd rather confront the invisible creatures than whatever protects these books. I glance down at the old leather book that has fallen to the ground. The text is faded, and I squint my eyes to read what I can before fleeing.

A shock rushes through me, and I do everything I can to focus. I bring the trembling candle closer to the text as the growls grow louder and closer with each passing second, and a heat fills the space, making my skin slick with sweat. A single word catches my eye, and my stomach drops, and my whole body freezes. I'm unable to move.

Kalix.

Another gust of wind blows through the room, shocking me out of my frozen state. Without thought, I rush toward the wall I came through, the single sconce serving as the only landmark for my exit. The wall begins to shimmer as I approach, welcoming me back. Looking behind me one last time, I see a solitary hand wrap around the end of the bookshelf nearest the table I stood at moments ago. Long black claws dig into the wood, and a deep growl reaches my ears, invading my senses with a surge of fear. I close my eyes and move through the wall. The darkness envelops me as I seem to travel back in time to my world, amidst the deep hallways of the castle.

The hallway is dark and silent, and thankfully, the over-whelming sensation caused by the presence of the invisible guards has disappeared. I sprint down the winding halls, doing my best to recall each turn I took only an hour ago. My heart pounds in time with my footsteps on the smooth floor, my hair whips behind me, and my lungs burn from running for so long.

The air starts to lighten, and I know I'm getting closer to our rooms. A rush of adrenaline hits me, and I push even faster around the last corner. I never thought I'd be grateful to see the bright, jeweled-eyed snakes staring back at me from the bedrooms.

I catch my breath outside the onyx-jeweled room and slump against the opposite wall. I lower my hand, resting it on my knee, and take the deepest breaths I can to slow my racing heart. I still feel the snakes slithering around me, causing me to shiver.

I hear a voice from down the dim hallway, and I jerk my head up.

"For fucks sake," I mumble.

Larkin stomps in my direction, light and anger radiating off his large body.

"Are you fucking insane?" He grabs my arms and pulls me upright in a single motion. "Do you have a death wish?"

"Don't fucking touch me like that," I clap back, ripping myself from his grip. "What is wrong with you?"

"What's wrong with me? You're the one who went off alone in this castle." He furrows his brow. "Do you have any idea how dangerous that is for you? The moment I slammed the door, I knew I shouldn't leave you alone, but by the time I opened the door, you were gone."

"Well, I'm sorry I didn't stay to continue being humiliated by your closed door." I cross my arms and stand a bit taller. "If you weren't such an asshole…"

Larkin leans closer. "You're lucky I didn't shift straight to Silas's house and explain your vanishing act."

"Oh, please." I square my shoulders. "Sorry to burst your bubble, but he's used to this."

"Do you know what he would have done to me for losing you?

"Killed you?" I move my face toward his. "Scared of your boss?"

"This whole kingdom would be in flames right now, with my body being the torch."

"Silas wouldn't kill you, Larkin." I roll my eyes. "Stop being dramatic."

Larkin gives me a look of incredulity. "You clearly don't understand how angry Silas can get. Especially when it comes to finding or protecting you."

"And you do?"

"Yes." His eyes shift into something I don't recognize from him.

Fear.

He continues, "Sorry for wanting to save my own ass and avoid being murdered."

"You wouldn't be killed. And you don't get to threaten me with him," I snarl, refusing to back down. "Especially if you are only looking out for yourself."

"I've worked too hard for my position here to let you ruin everything because you have a curiosity that will get you killed."

I feel the anger rising in my chest, and I grind my teeth in his face.

"Give it a rest, will you?" I snap.

I can't stand this guy.

"Just like your fucking brother," he mutters. "Always getting into shit."

I glare at him.

"Then maybe you should have better manners than to slam doors in people's faces."

"You are impossible." Larkin rolls his eyes. "That sarcastic mouth is going to get you killed."

"And slamming doors will do the same for you."

We stare at one another, neither letting the other have the last word, and for a split second, the corners of his mouth twitch alongside mine. Larkin creates distance and rubs his hands over his eyes and into his disheveled hair.

"So, you've been looking for me for the past hour?" I ask.

"An hour?" He angles his head. "I haven't seen you in almost three hours. Do you have any idea what fucking time it is?"

"No. That's impossible."

He shakes his head. "Apparently, it isn't. I was about to call in backup when I found you outside Silas's door."

"I don't understand," I say, baffled.

"I don't either." He scratches his head. "Where have you been?"

My mind drifts to the stone wall, the shimmering light, and the magic emanating from the nearly invisible entrance. I felt an overwhelming sense of power as I entered the neglected library. I know I haven't been here long, but I can't help but think that the library isn't common knowledge—like the darkness only allows you inside if you're invited.

"I just went on a walk," I say, shrugging.

"Now who's withholding information, Briar?"

Larkin refuses to talk about Barlowe, so until I can trust him, I'll withhold any information I see fit. Plus, I may sound insane telling him I walked through a wall moments ago.

"I don't owe you an explanation."

Larkin sighs. "You should shift to Silas's house. It's late, and I'm exhausted, to be honest. Looking for you is a task, and I didn't sign up as a fucking babysitter."

I huff. "No one asked you to look for me."

"I'm aware of that, but I can't let anything happen to you on my watch." He rubs his sagging eyes. "Please go so I can get some sleep."

"Are you always this angry?"

"Pretty much."

"Good to know," I reply.

"Are you always this impulsive and reckless?"

"Truthfully?" I ask with a smile. "Yeah."

"Go," Larkin snaps, waving his hand. "Before I lose my gods-damned mind."

I open my mouth to speak, but he spins, putting his back to me and making his way down the dark hallway.

I nod—feeling beaten once again in our war of words—and close my eyes, thinking of the black house on the cliff. I imagine the front door, the windows, and the smoking chimney that I saw when we arrived, and a calmness rushes over me.

I think of Silas—*my* Silas.

My magic tingles in my fingers and flows through my body like a warm breeze. I notice Larkin glance over his shoulder one last time, making sure I'm following his instructions.

I become a shadow, but not before I send a rude gesture Larkin's way, using both hands for emphasis. His face twists, and I let my pride carry me all the way to the person who matters most to me in this world.

The house before me is silent, dark, and lackluster. I exhale sharply; just the knowledge that Silas is nearby puts me at immediate ease. A candle flickers in the small front window as I step onto the old wooden porch. The large black door in front of me features an ornate gold handle among many serpents of all colors. As I reach for the handle, it unlocks with a crack, welcoming me home.

I enter the small sitting room and look around. The scent of worn leather mixed with the sea breeze greets me. A large staircase at the back of the room catches my eye, and I make my way across the hardwood floor to stand at its top. Darkness looms down the narrow stairs, and I hesitate out of habit, but push myself to descend the stairs that are built into the massive cliff.

You are safe.

Just follow your instinct.

As I descend the staircase, darkness envelops me, and I narrow my eyes, attempting to see in the dim light. My feet reach the final step, and my jaw drops.

The house opens up to the sea, as if it were built in unison. Wide double doors are flung open to a large balcony, making you feel as if you are inside the cliff itself. The sea breeze sends my hair dancing around my body, and the slapping waves awaken all my senses. I'm awestruck.

Black stone walls mix with the beautifully crafted Gothic furniture. An iron candlelit chandelier sways gently in the open air over a long wooden table. Remnants of dinner clutter the table, and guilt travels through me.

I wasn't here.

I glance left toward an intimate sitting area, followed by a long, narrow hallway—likely heading to the bedrooms where my friends sleep peacefully after a night together. A single tear falls from my eye, and I tiptoe to the balcony.

The crisp night air tingles against my face, and I press my hands against the rail, gripping tightly. The expansive balcony extends far from the cliff—as though I am soaring miles above the world—and the vast sea stretches endlessly before me. I take a deep breath and gaze at the stars, which I've never seen so bright, like thousands of shimmering diamonds flickering in the sky above me.

"You're here," a deep, pained voice whispers behind me.

I spin around, completely startled, thinking I was alone.

Silas stands behind me, shirtless, with his pants dipping low on his hips, eyes still heavy with sleep. The glowing moon illuminates his strong chest as he tussles his messy hair. He walks onto the balcony and joins me, elbows resting on the rough railing as he gazes across the dark sea.

I watch him. I memorize his profile for the hundredth time and let a tear fall down my cheek.

"I'm sorry," I whisper.

He doesn't look at me but nods, acknowledging my words.

"I'm so sorry," I say again. "I shouldn't have pushed you away, Silas. I…"

He cuts me off, "Briar."

I freeze, waiting for harsh words to follow.

He gazes at me, and his piercing green eyes glow under the full moon's light. "I'm mad at you."

I shake my head. "I know. I'm an idiot."

"I've been thinking about what you said in the dining room," he replies.

"What?"

His bright green eyes find mine, and he nods, his lips forming a thin line.

"What are you talking about?"

"I'm mad at you, Briar. So fucking mad." He places his head in his hands for a moment before standing. His large body towers over mine, and he grabs my hands. His touch sends lightning bolts through me.

"I'm sorry," is all I can say, my voice soft and broken once more.

"Do you want to know why I'm mad at you?" His mouth is set in a stern line, and he forces my gaze back to his. "You haven't asked once."

"I don't need to ask."

He tilts his head. "I think you should."

"Because I screamed at you. I made you leave when you were trying to help. I pushed you away and let my anger win." Tears fall like rain down my face.

He cups my jaw harder, holding my gaze to his. "That's not why I'm mad."

Shock dances across my face, and I'm incredulous as I ask, "What?"

"What angers me more than anything about this evening is what you said to my mother."

Shame floods me, remembering the declaration I made about Silas in front of the table, in front of his family and his commanders.

I clearly crossed a line.

"I shouldn't have said that."

I lower my head.

He lifts my chin with his knuckle, green eyes burning into my soul.

"No, you shouldn't have." Silas takes a deep breath before continuing. "I'm pissed because you said you loved me, and I didn't have a chance to respond, Briar. I didn't have a chance to tell you how I feel in return."

I stare at him, not understanding what he means.

"I love you, Briar Blackbyrne. Darkness and all. Soul and all. You are mine, and I am yours for eternity, even after we reach the darkest realm."

Silas's strong hand moves to the back of my neck, and he tightens his grip, pulling me closer, demanding every ounce of my attention.

"I'm angry that, for even a moment, you didn't know I felt the same. That you declared your love, and I wasn't able to respond with mine."

My mouth slightly parts as he tilts my head toward his.

"You will never doubt my feelings for you again. My soul burns for you. My purpose is only you."

I open my mouth to speak, but I pause, my brain slow to process his words.

"Do you even understand, my love? Do you understand what you do to me?" he asks, commanding an answer. "I will dedicate the rest of my life to ensuring you never have to say those words alone again."

CHAPTER 11

I can't control my breathing or the tears streaming down my face.

"Don't cry," he whispers. "I never want to be the reason you cry."

He wraps his arms around my body, pulling me in tight. I bury my head into his chest, my racing heart already starting to calm. His hand cups the back of my head, and he holds me tighter, allowing me a moment to catch my breath. Once I calm slightly, I pull my face back to look at him, my cheeks stained with tears.

"I'm still sorry I got so angry." I tilt my chin to look into his eyes.

"Don't apologize." He presses a soft kiss on my lips. "I'm the one who should be sorry. Since arriving, I've been distracted. I'd forgotten our reasoning for being here, but that's all going to change."

I rise up on my toes and kiss him again, deeper this time. I wrapped my arms around his neck, and his hands travel slowly down my back, stopping when they reach my ass. He lifts me up, and my legs move to wrap tightly around his waist.

Silas turns and sets me on the stone balcony railing.

My heart leaps in my chest as I face away from the dark drop below, worried that I will tumble over the edge at any moment. My entire body jolts for a moment out of reflex.

Silas laughs, our lips still touching. "I forgot you were afraid of heights."

"I'm not afraid of heights, Silas. I told you; I'm afraid of falling to my death."

"It's only a 300-foot drop, jagged rocks, and a deep ocean below. Nothing to be concerned about."

"Extremely funny," I say, as my palms begin to sweat.

He laughs again, this time a bit more wicked. "Do you trust me?"

I look over my shoulder, the distance to the ground below making my skin crawl. "Entirely."

His mouth crashes against mine again, and my body melts as I feel his hand slide between my thighs. The sensation of Silas's touch quickly fades as I feel myself slipping into the shadows rather than over the railing. Our linked bodies become mist, and I realize that Silas is moving us somewhere together.

As quickly as the realization hits me, we land with a soft thud against soft bedding. Black silk sheets wrap around my curves, still warm from his body, and I groan. Silas's bedroom—regal and dark—is just as sexy as him, with a large, four-poster bed and tasteful antiques filling the large room.

As we return to our bodies, Silas pulls away from our kiss. His gaze could set the kingdom ablaze. He notices my puzzled expression at the abrupt change in scenery and smiles.

"I plan to fuck you in every single room of this house, but with your fear of heights, my love, I'll impatiently wait until the balcony railing is your idea."

My core turns molten, and I prop my arms on the soft bed to bring my mouth closer to his. "I'm very interested in the plans you have for me."

He lowers himself over me, shadows rippling across his back. "Then, we should begin."

I suck in a steadying breath and watch as his eyes grow drunk with lust before he slowly trails his fingers all over my body. I lie back and close my eyes as he buries his head into my neck. I hear him inhale and press soft kisses all over my burning skin while both hands travel up my shirt to grasp my aching breasts.

"Take it off," he snaps. "Now."

I'm quick to obey, lifting both arms over my head to allow him to remove my shirt, freeing my breasts. Silas lays me back down and moves from kissing down my neck to pulling a nipple into his mouth. His tongue flicks against my skin, sending shocks to my center.

I lift my head against his shoulder and bite hard as he pinches my nipple.

He pauses and looks me in the eyes. "Hungry?"

"Starving."

Silas smirks, and his eyes darken. "As am I."

He returns to kissing my neck and slowly begins to travel down, licking and sucking every inch of skin available to him. He hooks both hands around the waistband of my pants and slowly pulls them off, tossing them across the room. I look up as he stares at me, completely bare before him.

"Fucking gorgeous," he growls.

Silas slowly moves both hands from my ankles to my knees, then pauses.

"Spread them," he demands.

I relax my body and part my legs at his command, his hands pressing them against the silk sheets. He leans in, kissing and licking up my thigh while I squirm under his hold. He presses harder against my legs—fingers digging into my skin—and for a second, I fear I may tear in half.

I close my eyes and fist the silken sheets. I press my hips

toward him, desperate for the touch I desire. I feel his breath against me, and the anticipation alone has my orgasm building in my core.

"Silas," I breathe, unable to stand it any longer.

His tongue does a full sweep of my center, and my entire body shudders. I arch my back into his face as he continues to lick and suck. He presses harder against my legs, pushing them even farther. Pain shoots through my hips, but is quickly overshadowed by the intense pleasure of his mouth devouring me.

I need more.

Another quick flash of pain hits my center, causing me to yelp.

He fucking bit me.

Silas muffles a laugh. "It's only fair."

I dig my hands into his tangled hair and squeeze as he returns to fucking me with his tongue.

"Fuck." I tip my head back, seconds from my undoing. *"Fuck."*

He increases his speed, knowing exactly how close I am, and thrusts his fingers deep into my core, hitting the spot I'm so desperate to feel.

My entire body ignites with a white-hot fire as the pleasure explodes, shattering me into a million pieces. My back arches as an orgasm slams into my body, and a loud moan escapes from my mouth. I try to squeeze my legs together, but Silas holds firm and continues to lick my hypersensitive clit as my body trembles under him. He places a hand on my stomach to keep me still, and I wince slightly under his hold.

Silas lifts his head—eyes wild with lust—and slams his mouth against mine.

"See how delicious you are?" he growls. "Do you understand why you drive me fucking wild now?"

His kiss is deep and feral, and he grabs a fist full of my hair as

I wrap my trembling hands around his back, my nails digging into his hot skin. I feel him reach down, lowering his pants, and another wave of excitement travels through me.

His eyes burn with an intensity that makes my chest heave.

"Do you even realize what you do to me?"

I feel his cock tease my entrance, and I shift my hips, trying to bring him closer.

"You've unraveled the deepest part of my soul and are putting it back together, piece by fucking piece."

And with one thrust, he slams his hardened length into my core. My eyes widen, and I gasp at the feeling of being this full. He glances down, taking in the sight of our connection as he continues to pump in and out, as if he can't get enough of us together.

"You will be my fucking undoing. My beginning, and my grim end."

I tilt my head back, and he catches my moans in his mouth. Our lips press together as he slows, each thrust becoming harder and longer. He reaches down and brushes my clit, and I jolt under his touch.

"Don't stop," I moan into his mouth again, before he pulls his head back.

Silas's gaze meets mine, and his eyes are heavy—drunk from the feeling of us together. A low groan leaves his throat, and pleasure builds in my core once more.

My eyes begin to roll back in my head, and his hand wraps firmly around my jaw.

"Keep your eyes on me," he demands. "I want to watch you lose control."

He thrusts into me, before pulling out at a torturously slow pace. His breathing becomes rapid, and he wraps his hand around the back of my neck, pulling me closer to him as he slams his pelvis against mine. Shadows begin to swirl around us—our delicious darknesses combining—and threaten to knock out every ounce of light.

A blinding heat spreads through my body, which sends a wave of pleasure crashing through my veins. Stars dance in my vision, but I keep my gaze directly on him. My senses come alive, like a vibrating shock moving through me and into Silas. I clench around him, and his head falls forward for a second before lifting to meet my gaze.

"Fuck," Silas moans into my mouth, capturing my lips in a long kiss.

He unravels with me, spilling himself deep inside me. His thrusts slow, but he remains inside me as I continue to pulse around him. The world around us seems to pause, and we lie together in a tangled mess.

Silas collapses next to me, our breaths ragged and heavy. My body feels completely drained—my soul shattered—as my racing heart slows. Exhaustion weighs heavily on me.

He props himself up next to me and whispers, "You should sleep."

"You should as well."

"I will, when you drift off."

He kisses me gently and pulls the soft sheets up, draping them over my naked body. The weight of the blankets, combined with his warmth, immediately makes my eyes heavy.

"I'm right here and not going anywhere." He moves his fingers through my hair. "Sleep. Morning will come sooner than we wish."

I keep my gaze on his for as long as I can.

The corner of his lips curls, and I trace my finger along the scar above his left brow. He nuzzles into my touch, and I drop my hand, curling into his chest. The large open window invites a cool breeze around us, and the sound of the crashing waves fills the still room, lulling me to sleep in the dark bedroom.

"*Help. Me. Briar.*"

I jolt awake in bed.

The morning sun paints the dark bedroom with golden rays, making the room seem to shimmer as the light and dark work together in perfect unison. Silas stirs next to me but doesn't wake. I rub my throbbing head and dangle my feet over the edge of the bed, relishing in the sea breeze flowing through the open window as I inhale the fresh, salty air. I walk to the window and push it open fully, staring out at the sea that stretches for hundreds of miles while the waves slap against the cliff wall below. I look toward Daramveer and let sadness fill my chest. The bright sun quickly chases the sleep away, and my senses awaken when the realization hits me.

Someone just screamed my name, and I know exactly who that voice belongs to.

Rohhit.

That was Rohhit.

Panic grips me, and I rush back toward the bed and shake Silas.

He jolts from sleep, eyes meeting mine as he asks, "What's wrong?"

Unsure of what to say, I tilt my head. "I'm okay, but…"

Silas frantically sits up, hands traveling over my body to ensure nothing is out of sorts. His concerned gaze finds mine, and he swings his legs over the edge of the bed.

"What is it?"

"I…I think Rohhit just tried to speak to me."

CHAPTER 12

"Can we have just one day of peace?" Oak asks from his place at the long table, voice muffled as he holds his head in his hands.

Maines pats his broad shoulder. "Oh, Oak. You should be used to this by now."

"I fled the mainland with the head healer of the House of Hedro, the Queen of Daramveer, and the Prince of the Forgotten. I'm in Andorwood to win over the king and his armies, and the Great Wiitch of Darkness possesses my best friend. No, darling, I'm not used to this yet." He lifts his head from his hands. "Oh, and I should add that this best friend is now hearing our other possessed friend's voice."

Maines huffs indignantly. "I thought I was your best friend."

"Can you two be fucking serious for once?" Silas grumbles from the head of the table, placing his head in his hands in turn.

Oak winks at Maines, and they try to hide their amused faces.

"Briar, tell us again what happened." Silas urges Oak and Maines to quiet and gives me the floor.

"Well, I was asleep and heard someone—Rohhit—asking for

help, and then I woke up," I say with a shrug. "I think I heard him when I was in the castle when we first arrived, too."

"Do you think you can speak back to him?" Oak asks.

I shake my head. "I'm not sure how to do that. I haven't tried, though. What if it isn't him, and instead it's Carobon trying to trick us?"

Silas rubs his temples. "It would make sense that you two are connected, seeing as you are both vessels for the Great Wiitches. Maybe that links you in a way."

Maines stands, pacing around the table for a moment—lost in thought. I watch her and can only imagine what her brilliant mind is coming up with right now.

"He's right. You are likely connected somehow. Although I've never read about this exact thing, I do believe that people can communicate on a spiritual level. If Carobon has fully possessed Rohhit's body, Rohhit could be somewhere else."

"Think of how helpful this could be. We could learn what they are planning if Briar can communicate with Rohhit," Oak chimes in.

"There's some positivity," Maines cheers, as Oak winks.

"It's true," Silas mutters. "But, I don't think we should mess with this until we know what we are dealing with. I'm not putting Briar in danger until we know how to control this."

They all nod.

I watch them continue their conversation as if I'm not here—coming up with plans, thoughts, and wild accusations about me and my dark magic as well as Rohhit. My mind drifts back to the library—to the scrolls, ancient books, and *Kalix* written on one of the faded pages.

"Well, maybe we could control the situation if we were with her. Silas, you can pull her out of any nightmare, right? And Maines will be there to help if anyone needs healing," Oak suggests.

Their plans begin to unfold, and I can't stand it anymore.

"Stop," I shout, louder than intended.

They all snap their heads in my direction, eyes wide at the sudden outburst.

"Stop talking as if I'm not here. Stop coming up with plans about what I will do with my magic."

Silas, Oak, and Maines halt.

"If you insufferable people decide to ever let me talk, I need to tell you something," I admit.

"Oh, Gods. What now?" Oak throws his hands.

"When I didn't immediately come to Silas's house last night, I went for a walk around the castle." I pause, waiting for Silas to lose his mind.

"You what?" Silas's nostrils flare.

I glance at him, making a pained face. "The creature that haunts me showed itself, and I followed it."

"Yeah, I'm not prepared for this." Oak places his forehead on the table. "Is there any ale around?"

Maines punches his arm, shushing with her finger, and ushers me to continue with a weary grin.

"I found something at the end of a long hallway, but thinking back, I have no idea which way I even went."

"What..." Silas sits straight up, and I can practically smell the anger leaking from his body. "What did you find?"

The memories of the books, snakes, and the undeniable darkness that slithers around that clearly forgotten library cause me to nearly shiver in my chair.

"I found a..."

A strong voice rises from the bottom of the staircase, interrupting me.

"She found the library, Silas. The Forgotten Archives."

Larkin stands on the last step with his hands tucked into his pockets. His face is stern, his hair messy, and purple circles rest under his intensely dark eyes—like he hasn't slept at all.

Silas stands, abruptly. "And you would know this how, Captain?"

He shifts inches from Larkin's face, seething with anger from the withheld information.

Larkin jolts at the sudden appearance, raising his hands in defense. "Fuck."

"Silas." I jump up, nearly knocking my chair backward. "Calm down."

"Speak. Now," Silas snaps, eyes still trained on his captain.

"I found her outside your bedroom, slumped against the wall after you ran away. I went looking for her because she had been gone for hours." He pushes Silas back. "You wouldn't know any of this, though, would you? Leaving me to babysit. That's not my job, *Prince*."

"Ran away?" Silas barks back. "That's the wording we are going with? Are you serious?"

Larkin's tone is challenging, and I can't believe he's standing up for me right now, even though *babysitting* doesn't sit well with me. His eyes narrow, and he leans toward Silas, not away.

"Am I wrong?"

"I left you to do nothing, Spiridon," Silas rages.

"Stop it," I say, trying to get their attention.

"And, had I done nothing," Larkin tries to push past Silas, but his shoulders hold firm, "she would have been in an entirely different situation—no thanks to you."

Silas tightens his brow, wrapping his hand around Larkin's throat. "You have three seconds to continue speaking, or those will be the last words you speak—in this house or otherwise."

"Then release your hand… from my fucking throat," Larkin mumbles.

Silas's grip tightens.

Larkin coughs under his hold. "Hard…to speak…with you choking me."

"Silas!" I shout, "He did nothing wrong."

"What were you thinking?" He peels his eyes away from Larkin—dropping his hand—and turns his rage on me. "You are going to get yourself fucking killed, make me kill someone, or both."

"I was thinking that I had just screamed at you, you had left, and I needed to clear my head. I am trying to figure out what's happening here and what I can do to save you all." I walk to Silas and grab his hand, forcing his gaze to mine. "I was thinking that if I can stop all of this, it will save your life—all of your lives—and I will happily risk my own to ensure that happens."

His eyes soften, but his tone doesn't. "You don't have to carry this burden alone."

"I know."

"But how did you know she was missing?" Silas returns his gaze to Larkin.

"I went to ask him if he knew where you went. He told me your house, so Maines and Oak came to speak with you first," I interject. "That's it."

I glance at Larkin, who mouths, "*Thank you.*" I chose to keep the part about him slamming the door in my face and leaving me alone in a dark, haunted castle to myself.

"Very well." Silas returns to the table and sits down with a new weight pressing down upon him. "Larkin, sit."

"Is someone going to explain this library?" Maines cuts in, hesitant to speak. "It sounds like it could have the answers we need."

Silas nods. "It's likely, but we can't go inside. The library doesn't welcome just anyone. It has to invite you in." He sighs, letting memories flood his mind. "Many have searched for the

Forgotten Archives for centuries and never found it. My grandfather nearly drove himself mad searching for it."

"Well, Briar found it." Larkin joins Oak, Maines, and Silas around the table.

"She's great at creepy, ancient things finding her," Oak says, chuckling.

Silas flashes a warning look.

I pull my chair out and sit down next to him.

"Silas is right. We can't go into the library."

They wait for me to keep going, but Silas's expression reveals that he knows more than he's letting on.

"I was led to the library by the creature that's been haunting me, and as I entered the room, I had no idea what I was about to discover. Something dark lives in the depths of the shadows. I've never experienced such a negative darkness oozing from anything in my life." I glance at each of them. "We can't go back in there, because we don't know what we're up against."

They all stare at me, and Silas gives me a soft smile. "And, who knows if it will ever appear again."

"So, that's it?" Maines stands, planting her hands on the hard wooden table. "Once again, we won't even try. At this point, we should pack up and fucking leave. Since we got here, all you have done is act defeated."

We watch, listening to her outburst.

"Do I really need to remind you of what we accomplished in Daramveer? We worked together, faced danger, and fucking succeeded—at least at saving ourselves. We can do it again, here."

Oak stands, "We just need to find someone who knows more about this library."

Silas glances at Larkin, a silent conversation moving between them, before he says, "We do know someone. Someone who has been inside the library, and someone who has found it more than once."

Larkin nods.

"My mother."

"Well then, we need to set up a meeting with her. Immediately." Maines claps her hands together. "Where is she now?"

Larkin stands, "She is with Fen and Warrick. I met with them this morning. They are going to discuss with Malachi the possibility of meeting with Briar—a formal meeting in his office. No dinner party, no distractions. Just a king and queen discussing the safety and future of our lands."

"Everyone has lost their minds," Silas laughs. "Larkin, do you think he is going to agree to that?"

"I do," he says, with a dip of his chin.

"Why?" Silas snaps.

"Because we are going to disclose some information to him that will either save or destroy Andorwood in a week's time."

"What the fuck are you talking about?" Silas's shadows begin to ripple around him.

Larkin clears his throat. "We weren't for certain, but a ship followed you from Daramveer. From our findings, it set sail a few days after you all left."

The color drains from my face.

"I didn't want to alarm anyone, so I sent a few of my men to assess the situation. It's not good, Silas. The people on this ship are different. They don't seem like normal Wielders. The men told me they were changed into creatures." He shudders as the words leave his lips. "I can't make sense of what they are, but if our findings are correct, the ship will arrive in Andorwood in a week."

"They used the resurrection stone," I whisper.

"Oh, Gods." Maines slaps her hand over her mouth, horror painting her features.

Silas storms toward the balcony, pausing to look across the sea, as if expecting to see the ship of the risen heading right for us.

"Silas," Larkin calls to him. "Without Briar and her knowledge of these creatures, I don't think our men can fight these things alone. Your father will agree to work with her to save Andorwood."

I watch as Silas's knuckles turn white from his grip on the railing.

"No," Silas turns, his eyes blazing with a black fire, "he won't."

I stand, watching each of their faces pale. "Then, that is his choice."

Silas nods and—for a moment—mourns Andorwood and the destruction to come. Even with the strength of the entire Andorwood army, they would be no match without warning.

"But not mine," my voice echoes in response to his dejection. "I will fight alongside Andorwood, regardless of Malachi's decision. I will battle to save these people, because that is what is right. Carobon is trying to turn us against each other when we should be joining forces." I narrow my eyes. "I will share my knowledge with anyone willing to listen. I will inform Malachi of what we need to do to win. And when that ship arrives, I will be on the front lines, greeting those resurrected creatures as they meet their fucking demise."

Silas looks at me, his face as hard as stone, and for a moment, I know all he sees is me. He bounds toward me, uncaring about the people around us, and his lips crash against mine—a kiss so intense that I lose track of where I am.

He pulls back, tucks a fallen piece of hair behind my ears, and cups my face. "I fucking love you, Briar Blackbyrne."

I smile wider than I have in what feels like months before

turning to the others. "We'd better get a plan in place. We are going to need a compelling story."

Maines smiles. "Oh, so stopping Carobon isn't compelling?"

"Apparently not," Oak chuckles. "Silas, any pointers for speaking with your father?"

Silas shakes his head. "My whole life has been dedicated to speaking with him as little as possible. We are going to need Fen's help with this one."

I catch Maines rolling her eyes and flash an annoyed look in her direction.

"How quickly can she be here?" I ask.

Silas opens his mouth to speak, but is cut off.

"Talking about me behind my back?" a cheerful voice sounds from the open balcony doors.

Fen steps into the living space with Warrick close behind, per usual.

"Well, that wasn't nearly fast enough," Oak jokes.

Silas smiles at the sight of his sister and Warrick shifting in at the perfect time.

"Where is Hux?" Silas asks. "We will need everyone on board."

"He stayed back to sweet-talk our father about this meeting. He knows what is going on. Don't worry, he's the best person for this job. Hux has a certain…pizzazz to him." Fenmore winks.

"If that's what you want to call it," Warrick chimes in. "He is persuasive and cocky as fuck. That's why Malachi likes him."

Fen shrugs.

"Tell me I'm wrong," Warrick responds, with a grin.

"I'm trying not to be pissed off that I'm the last to hear about this plan. My right-hand men and sister are making plans without me." Silas grabs my hand with a squeeze. "This has never happened before."

His commanders laugh.

"How does it feel, boss?" Warrick angles his head.

"Sour," Silas responds, stiffly.

Fen plops down at the table. "Oh? You don't like being the last to know? Now you see how we've all felt for years."

I chuckle before redirecting the conversation. "Alright, so we are all here. We will have to wait to find the library."

Fen coughs. "Excuse me, what?"

I glance back at Warrick, and he's as stunned at my words as Fenmore.

"When do we meet with Malachi?"

Warrick steps forward. "Tonight."

CHAPTER 13

We spent the rest of the afternoon discussing our past lives and the different worlds we grew up in. As the day nears its end, the bright sun begins to dip behind the horizon, casting a looming shadow across the room. The fading light seems darker, like it's threatening what's to come.

Our chatter fades.

When we can't wait any longer, we split up to dress for the castle. Oak and Maines return to their bedroom, and I slip into Silas's room while he stays behind to discuss a few things with his commanders quietly.

Nerves run through me as I make my way to the bathing chambers. I splash some cold water on my face and smooth my hair. With all of my belongings at the castle, my options are limited for clothing.

A soft knock sounds, followed by the creak of the heavy wooden door.

"Briar?" Fen pokes her head through. "You in here?"

"Yeah, come in," I call from around the corner.

Her steps are near silent as she approaches the large bay window, placing both hands on her hips. The fading sun casts golden rays of light that bounce around the room. I hear her sigh as I cross the room to join her.

"Are you alright?" I ask.

"Oh, I'm fine," she responds. "I've just had a headache I haven't been able to shake for the past few days."

"Are you not sleeping?"

"I am. I'm just having really vivid dreams—or nightmares—and they all end the same way. With..." she trails off, and starts to fidget with the stunning necklace she always wears.

"Ends with what?" I push.

She pauses, as if she doesn't want to speak the words into existence. "Someone screaming."

A chill runs up my spine, and I try to give her a reassuring smile.

"Who?"

She shrugs. "Someone familiar, and not at the same time."

"I also have nightmares." I nod, with a soft curl of my lips. "For years. They never get easier, and the fear you feel when trapped in them never fades. I've always known that darkness hides in our dreams, like something that can't reach us when we are in the light."

"I feel like I've been swallowed whole lately," she continues. "Like the darkness has shifted into something different, and as I run through my nightmares—as I race through the ruins—I only see a single light." She braces herself against the windowsill. "And no matter how fast I run, I can't reach it."

I look out over the dark sea before us. "It's a dream. Keep pushing forward, and maybe you'll reach it one day."

She blinks, fighting back a tear that threatens to roll down her cheek, and clears her throat as the memories fade. And just like Silas, she turns off that part of her—weakness—as if it's a sin. Fen spins around and notices that I'm still wearing the same outfit —black fitted pants and a wrinkled white shirt.

"Oh no." Fenmore shakes her head. "No."

"Hm, okay? You could pretend that I at least look decent. I'm comfortable in this," I respond, mildly irritated.

"You look stunning. Always," she laughs. "But, that outfit won't do. I had Warrick bring all your things. I came to make sure you knew that, and it's clear you didn't. My father loves the dramatics; if you show up over the top, he'll love you."

"Gods, you are as direct as your brother."

Fen laughs again. "You're going to whip him into shape quickly. I can already see a change in him—in a good way, I mean. He's softer."

"Silas Nastronde is softer?" Her statement takes me aback. "He threatened to slaughter Larkin in the living room."

"He wouldn't hurt Larkin," she says, rolling her eyes, before pausing to think about it. "Well, not too bad."

I chuckle.

She shakes her head. "Believe it or not, he is. And it's because of you." She looks out of the large window. "He was…angry before he left for Daramveer. He was so haunted by his dreams that he could barely function toward the end. He was slowly going insane."

"What do you mean?"

"He ripped this kingdom apart a month before the competition was announced, looking for you, not realizing you weren't here at first." She blinks back the memories. "He scared the fuck out of the people here. Larkin and Warrick did everything they could to calm him down, but it didn't work. Our father gave him a brutal beating afterwards, seeing the mess he made."

I gaze out of the window alongside her. "I had no idea."

My mind travels back to the words Larkin spoke about Silas and his anger, and how he witnessed it.

She moves closer. "I'm not surprised. He's not one to talk about his feelings, especially old ones. Warrick and Larkin finally had to restrain him after his largest outburst. They locked him in this house for days. I don't think either of them slept. It consumed him."

"He has a temper," I add.

"His is different." She nearly trembles. "Much different."

I keep my eyes locked on hers, and I swear fear dances in her eyes before her gaze drops.

She pauses, and glances back at me. "Silas has been through a lot. Our father spent many days practically torturing him. My brother has spent years building walls to keep people out."

"I know the feeling."

"Give him some time, Briar. He will let you in deeper than he's let anyone."

Tears form in my eyes as I look at Fen. Her face is so beautiful and reminiscent of Silas, but different all the same.

"What happened to him?" I ask.

She grabs my hand with one of hers, pulling the shoulder of her shirt down with the other. A thick white scar lines the top of her left collarbone. I flinch at the pain I can only imagine she endured to receive that.

"I know you've heard our father has interesting tactics for punishments. We fight here in Andorwood. There's a worn, wooden platform near the center of the kingdom. Crowds are forced to watch as people battle it out. Whoever wins, lives." She shrugs, as if the words are casual. "I was young when I got this scar—too young. Silas had to be restrained during that fight; he killed three guards trying to escape to stop me from getting hurt. He practically exploded with rage that day, and even as a child, I think our father feared him."

My heart shatters, and my lip quivers, as I try to regain my composure.

She continues. "My father was so disgusted by his reaction that I never had to fight again. Silas took every single one of my punishments for me. Beating after beating—for me. He's covered in scars—both inside and out—because of me." Tears well up in her large green eyes. "He deserves the world. He is selfless, loyal, and loves deeply. Just be there for him as much as you can. You have his heart—his soul—and I know he's stubborn, but it's real. I know that for a fact."

I stare at her, my chest tighter than it's ever been.

Silas.

My Silas.

"I've been selfish, Fen."

"No, you haven't, my friend." She returns the soft gaze. "You are about as far from selfish as you can get. You are resilient, kind, and humble. And even though you have a darkness deep within you, Briar, you are good."

I take her hand, our conversation fading into silence. She softly squeezes my hand in return, and a look of understanding crosses her face.

"You are going to change everything one day. Just trust your-self, and trust Silas."

She wipes a falling tear from her cheek and turns away.

"What is it?" I ask.

"I'm the one who has been selfish," Fen admits, and I watch her face turn from sadness to painful regret.

"What do you mean?"

"I think things are going to change soon, and I'm worried about him. I feel as if I'll be sick at any moment with this feeling twisting in my gut."

I angle my head. "Warrick?"

She nods. "Yes."

"Why do you say that? If you're worried about something, the best thing you can do is face it head-on. Trust your instincts. The what-ifs will drive you mad."

She wipes a tear and shakes off the unsettling feeling with a smile. "Maybe I'll do that, but not right now. Right now, we need to get you ready."

I nod, resigned to my fate. "What do you think I should wear?"

She strides to the large wardrobe and opens the doors. "First, let's move all of Silas's clothes. They aren't important." She flashes a grin over her shoulder before returning her focus to the wardrobe. "This. You'll wear this."

My jaw drops.

She holds a stunning, floor-length gown made from the finest fabric. I take the dress, gazing at it with reverence, before slipping it on and stepping out to show Fen. The black gown hugs my body perfectly—as if it were tailored just for me—with nearly invisible swirls that sit upon the fabric. The flowing fabric catches each ray of light as it moves. Two golden serpents adorn the dress; the snakes' tails start above the chest and wind their way up the fabric. The neckline features the snake's bodies dramatically entwined with their heads resting delicately on my throat.

"My fucking Gods." Fen smiles. "You could win over an entire kingdom in that dress."

"That's the point, isn't it?" I sweep my hair over my shoulders to really show off the neckline.

Another knock sounds on the door.

"What?" Fen shouts harshly, and I bust out laughing.

Silas steps into the room, and my whole body tenses, anticipating his reaction. His lips part slightly, and his brows lift.

I smile and curtsey, the long dress pooling around me.

"She looks fucking spectacular, doesn't she?" Fen points toward me and jokes, "Can I date her?"

I look at her with a dramatic eye roll.

"Fen," Silas says. "Can you give us a minute? Alone."

"Of course," she says with a nod. "But, we need to leave soon. I'll prepare the others."

Fen moves across the room quickly, reaching the door to exit, but not before she gives me a smile.

"Thank you, Briar, for the talk."

I return the smile and dip my head.

She closes the door behind her, and I turn my head to Silas. He stands before me, frozen, and I can't decipher the expression on his face just yet.

"If beauty could kill," he rasps, "I'd be fucking dead on the spot."

I move toward him and chuckle, letting the dress trail behind me—a shadow of black fog. I pause, and we stand pressed together for a moment, neither of us speaking. He tucks a stray piece of hair behind my ear. My eyes are level with his chest, and I pull his shirt down, revealing all the aged, white scars. I trace my fingers along each one, a new understanding of the pain behind them.

Every scar is an agonizing memory, forever marked on his body, that he lives with every single day. For an instant, I feel the same pain. Pain for what he endured, pain for the challenges he faced, and pain that I can never erase those memories for him.

He slowly slides his hand up to meet mine and holds it against his muscled chest. I close my eyes and feel his heart's strong, steady beats against my hand. His chest rises and falls in a rhythmic motion. Silas kisses my forehead and lingers there momentarily, inhaling my scent and savoring this moment for as long as possible.

We both know our time is limited.

I gaze up through my lashes, and he's smiling. The world is quiet around us, with the exception of crashing waves against the cliff-face, the gentle breeze, and the beating of our hearts. Together. Connected. Deeper than we can put into words right now.

"You ready?" he asks.

"I am."

"I need to talk to you about Malachi."

His face changes, and the soft expression fades as his father's name leaves his lips. Our hands are still connected, and he guides me to the sitting area. We sit facing each other on the small couch, and anticipation fills me as I wait for him to begin.

"There are many things I still need to tell you." Silas takes a long breath. "We don't have time for everything right now, but I promise you will soon know all there is to know about me and my world."

I nod.

"Malachi cannot be trusted, Briar. No matter what he says, he is deceitful, manipulative, and will haunt you. Do not believe a word he says."

I angle my head, gazing at him questioningly. "Haunt? Truly?"

"He has powers we don't understand. Powers and abilities I've been searching for my whole life. He...he can appear to people like mist—a spirit sent from the darkest realm to haunt you."

My mind snaps back to the dinner, his cloudy appearance when only I could hear his whispers. He was there to me, a manifestation, but not to the others. They couldn't see him.

"I know he appeared to you in that form at dinner. I saw your face change and turn pale. I knew he was talking to you, and I was horrified."

"I know you were."

"I'm so sorry I didn't warn you. I thought I was keeping you safe by keeping this information, but I see now that all I did was put you in danger." He drops his head, "I'm the entire reason you've been in danger since we've been here."

I cup his face, lifting his chin. "I'm fine. And I understand all about doing what you must to keep those around you safe."

He softly chuckles. "Yes, you are Queen of Daramveer. Well, you're more like the Queen of Withholding Vital Information, aren't you?"

"You know it, Nastronde."

Silas nuzzles into my hand. "I'll tell you everything once we get this over with. We're coming up with a plan together. Just please, don't think of me differently when I share everything with you."

"I won't. Let me help you as you help me."

He nods.

"It's okay to talk about your pain—visible or not," I whisper. "I have it too; you just can't see it."

Silas leans forward, pressing the softest kiss to my lips.

"We need to go," I whisper against his mouth.

He rests his forehead against mine, sighing heavily. "I know."

I stand, pulling him to join me. Our hands separate, and I head for the door with him trailing behind me.

"Briar," Silas calls, pulling me back from crossing the thresh-old. "I'm not finished. There's a way to stop him from haunting you."

"Well, great." I spin on my heels, turning to face him. "How?"

Silas hesitates, and my excitement twists into something more sinister.

"It involves the poison that killed your brother."

CHAPTER 14

When only a few hours separate me from facing Malachi, Silas and I join the others around the long, wodden table, ready to finalize our plan before my meeting. We have just a few days that remain until a ship arrives at Andorwood to wipe out the army I've yet to build.

They gawk at my appearance, Maines being the first to speak. "Damn, Briar."

My cheeks turn a soft shade of pink at the attention, but I laugh.

They are all dressed in fine clothing, because Fen likely forced them all to look their best. Maines wears a long, flowing emerald green dress, and Fen wears a dark red, tight-fitting gown that makes me flinch for a moment.

It's not blood.

The men are all dressed in what looks like fighting leathers, but elevated. Each suit perfectly hugs their defined muscles, and a jeweled gold serpent dances on each man's chest.

Maines catches my stare and raises her brows twice, then winks.

Silas steps forward, instantly garnering the attention of those in the room with ease. He stands tall, and I realize he's transformed from the Silas, the man I love, into Silas, Prince of Darkness. He stands before us, looking more like the future King of Andorwood than I've ever seen him before, ready to take charge.

Everyone falls silent and waits for him to speak. We sit around the table while he stands before us, and a surge of pride fills my chest. He can do this. He's going to face his fears, and one day he will reign as a noble king.

"In a few hours, Briar will meet with Malachi, and a decision will be made that is likely to change the course of our futures," he states, his voice booming like thunder. "The King of Andorwood will either work with us to stop Carobon, or he will not. Either way, we will not back down. We will do what we can to save our lands, with or without Malachi."

We listen in rapt silence as his towering figure stands before us. Shadows ripple around him like the threat of a storm on the horizon, and the salty sea breeze traveling through the room pauses as Silas speaks again, as if giving him its full attention.

"Briar can't walk into his territory unprepared. We must protect her against Malachi and his magic."

Larkin, Warrick, and Fen tense up around us, shifting in their seats. Oak and Maines glance at each other, waiting to be clued in on what's happening.

"Silas, no," Fen pleads, placing both hands against the hard table. "You aren't serious."

"We aren't prepared for this," Warrick sounds. "I'm siding with Fen here. No."

He ignores their words. "Malachi holds a power we do not understand."

Silas looks at Maines and Oak, recounting what he said to me just moments earlier. When he finishes the story, their jaws drop in disbelief.

Maines whispers. "How is that possible?"

"We don't know, but the people at this table have been searching for an answer for years. He can linger in a shift." Silas's brow tightens as he explains Malachi's power. "He can appear as a spirit and haunt you. He has driven many people mad with this power, and I fear he will start using it on Briar. I fear this, because he already has."

Maines and Oak snap their attention to me.

"What?" Oak says, standing with force. "Care to explain?"

I notice the others squirm in their chairs, already knowing how this awful man works.

"When we first arrived, I saw him at the dinner before anyone else did. He taunted me, but I was too afraid to speak. I didn't understand what I was seeing, and my body was being held captive so I could only focus on him."

Silas nods. "But, there is a way to stop this. We only discovered this a few years ago. Had we known sooner, this would have saved us many years of torment."

I glance at Fen, who refuses to make eye contact with anyone at the table. I know she's blaming herself for the years of pain Silas went through, and she gazes hard at her hands.

"But, Silas, like I said, we don't have time for this right now," Warrick says, standing with both large hands pressed against the table. "We don't need to rush this. We know where that may land us."

"Do we have a choice?"

"We always have choices," Warrick responds.

"Bullshit." Fen scoots away from the table. "I can't fucking believe this, Silas."

She glares at him and walks to the balcony in silence. We all watch her place her hands against the railing, squeezing it tightly —as if contemplating shifting away from this conversation as fast as she can. Warrick watches her leave, but gives her space to breathe.

"We will have to make time, I'm afraid. I'm not sending her in there unprotected." Silas's eyes travel to mine. "We need to make a decision soon. We're running out of time."

Warrick opens his mouth to speak again, but Silas dismisses him with a wave of his hand.

I hold my breath.

"We discovered a Rigil in a book located in the Forgotten Archives. Actually, my mother found it. It's a symbol that can shield you from precisely what my father is capable of. It can protect you from possession."

My brows shoot up. "What?"

He nods. "We spent months trying to get it to work, and many of our tactics failed. We tried ink, blessed ink, and ink mixed with blood, but nothing was strong enough. Nothing stopped him from entering our minds." He pauses, seeming to find the right words. "So, we looked further, deeper, and darker."

My heart races in my chest, and I can feel the panic rising. I grip the edge of the chair, fearing I may pass out.

Maines speaks, "And you realized that the poison that's linked to Andorwood is the strongest thing we've seen in centuries."

"Exactly," Silas adds.

Fen reenters the room, sweat beading on her forehead. Anger radiates from her as she glares at her brother, and the shadows darken behind her green eyes. As if out of nervous habit, she grasps the necklace around her throat and squeezes, her knuckles turning white. "Silas, we can't do this to her in just a few hours. Are you insane?"

His eyes narrow. "We don't have a choice, Fen."

Warrick stands to join Fen, offering a comforting touch to her face.

"We do," she snaps. "Stop saying that."

The stare between Silas and Fen could set the world aflame, and that's one fight I don't think either would walk away from.

They stand, challenging each other, their eyes narrowed and filled with fury. My chest tightens, and my palms begin to clam up with sweat. Silas may win this argument, but I can't help but feel a sense of relief that someone is on my side, even though it seems I don't have a real choice.

"I'll do it," I declare, standing to join the others. "What… do I have to do?"

Silas offers me a gentle smile tinged with concern as he gazes at the others sitting wide-eyed around the table. "The Rigil must reside on your body permanently. We need to tattoo the symbol on you with ink, blood, and the mixed poison to permanently mark the Rigil on your body, gracing you with the protective barrier."

They all look at me, and I swallow hard.

Silas moves around the table to stand next to me. Larkin keeps his head down, refusing to meet my eyes. Silas wraps his arm around my waist and pulls me close, kissing my temple.

"Briar, we all have one." Silas points at Larkin, Fen, and Warrick. "This is painful. You will want us to stop—you will beg us to stop—but once we start, we can't." Silas cuts his eyes across the table. "Larkin will tattoo you; he knows this poison better than anyone."

I snap my attention to him. It's clear to me that Larkin knows more than he's telling me about my brother.

How did the poison get all the way to Daramveer?

Silas continues, ignoring the building tension in the room. "I will be beside you, and Maines is here if something should go wrong."

My eyes swiftly scan their bodies for any signs of a tattoo. Larkin stays silent, his face devoid of color as he softly touches his forearm, as if the tattoo he has throbs.

"You don't have a tattoo, Silas." I look up at his face.

"You wouldn't think so," he says with a gentle smile. "But I do. It takes a few hours to heal, but the Rigil heals to nearly invisible on your skin.”

Silas lifts his shirt, and barely perceptible to the naked eye, a tiny Rigil is embedded in his skin, just below his pec. Mixed with his scars, it’s unnoticeable.

Fen looks at all of us. “Are you all fucking insane? Briar is already possessed. We have no idea how she will react.”

“I’ll take the risk,” I say.

“Larkin, you are not doing this right now,” Fen snaps. “As your superior, I’m saying n…”

She pauses for a moment and turns her head toward the balcony, as if someone just called her name. She stares at the empty space, like she’s waiting for a presence to walk into the room with us.

“Fen?” I question. “Are you alright?”

Fen rapidly shakes her head and returns her gaze to us. Her expression is filled with confusion and anger, and she clenches her fists tightly.

“I thought I heard something,” she responds. “It’s nothing.”

I look around, and my heart pounds against my chest like an animal trapped in a cage. The darkness inside me vibrates, as if Kalix can hear us right now and is urging me to walk away.

My hands tremble as Silas pulls me in closer, noticing the shiver.

“She can do this,” he declares.

“Maybe we should think about this,” Maines chimes in. “I agree with Fen. I’m not sure how she will react to this and what… what if something goes wrong and I can’t heal her.”

“We’ve been through this four times now,” Warrick answers. “I can prep you the best I can, Maines, while Larkin gets set up.”

Maines pales.

“From what I’ve heard, you are extremely skilled in healing, so I imagine you will pick everything up quickly.”

Maines shakes her head, and Oak steps to her side, wrapping his arms around her. He knows exactly what she's thinking as the fear courses through her body.

"I'm not going to sit here and let you do this to her," Fen shouts. "Silas, you are asking her to do something that almost killed Larkin and Warrick. How dare you put her in this kind of danger? After you've waited so long to be with her."

"Fenmore. Hush," Silas roars, slamming his fists on the table. "I won't let Malachi corrupt her mind. She's too valuable and knows too much. I'm trying to fucking save her." He grips the table in a feeble attempt to calm himself. "And this is the only way I know how."

Her eyes fill with rage, and she spits out, "If she fucking dies, Silas, I will never forgive you."

"She won't."

Fen's eyes lock on mine, and I see the fear behind her eyes. She lingers for a moment before shifting from the house, followed by a trail of shadows.

Silas stares at the space, but no regret shows behind his piercing eyes. He exhales harshly, rubbing his throbbing temples.

"Want me to bring her back?" Warrick asks.

"No." Silas shakes his head. "We need you here."

Warrick's shoulders sag. "She'll be okay."

"I know she will."

"We need to get started," Warrick says. "Larkin, get up."

Larkin raises his head, and nerves slam into my chest. His face is pale, and I notice his fingertips shake. He clearly does not want to do this, but I know he can't say no.

What about this bothers him so much?

"We will do it here," Silas says, pointing to the table.

"Briar should change," Maines steps in.

"There isn't time," Silas responds.

He begins clearing the plates and various objects off, making a large enough spot for me to lie down. "Larkin, get the supplies, and be back here within five minutes. Briar will be ready for you to begin then."

Larkin remains silent as he shifts.

Maines turns to me. "Are you sure about this?"

I take a deep breath, steadying myself. "If it protects us and what we know, then yes. I'm sure. I know Silas wouldn't do this unless it were necessary."

Silas nods. "Maines and Oak, you two will also need to do this, but another time. I fear you'll opt out after you see this, but please know this is for our safety."

"No chance I'm fucking doing this," Oak snaps.

Maines takes his hand, already anxious, and offers him an understanding smile.

I step out onto the balcony, taking a moment to think.

Memories of my brother flood my mind as I breathe in the sea air, and he's all I can think about. Then, I realize Silas faced this situation after Thatcher shot him with an arrow.

A large hand gently touches my shoulder, pulling me out of my thoughts.

"I believe I survived the fourth trial because my body had already endured some of the poison," Silas says, moving beside me to gaze over the horizon. "I would be lying if I said I wasn't scared to do this."

"I can do it," I say, with a weary smile and more confidence than I feel.

"I know you can." He grabs my hand. "But, when the needle touches your skin, it'll burn like you've been dropped on the surface of the sun. When the poison breaks through the skin, you'll want to tear your flesh from the bone. It will bleed, but once Larkin starts, he can't stop."

My chest heaves, and I have to steady myself again. "Great."

"I'm here with you, and I won't let you go. The pain you'll

feel isn't forever, but the pain I feel for doing this will last a lifetime." Silas's hand traces the length of my arm. "Where would you like the tattoo?"

"Here," I say, pointing to my shoulder blade.

Silas reverently kisses my jaw, neck, and shoulder, sending a shiver down my spine.

"You ready?"

I take a deep breath, then nod.

We reenter the living space. Maines and Oak sit in the chairs close to the head of the table, while Warrick stands over them. Larkin sits on the opposite side with a small workspace prepped, including various needles, towels, a bowl, and a small vial.

The vial holds a black liquid that appears to pulse as Silas and I approach the table. They all turn to us with soft, insincere smiles painted on their faces. Larkin still refuses to meet my gaze, even though I know he feels my stare blazing into him.

"She would like the Rigil on her left shoulder blade, Larkin," Silas informs him.

Silas directs me to lie face down on the table. He pulls my hair to the right, making space for Larkin to work. My heart pounds against the wooden table, like someone desperately trying to get into a locked room, and I lie flat, my face pressed against the hard surface.

Silas rubs my head gently. "He will begin shortly. Just breathe, my love. It will be over soon."

I feel Maines grab my hand from the opposite side of the table, and I try my best to steady my trembling body.

I turn my head, facing Larkin. He slowly lifts his head, finally making eye contact with me, and a wave of sorrow washes through his dark eyes. He grabs a dagger from his station and pauses, saying, "We need blood. I don't want to use Briar's because of how much she could lose in this process."

"Use mine," Silas says, quickly extending his forearm across the table.

Larkin nods and swipes the blade across Silas's forearm without hesitation. Bright red blood pools down into a bowl, and I already feel as if I may be sick. He retracts his arm, and Warrick offers a piece of fabric to wrap around the wound, but Maines grabs his arm, placing her hands over the cut, and closes her eyes. A small wave of magic leaks from her hand, and the bleeding stops just as quickly as it started.

Larkin pauses for a moment to silently pray to both Gods—Raddnoke and Kantore. The bowl lights up with a shimmering glow as he dips the needle into Silas's blood and then into the dark poison.

Everyone's attention lands back on me, and I inhale deeply. Larkin makes eye contact with me once more, worry painting his expression, and I dip my chin.

"It's okay," I whisper. "I'll be okay."

One.

Two.

My heart thunders.

Larkin inhales deeply, pulling his eyes from mine. "We're ready,"

"Begin," Silas says.

CHAPTER 15

Searing pain travels through my body, an electric shock ripping me apart. The pain shoots from my neck down my back, and I worry with each passing second that the pain will become too unbearable. Larkin presses the needle against my shoulder, moving it in a continuously pull, and my vision distorts, causing his face to blur. My entire body convulses under the unyielding grips of the others.

Maines, Oak, and Warrick hold me in place while Larkin works. A familiar, calming hand rests on my head, keeping me from slamming my head against the wooden table in an attempt to knock myself out.

Tears fall from my eyes, creating a tangible pool of my pain against my temple.

"Stop," I beg. "Please, Silas." My voice is already hoarse from the piercing screams that travel around the room.

In the distance, I hear sobs coming from Maines, but it's like I'm trapped in a long tunnel of my own agony. The needle lifts from my shoulder for just a second, causing another scream to erupt from my throat, nearly shaking the cliff around us. My heart races, and I feel a tingle at my fingertips before another wave of pain slams into my body.

Larkin presses the needle against my skin once more. The sharp tip tears my flesh apart, and I swear I can hear the skin falling from my bones. Blood begins to flow from my shoulder, the crimson liquid mixing with the murky poison to create a pool of darkness around me.

"Kill me," I plead. "I can't do this."

I sob uncontrollably, a dark desperation moving through my mind.

Help.

Me.

Someone.

The pain moves through my body like a wretched disease spreading so widely that I fear it will consume my soul. My throat is raw, as if one more desperate scream could tear it apart.

"Breathe, my love. Please." I hear Silas whisper, pleading with me. "You can do this. He's almost done."

His voice sounds like he's somewhere else.

They all feel so distant, anchoring me in another miserable life—a time that doesn't exist—where I scream in desolation and pain. I want to leave this body. I need to get away from my own flesh.

"Stop," I scream. "Stop!"

Larkin watches his work intently, never breaking his stare from the needle piercing my skin, and I attempt to focus on him. His eyes flash to mine, and a sadness fills them. A push of the needle sends another shock wave through me, and my eyes roll to the back of my head.

Someone.

Help.

A breeze moves over me, and my eyes snap open.

My autumn glow is replaced with the darkest despair. I look at

Larkin through a shadowed haze, and his eyes widen. I know exactly what he sees.

No.

No.

"You can't stop, Larkin." I hear Silas urging him, as the sob breaks from his lips.

"I swear he's almost done." Silas's handsome face comes into focus briefly, and I swear it looks as if he's been crying. "Hang on."

Through my fog, I hear Larkin speak. "I think we should stop."

"The pain is for nothing if we stop," Silas says, clutching his chest as if he can feel the searing pain vibrating my body.

Larkin whispers, "It's killing her."

A loud gasp leaves my mouth as a frozen whoosh of air enters my lungs. My back attempts to arch, and I thrash against the table, held down by my friends, who are also desperate for this to end.

The room turns cold, and the pain disappears, even as Larkin continues to tattoo my broken body. A numbness rises through my legs, spine, and to my hands, like the shadow creeping over a field on a summer day. My eyes flutter closed, and a tingle starts in my fingertips, offering a break from the pain.

Silas shouts, "Larkin, stop."

But it's too late.

A whisper flows into my ears, an angel of death coming to answer my prayers.

"*Hello, Briar.*"

I scream.

"*Welcome back.*"

My eyes burn as I adjust to the brightness surrounding me, standing in a field of golden flowers. A calm, warm breeze moves my hair in all directions, and the scent of a perfect spring day floods my senses. It's quiet, and the pain has stopped. It's serene.

It's…peaceful.

I drag my hand across the tall flowers. The delicate petals tickle my skin, their silken texture surprising me. I glance at my fingers, noticing the lack of black fingertips and dark veins traveling up my hands and forearms. My skin is smooth and sun-kissed, and my long, dark hair flows in gentle curls to my hips.

I move in a circle, observing my surroundings. The fresh blue sky shines around me, and billowy white clouds cast shadows as a break from the warm sun.

I squint my eyes to see across the field and smile. A tall, broad figure looms in the distance. His shoulder-length black hair is pulled back into a low, messy bun, and his eyes are the ideal shade of crystal blue. I step forward, angling my head. The brightness from the blinding sun stings, causing me to place my hand over my eyes to get a better look.

Barlowe.

The balminess of the sun caresses my face, and our surroundings provide a sense of tranquility. I step forward, the soft ground cushioning each step as I glide through the tall flowers swaying in the breeze. With every step I take, he moves further away.

"Barlowe?" I shout.

I start to run, my feet pounding against the ground. My legs feel heavy, making it impossible to move at full speed. His towering figure begins to fade like a distant memory.

"Hey," I say again, but muffled this time.

He turns toward me one last time, and even with the distance separating us, I see a tear form on his bottom eyelid. He reaches for me, but is pulled away by a force I cannot see. A desperate whisper leaves his lips, but the wind drowns out his words.

"Wait, no. Stop."

He turns to mist in front of my eyes, leaving my chest heaving as I try to catch my breath.

The golden flowers surrounding me begin to lose their color, their delicate petals curling at the edges, fading to a dull gray. The flowers droop all around me, dying, and I whip my head in every direction, watching the vibrant colors vanish along with my brother. The ground beneath me withers, and the soft grass turns to chalky ashen mud as the sun's warmth disappears, leaving a cold wind to bite at my skin. I stand in shock as panic floods my veins.

A murder of crows flies overhead, their cries filling the air with their screeching. My peaceful surroundings transform into a decaying wasteland as I stand, transfixed in horror.

"It doesn't have to be like this," a cold voice calls from behind me.

I close my eyes, tears streaming down my cheeks, but I don't turn to see who is speaking. I know.

"Would you like to live with your family here? With your brother? Your mother?" Her voice taunts and promises. "I can restore the serene lands you just saw. You can be happy here, unbothered and at peace."

I don't respond. I stand motionless—defeated and terrified.

"All you have to do is surrender, Briar. I'll take it from here, and you can stay in this place. No pain, no suffering, simply here with them."

I tip my head toward the gray sky, and when I open my eyes, I'm once again standing in a field of flowers. Their scent is overpowering, and the warmth of the sun once again warms my ice-cold skin.

I slowly turn to look at Kalix.

Her flowing raven hair sways in the warm breeze, and she's dressed in a sheer black dress that reveals her skin underneath. Her eyes—black as the darkest night—shine into mine, and I can't help but see how similar we look when my eyes shift. Crimson and black veins mark her skin, and a similar soft red flows through her hair, reminding me of blood leaking from her skin. A single crow perches on her shoulder, and she gazes at the large bird, petting it with her own claws.

"Aren't you tired? Tired of fighting? Tired of being in pain and worrying?" She smiles broadly, rows of sharp teeth glistening in the sun. "If you let me in completely, I can take it all away. You will live comfortably."

"This isn't real," I whisper.

"It can be," Kalix responds. "For you."

"It's all a trick," I rasp. "Just like the other illusions you've cast before."

I look at my hands, and through the bright haze, I can see my black fingertips starting to return.

Briar.

My gaze looks in all directions. *Silas.* I feel his voice desperately claw into my mind.

Kalix snarls, "Don't you grow tired of him. He's always ruining our fun. Typical of his kind."

"He wakes me from the dreams—the nightmares—you cast in my mind. How can he do that?"

"Magic," she quips, waving her hands sarcastically, and smiles.

"What is he?" I ask, my voice demanding an answer.

"He's a pain in my ass. That's what he is." She lowers her gaze, looking up through her black lashes. "And he's going to be the first person I kill when I fully take over your body."

Briar? Can you hear me?

"Why do you hate him?" I stumble back, creating distance. "Is it because he helps me? Is it because he can pull me out of this?"

"I'm stunned you haven't put it together yet. He rips you from my grasp every time, as they all have in the past." Anger flashes in her soulless eyes. "Bothersome fucking things."

I narrow my eyes. "I don't understand."

"You choose not to, Briar. You know these aren't nightmares." She laughs, coldly. "You can feel it. You continue to fear me instead of using me. Let us become one."

I stare, confusion and anger filling my chest like wildfire, accompanied by the harsh reality of what's happening.

Briar! Fuck.

I feel myself fading. The nightmare swirling around me begins to lessen. I hear Silas's call as a beacon of light in the darkest nights.

I squint my eyes, ignoring the pull, fighting with everything I have to stay.

Here.

In my own mind, I shout, "*Stop, I need to hear what she has to say.*"

Kalix narrows her large eyes, observing my internal struggle with a satisfied expression on her face. "You want to stay? You want to know the truth, don't you?"

I clench my fists and say, "Keep going."

"You can shift wherever you wish, my child. The world is yours. The realms are yours—past or present, never future. That's why you are my perfect vessel." She stalks forward, and I backpedal.

"With you, I could achieve so much. But that man—he's the

tether pulling you back from where I can reach you. Fate always brings a vessel and tether together to protect the cosmos." She pets the crow on her shoulder, savoring my shock. "It's unnatural possessing this power, and there must be a balance. He is your balance. Your tether of realms. He will always guide you home." She laughs cooly. "That is, until he's gone."

The memories of before crash into my mind. All the nights I was lost, and he found me.

He's kept me safe for years without ever truly knowing me, designed to protect and ground me. I felt stuck in that wasteland for what seemed like years while Silas was so severely injured that he couldn't come after me. I traveled so far without realizing it and had no way back. The morning I woke up on the ship, Silas had found me. He had healed and desperately searched through the shadows of all the realms to find me.

Kalix continues, "See, the thing is, Briar, you want me to take over. If you didn't, you wouldn't have traveled here. You are the reason you continue to see me—because you want to." She steps forward. "I didn't force you here. I can't. You came willingly."

I shake my head.

Stop ignoring me. Silas's voice shouts.

My chest throbs in pain, and I clutch my shirt.

"He's calling. Better run home, now. I'll see you soon. That tattoo won't keep me away for long."

Kalix fades into a haze with a wicked grin painted on her terrifying face.

I drop to my knees, my chest feeling like it's about to explode. The heat shines down on me before swiftly turning ice cold. I close my eyes and let the words guide me, taking me home—to Silas.

My bloodshot eyes rip open, and Silas hovers above me, his hands on my chest. His panicked face tells me all I need to know. They thought they lost me, and maybe they almost did. I can feel my eyes still heavy with darkness, unable to shake from her grasp just yet.

"Push her away. Shift back," he snaps.

"*Or don't*," Kalix's voice, barely a faint whisper, travels around me.

I gasp for air and thrash, as a single tear soaks into the veins that branch out from under my eyes.

Everyone is standing together—near the table, but pushed back—to give Silas the space he needs. The familiar sea breeze travels through the room, mixing with the sighs I hear coming from their mouths. My back is pressed against the cold wooden table as I gaze up at the tall ceiling. The pain settling in my shoulder slowly becomes more apparent, and it quickly snaps me back into focus.

Silas's hands wrap around my jaw, and he moves closer. "Push her down."

I slowly sit, gripping my upper back, and glance around the room. The exhaustion slams into my chest, but I feel her drift away as my eyes shift back.

The blood has been cleaned, and my gown remains somehow untouched by the mess. Maines and Oak's faces are filled with horror. Warrick's expression is as hard as stone, and Larkin is pale —utterly devoid of color—with small beads of sweat coating his face.

"You were going to do it. Weren't you?" Silas fumes, moving

back into my line of vision. "You were going to fucking listen to her."

I blink through the haze, my hazel eyes fully returning, and see how serious he is.

"Answer me," he bites.

His piercing green eyes are so close to mine that I can see the anger dancing within them. His chest heaves with fury, while the others watch us in confusion.

Tears begin to fill his eyes as he whispers, "Fucking answer me."

Silas remembers this time.

He knows what I was feeling in the presence of Kalix, and so do I. It all makes sense now.

I remember everything.

I know what Silas is to me.

CHAPTER 16

"Get out," Silas snaps, looking over his shoulder to the others, letting anger drive his words. "I need to speak with her."

Oak and Maines stiffen as Warrick and Larkin move almost immediately, reminding me that orders from Silas must be quite standard for them.

"Wait a second," Maines says, angrily stepping toward Silas and me. "Briar just blacked out from something you pressured her to do, and now you're kicking us out? Silas, we thought she was dying. I need answers about what the hell just happened."

Larkin and Warrick halt.

"Get. The. Fuck. Out," Silas orders.

He pauses and turns his glare back toward me. Shame washes over me, and I clench my jaw, just seconds away from my chest imploding.

"No, Nastronde. We're not leaving." Oak shields Maines with his body. Bolts of light flicker around his large frame as anger radiates from him. "And, I suggest you never speak to Maines that way again, either."

Silas bores his gaze into mine.

"We need answers," Oak barks. "Now."

Silas pushes away from the table and turns to face Oak, the challenge evident. Their eyes meet, and they stand face to face as fury leaks from Silas around the room.

Larkin and Warrick hang back, making themselves nearly invisible against the wall.

"I'm not fighting you, Silas," Oak says. "That wouldn't end well for anyone; I fucking promise you that."

A crackle of lightning zaps from Oak's hands, and Silas moves his gaze down to see the magic building around his friend. Shadows begin to build upon Silas's back.

"Stop," Maines orders.

Oak steps back to create distance.

"Do not push us away right now," Oak grinds out.

I've never seen Oak this angry, and Silas pauses for a moment, realizing that fighting him isn't what we need right now.

Silas exhales sharply, stepping back. "Fine. I'll give you an answer. Briar was ready to listen to Kalix. She was going to let her take over."

They all stare at me, their gazes burning into my soul. I slam my eyes shut, swearing I can still feel the delicate flowers brushing against my legs. I see Barlowe in the distance, his calm face watching me, and my heart splits in two. I let out a long, shaky breath. I crack open my eyes, and heavy tears rest on my bottom eyelids, threatening to spill over.

"I wasn't going to."

"I felt it." He glares at me, accusation in his stare. "I could feel everything you were experiencing. Barlowe wasn't real."

His words strike me like daggers. Maines and Oak look toward us in shock.

"B-Barlowe?" Maines gasps.

"I know he wasn't real, Silas. Believe me, I fucking know that," I respond, my voice rising. "But, it was calm, and I wasn't in pain. I'm tired. I'm so tired of fighting every single fucking day." My head falls into my hands.

Maines and Oak walk to my side, allowing me to cry momentarily, and give Silas a nasty look. Silas stands back, and I can see his chest rising and falling quickly. He's unbelievably upset with me. He understands that I'm not telling the truth—which keeps the others from panicking—because he's right. I considered it.

I thought about letting go and living blissfully unaware of the pain, and for a moment, I almost accepted that decision. The guilt hits me.

Silas tilts his head and walks to his bedroom. The door slams shut with a bang, and I don't chase after him. He needs a moment to process what just happened, as do I.

"Is that true?" Oak asks.

The others wait for my response, and the anticipation fills the room with a thick tension.

"No. I...I wouldn't do that."

They nod, but I can sense that no one in this room genuinely believes me. I don't even believe myself.

Maines pulls me into a tight hug, "Are you alright?"

I shake my head. She knows I'm not okay, physically or mentally.

"Just give him a minute. He'll be fine, but he needs to calm down." Maines's composed words ease my racing heart. "I'm not sure what happened, but you seriously scared him."

I grab my back, feeling the ache settling in. I glance at Larkin, and his face is still pale as he refuses to meet my stare.

"Your shoulder has almost healed. The tattoo turned out fine, and Larkin did an amazing job," she continues. "I can tell that it's healing on its own, but it'll be noticeable for a while. We'll need something to hide it from Malachi." Maines grins over my shoulder. "I can grab you a shawl to bring with you."

Oak smiles as he leans his hip against the table. "After

witnessing that, I'd prefer being haunted over experiencing getting that thing tattooed on my body. No offense, Larkin, but you're not getting anywhere near me."

Larkin moves closer to me while I'm still perched on the table. He walks behind me, examining his work. His rough hand grazes the fading ink, causing me to flinch. I hear him exhale, as if relieved that I'm sitting here with them right now.

"It's healing nicely. You did well, until you didn't, but right now, your body seems to be reacting well to the poison," Larkin's relaxed voice states. "And no offense taken, Oak. You aren't my type, anyway."

Oak's jaw drops. "What? I'm everyone's type."

Maines laughs loudly. "Finally, someone is helping me check Oak's wild ego. Do you know how often I tell him that?"

I glance at Larkin, a gentle smile spreading across my lips. "Did you just make a joke?"

For the first time, he smirks at me. "I do have the ability to be funny."

"Take note of this, everyone," Warrick says from across the room. "Larkin makes about one joke a year."

Larkin's bright white teeth gleam as he tips his head back, laughing.

"Noted," Oak says.

"You're tough," Larkin says, still studying the tattoo. "In more ways than one. I see why Silas is so fond of you."

His name makes me flinch.

With the others gathered around me, playfully arguing about Oak's ridiculous statements, Silas has remained in his room. His door stays shut, and Kalix's words echo in my mind.

Tether of realms.

I approach the edge of the table, taking my time to stand up. Given what just happened, I can't imagine rushing anywhere is a good idea. Larkin grabs my arm, helping me stand.

"You okay?" he asks.

I plant my feet on the hard floor, gathering myself before trying to stand on my own. My shoulder continues to throb, and I swear I can feel the poison pulsing through my veins.

"You should go talk to him," Larkin urges, glancing toward the hallway. "But, you need to be quick. We have to be at the castle soon. Malachi isn't forgiving of tardiness."

I nod, and Larkin gently pats my back, joining Maines, Oak, and Warrick around the table once more. Their hushed tones tell me precisely who they're discussing—me.

The hallway before me seems to stretch forever, giving me too much time to doubt myself and overthink what I need to tell Silas. I know he could sense what I was thinking, an unfortunate part of him being my tether. We're deeply connected on a level that others wouldn't understand. I know the tattoo worked—Kalix feels more contained than usual, which is a nice relief—but I know it won't last. That said, I can't help but think about one particular thing, and it weighs on me as I continue my strides down the narrow hallway.

I don't think I can hear Rohhit anymore.

I reach Silas's door, pausing to take a deep breath before knocking. My fist gently taps against the sturdy wood, and I listen for the sound of feet shuffling, but no sounds greet me. I crack the door open and peek my head in. Silas stands at the large bay windows, both of which are open to allow the cold night air to flow through the room. The thin black drapes move in the breeze, but Silas remains unmoving. He leans forward, gazing out over the dark sea, and doesn't turn around as I cross the ample space to join him at the windows.

I walk beside him, resting my hand on his back, but he doesn't move.

I make a pained face. "I know you're mad."

"I am," Silas bites out. "Is it that obvious?"

He turns his body toward mine, and that's when I notice it. Blood—my blood—soaked into his clothing. The amount is shocking, and my mouth slightly parts.

"My Gods, Silas." I reach out to touch his hand.

He pulls his hand out of my reach, and a new invisible pain overwhelms me.

"I know you are lying to the others to keep them calm, but do not lie to me." He finally meets my gaze, and his eyes are filled with hurt. "I could feel what you were thinking, and I know you wanted to give up."

I try again to grab his hand, and this time, he lets our hands mold together.

"That's not the Briar I know." His green eyes blaze. "You're the strong one, and I worry that if the others see you give up, all hope is gone. I don't want to burden you with that, but you need to understand what you mean to them and what you mean to me."

I gaze out of the open window. The sea below us churns, and with each crashing wave, the sounds thrumming in my chest.

"I never asked for any of this."

Silas releases my hand and moves his hand around my waist. "I know. None of us did, but it's what we've been dealt. We can either decide to face this head-on or give up and let the evil win." His embrace gets tighter. "It's time we turn this around and take things into our own hands. I've been afraid, and I can see in your eyes that you have as well. That fear stops now, and I'm so fucking ready for what's next."

He turns my body toward his and tips my head back, pressing a deep kiss to my lips.

Silas pulls away and cups my face. "The next time you feel like giving up, talk to me, and I'll give you a thousand reasons to keep going."

I nuzzle into his hold, and pride shines brightly across my face. Fear has been holding us both back, and we can no longer hide in the shadows of our nightmares. There's too much at stake to give in now. With all the evil surrounding us, it's time to show the demons who the feared ones truly are.

I nod. "We need to leave."

"I should change. As delicious as your blood smells, I don't think the castle staff would appreciate me tracking it in." He smiles.

I head for the door as he slips his clothes off, and I hear them slap to the floor with a wet thud. Before I cross the threshold, I turn back to his shirtless body.

"Silas," I call out.

"Yeah?"

"Did you hear everything Kalix said to me?"

"No." He gives me a puzzled look. "I could only feel and see you."

I offer a gentle smile and open the door to leave.

"Why? What did she say?" he asks, concerned.

I open my mouth to speak, but Maines calls from down the hallway, "We need to leave, now."

"Go ahead. I'm right behind you." Silas slips into a fresh black shirt, fastening a dagger across his broad chest. "You can tell me later. Malachi won't wait."

Every step down the hallway echoes in my chest, but I don't have time to panic right now. I need to concentrate on my meeting with Malachi, but I can't.

Silas doesn't know what he is.

My tether.

CHAPTER 17

We all shift into Silas's bedroom in the castle. Once everyone arrives, we stand together in silence for a moment. Fenmore still hasn't returned, so I can only hope she has been with Hux, preparing Malachi for my arrival. My shoulder continues to throb, which Larkin assured me is normal and will persist for a few days until it truly heals. The looming dark walls of Silas's room feel suffocating.

"You will meet him in his study. It's near the Great Hall, down a small, hidden hallway." Silas goes over our plans. "I will enter the room with you, but take my leave shortly after. Larkin and I will be outside the doors. Warrick, I would like you to stay back with Oak and Maines."

Warrick nods, accepting his orders. "Say the word, and I'm here to help."

"What?" Oak chimes in.

"I thought you might be upset," Silas says, treading lightly. "Neither of you has the Rigil's protection, so it's not safe. With what's coming in a few days, I believe we should get Rose off the ship and settled at my house. She can stay there. It's the safest option for what's ahead, since it's warded."

Oak steps forward to protest, but Maines grabs his arm. "He's right. We need to help where we can, Oak. Briar can do this, and we aren't protected. As a healer, I know messing with this sort of stuff is serious. This isn't something I'll argue with."

"Take care of Rose," I say, as I quickly hug Maines. "We will be back at the house as soon as we can."

Oak huffs as we exit the room, but we push forward on a strict schedule as we enter the spacious hallway. The flickering candle-light illuminates our presence, causing shadows to dance all around us.

I lead the way.

My black dress flows behind me, like a dark river of madness. The snakes coil around my neck, and my steps echo against the smooth floor. Silas and Larkin walk closely behind me, their large bodies towering over mine.

Silas's shadows compete with those in the hallway, growing larger as he focuses and channels all the magic he can. Larkin falls silent, and a steady stream of bright energy radiates from his body.

Together, we are a storm—a surge of darkness and light—working in perfect harmony.

Nearing the Great Hall, Silas points to a barely noticeable entrance leading to a dark hallway. Old paintings of past rulers of Andorwood line the hallways. The men are all graced with black hair and the same piercing green eyes that Silas harbors, clearly from his mother's side. A dense fog rolls over the floors, sending a chill up my spine. I look at Silas, his face hard as stone, but he gives me a reassuring nod.

The hallway ends with a single door on the back wall. A tall glass window extends high up to the ceiling, and intricate metal is implanted in the glass, twisting chaotically, causing the bright moonlight to shine like madness on the floor.

My senses perk up even more, expecting to see a serpent

embedded in the door. Instead, before us is a door with detailed wood carvings and a single painted crow with eyes as soulless as the man behind the door. Silas leans over me to bring his fist down against it, but just before he can, we hear, "Come in."

The door opens on its own, revealing only darkness.

Silas gives Larkin a look to back off. I glance at Larkin and try to smile, but my nerves take over, a worried expression overtaking my face.

"Be smart, Briar. You can do this," he whispers, squeezing my arm.

Silas enters the room first. He disappears into the darkness before I have time to cross the threshold. The dense black fog begins to fade as I make my way deeper into the study. Silas's silhouette comes into view, and the room opens up.

He stands before a large black desk encrusted in gold that is clear of clutter. In fact, the entire room is pristine. Thick drapes hang from each tall window, and a chandelier of a thousand candles sways gently in the breeze. The room is hauntingly beautiful, and I can't stop myself from looking around.

I join Silas at the desk and notice the empty leather chair. Malachi isn't here. Silas grabs my hand and holds tight. My heart pounds so intensely that I can hear it throbbing in my head. Even my eyes seem to pulse from the anticipation building in my system.

"Glad you could make it," Malachi's devilish voice calls from behind us. "You were nearly late."

Silas whips around, never releasing my hand, and my breath hitches in my chest as I catch sight of him.

"We aren't here to play your fucking games, Malachi," Silas fumes.

"Oh, did I startle you? You scare so easily." His eyes shine in the light of the roaring fire. "I thought we could have a bit of fun before diving into the serious topics." He laughs and moves around the large desk, sitting down with an unruly grace.

"I'm serious," Silas snarls. "Cut the shit."

Malachi slams his hands against the table, rising to eye level. "You cut the shit, Silas. I know why you are here. I know what you seek." His outburst fades as quickly as it sparked, and a sinister calmness runs over him once more. "And don't think for a second that I'm not aware of what sails toward Andorwood, or what you are about to dangle over my head. I'm the King of Andorwood. Your fucking king." He settles back in his chair, adjusting his fitted shirt.

Silas huffs a sarcastic laugh.

"But," Malachi interjects. "I will give Briar her time to speak. Once you are gone from the castle grounds." Malachi points to the door. "Tell your guard dog, Larkin, he can leave as well. I know he's here."

Silas's eyes darken, and his jaw clenches so tight I fear his teeth will shatter.

"You are a fucking fool if you think I'm leaving her in this castle alone."

"Haven't you once already?" Malachi laughs. "Last night?"

Out of the corner of my eye, I see Silas getting ready to lunge. I quickly grab his arm and dig my nails in deep to pull him out of the blind rage. He calms down—barely—but takes a deep, shuddering breath.

"Looks like Briar is your guard dog, not Larkin," Malachi observes, keeping an eye on the rapid exchange. "Mind if I borrow her?"

"I will fucking kill you," Silas barely whispers.

"Hurry up," Malachi says to Silas. "I have other things to do after this."

Silas turns to me, pulling me slightly away from the desk and behind his body. "Briar, this is your call. I told you, no fear, but this is up to you." His eyes burn with intense focus. "I will not leave you if you tell me not to. We can come up with another plan."

"It's just a conversation," I assure him. "Go."

Silas stares at me for a long moment, and I can only imagine the internal struggle he's facing about this plan. He closes his eyes and rests his forehead against mine. "Alright."

He turns to his father, and nothing but hatred shows on his face.

"Tick-tock," Malachi says, sarcastically.

"Briar will walk out of this castle unscathed," Silas fumes. "Understood?"

Malachi nods, smiling.

"And while we are at it, tell your fucking invisible guard dogs to back down. If they continue to stalk her, we will have bigger problems than we already do."

"Ugh, you are so dramatic, Silas." Malachi snaps his fingers, and the room instantly feels lighter. "Done."

As the curtains and windows fly open and the invisible creatures leave the room, I feel a chill run down my spine. I shudder thinking of the unseen guards who lurked in this room, watching us and protecting Malachi without me even realizing it.

Silas turns his back on his father and exits the room, the door slamming behind him. I feel Silas shift, and our connection dims as he and Larkin leave the castle. I slowly turn my focus back to Malachi, and a wicked smile graces his face.

"Alone at last, with a worthy opponent." He looks me up and down. "You look stunning, by the way. Good enough to eat."

"Of course I'm worthy." I steady my stance and calm my racing heart. "But, I don't think we need to become rivals right away, Malachi."

He studies me like a hunter finding his prey, but what he doesn't know is that I love a challenge.

I return his prying gaze and size him up, asking, "How old are you?"

For a second, he's surprised by my question. "Ouch, Briar. Do I look that bad?"

"Who said I was basing that question on looks? Not everything is physical, Your Majesty. I'm basing my question on the advanced abilities I've heard of, and now seen." I smile, and place my hands behind my back. "However, if we are talking about your looks, my question still stands."

He laughs. "Don't you know it's rude to ask someone their age?"

"That doesn't offend you, though," I bite back. "Does it?"

"No, it doesn't, but I'm glad you can recognize my wisdom. Many people don't understand my level of…knowledge."

I angle my head. "Is that what we are going to call it?"

"I'm not sure why I'm surprised that the daughter of Lornx Blackbyrne has a mouth that wicked." He stands, ensuring that we are on an even playing field. "Is that mouth how you won Silas over, or was it something else?"

Malachi stares directly at my lips, his eyes darkening, and a wave of repulsion hits my stomach.

"You are truly nauseating."

"Oh, take a joke." He points to the sitting area near a roaring fire. "Shall we?"

I let him take the lead, and I curl my fists at my side. I won't let him get under my skin. Silas warned me about his father countless times. I refuse to let fear take over my mind. Malachi gestures to an empty chair, and I follow his instruction to sit. He crosses his legs and studies me for a moment, his brows wrinkled. The crackling fire pops, and I can't help but flinch. He smiles, aware that I'm on edge.

"You are fascinating." Malachi chews his lip.

"Is that a compliment?" I spit back. "Or another insult?"

"However, you'd like to take it."

I huff a sarcastic laugh.

"The strongest vessel for Kalix to ever live." He taps his index fingers on his lips. "Tell me, can she hear us right now?"

"No, she can't. I can control her, and right now, she isn't here." I place my hands casually in my lap. "Right now, she isn't even a thought in my mind."

He laughs wildly. "You cannot control her. She only lets you believe that you can."

"And how would you know?" I question.

He pauses, thinking of his next words carefully, and the slightest change in his eyes lets me know that he's trying to enter my mind. I glance at his wrist, noticing a bit of grey discoloration on his skin. I tilt my head and let my thoughts swirl.

"That's a story for another wonderful meeting, Queen."

That title on his lips makes my skin crawl, and I can't help but fidget in my chair. I narrow my eyes, carefully considering my next move. He's currently playing a dangerous game of back and forth, and what he doesn't know is that I was made for this game. A subtle tap in my mind makes my insides squirm; the tattoo is blocking him right now, and I'm thankful for the pain I experienced at this moment.

"You know," he says, clearing his throat. "I was truly upset when Silas found a way to block my talents a few years ago. I had such a great time tormenting him as he grew older." He smiles, fully aware of the weight of his words. "Given how your mind is closed off, he must have shared this knowledge with you. Tell me. How much did it hurt?"

"Like hell," I respond. "But, all the pain was worth the miserable look on your face right now."

He leans forward in his chair, scratching his chin, "Do you think Barlowe felt it that much? When the poison entered his veins?"

The words hit me like a blow to the face. Anger rises within me, and the darkness creeps up.

And, it doesn't quiet down. The dark veins on my hands vibrate, and for a moment, I think that Kalix coming forward and wiping this man from this realm sounds like a great idea. He wants to provoke me, and I refuse to give in to his demands.

"Malachi, the only power you hold over me at the moment is your words."

"And other things," he smiles.

"I can promise there is nothing you could say that would hurt me."

"Is that so?"

I nod, crossing my arms.

"Then let me try," he insists, grinning maniacally. "I like games."

"Go ahead. I have all night, and nothing to do."

Malachi tilts his head. "Does Silas know?"

I freeze, and the air leaves my lungs. "Does he know what?"

"Oh, Briar. You know exactly what I'm asking. Do you think he loves you because of you? Or because he was designed to?" He leans forward. "It would be such a shame if his love for you wasn't real."

I stand with such force that my chair flips and I rush toward him. I bring my face inches from his and snarl, "You are a fucking child."

"Am I?" He laughs. "Seems like I just won."

"This isn't a game," I spit.

"But," he grins broadly, "it is."

"Instead of taking the fate of this kingdom and our realm seriously, you sit in your velvet chair of misery and taunt people, because after all these years, you've realized that's the only control you truly have."

Before I can react, his large hand wraps around my throat and squeezes. He stands and pushes me backward against the wall. His hot breath brushes the nape of my neck, and I try to fight against his grip, but it holds. His eyes pierce into mine, and in this moment, they are unlike any Wielders I have ever seen. They are dark, ancient, and animalistic.

They are inhuman.

"You don't know what you're up against," he whispers in my ear. "I'm not the only one playing games; you are, too. You think you can win, but you're wrong."

I gasp against his hold, feeling the burn in my lungs.

"You're living in a delusion, and I will make sure that I'm the one who snaps you back into this harsh reality," Malachi says.

He releases my neck, and I fall to the ground, inhaling as hard as my lungs will allow. The handprint around my neck burns, but I don't touch it. I don't dare give him the satisfaction of knowing he can hurt me. Malachi sits back down in his chair and gazes at the fire.

I stand on unsteady legs and grasp the edge of the dark velvet chair. He ignores my struggle, and I pull myself up again, sitting across from him once more.

"The only one living in a delusion is you," I say. "I think you are scared, and I'm going to find out what of."

This meeting is over.

Taking a deep breath, I stand. "You might think we don't have a chance, but at least we're trying, Malachi."

He places his elbows on his knees, listening to every word.

"Carobon has possessed the Prince of Eddris, Rohhit Harte, while Calia Thornfield is orchestrating plans that have been years in the making with my apparent half-brother, Nolan. They have the resurrection stone and are planning to raise an army."

He snaps his head from the crackling fire. "Lornx had a child with Calia Thornfield? There's another Blackbyrne son?"

"Is that what caught your attention? My father's infidelity?"

He nods, facing the fire once more—lost in thought.

"If you're not going to help us, then Andorwood will cease to exist. Carobon plans to rid the realm of all Shadow Wielders."

He shrugs, but I continue.

"You know a ship is sailing here with those creatures aboard. We need to be prepared to fight in four days. Are you willing to help us? Are you going to prep the Andorwood army to fight? Or, will you let Silas lead?"

"No. They won't fight," he replies, still focused solely on the flickering flames in the fireplace. "I won't allow it."

I step into his line of sight. "You're a coward. I hope you spend what's left of your miserable life trapped in this castle. When the time comes, I'll gather whoever I can to protect this kingdom. When you don't show up, they'll see who will truly rule and who chooses to languish in the shadows." I step back, leaving him with my words. "I used to hide there, Malachi, and I can promise it's not the way. The people of Andorwood will see Silas as the future, and you will be forgotten."

He doesn't turn his gaze to meet mine, and I exhale sharply, creating distance.

"Who will you haunt then, Malachi, when no one remembers your fucking name?"

I move toward the door and reach for the handle.

A shift in the room causes the candlelight to flicker chaotically, but I ignore it and move faster to exit. An unseen breath brushes my hair aside, inches from my face, and I freeze. Fear envelops me, and even though I can't see the threat, my senses scream at me to look around. An invisible claw grazes my shoulder as if tracing the spot where my tattoo is marked on my body. The claw begins to dig in deeper, and I spin around to see Malachi standing there, facing me. An unnaturally broad smile spreads across his face, and I watch madness creep over his aged features as the flames crackle behind him.

"It would be so easy, Briar, to end your life right now." Malachi rests his hands on the chair before him and leans into it. "You are distracted and only worry about the things right in front of you, when you should be concerned about the things that creep in between."

The claw digs deeper into my shoulder, and I grit my teeth against the sharp pain shooting down my back. I don't move; it's as if fear has trapped me once again, taking me back to the dinner table the day before, when I couldn't move, only blink in horror.

"I will not fight alongside you, because you are reckless. You are not prepared, and associating myself with you would be suicide."

I fumble behind me, trying to get a good grip on the door handle to yank it open and make my exit.

Malachi steps closer.

"I haunt and dwell in the shadows to remain hidden. You have no idea who—or what—I've dealt with in my life. I'll torment, hunt, and torture for the rest of my life if that keeps me safe." His face moves closer to mine. "I'll continue to hide, and I don't intend to be found. You should know all about hiding in the shadows. You are a coward, just like me."

I angle my head, unsure of how to interpret that statement. Malachi steps back abruptly, giving me space to open the door.

"I've worked hard to be here, and I don't plan to go back," he mutters.

I cross the threshold and glance back once more. He remains frozen in the doorway, watching me walk down the long, dark hallway. The shadows around him distort his face, and for a moment, all I see is a monster as a broad smile spreads across his face.

He calls down the hall, "That tattoo won't protect you for long. She'll come forward, and you won't be able to stop her."

His words echo in my ear as my steps pound against the floor, making my way down the hallway once more. Just the mention of the tattoo makes my shoulder throb as the poison continuously burns through my veins. The hallway ends, and I stand in the wide opening of the castle. The corridor behind me resembles a tunnel of darkness, and I quickly turn to ensure my back isn't facing that direction.

The dark castle looms above me, and the vaulted ceilings creak from the roaring wind outside. Each noise has my senses on edge, and no matter how hard I try, I can't steady my racing heart. Something about this castle scares me—as if each shadowy corner holds a secret just waiting to be revealed. Even though my curiosity sometimes gets the best of me, I believe that most of the secrets should remain just that.

Andorwood has been as confusing as I imagined it would be. Nothing since we have arrived makes sense, and I fear the longer we remain on this island, the more the tension between the group will rise.

I continue through the large room, my defenses dropping as I continue up the stairs, lost in thought.

The towering chandelier at the top of the stairs is decorated with black and silver jewels that snake to the ceiling. The tall windows are stained with dark-colored glass, and the moonlight casts in, creating more shadows. The shadows around me seem to build in my presence, and fear rises in my chest. My steps quicken as I turn the corner toward our bedrooms. I glance over my shoulder, and in the darkness, I can make out faint movements —something dark is following me.

I bound forward, and each time I whip my head around, the shadow quickly slips into a pocket, making it impossible to distinguish the figure stalking me. I start to run and whisper, "Gods, just give me some light in this fucking darkness."

Did I just pray for light around me?

I hear a muffled growl behind me, and I shout, "Stop!"

Turning on my heels, the looming figure behind me steps out of the shadows, towering over me by three heads. My eyes widen, and I freeze in fear. I widen my stance as the nearly invisible creature crawls toward me on all fours.

"Leave me alone," I scream, while pushing my palms forward, expecting a surge of black magic to erupt from my body. My jaw drops when darkness doesn't emerge from my hands. Instead, a bright white light sends my entire body flying backward. The hallway fills with a blinding radiance, and the creature shrieks in agony.

Stunned, I lie on the floor, gasping for breath.

Light.

I wielded light.

A small hand wraps around my arm, and I scream as I'm pulled through an open bedroom door.

CHAPTER 18

The dark bedroom engulfs me as a hand clasps over my mouth.

"Shhh," a soft voice whispers in my ear. "I'm sorry to startle you, but please don't scream, or it may follow us."

I push the hand away from my face and quickly get to my feet. "What the fuck."

A light clicks on in the room's far corner, and a small figure remains half in the shadows. "Please don't be mad, Your Majesty."

A woman emerges from the darkness, causing me to squint.

She looks familiar. Long white hair cascades around her petite hips, and her large, round eyes are as black as the shadows enveloping us. I lean in for a closer look, still trying to steady my blurred vision.

Before me stands a dancer from the dinner on the first night, an evening I wish I could erase from my memory—the woman who couldn't take her eyes off Silas. The memory strikes me, and jealousy surges through my veins for a moment. She offers me a soft grin and points to an old chair. I wearily tilt my head and move to join her.

She continues to stand. "Please have a seat." She bows.

"Oh, you do not have to do that," I say, as I sit on the worn furniture.

"Apologies, Your Majesty." She smiles. "It's just in my blood to treat royalty as such."

The woman sits in the chair across from me, smoothing out her dark dress. She tucks her long hair behind both ears and settles in. I focus on her, but I can't shake the urge to glance at my hands. She appears exhausted, and I immediately feel a soft spot for her. She's older than I am, but her eyes tell the story. Years of hardship linger behind her shadowy gaze.

What the fuck just happened in the hallway?

"I don't mean to be rude, but who are you?" I ask.

She chuckles at my forwardness, but doesn't seem offended in the slightest.

"My name is Yara. I was one of the women providing the entertainment the other night during your arrival dinner." Her white smile dazzles in the dim lighting.

She's a stunning Lumor Wielder.

"Yes, you look familiar," I reply, stiffly.

Yara dips her head and settles into the chair, relaxing her shoulders. Her eyes soften, and I can tell that she's holding back, saying what is desperate to roll off her tongue.

"What exactly can I help you with, Yara?"

She nods. "I want to apologize for grabbing you. I heard shouting, so I came to see what was going on. I...I saw what you did back there—wielding light. That was really impressive, to say the least, and interesting."

I nod, letting my own confusion slam into my chest.

"Interesting is a great word for that," I say.

"Do you often practice Shadow and Lumor Wielding? It's quite rare."

I open my mouth to speak, but no words come out.

No, I didn't know I could fucking do that.

I look at my hands, and they remain unchanged. My black fingertips tingle, and subtle black veins emerge beneath my skin. "Yara, please don't tell anyone about that."

She gazes at me with an understanding look. "I won't."

The dimly lit room is filled with a musty odor, yet the open window allows a breeze of fresh night air to flow in. It's smaller than the other rooms I've seen and certainly not as ornate. "Do you live here?" I ask.

"Yes, for many years now. I work here as a dancer and help with various castle staff needs, among other things." She looks toward the ground, and a flash of shame hits her dark eyes.

"Your dancing is quite beautiful. You should be proud of the talent you have," I say, and chuckle. "I would have crashed into everyone sitting at the table."

Yara returns the laugh. "Oh, I doubt that, Your Majesty, but thank you. I've danced for years."

"Please," I respond. "Call me Briar."

"Okay, Briar." She nods.

The tremor in my hands begins to subside as the adrenaline of recent events fades in my system. I take a deep breath to slow my heartbeat and convince myself that I'm safe in here.

At least, I hope I am.

"Thank you for bringing me into your room. I'm relieved I'm not still outside with that creature."

"We call them *Travelers*."

I tilt my head. "The invisible creatures?"

"Yes." She shudders. "I'm not sure anyone knows their real name. They move unnaturally and silently until it's too late. All I know is that they are deadly and not of this realm. They have a way of shifting in the shadows that no one truly understands."

"How wonderful," I say sarcastically, but her words stick in my mind.

"I can't fathom how ancient these creatures are. The king seems to be the only one who has full control over them," she adds.

I grimace; the memory of the hot breath against my skin makes it crawl. "Yes, his guard dogs. I have had the pleasure of running into a few of them already."

"It's not a coincidence that I ran into you, Briar." Yara's eyes meet mine. "I was looking for you. I heard rumors that you were speaking with Malachi tonight, and I needed to speak with you, too."

Anticipation rolls in my stomach. "What did you need to talk about?"

She pauses and takes a deep breath, as if carefully considering her following words.

I can't help but pray this doesn't involve Silas. I think back to dinner and how her gaze burned into his skin, as if she was trying to set him on fire—like something was left unsaid between them. I know there were women before me, but I never thought I'd have to encounter one.

"There is no easy way to say this," she breathes.

My palms begin to sweat, and my once steady heartbeat increases with every passing second that she hesitates to speak.

"Does this have to do with Silas?"

She drops her gaze. "In a sense."

"Well," I shift in my chair, not letting my nerves show, "let's hear it."

"I'm having an affair…" Yara blurts. "With Malachi."

My mouth slightly parts, and I can't help but widen my eyes. For a split second, relief hits me that it's not Silas, and that my assumptions upon arriving were wrong.

"I'm sorry," I snap. "What?"

Yara fidgets with her long hair as her cheeks flush.

"Don't make me repeat it."

I speak again. "I think I misheard you."

"It's not uncommon for him," she says, as she grows uncomfortable. "We've been sleeping together for close to five years."

My eyes widen more, and I can't help but place my hand over my mouth. "You win for most shocking confession, Yara."

"Thank you?" she says, questioningly. "I guess."

I shouldn't have said that.

"How does this concern me?"

She stands, pacing the room. She moves to the open window and takes another deep breath. She slowly turns, and her eyes are filled with heavy tears.

I stand abruptly and walk to her. "I didn't mean to react that way. It's just shocking to think someone as stunning as you would sleep with someone like him."

Shit, I shouldn't have said that either.

"No," she chuckles at that. "It's not your reaction."

I move her back to the chair and sit beside her on the couch this time.

"Malachi has always done this. Aerona is very much aware of the extra attention he requires. I think she appreciates someone else keeping him company in that way. Malachi is awful, I know, but he has a way of charming you to fall for him."

Here comes the reaction again.

"You are in love with him?" I snap, louder than intended. "Sorry."

"That's okay," Yara reassures me once more. "After all these years, I've developed a sort of attachment to him, you might say. Whether it's genuine or not, I question that every day."

"Gods," I mumble.

"He sometimes confides in me, and our relationship has grown quite a bit."

"Is he nice to you?" I can't help but ask.

"He has his moments, but I would never put Malachi and nice in the same sentence," Yara confesses. "But…"

She pauses, and I can't help but lean in, impatiently waiting for her to continue, like this is the best gossip I've ever heard in my life.

A brief flash of doubt sits behind her large dark eyes.

"Every few years, Malachi picks a new…companion," she says, cringing. "We all assume it's because he tires of them. Lately, our conversations have felt less meaningful, and our meetings have become more…straight to business and uncomfortable, if you know what I mean."

"I understand," I respond, grimacing.

"It started when we were interrupted one evening. I was in Malachi's study, where most of our meetings happened."

"And?" I push.

"Silas walked in."

"Oh, fuck," I can't help but blurt out. "When did this happen?"

"A few days before he left for Daramveer. I didn't get a chance to talk to him, and I felt terrible." Yara lowers her head. "I've known Silas my entire life, so it was awkward—to say the least—when he walked in on me and his father in a most compromising position."

"That's why you were staring at him during our first evening in Andorwood?" I ask.

"Yes," she says, with a nod. "It was the first time I had seen him in a long while. When he wouldn't look at me, I knew right then Silas knew it was me. From that moment before Silas left, Malachi and my relationship began to crumble on both our parts." Shame floods her face once more. "What I once thought was my future isn't what I want anymore."

"Maybe I can talk to Silas for you. Is that why you are telling me this?"

She shakes her head. "I think my time is running out, and I'm scared. The girl before me went missing when Malachi grew tired of her."

Nerves twist in my stomach.

"Ella was her name," Yara continues. "She was a good friend of mine, and she told me similar things one day. She started to grow afraid of him and their meetings. I shrugged it off, thinking a breakup was coming, but then I never saw her again. Rumor has it that she left Andorwood to escape Malachi, but I know that isn't the truth."

"Well, we can get you out of here, then." I narrow my eyes and nod in understanding. "You don't have to stay if you are in danger."

Tears sit heavy in her bottom lid. "Malachi is planning to leave, Briar. When the ship nears, he will leave Andorwood and head into the mountains. I overheard him while I was in the office the other day." Her hands tremble. "He plans to abandon every-one, because he knows the ship sails toward us. He is willing to let Andorwood fall as long as he can stay hidden."

Anger bubbles in my chest. "What else did he say? Why is he so determined to stay hidden?"

"He is old, Briar." Yara's fearful eyes meet mine. "Older than we can imagine. I don't know how he's been able to live this long, but it's something dark."

"Yara, what do you know?"

A tear falls down her smooth cheek. "He mentioned some-thing about a tether."

"That isn't surprising." I sit back, releasing a heavy exhale, "Was it regarding Silas?"

She shakes her head. "He did mention Silas's name, but I have no idea what tether even means."

Because Silas is my tether, I think to myself, but don't share that piece of information.

It seems unfair to share that with her before telling the person it truly affects.

My jaw slacks, and I rub my temples for a moment, processing the wealth of information Yara has thrown at me. My head spins, and my heart breaks for her. She is scared, and I'm going to do everything I can to help her.

"Do you know anything about the Forgotten Archives?"

More tears flow down her beautiful face.

I grab her hands. "Any information you know could help us save Andorwood."

"I know it's guarded by something dark." She sighs, "If you enter, you'd better be prepared to fight. Malachi has spent countless nights searching through scrolls and books for the entrance. Whatever is in there must be important."

"Yeah, that seems to be common knowledge about it," I reply.

"But," she wipes her wet eyes, "I've heard only rumors, of course, that the Archives opens itself upon the full crimson moon. Malachi has an ancient book of Rigils that can protect you from the darkness inside."

"Yara, the crimson moon is in two days."

The first crimson moon signals the approach of warmer months, and the large, glowing orb shines brightly in the sky. It always happens around my birthday, so I'm quite familiar with the date. I often spent my birthdays on the roof of the castle in Daramveer, awestruck by the beauty of the sky. I always said it was my personal gift from the Gods.

"Yes, it is, Your Maj—I mean, Briar," she says, and smiles. "I told you this meeting wasn't a coincidence."

"Wait," I pause. "I never asked who Malachi was speaking with about all of this information regarding Silas."

"Oh," she says casually, unaware of the weight her words carry. "He was having a meeting with Hux."

I refuse to let my expression contort into disgust, and I nod my head in thanks to her once again. I stare, allowing the information to sink in for a moment. Silas's supposed right-hand man is withholding all of this information deliberately.

He knows what Silas is, and I bet he knows a lot more.

"Thank you for telling me this," I say, as I lean forward and wrap my arms around her tightly. "I need to get back to the others to form a plan, but please come with me. We can keep you safe."

Yara embraces me momentarily before pulling away. "I have a plan, Briar."

"A woman with a plan." I smile. "You are quickly becoming my favorite person."

"I'm supposed to meet Malachi tomorrow night. Once he falls asleep, I can grab the book and meet you. It will be in your possession, and you can enter the Archives to find whatever you're looking for."

"Absolutely not," I snap. "That is too dangerous and puts you at too much risk."

"It's important," she snaps.

"He will kill you if caught."

"Don't worry. I promise I can take care of myself. I'll work extra hard to put him right out," she winks. "I'll try to pry a bit more and see if I can uncover anything else."

"Why are you doing this?" I angle my head.

She stands, pulling me along with her. We walk to the large, open window and let the cool night air brush against our faces in complete silence for a moment.

She gazes out over the dark kingdom.

"Andorwood is my home. I was born and raised here. I didn't live the exact life I wanted, but I won't complain." Yara turns to me. "I know what lurks deep within you, Briar, and I know you fight every single day to make this world better for everyone—even people who don't deserve to be saved. You are a fighter, and if I can contribute even a small part to this war, I'll do whatever it takes to improve the future for women just like us."

I stare at her, and her return gaze strikes me in the heart.

"Thank you," I whisper. "When we leave Andorwood, would you come with us? Back to the mainland? I can't promise what we'll walk into, but you're exactly the person I want on my team for any future battles, big or small."

"I would love to," she says, a genuine smile painting her exhausted face. "But…"

I wait for her to continue.

"I won't leave my mother."

I smile, knowing exactly the feeling of having someone you love so much that you are willing to stay in a horrible situation, just to keep them close.

I return the smile. "Tomorrow evening, we will meet in Silas's room here in the castle."

She winces at his name. "I'm not sure that's a good idea."

"Don't worry about him. I'll talk to Silas, and it will be fine." I walk toward the door. "Besides, he listens to me."

"If you need any help controlling your Lumor magic, just let me know, but that will stay our secret," Yara says.

I pause, feeling like I'm back in the hallway with the invisible creature. I glance at my hands once more, half expecting the black veins to disappear and be replaced with bright white ones, but the darkness persists.

"Thanks." I turn before crossing the threshold.

"Miss Briar," Yara calls, as I step into the dim hallway. "There was something more."

I freeze.

"Malachi talks of a stone—beautiful, dark green, and oozing something powerful—that resides in Andorwood somewhere. I don't think it's safe to use." She hesitates, and warmth rushes to her cheeks. "But, I thought it may be important to know."

My mind snaps back to the moment in the forest when I came upon another stone with power. The dark influence radiating from the striking, onyx stone, the smooth sides that felt like silk against my pale skin, and the darkness—that sheer darkness—that made my entire system scream at me to run away.

Gods.

I stare at her, realizing there is more. I don't move, and bore my gaze into hers. What's left seems harder to speak about than the previously revealed information. She seems afraid to let the words leave her lips.

"And…"

"Yes?" I reply, and this time I can't suppress the quiver that runs through my hands.

"Malachi isn't Silas and Fenmore's real father."

CHAPTER 19

My body feels like it's dragging as I shift, using all my strength to get back to Silas. I played it cool as best I could leaving Yara's room, but the moment I heard the lock click from the inside, I bolted faster than ever. The cool air whips against my face, but I press on. My chest heaves, and I know it isn't the exhaustion hitting me—it's the information I now hold like a crushing weight.

I land outside the deceptively small house, and despite my throbbing head, a sense of calm washes over me, knowing I made it. I'm close to Silas, and I have to tell him about being my tether. I quickly decide not to inform him about his father just yet; I need to speak with Aerona first. The small lanterns outside flicker in the rain, and I swear that before my feet even fully touch the ground, the front door swings open.

Silas steps out of the dark doorway and sprints toward me, as though he felt my presence. I freeze at his sudden appearance, watching his figure grow larger with each passing second. He looks frantic, his hair falling messily over his forehead, and relief washes over him completely when we lock eyes. I can't imagine the horror he felt at leaving me alone with the man who had tormented him his entire life.

His arms wrap around my entire body as he crashes against me with a force that makes me stumble backward—yet he keeps me steady. His face falls into the curve of my neck, and he breathes deeply. The rain continues to fall, soaking us both. He pulls away and runs his hands up and down my body, checking every inch of me for even the slightest scratch.

"Are you alright?"

"Yes," I breathe. "I'm fine."

He freezes when he sees the fresh claw mark on my bare shoulder. "What the fuck is this?"

"I told you, I'm okay," I say, trying to reassure him. "Nothing to worry about."

"Briar," he seethes, and his eyes darken. "Did he touch you?"

"No. One of his guard dogs tried to scare me, and succeeded, I might add. I promise I'm alright, though." I cup his face, and his eyes are wild with rage. "Calm down, Nastronde. I'm here and in one piece."

I rest my forehead against his and place my hands on his strong chest. I give him a moment to calm his pounding heart. It beats erratically beneath my hands, and I fear it might beat right out of his chest.

"I've been going fucking insane since I left you," he whispers.

"I can tell." I grin against him, but it quickly fades.

"The outcome," Silas says, interpreting my body language, "isn't what we wanted."

"He won't fight with us. He's choosing not to because of me."

Silas exhales heavily and replies, "Hux told me the decision was made before you ever went. Had I known that, I would have never let you meet with him to begin with."

"How did Hux know?" I can't help but snap.

"He knows how to get my father to talk to him. He's been our insider for many years now. You can trust him."

My breath catches, and fury makes my fists tighten as they fall to my sides. Silas may trust him, but everything in me screams to get this man away from us.

Hux knows.

He knows everything, and he's hidden it from Silas for years. My shadows begin to thunder around me, deepening into darkness that rivals the night surrounding us.

Not quite understanding my reaction, Silas places both hands on my shoulders. "You are here—safe with me—quiet your shadows."

I gaze up at his strong face and can't hide the anger I feel bubbling in my veins. Mess with me, that's one thing. But jeopardize those I love, and I'll fucking end them. Hux doesn't know it, but he just gained a new enemy, and I don't see it ending well.

Silas wraps his arms around me once more and pulls me close. His warmth envelops me, battling the freezing rain falling around us. I feel his lips press against my head, and without even trying, my body relaxes into him. My shadows dim, and the feeling of losing control fades with each passing second. I close my eyes against his strong chest and take a deep breath.

"I could tell you were frightened," Silas confesses. "I could feel it."

My tether.

Our souls are connected to always find one another, to crave each other's closeness. I have to tell him.

The rain continues to beat down, and Silas gently grabs my face. "Let's go inside."

"Silas, I need to talk to you about something else." I lean forward, kissing his lips. "Well, I need to talk to you about many things."

He pulls back, looking me in the eyes. "Alright, anything. Can this wait until we get inside? It's freezing out here."

"No, it can't wait any longer."

He angles his head, waiting for me to continue. Silas's strong face hardens, and he is afraid of what I might say next, but he allows me time to think carefully about my words.

"Go ahead," his voice deepens.

"Silas. I know…"

I stop myself.

Malachi's words float into my mind, and I struggle to ignore what he said. What if Silas discovers the truth and realizes it's not love—that I've been forced upon him? His feelings for me could change. He might start to resent me, and that thought is worse than death.

I step back, freeing myself from his grip, and he angles his head, feeling the unwanted distance creeping between us.

The cold air wraps around me, and even though I crave his warmth, I can't touch him without knowing if it's real.

Silas reaches for me. "Hey."

"I can't," I say, as I step back.

A noise from the house breaks my stare, and Silas glances over his shoulder.

Oak bursts from the doorway. "Thank Gods, you're back."

Maines, Larkin, Warrick, and Hux follow him. I narrow my eyes at Hux and do my best to hide the snarl on my face. Silas notices my tension and moves toward me, rubbing my shoulders. He steps behind me, facing the others approaching, and plants a soft kiss on my head.

"Come on," he says, nudging me.

I don't move.

"We will continue this inside once we get dry."

I cut my eyes upward at him, and a soft smile graces his face, but his eyes show anything but gentle amusement.

I step forward, and we move inside, the warmth of the house calming my shivering body. After giving us a few blankets to warm ourselves before we can change, the others file down the stairs to the open space below the cliff. Hux stops halfway down the stairs and turns to us. My gaze pierces his, and he narrows his eyes. I clench my fists and ignore the pain of my nails digging into my skin.

"Do you two need anything?" Hux asks Silas.

"We don't need anything, Ackerley," Silas responds. "Give us a minute. We'll be down shortly."

"You sure?" Hux's deep voice floats up the stairs like pure darkness.

"Tell the others to relax," Silas says. "You included."

Hux hesitates to continue down the stairs, and his eyes lock on mine again.

His piercing blue eyes hold nothing but deceit. "Alright, boss, I will. I'll go check on Rose."

Anger surges swiftly in my chest, and the offer carries a heavy threat that hits me like a blow to the sternum. I fight the urge to go after him and take a deep breath to calm my racing heart.

Silas shakes the blanket through his wet hair and drops it to the ground with a thud. He wraps a fresh one around my cold body before taking off his damp shirt, socks, and shoes. He leans in and kisses me before pulling back. His green eyes lock onto mine, and the information I carry feels like a burden worse than death.

"Need help removing anything?" he asks cheekily, as he stares at me.

I don't smile—I can't. I close my eyes as tightly as they will allow and wrap the blankets around me tighter. Silas notices my recoil and hardens his brow.

"Tell me what happened."

Tears begin to well in my eyes as he grabs my hand, pulling

me toward the small sitting area near the front door, but I wince in his hold.

"Don't push me away," he whispers, his words filled with hurt. "What happened?"

The crackling fire fills the small room, and each sound sends a wave of anxiety through me. Before we can sit down, a high-pitched scream echoes from downstairs, causing both of us to jolt and move deeper into the house as quickly as we can.

We stop at the bottom of the stairs to see the others gathered around the table. Instead of screaming, the room is filled with laughter. Fenmore, Rose, and Larkin chuckle while huddled next to Hux and Warrick. Maines sits on Oak's lap. Various coins lay scattered across the table, and I quickly realize they were playing a game.

"Who the fuck screamed?" I snap.

"Oak," Maines says, as she points. "Couldn't you tell from the girlish shriek?"

"It was not," he snaps back, poking her side.

They laugh together, and it only makes my pounding heart race more. I glance at Rose, and she quickly stands, hurrying over to the bottom stair.

"Fenmore screamed because she had just lost the entire pot," Rose adds. "To me."

"It's such bullshit." Fen rolls her eyes and says, "I'm going to kick everyone's ass if I don't win the next round."

Rose wraps her arms around me, and I return the embrace. The feeling of her closeness calms me for just a moment before the harsh reality of what I know crashes back into my mind.

"We just started playing a moment ago, my shadow. Once Hux let us know you had returned, we all relaxed." She squeezes my shoulders, seeing my worry. "I promise this wasn't the case while you were gone. That boy over there almost lost his mind." Rose smoothes my hair, nudging her head toward Silas.

I flinch at Hux's name.

"It's okay," I reply. "I'm glad you are here."

"Go change and come back to sit with us," Maines calls from the table. "We want to know everything,"

I shake my head. "I really need to speak with Silas for a moment."

Hux stands abruptly. "First, I need to speak with him regarding a few things in the coming days."

I offer them a smile that doesn't reach my eyes.

I glance at Silas, who nods reassuringly. "Go change, Briar. I will be in the room shortly. You will have my full attention then."

He leans in and kisses my forehead before stepping off the bottom stairs to join Hux, Larkin, and Warrick on the balcony. They turn the corner and disappear from our view.

Panic washes over me at the distance between Silas and me. I have to tell him, no matter what that means for my own heart. I didn't have time to warn him. He's not safe with Hux, and I didn't stop him from leaving. Disappointment sinks into my core, and I feel the color drain from my face.

I made a mistake.

"Are you alright? You look like you are going to be sick." Maines gets up and rushes over to me.

"I... I need to go to my room." I wobble, the pressure of everything being too much to handle.

"Come on, let's go." Maines grabs my hand to keep me steady as we walk down the hallway.

"Let me know if you need anything," Rose calls from the main room, and the others watch cautiously.

The hallway stretches on and on, and time passes slowly. Each step thunders in my ears, and the words continuously crash into my mind—like waves against the cliffs in a storm.

We enter the familiar bedroom, and fortunately, the large bay window is open, letting in a cool breeze that refreshes my clammy skin.

"Go slip that dress off. You are freezing," Maines says as she ushers me to the bathing chambers. "I'm going to grab you some fresh clothes."

She rushes over to the large wardrobe, pulling out a fresh shirt and black pants, before tossing them to me. I slip off the heavy dress and dry the remaining water from my skin. Even though my skin is ice cold, the warmth of my anxiety envelops me, causing me to shake from the contrasting temperatures.

I quickly slip into the pants, throw on the billowing top, and button up the shirt, leaving the top two buttons open.

"How is your tattoo feeling?" Maines enters the room once I've fully dressed. "Do you want me to check it?"

I tighten the shirt around my shoulders and smooth my hair.

"No, it's fine," I lie.

The throbbing hasn't lessened, and the fresh claw mark sitting on my skin would only alarm her. I run my hand over the marking and can feel the raised, irritated skin underneath. The pulsing that hits my hand causes me to jerk it away, as if something inside me is trying to rip it from my body.

"Okay. I'm going to sit and get a fire going." Maines smiles and starts to pull the door shut behind her. "You look like you need a minute."

I hear muffled shuffling outside the door that quickly fades as Maines makes her way across the room to attend to the fire. I glance in the mirror and take a shaky breath. My black hair is still soaked and plastered to my head. My eyes are heavy—not just with exhaustion, but a weight desperate to leave my body. My eyes are my normal autumn shade, and I'm thankful the brilliant hazel is settled.

My eyes.

They have always been different than other Shadow Wielders,

and tonight, I think I've learned why. I'm different, and I don't think I'm just a Shadow Wielder. I glance at my hands, the black veins still visible.

I close my eyes and concentrate on the words.

Give me light.

But nothing happens.

Nothing brightens the room, and the black veins mock me against my pale skin. Maybe I'm losing my mind after all that's happened. That would almost comfort me if it were true. I reflect on my mother's remarkable ability to adjust to the darkness after marrying my father. My mother was strong—just like he was—but, I can't shake the feeling that this ability may not come solely from her. My father was private to a fault, and I'm beginning to think there is more about my parents that I never understood. But, I know someone who might have the answers.

Rose.

I focus once more and try to dive deeper into the steady flow of magic I feel, but nothing speaks back. We have to figure out what's going on, and regret hits me again. I may have successfully blocked Malachi from haunting me, and Kalix is more dormant than usual, but I can't hear Rohhit, and it feels like I desperately need to.

I do my best to compose myself and present a calm appearance. I open the door and join Maines around the simmering fire. She looks up from a book she's holding and smiles gently.

She pats the seat next to her, an invitation to rest. Without protesting, I plop into the chair and let a wave of exhaustion settle into my bones.

"What happened?" Maines asks on a sigh.

I rub my eyes and avoid her gaze for a moment. Maines has a knack for extracting any information she desires from people, and I know if I slip up, I'll reveal everything to her before I can tell Silas.

"I don't even know where to begin, Maines." I exhale heavily. "This has been a disaster."

"Then, tell me what you feel comfortable. I know I'll learn the rest when you are ready."

I immediately relax a bit.

"Just promise me you are safe first."

My shoulders slump, and the tattoo pinches, causing a pained expression to cross my face. "You know I can't make that promise, Maines. None of us are safe."

She inches closer. "I know."

I turn to look at her, and Maines's familiar, beautiful eyes stare back. I can't tell her before Silas, but I can be honest with her. It won't do us any good if I keep everything in the dark any longer.

"Malachi isn't going to help us."

She nods. "Hux told us."

"You cannot trust him. Do not tell him anything important. I don't care what the others say right now," I say, sharply. "Promise me that."

My reaction catches her off guard. "What happened with Hux?"

"Just promise me, Maines."

She drops her gaze. "I promise."

The fire before us dances in the shadows of the room. The blazing heat quickly becomes sweltering as growing tension fills the space. There's a crack, and a log falls to the bottom of the fireplace, making me jolt in my seat. Maines darts her eyes toward me, sensing my unease, and leans back against the couch, crossing her arms.

A heavy exhale leaves my chest, and the words bubble in my throat. "I met one of the dancers tonight in the castle—Yara. I got into a bind, and she helped me."

"Briar Blackbyrne—what aren't you telling me?" Maines's posture straightens.

"It wasn't anything I couldn't handle." I roll my eyes as she relaxes.

"Then, keep going," Maines says. "Make me believe that."

"Yara shared more information than anyone should ever have to process in one sitting. Andorwood has a stone, and from her description, it seems to be something similar to the resurrection stone."

Her jaw slacks. "Did she have any idea what it does?"

"No. She said it wasn't something to mess with. She also knows what can protect us when we get into the Archives," I explain. "We are meeting her tomorrow night for the Rigil and more information."

"Gods, who is this woman?" Maines curses.

"A brave bitch."

She laughs. "I believe it."

"There's one more thing I need to tell you. You are the perfect person to come to with this because you've studied more than anyone I know."

She nods, uncomfortable in her own seat suddenly. "Okay?"

"Before I met Yara, I was standing in the hallway when a Traveler approached me from behind."

"A what?" she snaps.

"The invisible creatures that guard the castle," I say, casually brushing over the name. "I nearly drowned in complete darkness and just prayed for light. And...well...that happened."

"Wait? What are you talking about?"

"I wielded light, Maines."

CHAPTER 20

" Are you fucking joking?" Maines's mouth falls open.

"Yes, Maines. I'm kidding," I say sarcastically, as I slap her arm. "Why would I joke about that?"

She stands, rubbing her temples, and strides to the bay window—as if she needs to create some distance between us. She rests both hands against the wood and drops her head. Maines has studied countless textbooks about our powers, ancient and present. She would know about this, or at least be able to offer some wisdom on whether I'm insane or not.

Maybe I'm crazy, and this will all be so much easier.

She turns to me, and shock still paints her face. I watch her, waiting for a massive reaction to fill the room. Her hands move through her hair as she tosses it to the side, her bright eyes shining as they gaze into mine.

"This is huge."

"That's all you have to say?" I ask. "Is this even possible?"

"Of course, it's possible." She throws her hands. "Shadow and Lumor Wielders have reproduced for centuries. But, it's rare, Briar. Like, really rare."

I let out a heavy exhale.

"Many people might try to tap into both powers their entire lives and still never produce a light or shadow," she explains. "As far as we knew, Dusk Wielders didn't really exist anymore, because people stopped trying when magic fizzled out."

"Okay, so I'm somehow just able to do that without even knowing I can?" I stand, unable to sit through the nerves coursing through me.

"I guess so, but we all know you are powerful, and clearly, fear was amplifying your magic even more, which makes sense." Maines shakes her head. "Did anyone see this happen?"

"No, but Yara knows about it," I admit.

"That isn't ideal." Maines rubs her head once more, tunneling back into thought.

"I don't think she would tell anyone. Plus, who cares if she did? Maybe it would persuade Malachi to help us."

"I don't want to alarm you, Briar, but if people feared you before..."

I close my eyes and let a moment of darkness fill my vision as thoughts flood my mind. My heart pounds against my ribs, and a headache begins to twinge between my brows.

"Great. Let's add this to the list of reasons people want me dead."

Maines makes a distressed face and nods.

My mind drifts back to my childhood in Daramveer. We had various training sessions and schooling opportunities as young children. I especially remember a few lessons about Dusk Wielders. They were born from a Shadow and a Lumor Wielder. The infant often showed clear signs of power at birth, usually with hair that was either coal black, representing shadows, or icy, symbolizing Lumor magic in their veins. However, as the child grew into their powers by early adulthood, a specific aura would take over, casting the child in a different light. Either streaks of the opposite power appeared from the child's head, or their eyes changed color.

If my feet weren't rooted to the floor, the urge to rush to the bathing chambers would take over. My eyes, like autumn leaves, have become increasingly noticeable since I reawakened my powers. Perhaps the lapses in my abilities after my mother's death caused the change to happen more slowly. People in Daramveer mostly avoided making eye contact with me over the years, so it's possible that no one noticed my transformation. Or maybe no one cared.

My father rarely looked me in the eyes, and I always assumed it was because I favored my mother so much. But, what if it were for deeper reasons—a gut feeling he had over the years that caused him to envy me?

A loud knock on the door echoes through the room and makes us jump. Maines snaps her attention to me and waits for my approval for someone to join us.

"Come in," I shout.

The door slowly opens, and Fen pops her head in.

It relieves me that it isn't Silas just yet. I haven't even begun to think about how I'm going to tell him this news. However, one piece involves Fen, and seeing her makes me uncomfortable.

"Am I interrupting?" she asks with a smile, her expression is so similar to Silas's that I feel anxiety once more.

"Nope," Maines answers. "Briar was just getting changed, and we were catching up."

Fen nods and asks, "Could you two join us at the table again? Sorry to rush you, but we need to talk about the plans for the ship that's on its way."

I pause for a moment, recounting Hux pulling him away. "Where is Silas?"

Fen peeks down the long hallway as if checking to see if they've come back inside.

"Still speaking with the guys on the balcony," she replies. "Hux told me to come get you so he could speak with Silas a bit longer."

My blood boils. He's keeping him away from me on purpose.

"Just give us one more second," Maines says with a smile. "Then we will join you."

"You got it."

Fenmore shuts the door quietly, and her steps quickly fade down the long hallway.

I turn to Maines, and the color has drained from her face.

"Are you alright?" I angle my head. "She can't bother you that badly?"

She lets out a heavy exhale. "It's not Fen. I'll admit, she's growing on me." Maines looks out of the large window. "This ship. It's filled with those creatures. I can't stop thinking about Barlowe and what he looked like that day. I'm supposed to heal, not kill, and I murdered him."

"You did what you had to."

"And Graven?" Maines asks. "You'd argue I did what I had to when I ripped his head off his body?"

"Yes, I would."

She shakes her head, trying to rid her mind of the thoughts swirling.

I reach for her hand. "You did that to Barlowe to save a life—mine. And the other was self-defense, Maines. If you think about it for too long, your feelings will drive you crazy."

"I think it's already driving me crazy."

"You did what had to be done in that moment, just like we all have."

"That doesn't make me feel better," she adds.

"Then we can work on that."

"I don't think I can fight, Briar, and I feel so weak for saying that." A tear falls down her cheek. "But, if I don't fight, and something happens to one of you, I'll never forgive myself."

"Why are you doubting yourself?" I ask. "This isn't you."

She shakes her head. "I'm not sure. Lately, I've felt... I don't know how to describe it. I've felt off, unwell—almost heavy"

I try to offer her a soft smile. "Then, don't fight."

Her bloodshot eyes find mine.

"I think being a smart person is knowing when to fight and when not to. We need you healing anyway," I say, reassuring her. "No one will think badly of you for this decision, and if you'd like, I'll announce that as my idea."

Maines gives me a relieved nod. "Thank you."

"Let's go see what these men have come up with," I say with a wink, pulling her to stand. "Then, we'll let them know how things are actually going to run."

She laughs, and we cross the threshold down the hallway, leading us back to the others. Hushed whispers fill the room, and the scent of warm baked goods hits my nose in a delightful tingle. Rose stands in the open kitchen, working her magic on something. I feel gratitude fill my chest, knowing that she is here and safe.

Lang enters my mind, and I say a silent prayer that the Gods are keeping him safe right now.

Silas stands at the head of the table. Fen sits to his right, with Warrick next to her. Larkin and Hux sit across from them. Oak sits at the opposite head of the table, with Maines taking a seat next to him. A chair remains unoccupied to the left of where Silas stands, and he motions for me to sit at the head of the table with him.

I walk over to Silas, smoothing my clothes as I take a seat. My gaze cuts to Hux, and he watches me intently—clearly trying to figure me out. I lock eyes with him and raise a brow, letting him take in everything he wants. I push away the anger and exude only confidence as he drinks me in. Hux jerks his gaze from mine, and I smirk, returning my focus to Silas.

He remains standing and gently kisses the top of my head.

"In four days, a ship will arrive in Andorwood. This ship is accompanied by creatures that could haunt your darkest nightmares. Malachi has chosen not to rally with us and fight."

I place my hands in my lap to hide the trembling.

Silas continues, "We must have a plan in place to protect the people of Andorwood and emerge victorious. We need to send a message to the mainland that we are not to be fucked with." Silas's deep voice booms around the room, and those around the table listen to him intently. "The people at this table are those I trust more than anything."

I struggle not to make a face, knowing Hux is among the few Silas speaks about.

Silas continues, "What I am about to say may never leave this house. If word of this leaks, I promise what will happen next will be worse than anything you can imagine."

The table tenses, and I shudder at the thought of being on Silas's bad side. I glance up at his face, and he meets my gaze. His piercing green eyes are hard, and I nod directly to him.

"For years, I have expected an attack on Andorwood. My dreams showed me many things, and they always ended in destruction. Briar knows the destruction I speak of." Silas gives me a quick glance. "I also knew my father would never help if something arose."

Oak and Maines watch Silas speak with intense focus. The others seem somewhat aware of what's happening, but still give him the attention that the Prince of Darkness deserves. That makes sense, given that they've been with Silas in Andorwood all these years.

"Someone we know has been building an army behind Malachi's back for nearly four years. With the news of the ship, I can only pray they are working behind the scenes to make sure their army is prepped for battle. They are tactile, deadly, and every bit of what makes people fear Andorwood. They may have recruited every man and woman willing to fight."

"Women?" Maines asks, surprise lacing her tone.

Silas nods and says, "In Andorwood, and especially our army, everyone is free to fight if they choose. In my opinion, women should be feared more than men. My point is supported by the women who sit in this house right now." He smiles. "If you all wish to fight, you have my blessing; if you choose not to, you will be greatly valued elsewhere."

Oak chimes in to ask, "Who is raising this outside army?"

Silas smiles and shoots a look toward Warrick. "The Rebels."

"Do you work with them?" I cut my gaze toward Silas.

"No," he says. "Not yet."

Warrick shifts in his chair.

Maines shoots me a concerned look, and I stand. "What sails toward us on the ship is unlike anything you all have witnessed. They are strong and large and do not fear death, as they have already been to the darkest realm and back. You will have to be quick and precise when killing them. They do not go down easily, but they each have a weak spot. You must find it and strike hard."

"Briar is right," Silas says, wrapping his hand around my waist. "That is why she will lead us on the day of the battle."

Fenmore grins broadly, and I snap my gaze at Silas.

"That may not be smart," I say.

"And why is that?" Warrick interjects.

"They won't follow me."

"They will. We all will," Warrick reassures me. "You have a hold over people. Don't doubt yourself."

I gently smile in his direction.

Silas steps back in. "You've fought these creatures. You're great at making plans, even if I'm not always in the loop," Silas huffs. "And you're strong. Stronger than all of us, and we will fight alongside you. You will lead Andorwood to victory, and you will win over the entire kingdom."

I glance around the table, and the others nod approvingly—as if they've already discussed this many times. Anxiety fills my core, and I can't help but wonder what my brother would think. His entire life was devoted to becoming a top army commander, and now, years later, I stand on the brink of battle, preparing to give my orders when the day comes. The salty sea breeze flows through my hair, and for just a second, I feel he's with me, urging me to be brave and lead this kingdom to victory.

"Alright," I start, glancing at Silas before scanning the table again. "First, we need a plan for those who choose not to fight and the children. We will need a way for them to escape if things go wrong."

They all nod, and Fen speaks, "That's something I can take over. I have a few contacts who can ensure a plan is in place to relocate those people to safety hours before the ship arrives. The children will go first with their family members who choose not to fight." She nods confidently. "We can lead them toward the mountains, then I will join you to fight."

I flash a soft smile in her direction. "Thank you, Fen."

The room quiets again, so I continue.

"Next, we will need healers to assist with any of the injured or fallen." I look directly at Maines. "You will lead this operation."

She smiles proudly.

"Silas will provide you with the names of every healer in the city who is willing to assist. Maines, you will be our top healer and ensure that everyone stays calm and focused."

She nods and mouths, "Thank you."

I stare back at the others. "I think having an armed ship in the waters would be beneficial. They can initiate the attack and attempt to prevent the ship from docking. The longer we keep the creatures away from shore, the better our chances of defeating them." I can't help but glance at the balcony and the vast sea surrounding us. "This will need to be an attack of destruction. We can't let their numbers find landfall. It will be ugly, but I know we have strong people who can do this."

"Lark…" Silas begins to speak, but I cut him off.

"I would like to be on the ship for the first attack."

Silas snaps his head toward me. "Briar."

"You said I am the strongest—"

"I'm regretting my words," he protests.

"—let me prove that."

I watch Silas's chest cave in. "I promise you don't have to prove anything to me, my love."

Warrick stands. "I will assist Larkin in recruiting for the ship, but will remain on land during the battle. We will have our strongest on the ship and be prepared on the dock for attack."

I nod in appreciation.

"Silas and Oak will also remain on land and prepare in case the ship docks. We will need our barrier strong and ready to strike. We can't let the creatures far into the city, or I fear the battle could turn on us."

Oak gives me a hesitant thumbs up, and I cut my gaze to Silas towering over me.

"You created a wall of shadows once before. I'm going to need you to do that again."

"That would create a wall to separate us," he says, sharply. "Those of you on the ship would be alone and leave us blind to what's happening."

"Correct, but it will buy you all the time to prepare. If things go wrong and they dock, lower your walls and fight. Blindside them."

Silas blinks rapidly, and I know he hates this as much as I do.

Hux speaks, "We will lead that and prepare our men."

I tear my gaze from Silas's worried face and turn to Hux. "Don't you think you should stay back with Malachi?" Anger pulses around me. "He seems to be more your speed."

Silas snaps his gaze to mine. "What is that supposed to mean?"

Hux narrows his eyes and places both hands on the table. "I'm not entirely sure what you mean, either. I am head of land operations for the Andorwood army." He leans forward. "It makes sense that I help Silas."

"There are many things that make sense to me, Hux, but having you beside me on the day of the battle isn't fucking one of them."

"Whoa," Silas interrupts, placing his hand on my arm. "What the fuck?"

I look at him, trying to calm the rage swirling inside me. I glance at the others, and they stay silent, their eyes widening. Even Warrick appears shocked by my outburst.

"I'm not sure what's happening between you two, but this needs to be resolved before the ship arrives," Silas says.

Hux relaxes his hands. "I have nothing against her, but clearly I've done something to offend her, somehow."

I huff.

"If we don't fight together, we'll have gaps in our strength," Silas warns.

I glance at Hux, feeling my darkness rise. The tattoo on my shoulder throbs as my inner shadows pound against the ink, desperate for me to lose control. With their gazes turned from ours, Hux winks in my direction, and it takes everything in me not to lunge across my seat.

"If everyone can calm down, let's please finish going through everything," Fen chimes in. "We have a lot to get started on and not much time."

I take a deep breath and refocus on the task at hand. Silas

urges me to continue, giving me the floor once more. I take a deep breath, ignoring the stares from the room, and swallow my anger. I smooth my clothes, and focus on the task at hand.

"Lastly, I want to learn more about this ancient poison that comes from Andorwood, and Larkin will teach me."

Larkin's eyes widen at my statement, and for a moment, I swear a look of dread crosses his face. I smile widely, proud of my final demand. Larkin has been avoiding me since we arrived, and I want to know why. He runs his hands through his messy hair but stays quiet, staring at the table.

"It's settled." Silas claps his hand. "You all need to start on our plans for the tasks you've been given. We only have a few days, so time is not on our side."

Fen, Warrick, and Hux file toward the stairs, taking their leave to prepare for the long days ahead. Hux pauses, and he turns to me, letting the others move past him. His eyes convey an unusual anger—an intense rage that chills me to the bone for a moment. He knows I'm onto him, and he's not pleased.

"Anything left unsaid?" Hux asks.

"To you?" I fume. "Yes."

"Anyone else?" His lips slither into a smile. "Maybe Silas?"

I furrow my brow, unable to back down from his intimidation.

"Are you threatening me?"

"Now why would I do that?" Hux smiles. "You sure are paranoid."

I get ready to step forward when I hear Larkin call my name from the balcony.

Hearing my name pulls me out of the stare. I turn my attention toward him, and wave for him to wait a second. I waste no time jerking my attention back to look at the bottom step, ready to either scream at him or punch him in the face.

Hux has vanished. I stare at the empty space and grind my teeth. He's not going to fuck this up for us. I'll make sure of that.

Silas, Maines, and Oak are speaking at the table, and I pass them, heading to join Larkin outside. The cold night air stings my face, but its bite helps cool the anger rushing through me.

Larkin gazes out at the vast sea. His white hair billows in the wind, and although Lumor magic creates a steady halo of light around him, his tall frame casts a shadow on the ground.

"Silas is adamant I do this, just so you know."

"Good."

"We leave in the morning," Larkin's strong voice snaps. "It's a few hours' ride on horseback. We won't be shifting, so we can reserve our magic for the battle and not draw attention to ourselves where we are going. I'll have the horses prepped, and we will leave at dawn."

"Sounds great."

Larkin shoots me a look and says, "Okay."

He turns to leave the space, and I speak, stopping him in his tracks. I plan to have the last word.

"I know you don't like me, so I appreciate you taking me." I shrug my shoulders and turn to walk back inside when he grabs my arm.

"Who said I didn't like you?"

"Hm," I pause. "Pretty sure you did. Many times at this point."

"That's your own perception, then."

I roll my eyes, and he crosses his arms.

"It's me and the decisions I've made that have led me here, not you." Larkin's gaze is heavy, and I watch his demeanor. He seems anxious, and his shoulders slump inward—like he's hiding information that's eager to be revealed.

"So?" I smile. "You do like me?"

He chuckles reluctantly. "Unfortunately, you are growing on me—like a wart, or something else unpleasant."

I punch his arm.

"I'll meet you outside the house before the sun rises. Don't be late, or I will be forced to not like you." Larkin turns on his heels without looking back. "Again."

He moves from the balcony through the wide door and back into the living space. He walks to Silas and slaps his shoulder, telling him a quick goodbye. Maines and Oak wave as he walks up the stairs and disappears into the darkness above. His words play over and over in my mind, and I can't help but think it does have something to do with who I am.

I plan to learn a lot tomorrow, including what he knows about my brother.

With the house quiet, Oak and Maines settle in one of the chairs near the opposite wall's fireplace. Rose finished making her various dishes and excused herself for the night, leaving me alone with Silas finally.

His heavy steps echo as he approaches behind me. He wraps his arms around my shivering body and presses his torso firmly against my back. Silas leans down and burrows his face in the curve of my neck and kisses my skin gently.

"I'm so fucking proud of you," Silas whispers.

His soft lips send a tingle through my entire body, and as badly as I want to lean into him, I know I have to tell him who he is to me—what he's destined to be.

I just pray to the Gods that this doesn't change everything.

CHAPTER 21

I remain in his embrace and close my eyes. The crashing waves fill the air outside, and I try my hardest to hold back the tears that are eager to leave my eyes. Silas notices my tension and pulls away, turning me around to face him. He places both hands on my shoulders and slowly traces his hands down, reaching my trembling hands. His face turns to stone, and he can immediately sense the emotional distance between us.

"What is it?" he asks.

"It's so much," I reply.

"I have time."

I open my eyes, and tears stream down my cheeks. Silas brushes my tears away with his thumb and cups my face. His piercing green eyes lock onto mine, and I fear my legs might give out. I want to speak, but I don't know where to start.

I open my mouth, but no words come out.

"Come with me," he says, as he furrows his brow. "I want to show you something."

"I can't. Larkin and I are leaving in a few hours."

His hand squeezes mine tightly. "I don't really care."

"Silas."

"Larkin can wait if needed."

My gaze turns hard, and I stare at him for a moment. The corners of his mouth curl into a devious grin.

"You know you want to," he says, tugging my wrist. "You are too curious to let this pass."

"You're right."

His smirk grows larger this time. "Say that again."

I let myself go with him, and we become mist together. The world around us seems to pause, and the weight of the secrets I know vanishes along with our physical bodies. The figures around us blur as we move through the shadows of the night. I snap my eyes shut and let him lead the way. Even though we are weightless, I can feel Silas's strong hand wrapped around mine—a perfect fit.

We land with a thud, and I try to catch my breath quickly. Silas continues to hold my hand, as if he's afraid that if he lets go, the distance will grow between us once more. The darkness around us becomes overwhelming, and I quickly realize we are deep in the forest on the outskirts of Andorwood. Fear floods me, and I remember the third trial—lost in unfamiliar woods and darkness.

Silas notices my flinch.

"We're safe," Silas whispers. "This part of the forest is warded. There is absolutely nothing here that can touch you."

I glance around the dense trees that sway gently in the night, grabbing his hand harder. The forest around us pulses as if welcoming us—or Silas—back.

"There are a few acres around the entire kingdom that are permanently warded." He grins and walks me a few paces forward. "Even if something tried, it would be dead before it got close to you."

"Larkin told us not to shift. We need to save our energy."

"Since when do you follow rules?" he asks. "And don't worry about my magic. I'll be fine. So will you."

I blink, my eyes quickly adjusting to the darkness. Tall trees crowd the sky above us, making it impossible for the moonlight to grace us with its silver glow.

"Come on," Silas says, as he pulls me forward. "I want to show you something. You fine with a quick walk?"

I nod and let him pull me forward.

We walk silently through the dense forest, venturing deeper into the woods and closer to the towering mountains overhead. Silas walks with such confidence in front of me, having clearly made this exact journey countless times. He glances back and smiles when our eyes meet. Even in the darkness, his eyes shine brightly enough to light our way, his thumb tracing small circles on my hand.

After passing what seems like hundreds of the same trees, we come to the opening of a clearing. A memory immediately sparks, and I'm back in Daramveer in my favorite forest clearing, and my chest aches. I look to my right, half expecting the carving of mine, Maines, and Barlowe's name to be there. A pinch of sadness crosses my expression when it isn't there.

When the clearing opens, I realize we are at the base of the mountain. Bright white snow sits at their peaks, and finally, the moon's glow provides us with some shimmering light.

"Almost there," Silas says with a smile, and quickens his steps.

My eyes spot a small sitting area that appears worn from years of visits. A lone tree shades the spot, and Silas guides me directly to it. He halts and brushes off a fallen tree trunk that lies perfectly on the forest floor. He sits without warning and stares at the sky behind us, exhaling a heavy breath. I watch him for a moment, then turn to sit beside him.

My mouth parts slightly when I see the stars. The vast sky takes my breath away. Thousands of diamonds shine in the night sky above our heads, some so bright that I squint my eyes when looking at them. Others barely dance in the night sky, but together, they all work in perfect harmony, illuminating the sky if only for us. The bite of the cold night only adds to the beauty around us, and the stars above remain timeless, shining forever in an endless realm.

"I've wanted to show you this since we got here." Silas turns his gaze to mine.

"It's so beautiful." I keep my gaze fixated on the galaxies around us.

"You put every star to shame, Briar," he breathes. "Easily."

I tear my gaze from the sky and look at Silas. The subtle glow of the stars illuminates his handsome face. I realize that, unlike the stars, our time together in this realm is limited, and he deserves to know the truth.

"I need to talk to you." I try to keep my racing heart steady, but fail spectacularly.

Silas nods, "I know. I'd be lying if I said I wasn't worried about what words will leave your perfect lips."

He's concerned, and my chest feels tight, realizing this news could truly change things. I turn to face him, reluctantly. There are a few things I need to tell him, but for now, I'll decide which ones to disclose.

"After I met with your father, I went walking around the castle again."

"Fuck, Briar." Silas rolls his eyes. "How many times will it take before you listen to me?"

I shrug. "A few more times, I imagine."

"Go on," he groans.

"I ran into Yara."

Silas freezes, averting his gaze from mine.

"After I wielded light," I slip in. "She told me about you walking in on her and Malachi." I flinch at the thought.

He nods until my words hit him like a blow. "Hold on. What the fuck did you just say?"

"She told me about her and Malachi," I reply, simply. "And that you know about it."

"You are impossible." His gaze grows angry. "You wielded light? And you didn't tell me?"

"I haven't had time to talk to you. As soon as I got back, Hux whisked you away."

"But you let him," he replies.

Dread fills me because he is right. I've known this and let other moments get in the way instead of making him a priority.

"You're right."

"You're saying that a lot these days," Silas says.

I sigh.

He cups my face. "Stop fucking keeping things from me."

"Okay."

He tilts his head back to the stars and sighs heavily. "It's impossible to stay mad at you."

"That's a good thing," I say. "For my sake."

He chuckles. "And miserable for mine."

"Maines says this ability is rare."

"Fuck yeah, that's rare, Briar. Have you tried to do it again?"

I shake my head.

"I don't know what to say." He pauses to take a deep breath. "Briar Blackbyrne, a Dusk Wielder. With your power, I'm not surprised. Oak and Larkin can help you, if you'd like." Silas takes a long breath. "I've officially heard it all now."

"Nope." I make a pained face. "Not everything."

Silas rubs his temples and leans his head forward, crashing into my chest. He lets out a deep sigh and turns back to me.

"Why would Yara tell you that? That's wildly inappropriate."

"She's in trouble, Silas. Yara told me about the woman before her, and when your father grew tired of that woman, she went missing. Yara thinks that she's next."

"We didn't need this added to our plate," he snaps. "Yara made this decision with my father. Actions have consequences, some worse than others."

"We are going to help her. End of story." I lift his head from my chest and burn my gaze into his. "But...there's more."

"Of course there is."

He attempts to rest his head back on my chest, but I stop him, forcing his gaze to mine.

"Malachi has a book of Rigils that can protect us when we enter the Forgotten Archives. We need to speak with your mother about what truly resides there, and we don't have much time."

"Well, there's no way that he would give us any of that information," Silas admits.

"I agree. But that's where Yara comes in. She's going to take the book and meet us tomorrow night. The Archives will be easiest to locate during the crimson moon in two nights. This may be our only chance to get in and find out more about how to stop Carobon."

"Alright." He thinks to himself for a moment. "That's risky, though. If she gets caught, it will likely expose us as well."

He's right. Malachi may be onto us, but we will have to take the risk.

"She also mentioned a stone. Its description made me think it was a resurrection stone or, at the very least, something similar and powerful. We need to get that stone and find out what it does."

"Fuck. You have a lot of information tonight, don't you?"

"Oh, you have no idea," I reply. "My head feels like it might explode."

"Do you trust Yara?" he asks.

"I do." I pause, letting my words sink in.

Silas nods, absorbing the information.

"Do you trust Hux?"

My question surprises him, and he sits up straighter, "I do."

"Even though he's close with Malachi?"

"Yes," he says, and tilts his head, aware that I'm going somewhere.

"I don't think we should trust him, Silas," I blurt out, and crinkle my nose. "Yara saw him speaking with Malachi in private about all of this."

"He's been with me for many years, Briar, even though he tends to keep to himself. Hux typically knows everything, which is why I keep him close," Silas explains. "But, if you think something is wrong, I will talk to Warrick and Larkin to get their thoughts."

I nod, but keep a stern look toward him. His face remains firm. He doesn't like this one bit, and I know it. His eyes hold patience, but I know his mind is racing.

"Go ahead and tell me the other piece," he insists. "I know there is more that you are withholding. There is something that you aren't telling me regarding us, isn't there?"

I fidget for a moment and can't help but touch my shoulder. The throbbing tattoo responds to the graze, causing me to flinch. "I should have mentioned this to you earlier, but everything unfolded so quickly, and you were upset with me."

He leans in closer and ponders for a second. "This happened when you saw Kalix. During the tattoo?"

I nod, momentarily speechless. I open my mouth, but the words come from Silas's lips, not mine.

"She taunts you, doesn't she?" Silas doesn't break his stare. "Even when I can't feel it."

I nod, and my stomach churns.

"Always."

I glance at my hands, and the dark veins appear even darker against the night.

"Let me help you carry this burden," he whispers. "Let me help you."

I gaze into his eyes, letting the green of his irises feel like they are bleeding into mine. Silas can help me, and it's time I let him.

"She told me something."

"About?"

"Us," I mutter.

"She told you what connects us." His brows tighten. "Didn't she?"

Tears well in my eyes and sit heavy on my lower eyelids.

I nod again.

Silas exhales and glances back at the night sky for a moment. He traces his fingers through mine as he holds onto me and this silent moment. As badly as he wants to know this information, I can sense the hesitation as clear as the cool breeze around us.

"I knew it. You were different after that, and I feared it had something to do with me. With us."

"Everything has been so fucked up," I say.

"Then, let's change that."

"I'm scared that this knowledge is the reason everything could change," I mutter.

His gaze snaps back to mine, and shock dances across his face. "Change me and you?"

"Yes. What if knowing only changes the way we feel about each other? The way you feel about me?"

He grabs my face, trying to force my eyes to his. "Nothing will change the way I feel about you. Nothing, Briar Blackbyrne."

I look down, unable to meet his gaze. "Even knowing that you were created to be drawn to me? Even knowing that you are my tether? You must keep me grounded in this realm."

Silas sighs and remains silent.

He lifts my chin, forcing me to meet his gaze. "I knew those weren't nightmares. We can travel to different realms, can't we?"

His eyes grow distant, and I know he's retracing his steps each night he's dreamed of me.

I hum.

"I chased you all those years, pulling you back each time."

"Kalix referred to me as a Realm Walker. You, being my tether, were meant to pull me back. So yes, technically, you can too. Without you, I could get stuck—and I did get stuck. When you were injured, I found myself trapped in a realm with Kalix."

"I searched for you desperately, Briar. I used every ounce of my power to find you. You know that." Silas angles his head. "Why would you be afraid to tell me this?"

"What if our feelings are forced? What if they aren't genuine, and we only feel this way because it was our destiny?" A tear rolls down my cheek.

He places my hand on his strong chest, and a calming thump responds in return. "You taught me that we are in control of our own destinies. Fate may have brought us together, but each day, I choose you because I want to."

"But, what if that isn't real?"

Silas presses my hand to his chest tighter. "Do you feel my heart beating? Can you sense its steady rhythm? That's real, and it beats only for you." He presses my hand harder against his heart. "Tether or not, Briar Blackbyrne, I am yours. I want to walk through every realm with you. I want to know every part of you, and I swear to the Gods and beyond to love every fucking inch of you until my body—until my soul—turns to ash."

I can't control the tears streaming down my cheeks. Silas leans forward and kisses each one away.

"I started chasing you as soon as I felt you all those years ago," he rasps. "I'll chase you—even blindly, if I must—to the darkest realm. I'll never stop following after you."

His mouth moves from my cheeks to my lips. The kiss is gentle and slow, allowing me to find his calm. His hand releases mine, travels up to find its place at the back of my neck. He pulls me even closer, deepening the kiss. His warmth envelops me, and I open to him. His tongue swirls around mine, as if tasting me for the first time. Something in my chest tingles as both of us finally recognize the connection, causing something to click. I swear for a moment that if I looked down, I would see a physical rope connecting us.

In one fluid motion, Silas grips my hips and pulls me to straddle him. Our chests collide, and he slips a hand to the back of my neck, pulling me as close as possible. Our kiss grows more fervent, and I rake my nails into the back of his shirt.

I pull away and grip the back of his neck. "There doesn't happen to be a cave around here anywhere?"

Silas leans his head back and lets out a deep laugh that resonates around us. The infectious laugh moves around us, mixing with the breeze, and my heart flutters. It's been so long since I've heard that delicious noise, and I smile wider than I have in a long time.

"There she is," he declares. "My sarcastic girl. Would you like me to find one quickly?"

"I don't think that will be necessary, Nastronde." I laugh and respond, "I have a feeling that cave or no cave, you'd do just about anything I asked of you."

He smiles. "For the rest of my life, Briar."

Silas rests his forehead against mine and closes his eyes. I watch him and admire his beautiful face. His scar glimmers in the moonlight, and I softly trace it with my thumb. His breathing steadies, and we remain in this moment—only us. Silas slowly opens his eyes, and the stars reflect off his green eyes.

"We are one step closer to finding out what we need to know," he whispers. "I just need you to stay with me."

I shift off his lap and sit next to him again. "Then, why don't I feel better?"

"Because even after everything, I fear that the worst has yet to come."

Silas grabs my hand and holds it tight. I look up, and the stars continuously twinkle against the black velvet sky. "I think you are right."

"I usually am," he whispers, and I nudge his shoulder.

"I'd be lying if I said I wasn't afraid."

"I'm terrified," He responds.

"Silas?" I ask. "Afraid?"

"Not for myself, but because I'm worried about what might happen to one of you. I'll do everything I can to protect you all, no matter the cost to me. But still, in the back of my mind, I know I can't do this perfectly." He lets out a shaky exhale. "When the ship arrives, it's going to be ugly. I need you to promise me that if things go wrong, you will run. You have to be safe, Briar. You are this realm's future, even if I don't make it out with you."

I allow myself to think about what it would be like to run. What it would be like to explore the realms without Silas— without my tether. Completely lost in this life and all the others. A chill runs through me, and I scoot closer to him.

"I'm never leaving you, Silas. We are doing this together. Until the very end."

"Until the very end," Silas says, in my mind.

I pause, letting the realization of our power together flow into me like his deep voice. He smiles, as if knowing we could do this, and for the first time, Silas had information before I did.

"You knew we could do that?"

"Yes," he says, proudly.

"And you haven't tried before now?"

He laughs, "I didn't want to terrify you."

I lean forward, slapping his shoulder. "You kept something from me."

"*How does it feel, my love?*" he says, only in my mind.

"*Terrible,*" I respond. "*And exciting.*"

"*Of course, your twisted mind would enjoy that.*"

I laugh, letting the ease of this moment travel through me. I'm happy. With Silas, I am happy. My eyes close as the chuckle fades, and I glance at him.

He stares at me, and a flash of fear shows in his eyes, stopping me in my tracks.

"Us. Together." He cups my face, "Until the very end."

"Promise?" I respond.

"Promise."

He knows I'd never run, and I think that's what scares him the most. Silas knows that I would fight alongside him until our last breath, and with everything that we are, we both pray that it isn't soon.

"We need to head back soon." I brush a fallen piece of hair from his face.

"Nope." He moves to lie on the soft grass. "We deserve a night alone."

"*Thank Gods,*" I say in my mind.

"I think I'm going to enjoy being able to cast thoughts into your mind. Think of the conversations we can have about the others without them knowing? Or all the filthy things I can say to you."

I join him, stretching my legs in the opposite direction. I prop on my elbows and cup his face as our gaze meets. The blades of grass bend under my weight, feeling soft against my skin.

"You wish to speak about the others in a poor light?" I laugh.

"You have no idea how many times I've wanted to say horrible things under my breath the past few days about those wonderful fools." His arms stretch wide over his head, his hands moving down my sides, and I laugh again.

"I can't wait to hear that more."

"What?"

"That delicious laugh," Silas says, a massive smile on his face.

We lie in silence, watching the stars.

Some twinkle, some remain still, while others shoot across the black sky, and in this moment, the world seems at peace. There is no threat, no urgency; it's just us. Together by fate, destiny, and sheer luck. My eyes begin to feel heavy as I notice Silas turn, shifting beside me to wrap his strong arms around me.

"*Briar?*" Silas silently speaks.

"*Yes?*"

"*You are mine.*"

I smile as I respond, "*Until we reach the darkest realm and further.*"

He nuzzles into my back, and I close my eyes, floating into the sky alongside the stars.

CHAPTER 22

I wake to the dim morning light pooling through the tightly packed trees.

Silas remains motionless except for his chest rising and falling as gently as the morning breeze. I pause for a moment, taking in his features. He's peaceful, the world around us is silent, and for just a second, I feel peace, too.

For the first time in so long.

Through the dense forest before us, something catches my eyes, jolting my entire system and pulling me from the calmness I felt. A subtle movement in the shadows makes me sit upright. A familiar black cloak moves in the wind, and the creature steps into the open, clearly unaffected by the wards shielding us from our surroundings. Even after all this time, fear still swirls in my senses. I breathe heavily through my nose and try to keep my heart steady.

It can't talk to me. I have the mark.

It moves closer, seeming to float above the ground, and I backpedal, my back pressed firmly against the fallen tree. Silas remains motionless—still deep in sleep—and I pray he stays that way. I watch the tall, thin figure approach, its hood casting a shadow where its eyes should be. A wide mouth peeks from beneath the hood, and its skin is a lifeless gray.

My shoulder begins to throb in its presence, and I can't help but grab at the Rigil in response.

The creature notices my movement and shifts inches from my face, faster than I can comprehend. The breeze from its movement whips my hair in my face, causing my vision to blur. I try to scream, but its bony hand slaps across my mouth. Fear grabs me, and a single tear escapes my eye, landing on its decaying hand. With the other hand, the creature slowly pulls back its hood, and for the first time, I see its face.

The gray, ancient skin continues upward, and a hollow spot exists where a nose should be. My jaw drops, my chin connecting with its grip, when I see its eyes. Glowing, bright green eyes with vertical slits meet mine, and I feel lost—hopeless and soulless—as its gaze burns into mine with an intensity that could set the world ablaze.

The creature slowly shifts its gaze to Silas sleeping beside me.

"Don't touch him," I mumble under its grip.

The creature reaches out its free hand toward Silas, and I thrash against his grip. A single black claw gently brushes along Silas's head. He watches Silas sleep beside me, and a wave of nausea washes over me.

"*Silas*," the creature whispers into my mind. "*So much potential.*"

My eyes widen in horror.

"I said, don't fucking touch him."

The creature slowly pans its haunting gaze toward mine, and I fight the urge to break my stare from the soulless green eyes.

"*I can,*" the creature whispers again. "*And I will.*"

"Why?" I snap. "Leave him alone."

The creature smiles, and rows of decaying teeth lie scattered in its mouth.

"You'll see," the creature breathes, and my entire system shivers as the words slither out like a promise and threat.

How can it communicate with me when I have the Rigil tattooed on my body?

"You need the book," the creature hisses into my mind. *"Crimson will catch your eye."*

The creature gradually withdraws its hand from my mouth, and I stay silent. I wipe my lips, fighting the urge to gag at the creature's hot touch. Even though the creature seems hollow, a dust coats my lips, and my stomach churns.

"Where?" I ask in a whisper. "The Archives?"

The creature looks back at Silas, and I freeze. He stirs but remains asleep. Thank Gods this man sleeps like a rock.

The creature nods.

"What is in the book?" I hesitate to ask.

"Answers," the creature says, before it steps back.

"But, what answers?" I pry.

The creature begins to create distance between us, and I resist the urge to follow it into the dense forest surrounding us.

"To everything," the haunting voice says, snaking into my mind.

I lean forward, desperate for the creature to stay. "Wait," my voice yells, louder than intended. "Just tell me. Please."

The creature slowly fades into the shadows and nods its putrefying face. *"They are coming."*

The creature vanishes, shadows swirling into the darkness, and the air lightens. I remain still for a moment, my chest rising and falling rapidly. Its face was so disturbing, but its eyes—they were so green. I've never seen eyes that green, and the image is burned into my mind.

Silas stirs beside me and groans. He cracks open his sleepy eyes, and green eyes once more stare into mine. The good thing about being frequently haunted is that it doesn't take me long to calm myself, but annoyance lingers.

The words play over in my mind: *you need the book.*

I shake the fear from my mind and lean down, kissing his soft lips.

"Good morning to you, my love," he says, with a smile as he stretches.

I glance back at the distant trees, and the shadows remain still. No motion—no movement at all—other than the subtle dawn breeze.

"What's wrong?" Silas notices my state.

"I'm going to be late meeting Larkin," I say. "But for once, I'm glad for your insane ability to sleep through anything."

Silas wipes the sleep from his eyes, and before I can react, he playfully pulls me down. The sudden tug causes me to land on top of his strong body.

"Larkin can wait," he grumbles and tries to pull me even closer to him. "I want you all to myself."

"No, he can't. He already hates me for some reason, and this won't help my case."

Silas groans against my neck.

"Briar," he grumbles.

"Get up, Nastronde." I tug at his shirt. "Shift me home."

He smiles, leaning in to kiss me. His hands brush through my hair, and a soft exhale leaves his chest as we tangle together for a moment, completely lost in one another. My body calms, but my racing heart doesn't ease up.

"Your heart is pounding," Silas says. "Did you have a nightmare?"

"Something like that," I smile, pressing my lips to his again. "We need to go."

Silas pulls away with a grin. "You know, I should be mad that

I'm taking you home so that you can spend the whole day with another man."

"I don't have time for your ridiculous jealousy."

Silas grabs me again, making me yelp as he flips us, landing on top of me this time. Both of his hands land next to my head, and he presses his hips against mine. An excited thrill rushes through me, and the urge to stay here churns inside me.

"I'm not jealous." He kisses my neck.

"Oh, yes, you are."

He continues to kiss me, moving up to my jaw.

"Me, running off with a handsome man. You should feel envious."

He hums.

"What if Larkin captures my heart and I leave you for good, Mr. Nastronde?"

His eyes narrow. "You're pushing it, Briar," Silas teases. "Don't make me kill Larkin this early in the morning; that would really put a damper on my day."

I press my lips against his. Silas's hands quickly become tangled in my hair, like he's making sure to mark me before my day begins.

"Let's go. I have a hot date," I joke.

"That's it." Silas tickles my waist, and a laugh leaves my throat. "I'm killing him."

Silas moves off me and extends his hand to help me stand.

"You can come with us if you'd like," I offer an invitation.

He messes with his hair. "I'm going to stay back and talk to my mother about the Archives. We need to cover as much ground as we can these next few days."

"Please don't say anything about Yara," I plead.

"I won't." He huffs a laugh. "Trust me, that's not a conversation I want to have with my mother. I'll make plans for Maines and Oak today, too. It's going to take all of us to get ready for what's coming."

"Can you ask your mother about the red book?"

Silas angles his head. "Red book?"

"Just trust me," I casually respond, praying he doesn't pry.

"Hmm," he groans. "Once again, always up to something and keeping fun little secrets. What am I going to do with you?"

I shrug. "Get used to it, I guess."

Silas laughs. "I'll see what I can find out for you."

I stand on my toes to gently kiss him. "Thank you."

"Of course, my love," Silas says, smiling gently. "Please be careful today. Larkin will keep you safe, but keep an eye out for him as well, will you? You both need to have your wits about you."

I nod and say, "I'll be alright."

"I have no doubt about that."

"We will meet in your bedroom tonight when Larkin and I return. We'll wait for Yara there before we search for the Archives," I instruct.

Silas agrees.

He grabs my hand and shifts. We become mist together, traveling through the dim morning shadows that tuck behind each tree. With each second, the morning sun becomes brighter, and I can only hope that Larkin doesn't hate me even more for being late.

We land in a small pocket of trees just outside the house grounds. Silas pauses for a moment, catching his breath, and I step forward, gazing through the trees toward the house. A tall figure rests on the porch, long legs spread out across the wood. Two horses dip their heads to the ground, sniffing and chewing.

Nerves crash into my stomach, and we step out of the shadows.

As we approach the house, Larkin sits up and crosses his arms over his propped leg. I am delighted to realize that Myah is one of the horses. Her bright white coat shines in the morning light, and a smile spreads across my face. I rush up to her, placing both hands on the bridge of her strong nose.

Myah huffs, and I chuckle. "Hello, sweet girl."

I glance back at Larkin and notice a few shining weapons in the morning sun. A sword the length of my entire torso lies next to him. The beautifully decorated hilt is adorned with orange gemstones, and I gawk at its beauty. Next to the sword, I see my axes. The stunning gold shimmers like the sun's rays.

"I can't say I'm surprised you two are late," Larkin snarks.

"It's literally all his fault," I say, wasting no time playfully ratting Silas out.

"Oh, quit your bitching, Spiridon," Silas barks back. "We are barely late."

The horse next to Myah is as dark as the fresh night sky. Black hair is brushed perfectly alongside the horse's velvety neck, and a few braided strands decorate its mane. I reach gently toward the beast, and it huffs in response before turning its large head away from my touch.

"Wow, Larkin." I cross my arms. "Your horse hates me, too."

Silas laughs. "That's Atlas, and I believe he's grumpier than Larkin most days."

"Impossible," I reply, extending my hand toward the horse's nose.

"Watch him," Silas says, still smiling. "He bites."

"Larkin or the horse?" I respond, causing Silas to boom another laugh.

"Alright, for fucks sake," Larkin barks. "That's enough. We need to get going. I don't want to be anywhere near this place come late afternoon."

The morning sun begins to warm us, and Silas helps me mount Myah, handing me both axes so I can secure them tightly on my back. Larkin leaps, easily throwing a leg over Atlas with his sword strapped to the side.

Silas hands me the reins and pets Myah for a moment. I can see sadness swell in his eyes, and I know he's thinking about Xena.

"We will get her back," I whisper.

He shakes his head, clearing his thoughts. "Be careful. Leaving the kingdom's limits isn't safe, and where you are headed is worse. Stay alert every single second, and if your senses flare, listen to them. Don't do anything stupid."

I smile. "I would never."

He chuckles, slapping my ass. "Go, before I change my mind."

I nod.

"Larkin, if you let anything happen to her, I'll kill you."

"You got it, boss," he responds.

Larkin gently taps Atlas's ribs, prompting him forward, and I follow behind. We head toward the dense forest, deeper into the island. I glance over my shoulder to see Silas watching us from the front yard. I wave, and he returns the gesture.

I blink, then he vanishes, shifting into the shadows to talk to his mother.

Anxiety fills me as I turn back to Larkin, who is riding ahead of me. I gently kick Myah to speed up so I can ride beside him and Atlas. Larkin doesn't meet my gaze; he continues to look forward at the small opening into the forest.

"We will ride the horses for as long as we can, but we will reach a place they can't enter," Larkin says.

"Will they be okay alone out here?" I ask.

"Yes, they are protected like we are. Plus, I will ensure an additional ward is around them. They will be fine."

I nod, and we fall back into silence. The horses' steps are the only thing that fills the air around us. We head deeper into the forest, and the morning sun dims through the forest canopy. Each shadow causes me to flinch, and I remind myself that it's my paranoia.

"Thank you for doing this," I awkwardly say. "I can only imagine this will help us in the future."

"Welcome," he replies, tersely.

This man is impossible.

I lean forward and run my fingers through Myah's mane. She gently tosses her head in response, and I can't help but chuckle. During the ship's journey here, my days were filled with time spent with Myah. For some reason, she could calm my racing thoughts, and I believe I helped ease her anxiety on the rocking boat. We bonded during that time, and I feel grateful to have her with me again.

"There are things in this forest that are invisible. Silas was right to tell you to keep your senses sharp. If something feels off, I need you to do as I say."

"Alright," I say. "No issue."

He huffs.

"What?" I snap.

"I've heard you have a problem with following orders, so please don't take this lightly."

"Who told you that?" I protest, and can't help the slight smirk that crosses my lips.

"Literally everyone."

I gasp. "You've talked to people about me?"

"Yes."

"All good, I hope?"

"Fucking Gods. You are insufferable," Larkin snaps, rolling his head on his shoulders.

"Fine," I huff. "Where are we headed, anyway?"

A cool wind picks up around us, and the trees sway in the chaotic breeze—like hands reaching down to grab us as we pass by.

"Death's opening." He hesitates before continuing, "Just about the closest we can get to the darkest realm."

CHAPTER 23

"Are you sure we should be doing this alone? What if something goes wrong and we need backup?" I can't help but ask.

"I've taken this journey many times on my own without any issues, and from what I've heard, you're quite powerful. If anything, I'd say we're more prepared than usual."

"I'll take that as your first compliment, Larkin," I say, smiling at him.

The corners of his mouth twitch briefly before disappearing back into his harsh façade.

We continue down the winding path through the dense forest. The dim sunlight has transformed into a blazing glow that spills through every crack in the forest canopy. The birds around us keep to themselves, singing a pleasant tune in the distance, and I catch myself humming along with them. The horses seem relaxed, and I can't help but take a deep breath.

Being back in the forest and away from the gloom of Andorwood Castle has made me feel calmer than I have in days. The forest buzzes around me, my axes are a comfortable weight on my back, and dare I say, I'm truly enjoying myself.

However, the silence between us is slowly killing me. It's been over an hour without him speaking to me, and the awkward tension grows by the second. Larkin keeps his calm composure as he rides Atlas with ease—like the two of them were made for each other. Something about the bond between an animal is so special to me. I lean down to pet Myah and turn to Larkin again.

Every so often, I see him swat away a small pesky insect that makes me chuckle to myself.

"Not fond of nature?" I ask.

"I appreciate nature. I spent most of my childhood outside, but I'm not a big fan of bugs."

"Snakes?"

He cringes. "Even worse."

I laugh as another insect attempts to land on his hands, and he bats it away.

"You know they can hear that, right? They will be more drawn to you because you just made that statement."

He snaps his head in my direction. "That isn't true."

"Oh, yes, it is. A thousand of his buddies will come visit you now," I tease.

Larkin rolls his eyes and grips Atlas's reins a bit tighter, glancing over his shoulder. The horse snorts, and Larkin leans forward, giving him a quick pet.

"There is a spider on your shoulder, by the way," Larkin says, with a grin.

I scream and jerk sideways in an attempt to rid my body of the unwanted traveler.

Larkin bursts out laughing as I struggle to stay on top of Myah, who is annoyed by my movements on her back. After a few seconds, I realize there is actually nothing on my shoulder, and I glare in Larkin's direction, irritated by his teasing.

"You're fucking mean," I snap.

"And you are just as afraid as I am."

I brush the hair from my face and settle myself back on Myah's large back.

"This part of the forest is still mostly warded," Larkin says, changing the subject. "We have a bit farther to go before we pass through the wards, and our senses must be sharp. The creatures will primarily stalk us in the shadows. They don't tend to attack first. It's the creatures we won't see until it's too late that I worry about."

I nod. "Got it."

Silence hits again.

"Has Silas told you anything about the trials?" I ask.

Larkin looks at me, his dark eyes shooting daggers into mine. He nods and says, "Yes, a bit, but I didn't pry. I only listened to what he was willing to disclose."

"Why didn't you come with him to Daramveer?" I flinch at my own questions. "He traveled there alone."

Why would I ask that?

Larkin stirs on the saddle, obviously uncomfortable at my question.

He doesn't respond.

"I'm sorry. That was an odd thing to ask. I just...I know you two are very close, so I thought maybe he wanted some company."

The mid-morning breeze wraps around us, and even the birds seem to stop singing as I await his response.

Larkin clears his throat. "I was on a ship about twenty miles from shore when his boat docked in Daramveer. I had a small fleet follow behind him, in case he ran into anything and needed assistance." He pauses, as if reliving the memories. "When the ship arrived safely, I turned around and headed home. Silas didn't want help. He went to Daramveer with one purpose and one mission only."

"To win the trials?" I ask.

He shakes his head. "To find you."

My heart flutters for a second, and I quiet my questions. Larkin won't open up to me easily about what I really want to know, so I need to be cautious with my inquiries.

"It seems as if all of Andorwood knew who I was before I ever knew about you all."

The thought of that makes me uncomfortable.

"Hardly, Briar. Silas speaks to his close circle and rarely to anyone outside of that. Your reputation spread fast because of your skills and power."

"Is that what we are calling it?"

He nods, continuing, "Silas is extremely guarded and doesn't trust people easily. It's taken us years to get as close as we are now."

I raise my eyebrows. "Oh, I've noticed."

Larkin huffs a laugh, and I flinch at the sound. I see his head tilt back, and the bright sunlight reflects off his white hair. His shoulders relax a bit, and he lets loose of the reins, stretching his arms.

"We hated each other when we first met," he adds. "I think I knew Silas all of fifteen minutes before he punched me in the face in a local bar."

My mouth slightly parts. "You're joking."

"Nope." He laughs to himself at his own memory. "I drunkenly hit on Fenmore and spilled a bit of ale on her. It made Silas upset, if you can imagine."

"You can flirt?"

"Of course, that's what you take away from that story," Larkin huffs, cutting his eye toward me. "I do have a life, Briar."

"Were you and Fenmore an item? I don't mean to draw attention to it, but Warrick is always the one who's around her."

"No," he shakes his head. "Silas pretty much killed any chance of that happening after Fen had to pull him off me. It also didn't help my case that she was drenched in ale." He cringes. "After that, Silas and I became friends—sort of—and I thought it would be too inappropriate and uncomfortable for me to pursue anything further."

"I'm sorry it didn't work out between you two," I respond. "She's great."

"Fenmore is fantastic. She's strong, fearless, and stunning, but I promise I'm not lonely." Larkin laughs. "I can fill my time with others."

"Who? What's her name?" I can't help but ask.

He angles his head in my direction. "Who said it was a female?"

"Oh. I'm sorry, I just assumed that since we were speaking about Fen, you preferred women."

"It doesn't matter to me. I like someone for who they are as a person," Larkin smiles.

I nod and smile in return. "Oak would really be furious that you said he wasn't your type if he knew that."

We both boom a laugh.

"So, Maines and Oak are together?" Larkin asks.

I shrug. "They're something. But yes, I'd say they're together." I pause. "She...had a thing for Barlowe before Oak."

Larkin tenses. "I see."

"They grew apart when he left for the Northern Training Camp on the mainland, so to my knowledge, it never turned into anything deeper. They had different wants at the time, but you know, everything happens for a reason," I add.

He doesn't respond, and I watch his knuckles tighten around the reins at the mention of my brother.

"How long were you at the camp?" I ask, hesitantly.

He stares forward, and that familiar composure creeps back as I watch his shoulders cave inward. His harsh face returns, and any ounce of entertainment he was experiencing moves past me like the fading breeze.

"Why won't you talk to me about anything regarding my brother?"

"Because it's not your business," he bites back.

I jerk my gaze to his. "My family is my business."

"Briar," Larkin whispers.

"I'm sorry. I just need to know more," I say, louder than intended, startling Myah.

"Hush." Larkin raises his hand, placing his finger to his mouth. "Right fucking now."

"Why?" I snap.

Larkin's gaze turns to mine, and his eyes are filled with worry. "Because we aren't alone."

I quickly snap my mouth shut and glance around.

The forest surrounding us has transformed, and even though the sun shines above, darkness looms as we move deeper into the woods and farther from the heart of the kingdom. The trees have lost their vibrant green hue, the grass is parched, and I no longer hear the soothing melodies of the birds. The trees now appear as if they are rooted in decaying soil, and long, thin fingers have replaced the once-full branches. Only silence exists here, and as much as I want to ignore it, the invisible tattoo on my shoulder begins to pulse.

Larkin motions for me to fall behind him, and we continue forward.

The path becomes narrow, and I often have to dodge limbs that extend onto the path—as if the trees are desperate to pull us toward the forest on both sides. He glances behind him, checking to see if I'm keeping up, and I throw a quick thumbs-up in his direction. My eyes shift from left to right, and an uncomfortable tingle starts in my fingertips.

This is it.

Silas said to listen to my body's reactions.

Larkin raises another hand, signaling me to stop. I pull on the reins, bringing Myah to a halt. Even she senses something lurking around us, and her ears lay flat. I lean forward, brushing her mane, trying to give her any comfort I can in this moment.

Larkin swiftly swings a leg over Atlas and dismounts him gracefully, landing on the dirt with a thud. I quickly do the same and move to Myah's nose, wrapping my arm around her gently.

"Shh," I whisper. "You're okay, girl."

Larkin scans the surroundings.

His dark eyes sweep across the dense forest, and I look in the opposite direction to cover every pocket of shadows. He draws his sword, but I keep my axes tightly secured, placing my hand on one of the throats over my head, just in case.

"We will leave the horses here." Larkin points to the last bloomed tree. "Ten steps ahead of us is where the wards end, so they will be safe. We won't be long."

I give him a worried glance and rest my forehead against Myah's nose. "You'll be okay, sweet girl. I won't be long."

We carefully guide them to the nearby tree and tie their reins with enough slack so they can enjoy their rest. I watch Larkin lean into Atlas and whisper something. The horse flicks his ears in response, and Larkin leaves his hand pressed against the beast for as long as he can. I walk next to him and offer a soft smile.

"Once we pass that final tree, I need you to listen when I say something and react if I tell you to without a second thought."

I nod, letting the unease fill me.

"It's a two-mile walk from here, so it shouldn't take us too long," he orders. "Be careful what you speak of once we pass through the wards. Malachi has spies everywhere."

"The Travelers?"

He nods. "And crows."

I cringe at the thought of the invisible creatures that Malachi controls, but I'm thankful for the protection tattoo—even if it does cause me a constant dull ache.

"Larkin," I say to get his attention. "Can the invisible creatures show themselves?"

He nods. "Yes."

"Have you seen one?"

His face turns to stone. "Few people have. But, yes, I unfortunately have."

"What does it look like?" I ask.

"I hope you never know," Larkin says, sliding his sword into the sheath at his waist as he walks along the narrow path.

I fall into step behind him, jumping at every sound as we approach the last moments of warded protection. A tall tree stands before us, its trunk stretching wide, and not a single leaf clings to its branches. The bark is white and gray, and all I can think of is the creature that haunts me. Its skin is so similar, and that's when I realize: once we pass that, all wards are down, and we will be fair game.

The air thickens as we step past the tree. The silence is deafening, and I do my best to avoid any fallen leaves. Larkin keeps his senses sharp and moves his head slowly. Any sudden movements could attract unwanted attention, so I do my best to follow in his footsteps. My heart begins to race, and I speed up to walk beside Larkin. A loud growl in the distance makes my senses even more heightened, and I snap my attention to Larkin.

He places a single finger to his lips before pointing to a dense area of trees, turning in their direction and away from the looming threat. I hurry alongside him and silently curse that I'm acting like Oak right now.

Get a grip, Briar.

We step forward, and once the dead trees provide some shield for the open path, Larkin turns to me. "The forest will end soon, and we will confront Death's opening."

I glance around him, as if I can see the towering place through the dense forest canopy.

"This is where two mountains have split apart but connect at their peaks. No one knows how this happened, but legend says this is where the creatures of the darkest realm escape from."

I shudder.

"The poison you want to learn about is called Arxbayne. It comes from Death's Opening and is lethal within seconds."

My brother's lifeless body flashes in my mind like a lightning strike, and I close my eyes for a second, blurring the image.

Larkin notices my flinch but continues, "We'll enter the mouth of the mountains and visit a trap I set to catch the creature I extract it from. I'll teach you everything I know about it then, and once we finish, I will harvest it."

Shock ripples through me. "Why?"

"Because it's lethal, making Andorwood almost unbeatable to outside Wielder threats if we use it. We'll return to Silas's after that."

"Larkin, this is what killed my brother."

He tenses. "I know."

"How? How did this get to Daramveer?" I ramble, my thoughts going a million miles a minute. "How was this on the mainland?"

"Because I sold it to him."

CHAPTER 24

I step back a few paces. "What did you just say?"

Larkin lowers his head. "I'm sorry I didn't tell you."

"Repeat your fucking words."

"I sold it to him, Briar. Your brother asked for it, and being his friend, I gave it to him."

My mouth falls open, and tears begin to well in my eyes. I shake my head and continue to step backward, desperate to move away from him. Why the fuck did I agree to come out here with him.

I trusted him. *Silas* trusted him.

No. No. This can't be happening.

"Briar," Larkin starts, reaching for me.

I widen my stance outside of his grasp, and narrow my eyes.

"I would have never given it to him had I known what would happen. Please, believe me. I cared for your brother."

"Liar."

"We were friends."

"Get the fuck away from me," I rage.

"Briar, please just listen to me," he says, as he reaches for me again.

"You fucking killed him. You killed my brother."

"I didn't know that would happen. I...I was trying to help him." The color drains from his face. "He told me he needed to be prepared to return to Daramveer."

"For what?" I shout.

"He was going to kill your father, and now, knowing what I know, it was to protect you. I swear."

"Shut the fuck up!"

"Please don't yell. We aren't safe out here," he begs, in a failed attempt to calm me.

I continue to backpedal. "You are the only reason I'm not safe out here."

Shadows start to swirl around me, like a thick fog spreading across the forest floor, and an uncontrollable sensation starts to rise in my throat. My tattoo throbs with pain, and I grit my teeth, trying to ignore it.

I slam my eyes closed.

Breathe.

One.

Two.

Three.

Fuck. It's not working.

Larkin whispers, "Just let me talk."

A deep, thunderous scream breaks me from my daze. The forest seems to pulse like a slow heartbeat, and unease rises around us. Larkin rushes forward and grabs my arm, pulling me back into the small pocket of trees. He claps a hand over my mouth and crouches behind a large tree trunk. His large body presses against my back, and I can feel his rapidly beating heart. I attempt to slap his hand away, but he holds me tight.

"Get off me," I mumble under his hold.

His gaze snaps in all directions, and tears flow from my eyes and onto the back of his hand. I relax my jaw to bite down on his hand, but he pulls it tighter, stopping me.

"Be quiet," he whispers.

The clearing before us seems to pause, and a single crow squawks as it flies from a nearby treetop. The sun overhead dims, allowing more shadows to pour from the tightly packed trees across the clearing, and a horrifying darkness settles into my chest.

My eyes widen when I see it, and I fight the urge to whimper against Larkin's grip.

A creature that would stand three heads taller than Larkin if it weren't for its hunched back crawls into the clearing. Tattered white fabric clings to its lanky body, and its skin appears cracked, as if over time, the creature has slowly started to shatter from despair. Black, hollow eyes slowly scan the clearing for any signs of life, and it sniffs the air. Its movements are fidgety and unnatural—like the muscles in its body are also screaming—as it stalks forward.

I dip my head against Larkin, no longer caring about the news and instead fearing for our lives. The creature gradually turns toward us and points a long, clawed finger. A tear rolls down my cheek, and I feel Larkin behind me holding his breath. He slowly removes his hand from my mouth and places both hands on my shoulder, demanding my attention, as he spins me to face him.

"When I say run," Larkin pauses, glancing at the creature, "run as fast as you can to the right. When we make it past that sixth tree, I'll shift us to the mouth of the mountain. There's a spot we can hide there."

I stare into his dark eyes, allowing the tears to fall from a mix of fear and betrayal.

"I know you don't trust me right now, Briar, but please listen." He leans closer. "I'm not going to let anything happen to you, but we cannot fight this thing."

"Maybe we can," I say.

"We can't."

I turn my gaze toward the creature and flinch when I see it has moved closer, much closer. Its towering body looms over us like the tallest tree, blending into the gray sky, and trees that remain breathless in the dead breeze. Its body slumps forward, curling its bony back, and its head rolls around its long neck, scanning for us.

I slowly nod in understanding to Larkin. My mind snaps back to the trial: the darkness of the forest, the creatures, and my fear that I would never make it back to the castle alive that night.

The creature starts to lean forward through the dense trees we hide behind. Its long fingers grip completely around the large trees as its head peers between the branches toward us. Its stench fills my nostrils, and I fight not to gag. The smell of rotten flesh overwhelms my senses, making my eyes water. My vision blurs with tears, and I wipe away what I can, preparing to make a run for my life.

I watch Larkin steady his breath and nod, signaling that it's almost time. He observes the creature moving deeper into the tightly packed trees, and that's when I realize he's hoping the creature gets stuck once we bolt.

"Be swift," Larkin mouths, and squeezes my hand.

I reply silently, "You too."

"Ready?"

I nod.

Larkin springs from behind the tree and blasts a surge of light toward the creature of darkness. A deadly scream fills the air as the attack momentarily blinds the creature, sending it stepping backward slightly. Its shriek rattles around us, and I clasp my hands over my ears.

"Run!" Larkin shouts.

I dash through the trees, heading precisely in the direction he indicated. Larkin quickly catches up, and we rush forward together. Larkin is quicker, but he doesn't rush ahead, only sprinting a few steps in front as we race toward the far clearing of the forest. The trees behind us begin to snap, and I know the beast is breaking them with its sheer power and determination to catch us. Terror fills me, propelling me faster around every tree in my path.

"Keep going," Larkin yells.

My hair whips behind me as my lungs begin to burn from the surge of power coursing through my muscles. With each pounding step, the cracking of the trees grows louder. A growl fills my ears, momentarily overwhelming my senses and prompting me to look behind me. The large creature propels itself forward with its long, thin arms—breaking through the trees as if they weigh nothing. My eyes meet the creature's devious, glowing eyes, and a rattling shock moves through me.

It can't be.

I know those eyes.

A distressed scream escapes my lips as the creature closes in, and I reach behind me, still in motion, desperately trying to grab one of my axes. The stuttering of my steps makes me clumsy, preventing me from fully grasping the axe for my defense.

Larkin dashes ahead into the clearing, and that's when I notice it.

Death's Opening.

The vast space before us is both beautiful and horrifying. A broad opening rests at the base of two twin peaks, and thankfully, it is only a few hundred yards away.

Not much longer.

Larkin spins ahead of me, opening his arms for me to crash against him, and I keep pushing, faster than before. His eyes widen, and once again, horror fills me. A low growl reverberates in my mind, and I know the creature is right behind me from the rancid, hot breath that moves my hair. I lunge forward out of the trees and into the clearing. Larkin stands, opening his arms wider, and steps forward, ready to shift as soon as our hands touch.

I leap forward, and time appears to slow down. Larkin reaches out his hand, and that's when I feel it. A sharp pain strikes my shoulder, and I hear my flesh rip open like rushing water.

The scream that leaves my throat could crack the mountains around us. Adrenaline keeps me going, but I feel a hot liquid quickly soak into my clothes. Larkin's eyes go wild, and the smell of iron fills the air, drowning out the stench from the creature behind me.

"Don't fucking stop!" Larkin screams.

My hand finds his, and we shift into a brilliant light of mist.

We land in a dark, musty opening just a few yards inside the mountain's mouth. Before I have time to react, Larkin is on his feet, pulling me into his arms. He moves in quick bursts deeper into the mountain, carrying us as far away from the opening as he can. The darkness envelops me, and I feel myself slipping away, each movement tearing my shoulder more. My eyes can't focus, but I can see shapes of jagged rocks warped by time deep within the mountain. I'm not sure how, but a light aura cloaks me, and I feel warmth even against the cold stones.

"Fuck, Briar," Larkin mumbles. "Hang on."

Pain surges through my entire body, and even though he holds me tight, my body trembles. Screaming isn't an option anymore.

I'm too tired, but I can't help whimpering against the pain. I glance down to ensure my arm is still there, and luckily it is—although I can't feel it. The weight of my axes on my back sends an additional shock through my system, and my head slumps forward.

"My arm," I call to Larkin, my voice barely a whisper.

"I know." He offers a reassuring smile that I don't believe. "We're almost there."

The passing seconds feel like hours as the agony sets into my bones. I can't help but thrash against the pain and grind my teeth, not caring if they shatter any moment. The darkness of the mountain starts to take over, and I close my eyes.

"Don't close your eyes, Briar," Larkin orders. "Keep them open."

Even in pain, I've heard those words before. I've spoken those words to Barlowe when I begged him to hold on. He did the one thing I asked him not to do. He let himself slip into the darkest realm. I'm not one to follow orders, but I'll try. I keep my eyes cracked open as much as possible and catch Larkin glancing down to check every few seconds. His face contorts through the haze, and sweat beads on his forehead as he pushes harder to get me somewhere safe.

He starts to slow down near a shadowy patch of stone. A few candles rest on the ground as he lays me down on a smooth surface. The cold stone sends a shiver through my body, and my teeth begin to chatter. I quickly realized that the warmth I felt was from the thick blood running down both Larkin's and my entire body. A chill begins to creep up my core, and a concerning numbness tingles in my legs. Larkin works quickly to light a few candles using basic Lumor magic, granting us access to a dim light around the mountain cavern.

This tiny room is well used. Many items line the far walls, and I now believe Larkin when he said he's been here numerous times before. He rushes to my side, removes the axes, and peels away the shirt stuck to my blood-soaked body. I grit my teeth from the fabric taking my skin with it as he lowers it down my arm.

"I'm sorry," he says, as he flinches. "I need to look at your shoulder."

I give him a nod, not really concerned about what he does right now, as long as it puts an end to the pain. The chill seeps in deeper, and my eyelids grow heavier, flickering shut occasionally. The tingles travel up my legs, settling into my chest, and moving outward to my arms. I know once it covers my entire body, I won't be able to hold on.

Sleep. I want to sleep.

Larkin snaps his fingers in my face. "No way. Don't you dare go to sleep."

"I'm tired," I mumble.

"I don't give a shit. Keep your eyes open."

He touches the wound, causing a jolt of pain to shoot through my body. I thrash against his touch and arch my back. A scream escapes my lips this time, and my eyes fly open. My eyes find his, and concern sits in his dark eyes.

"That's more like it," Larkin says.

"Fucking," I barely rasp out, "asshole."

He works silently for a moment, using his own outer shirt to wipe the blood away. His hands move calmly, as if he's done this many times, and even though his nerves are shot, he keeps them steady.

"Tell me a story."

I blink at him.

"Tell me something about you and Barlowe as children," Larkin insists. "Something that makes you happy."

"I. Can't."

I can't tell him any stories that are happy, because the only thing that fills my mind these days are thoughts of all the despondent things that have happened. Tears begin to roll down my face, and I sit on the edge of consciousness, my eyes fluttering closed for a second, then snapping open seconds later. Larkin attempts to roll me more on my opposite side, and another flash of pain tears through my body.

"Then, I'll talk, and I want you to nod after everything I say so I know you are still with me."

I stare at him.

"Okay?"

I only blink.

"I said, nod, Briar," he demands.

I gently move my head up and down, battling the pain, sleepiness, chills, and nausea that hits me.

"I grew up in Eddris," Larkin begins. "My parents are both healers at the House of Havengart, which you'd think would come in handy right now for patching you up. I wish I had listened more." He leans over, checking to see if my eyes are open. "Sorry, I shouldn't say that right now. You're going to be fine."

He glances at me with a fake smile, and I nod.

"I never wanted to be a healer. I was about seventeen when I decided I wouldn't follow in their footsteps. I heard stories of warriors from various kingdoms who went to the Northern Training Camps to train, but one kingdom in particular dominated the camps: Daramveer." His brows raise. "But, another kingdom had an even worse reputation: Andorwood."

He pauses, and I do as I was told, moving my head slightly.

"Just checking," he continues, as he works behind me. "See, Briar. I think we're more alike than you realize. I also don't like being told what to do, and when you're young, the idea of joining an army of notorious rebels didn't sound scary; it sounded amazing. Thrilling. Challenging. Sounds like something you'd like."

I move my head, processing his words.

"Everything about my life in Eddris was the opposite, so a stupid seventeen-year-old boy chased his dream and later ended up at the training camp around the same time your brother arrived."

"Hmm," I whisper.

"I had a bad taste in my mouth about Barlowe Blackbyrne, just from what I had heard. He was cocky, a rising star, and already had the perfect life set up for him—the future I wanted."

He pauses, not to let me respond but to gather his thoughts. Even through the pain, fury rises in my chest at his words about Barlowe. It's his fault he's dead.

"I was a nobody. The son of two healers from Eddris was disowned for following his dreams. No royal status, nothing." He sighs. "I was just Larkin Spiridon, and I had a bad fucking attitude."

"Worse…" I cough, pain throbbing down my back, "than now?"

"You think you dislike me now?" He chuckles. "You should have met twenty-one-year-old me."

The sides of my lips faintly curl.

Larkin pats at the wound and draws a healing Rigil near his workstation. "I met Barlowe shortly after his arrival, and Briar, I couldn't have been more wrong about him. Your brother was an amazing person. He didn't care about all the things I assumed he would. We became fast friends, and I spent almost three years of my life at the Northern Training Camp with him."

I attempt to turn to glance at him, but he keeps me still.

"When the opportunity arose for me to travel to Andorwood, Barlowe did everything he could to ensure I was on the ship that day. Barlowe helped create the future I had always dreamed of. Upon my arrival in Andorwood, he had persuaded your father to send word that someone of significance was coming and that I was to be appointed a top Commander of the Andorwood army."

"That sounds like Barlowe," I whisper.

"He's the reason I'm here, living my dreams. Well, I can't say this very moment is my dream, but you get the point," Larkin says, and pauses. "After everything he did, I'm the reason he's dead."

I fully turn this time, and tears fall from his dark eyes.

I wanted him to admit what he had done, but now that I'm hearing it, it doesn't give me any satisfaction. I feel heartbroken for him.

"Hold still," Larkin pleads, before he continues his story. "We kept in touch over the years as often as we could, and when he reached out wanting Arxbayne, I was hesitant. But, he was persistent—almost desperate. He had done so much for me, and I caved. I wanted to help him because of how much he helped me."

I lazily blink up at him, my mouth slightly parted.

"He told me he needed it to save his sister. Barlowe had a plan, and he was determined to do everything in his power to ensure nothing happened to you. He risked everything to get that poison. When I heard about his passing and the circumstances, I couldn't bear it. I knew his blood was on my hands, and I still struggle with that guilt every single day." He pauses as the emotions crash into him. "Every day it haunts me."

"Larkin," I whisper.

"Then you arrived unexpectedly. Briar Blackbyrne, sister to someone I cared deeply for. I couldn't even bear to look at you. Even your voice triggered me, because I hadn't come to terms with what happened." His eyes find mine. "I've been rude to you, but I believe your presence is a sign from the Gods that it's time I come to terms with my actions."

The room begins to spin, and I squint my eyes closed for a second to refocus.

He pauses for a second and watches me. "I won't let anything happen to you, not out of duty to Andorwood or fear of Silas and what he would do to me, but because I owe everything to Barlowe. And I'll spend the rest of my life trying to pay him back."

My heart shatters, but pain quickly overwhelms all my functions. I feel myself drifting, unable to keep my eyes open any longer.

"Briar?" Larkin leans forward. "Can you hear me? I need you to nod."

The pain in my shoulder and his confession are too much. My vision blurs, and the candlelight around us turns into muted flickers in the distance. My heart rate increases, then slows at such a rapid pace that I can't take a good breath. My breathing turns into frantic gasps, and comfortable vibrations move around me. I hear Larkin curse, but I can't see him or move. I completely relax into the numbness.

"Don't you fucking die!"

For a moment, I wonder if this is what death feels like—a peaceful slip into nothingness, devoid of fear and sorrow, just your body drifting into the darkest realm to be embraced by a world of calm. I'm weightless, the world is soundless, and I let my eyes close. This time, I don't fear whether they will open again.

"Briar?"

I hear the whisper, but I still can't see anything. My eyes won't adjust to the darkness, and my head throbs. In the shadows, I feel around, reaching for my shoulder. The pain has subsided, but a tenderness lingers on my mangled skin over my tattoo. I try to speak, but my throat is too raw and dry to make a sound.

"Is that you?" the voice calls, as if coming from down a narrow tunnel.

My mind races. That deep voice is familiar, but it's not Silas's. I blink, hoping my eyes adjust, but only darkness fills them. I open my mouth to speak, but the words stay trapped.

"Hello?" I think to myself. *"I must be dead."*

"No, you aren't. At least, not yet," the voice chimes in.

"What the fuck?"

"Yeah, that's you alright."

"What is happening?" I ask in my mind.

"Briar, it's Rohhit."

CHAPTER 25

I remain surrounded by total darkness, hoping my eyes will adjust so I can see where I am. I know I heard Rohhit a few times before, but that stopped once I got the tattoo.

The tattoo.

The creature tore my left shoulder apart. The protection has been shattered.

Oh Gods. Kalix.

"Rohhit?" I speak aloud this time.

My voice escapes my mouth, feeling like needles shooting through my throat. I try to swallow, but the pain and dryness are overwhelming.

"Briar, I don't have much time, so I need you to listen," Rohhit's voice echoes in panic.

"Wait, how is this possible?" I interrupt.

"We are vessels—Realm Walkers. Carobon has completely taken over my body, but I can still hear him—his plans. You need to locate the Forgotten Archives. Have you heard of it?"

"Yes, it's here in Andorwood," I respond quickly.

"The answers lie within, Briar, about how to eliminate Kalix and Carobon for good. A ship is making its way to Andorwood, carrying resurrected creatures. Carobon, Calia, and Nolan have been working tirelessly since you departed from the mainland. They are trying to rebuild Cammon. It isn't good. They are coming to Andorwood to destroy what the Archives hold. You need to be prepared to protect it."

"We know, and we are as best we can be." I pause. "Rohhit, are you alright?"

"For now."

"Keep holding on," I beg. "Don't stop trying."

"Each day gets harder to hold on. I feel myself slipping, like I'm getting farther away from my own mind each day."

The darkness starts to overwhelm my senses, and I can barely hear Rohhit anymore. I feel like I'm blinking, but my eyes don't move. I try to lift my arm once more, but it feels stuck, as if it's being weighed down.

"Rohhit," I shout. "Can you hear me?"

"You need to leave, Briar. You can't stay here. Follow Silas's voice." His voice, barely a whisper, slithers into my mind. "Follow your tether."

Tether.

He must have a tether.

"No. Wait. Please tell me how I can save you."

"The Archives," a soft voice fades into the darkness.

A bright white light shines in my face, mingling with dark streaks of shadow. The light pulses with a light yet dark energy as I hear him.

"Briar, don't give up on me."

I feel as if my body is being lifted off the ground, but no matter how hard I squint, I can't see anything. I struggle against the pull, desperate to hold on a little longer. I need to talk to Rohhit. I can't leave him in this darkness. Silas's voice grows louder and more frantic, as if he's also searching for me in the dark.

I yield and let the silver string of light draw me toward his voice. The white light fades away, and everything becomes silent.

A gasp of air fills my lungs, and my body slowly starts to feel whole again. My legs aren't numb, I can hear things normally, and the pain from my shoulder comes crashing back into my body. My eyes remain shut as I feel two strong arms wrap around my body. Silas's scent fills my nose, and I inhale deeply once more.

I must be dreaming.

"She's breathing, again." I hear his voice.

"Thank fucking Gods," Larkin responds.

I lay there, wrapped in his warmth, before I dare open my eyes. A gentle hand brushes a fallen strand of hair from my face.

"Open your eyes," Silas speaks to me this time. "Please open your eyes, my love."

I slowly open my eyes. The cave's dimness confuses me for a moment, so I sift through my last memories to grasp where I am. Silas's face comes into focus, and I blink rapidly to clear my vision. His handsome face is smeared with thick black blood, and his eyes are filled with both rage and concern, but when our eyes lock, that all disappears.

"Hey," he whispers.

I softly smile. "Hey."

"I asked you not to do anything stupid," Silas grins.

"I didn't, technically."

He leans forward and kisses my forehead. "Sarcastic, even on your deathbed."

My lips quiver, but I smile.

"Unfortunately, since you got hurt, I have to kill Larkin now for a few reasons," Silas speaks again. "I've recently been filled in on everything."

"Look, Silas." I hear Larkin huffing from a few yards away. "I feel fucking terrible as it is. It would almost be a favor if you killed me right now."

"Don't kill him," my voice rasps.

A heavy exhale escapes Larkin's throat as I shift my gaze around the small pocket I occupy, deep inside Death's Opening.

"No, you definitely can," Larkin responds.

The surrounding caverns remain silent except for the faint sound of water trickling deeper through the winding tunnels. Silas continues to stroke my head, giving me time to collect myself. With each passing second, my senses return to my body, and the trembling begins to ease.

"How are you here right now?" I ask.

"I felt you slipping away. I was with my mother and Fenmore when it started." His jaw tenses. "My chest felt like a boulder was being pressed down on it, then I heard you scream, as if my night-mares were becoming reality. I started shifting as fast as I could to find and reach you."

I blink up at him. "Is that my blood?"

"Yes." He pauses, looking at Larkin. "And the creatures that hurt you."

I sit up slightly. "Larkin said we couldn't fight that thing."

He glances at Larkin again. "He was right to say that. It could have been much worse if you had tried to."

Larkin stands and approaches where I rest in Silas's arms. His tall frame is slightly slumped, and his white hair appears dull.

Silas watches him closely, and I can feel the anger radiating from his body. It doesn't take long for me to realize that Larkin likely informed Silas about everything, driven by fear, shame, and a hint of trepidation.

"I'm so sorry." Larkin hangs his head. "So much of this is my fault."

I shake my head. "Larkin, it's not your fault Barlowe died."

His expression turns to shock.

I attempt to sit up, and Silas helps me. My left arm hangs limply beside me, but it's gradually healing. I look around and see a few ritual items alongside the Rigils Larkin drew. I notice blood trickling from his hand, and I realize that he cut himself to strengthen the ritual to save me.

"It's Thatcher's fault that my brother is dead, not yours." I pause, still struggling to speak loudly. "I want you to know that. You thought you were helping a friend, and I'd be lying if I said I wouldn't have done the same."

Larkin lowers his head and crouches next to where I sit. "I'm sorry, Briar. I wasn't lying when I said I would do whatever I can to protect you for the rest of my life."

I nod and say, "Thank you."

"You're still on my shit list, Spiridon," Silas cuts in.

I turn my attention to Silas. "Leave him alone."

Silas casts a sly grin my way, with a wink.

"Did I die?" I cut my eyes at both of them.

"Almost," Larkin says. "You stopped breathing for a minute."

"Try five," Silas barks.

"That's about the time he shifted here."

I sit up higher this time and try to get to my feet. I stumble a little, and Silas is there to catch me. I stand on shaky legs, but at least I'm upright. My clothes are drenched in dark blood, my hair is tangled, and a chill courses through my body. My shirt barely clings to my shoulder, and Silas removes his, wrapping it around me.

"There's something else," Larkin says, his mouth forming a thin line.

"What?"

Silas wraps his arm around my waist to keep me upright. "Your tattoo is gone. The creature's claw went straight through it, slicing the ink in half." He glances at my back. "Hopefully a bit will still protect you, but you are going to have one insane scar, my love."

"I figured it was gone," I admit.

Larkin angles his head. "What do you mean?"

"When I…passed out," I start.

"You mean died?" Larkin cuts in.

"Semantics," Silas snaps.

"Yes, when I died, I heard Rohhit again." I pause, waiting for their reactions. "He's alive, Silas. He's still in his body."

Silas rubs his hand through his hair.

"He can hear Carobon. Carobon is working with Calia and Nolan to rebuild Cammon. The ship is heading to Andorwood to destroy the Archives. Whatever's in there is important, and we have to get there first."

A sharp claw drags its point along my mind, and I flinch, earning a look from both men.

The tattoo is severed, and Kalix is back, silently taunting me.

Silas says, "My mother told me that ancient texts are stored there, dating back to before and shortly after the Great Battle. Many records concerning the Great Wiitches were burned, resulting in the loss of a lot of information. However, there was a group of individuals who collected everything they could and established the Forgotten Archives to keep the information safe in case it was ever needed again."

"So, that's why something dark guards it," I add.

"Exactly. What's inside was meant to be burned, forever lost to the flames. Not even my mother knows exactly what's in there. She's been fortunate enough to be granted access, but has always been driven out by the lurking shadows within."

"Did she know anything else?" Larkin asks.

"I didn't get much information beyond that because, well, you know. But Fenmore stayed back to continue the conversation."

"We should head back," Larkin says. "We need to get into the Archives."

Realization hits me, suddenly. "Yara. What time is it?"

"When I left the castle, it was late afternoon. Since it's dark outside, I'd guess it's nearly 8 P.M.," Silas responds.

"We were supposed to meet her in your room." I stumble toward the small exit leading back into the opening. "We need to leave right now."

"First of all, you aren't rushing anywhere." Silas raises his hands. "Secondly, Maines and Oak will be in my room in case she shows up early. Fortunately, we prepared for situations like this to happen to you, Briar." Silas grimaces. "We can head to the castle, but it's going to be at a slow pace. I won't push your body right now. You nearly died."

I groan. "You're such a worrywart."

"I might be, yes, but at least I'm prepared. Warrick is taking care of Myah and Atlas. So, it looks like the three of us will be heading to the castle."

"How long will it take us to get there?" I snap.

"If Larkin and I take turns shifting you, we should be able to get there in under an hour," Silas calculates.

"That's too slow."

"I'm sorry, but I'm not pushing you," he says, as he walks behind me and wraps his arms around my waist. "Only you would return from near death, demanding things."

I nudge him. "I'm fine."

"And only you would come back from near death and lie straight to my face," he smirks.

I lift my arm to prove my statement and wince.

Shit.

"Let me see your shoulder," Silas demands, as he pulls down the fabric to examine the healing gash. "Welcome to the scar club. It looks like you were mauled."

"Well, it's fortunate that's exactly what occurred, isn't it?"

He kisses around the injury. "It makes you even more perfect."

"Can we go?" Larkin snaps from behind us. "I'm ready to get the fuck out of here."

"What about your trap?" I ask. "Don't you need to harvest the poison?"

"I'll be back in a few days. It's not going anywhere," he replies. "And no, you won't be coming with me."

I roll my eyes. "I wasn't even going to ask."

We walk toward the large opening between the two colliding mountains. Faint flashes of memories flicker in my mind, but they are as blurred as my vision once was. Jagged rocks jut out from the sides, and that's when I realize why they refer to it as Death's Opening. The rocks resemble razor-sharp teeth emerging from the mouth of a creature made of stone.

Silas halts me. "I'll shift with her first. Larkin, you stay close behind. We'll stop near the clearing to gather our bearings."

We all nod in agreement, and Silas takes my right hand.

"Ready?"

"Yes," I respond.

We turn to mist, and the world around us fades. The fresh air heightens my senses as we emerge from the cave into the night sky. The clearing is not far away, so it doesn't take us long to reach the spot that nearly killed me.

Larkin lands first and steps forward, ensuring that our

surroundings are safe. Silas and I land softly next, and before I know it, he is already there to catch me. Larkin pushes through the dense patch of trees, moving closer to the center clearing where the creature emerged. A crackle of light surrounds Larkin as he draws on his magic in case a second beast lurks somewhere in the shadows. He moves out of sight just ahead, and I hear him curse.

Silas turns to me. "The creature's body is ahead. We can go around if you don't want to see it."

"I want to see it," I reply.

He grabs my hand, and we move in the direction of Larkin through the tightly packed trees. Larkin stands before us, his mouth hung open, and before him, the creature lies dead. Its long, thin body is stretched across the forest floor, and its once cracked skin now appears shattered. A long tongue hangs from its wide mouth, and the creature's body is nearly split in half. Black steaming blood coats the ground around it, and I quickly cover my nose. The smell is unbearable.

Larkin turns, hearing us approach. "Gods, Silas. How the fuck did you do this?"

He walks beside Larkin, staring down at the creature. The shadows around him begin to pulse, as if seeing it revives all the rage he initially felt. I notice his fists tighten, and he glances back at me. His piercing green eyes reflect hatred, not for me, but for what the creature did to me.

"I wanted it dead, so I made it happen." Silas glances at the creature again. "No one will touch Briar and live to tell the tale."

"Damn, Silas. No one has killed a Traveler in centuries," Larkin says with a grimace.

Silas walks away from the creature and back to me, grabbing my hand.

"Until now." His voice is low and deep, revealing no regret. "Let's keep moving."

"I'll shift her now," Larkin says, quickly moving away from the beast and stepping closer to the line of trees where I stand, near the base of the mountains. "We need to rest whenever we can. We can't exhaust our magic with what's coming."

"Alright." Silas lets go of my hand. "We won't stop again. Head to the castle, and I'm right behind you." He leans in and kisses my forehead before disappearing into the shadows.

A part of me feels excited to shift with Larkin. Being a Lumor Wielder, the shift feels both familiar and different, as though a warm glow wraps around me when in motion. It's lighter—airier —and this time, I won't be in excruciating pain.

I extend my hand for him to grab. "Ready?"

Larkin hesitates to touch me.

"I'll never stop apologizing to you. I hope you understand that," he says, instead of taking my hand.

I softly smile at him. "I just wanted to say that I, too, would do anything to help my friends."

Larkin's jaw tenses.

"And, I'm sorry I screamed those hateful words at you. Barlowe cared for you as well. He talked about you."

Larkin glances at the ground.

"Please don't ever think that your friendship was a waste or that you let him down."

He smiles. "Thank you for saying that."

"You're welcome."

I push my hand out again for him to take, and he squeezes it before glancing toward the towering castle in the distance.

Larkin shifts into a bright ball of light, taking me with him. We swiftly move closer to the castle, and I can feel his magic starting to dull as we cover the distance. Somehow, during our journey, I burrow down and use my own magic to propel us forward.

After landing in Silas's room, both of us take a moment to

catch our breath. Moving such a distance would wear anyone out, especially after what we just experienced. A large, roaring fire lights the room, and the familiar dark space comes into focus.

Before I know it, Silas is there, leading me to the vintage furniture beside the warm flames and Maines.

I sit, and Maines rushes over, throwing her arms around my neck. I wince at the pain shooting through my upper back.

"Oh Gods, I'm sorry." Maines pulls away. "Please, can I look?"

I offer her my left shoulder. "Go ahead."

Maines pulls down Silas's large shirt, assessing the injury. She makes a few hushed noises, thinking to herself before speaking. "Who healed this?"

Larkin raises his hand, joining us around the sitting area. "That would be me."

"It's truly horrible," Maines hisses.

Larkin huffs.

"It will leave bad scars, but I believe I can help minimize them, so you won't be mangled for your whole life. But..." she adds. "You saved her life, Larkin, and for that, I'll forgive you for your foolishness."

He dips his head. "Thanks. I think."

Maines covers me up again and settles back into the couch. Oak sits across from us with a grin on his face while Silas throws a fresh shirt over his head and occupies the other chair.

"It looks like we have a lot to catch up on," Oak says, glancing at Larkin. "Come on, Spiridon. Join us."

Larkin remains planted in his spot.

"You don't have to act like you're in trouble forever."

I scoot over, letting Larkin sit next to me on the long couch and giving his back a gentle pat. The crackling fire swiftly fills the space with popping sounds that startle me each time. They chat among themselves as I keep a close eye on the door.

"Has Yara been here?" I ask, waiting for a response. "She should have been here by now."

Silas, Maines, and Oak exchange glances, deciding who among them will answer me.

"What?" I demand, and nerves immediately flood my core.

Silas leans forward. "No one has seen or heard from Yara, yet."

CHAPTER 26

I stand, making the others around me jump.

"She wouldn't just not show up," I snap.

"Maybe she's running late. We can wait a little longer." Maines grabs my hand, trying to pull me back down. "Who knows what Malachi has her up to?"

I jerk my hand away. "No, she wouldn't. You didn't speak to her; none of you did."

"Did she tell you what time she would be arriving?" Silas asks.

"No. Just that she would be with your father, and when he fell asleep, she'd be here."

"Then we're all set. It's not even 10 P.M., so there's no way he's asleep right now," Silas assures me. "We can wait a little longer."

He's right. It's still early, and I'm just rushing because I'm nervous. I sit back down and feel the others staring at me.

Oak clears his throat and strikes up a conversation with Silas. Maines settles closer to the fire, closing her eyes to prepare for the long night, while Larkin tips his head against the back of the couch next to me.

I continuously fidget in my chair, unable to sit still from the anxiety and adrenaline flickering through me like the roaring fire.

"Rest," Larkin mutters, keeping his eyes closed.

"I can't stand knowing that she is with him."

"Yara is tough and has been with him for years. She can handle herself for another night." He lifts his head off the back of the couch. "Gods, you are so much like Barlowe."

I snap my head toward him. "No, I'm not."

"Oh, yes, you are." He laughs. "You look like him when you're mad, too."

Maines sits up at that. "Oh, my Gods. She does."

Larkin gives her a soft look. He knows how close she was to Barlowe, so Maines has now become someone he cares about as well.

She settles onto the couch, getting comfortable again. The fire continues to burn as the minutes go by, and a rising anxiety begins to consume me, and every snap of the wood makes me jolt. Maines sleeps quietly to my left, Larkin rests to my right, Oak snores in the chair across from us, and Silas stands at the window.

I stand up, unable to sit any longer, and move next to Silas, to the large bay window that overlooks the kingdom and the vast sea surrounding Andorwood.

"Something isn't right," I whisper.

He looks at me, and from his gaze, I can tell he feels the same. He opens his mouth to speak, and a soft knock on the door echoes.

The sound awakens the others, and we all jump to attention. The large door slowly creaks open, and I inhale sharply, waiting for Yara to enter.

Fenmore pokes her head through the doorway, and dread floods my body. It's still not Yara. Fen enters the room and sits next to Larkin and Maines on the couch.

Silas cuts his eyes to me, knowing the devastation I feel, and he grabs my hand, pulling me from the window to join the others.

"It's nearly 1 A.M.," Fen informs us, and my stomach drops. "Did I miss the meeting?"

I look at Silas, and his gaze burns into me. He knows something is seriously wrong.

"She should be here," I say to him.

Silas responds, "I know."

"I'm heading to Malachi's office," I say, loud enough for everyone to hear.

Larkin jumps to his feet. "No, you're not!"

"He's right," Silas adds. "No fucking way are you storming into his office right now."

The others watch us, aware that an argument is about to erupt. She wouldn't be late. Yara was too serious about helping when we spoke for this to have slipped her mind. She was scared, and she needs us.

"You can both try to stop me, but I won't hold back against either of you." My eyes darken. "You can come with me or watch me walk out of that door. Alone."

Larkin crosses his arms and cuts his eyes toward Silas.

"I'm going to check on her, and I'll deal with the consequences once I know she's alright," I add. "I'm not afraid of Malachi."

"Well, you should be," Fen whispers.

Silas rolls his eyes, placing both hands on his temples. He begins to pace in front of the fire. The dancing flames bounce off his large silhouette, and the room goes silent—waiting for what's to come out of this mouth.

"Fine," Silas grumbles. "I'll go."

My brows shoot up.

"Oh, you have to be fucking joking," Larkin barks.

Silas shakes his head. "I'm not, and neither is Briar. She would leave us all, so I'm going too."

"Well, I'm not just sitting here," Larkin chimes in.

"Then either stop bitching," Silas says, "or come with us."

I watch Fen, Oak, and Maines, waiting for them to try to join in so I can shut them down. Not everyone can come in case something goes wrong, and I need to keep them safe. They are too important for our future.

"I'm coming," Maines whispers.

I jerk my head toward her. "No, you are not."

"Yeah, you are not going," Oak adds.

She nods her head. "Yes, I am. If something goes wrong, you will need me. After Larkin's shit job at healing you, I'm not letting you do this without me."

I let my thoughts swarm as I weigh the options. "Fine. You can come, but you are to stay outside the office door."

Maines smiles, and Oak sighs heavily.

"Oak and Fen, please stay back and be ready for anything," I instruct. "Hopefully, we will be back soon and can forge a plan to enter the Archives tomorrow night. If we aren't back shortly, you both shift to Silas's house and wait there."

They nod, and Oak strides across the room toward Maines. She goes tense as he approaches, but immediately relaxes as he cradles her face. His expression turns so serious that for a moment, I don't recognize him.

"Don't you dare get hurt, Miss Madden."

He gazes into her bright eyes, and for a minute, I watch Oak become completely lost in the blue sea they mirror. She smiles at him, and happiness fills her face as her cheeks turn a soft shade of pink. I turn my gaze away, feeling like I'm intruding on their moment.

"I won't," she says with a smile, leaning into his touch.

His large hand covers her entire cheek, and he hums as she closes her eyes against his touch.

"If you need me—" Oak begins to speak, but is cut off by her pouty lips crashing into his.

Her arms wrap around his neck as he dips her deeper into the kiss.

"—I'm here." He finishes his sentence as they part.

"Get a room," Fenmore laughs.

Her arms remain around his neck, and she takes her time dragging her gaze away, followed by her grip. Maines begins to walk toward the door. Just before she moves out of reach, Oak playfully slaps her ass, and she yelps playfully.

"See you soon," he calls.

"In your dreams, Hombern," she teases.

We all step into the dim hallway.

The silence of the castle surrounds us, and the flickering candles along the walls cast an eerie feeling through my veins. Our footsteps echo in perfect unison, and an unsettling chill rushes around us. The jeweled serpents on the door seem to watch us as we pass by.

Silas and I lead the way, with Larkin on my right and Maines slightly behind. Unintentionally, my shadows have already emerged, complementing the darkness around us. Faint whispers echo through the halls—barely audible—and they only add to my racing heart.

We round the corner and face the large staircase that leads us down toward the Great Hall and one step closer to the dark hallway to Malachi's office. With each step down, we descend further into darkness, and even though the room around us is expansive, the walls seem to close in around me. The bottom of the stairs is black, as if we are about to sink into a pit of darkness and despair. Silas's fingers brush against mine, and I can feel the dread surrounding him as well.

We pause just before the hidden door that leads to the hallway, followed by his office.

"Maines, you will stay outside, but nearby should we need you," Silas orders.

She agrees. "Got it."

"Larkin and I will enter first, then you behind us, Briar. Whatever we find, we will prepare as best and quickly as we can. In the best-case scenario, they both fell asleep, and the office will be empty. In the worst-case scenario..." He hesitates. "Well, we will deal with that as well."

"Yara is going to be fine." I force a smile.

"She will be," Silas reassures.

We turn and slip into the shadows.

The long stretch of hallway distorts as we move forward. The flicker of lit torches casts unnerving shadows across the walls. My senses are heightened and focused, yet I feel myself seconds away from breaking down. The large stained-glass windows glow in the moonlight, and each step feels heavier, like I'm walking into something far more grim than I know. I glance at Silas and Larkin, their faces expressionless. Both of their eyes are sharp and intensely focused on the task ahead of us, and neither shows an ounce of fear.

As we near the end of the hallway, the large door in front of us remains closed. A crow, the darkest shade of black, stares at us with jeweled eyes that seem to draw in our souls. Larkin presses his ear against the door, leans back, and shakes his head.

"I don't hear anything," he mouths.

Silas reaches for the handle, and I fear my heart might break through my chest. I glance at the others, half-convinced they can hear my pounding heartbeat. The latch clicks, and he gently pushes the wooden door. Silas steps a foot inside the office and pushes against the door harder, revealing only darkness within. Relief rushes through me immediately.

They aren't here.

Silas turns back, giving us an optimistic yet cautious look, and asks us to keep close.

Larkin trails behind him, glancing in all directions. I look at Maines, who gives me a reassuring nod before positioning herself in the small corner, ready to jump in if needed. We enter the dark office, and it's silent. The windows are all closed, and the fire was extinguished hours ago. A musty smell fills the air, and we travel farther into the darkness.

"See?" Larkin whispers. "They aren't here."

Silas moves across the room to Malachi's desk and quickly begins to look through the stacked papers. Larkin heads to a nearby bookcase, examining each spine to see if we can find the book that Yara mentioned containing the Rigil. If she isn't here, she must have returned to her room once Malachi finished with her.

I make a quick mental note to find her tomorrow to get an explanation for standing us up. Even though relief fills me, my hair stands on end, and my senses scream at me to pay attention. The office looks the same as when I first entered. Nothing is out of the ordinary, and nothing seems to be misplaced or disheveled.

I look up at the large painting above his desk that I didn't notice during my first visit. A family portrait hangs there, and I see Silas as a child—no older than twelve. Instead of a scar above his left eye, a deep wound rests freshly above his swollen, black eyelid. He doesn't smile, and he doesn't have the face of a happy child.

My stomach rolls.

I turn and face the fireplace, unable to look at the painting any longer. Only a monster would force a child to sit through that, only days after almost losing their eye. Disgust fills me, and I focus on the area before me, squinting.

A darkness—darker than the other dim pockets in the room—radiates from a chair directly facing the three of us.

I freeze.

An outline of a prominent figure sits in one of the tall chairs, and fear courses through me. I attempt to yell to get Silas and Larkin's attention, but I'm too stunned to react. I can only stare at what I see.

"Your tattoo is gone," the dark figure's voice says, as it slithers into my mind.

Tears begin to well in my eyes.

"It's a shame the creature didn't get more of its claws into you," he hisses. *"But, lucky for me, beautiful, I can sink my claws into you just fine now."*

I feel as if a razor-sharp claw drags down my freshly healed wound, and I cringe against the pain, my shoulder blade dipping in response.

The fireplace ignites, quickly filling the room with a bright light that stings my eyes. Silas and Larkin spin and rush toward me as I stand in shock. Malachi reclines in a chair with his legs crossed—as if he's been waiting for hours. A large, ancient book rests on the table before him, and my eyes widen.

That's it.

I pan my gaze to the left, and tears roll down my cheeks, noticing the figure on the ground I didn't see before. Yara lies motionless on the couch beside him. Her white hair pools over the edge of the sofa. Her body seems unharmed, but knowing Malachi, it's her mind I'm worried about.

Larkin and Silas move around me, like two opposing forces of nature. One pure darkness, the other a brilliant light of protection.

Malachi lets out a deep, haunting chuckle and says, "Hello, boys."

"What the fuck is going on?" Silas rages, and I notice his chest begin to heave.

"Do you know how long I've been waiting? I've grown impatient as I've gotten older, Silas." He casually picks at his nails. "You know you shouldn't do that, boy. It only makes me angry and creative."

"Stop toying with us, Malachi," Larkin growls. "It's obnoxious."

"Me?" Malachi snaps. "I'm sitting in my office, minding my own business. You three are the ones who charged in."

"Yara?" I whisper toward her, before glaring at Malachi.

"Poor thing isn't very sly," Malachi says, tsking as he looks at Yara's still body. "You should have prepped her better, Briar."

I step around Silas and Larkin's large bodies. "She's breathing, right?"

"Yes." Malachi stands and traces his fingers along her profile. "I knew something was at play when she arrived tonight. She had a pep in her step and asked more questions than usual, not about anything in particular, of course." He sighs, annoyance leaking off him. "She's not stupid, but she was inquisitive, which isn't why she's here. You know why she's here." He winks at the men. "Once she fucked me, quite well I may add, it was easy to slip some Dyisen in her water."

I fight the urge to gag and step toward her.

"I wouldn't do that," he warns, and I freeze. "You all will stay right there and fucking listen."

Larkin and Silas stay still, and he nods in approval at our obedience.

"I'm offended that you all think I'm the stupid one here. I know what tomorrow is, and I know Yara was going to offer you something." Malachi traces his jaw with his fingers. "There are things in the Archives that I've wanted my entire life, and if you think I'm letting you in there, you're wrong."

Malachi reaches forward, grabs the dark leather book, and tosses it into the fire.

"Wait," I shout, and defeat hits me like a blow to the face.

The book sizzles in the flames, slowly beginning to wilt around the paper edges. The leather cover turns a charred shade of brown, and the spine quickly catches fire. I watch in horror as the book slowly turns to ruin before my eyes, and realize that our chances of getting into the Archives burns with it.

I glance at Yara, and she stirs.

I need to buy us some time to get her out of here.

"What's so important in there?" I ask.

I take the split second to quickly snap my fingers toward Silas behind me to get his attention, and he notices her small movements.

"You truly have no idea how rare this is, do you?" Malachi tilts his head. "Two tethers and vessels alive at the same time? This is one in a million."

"Two tethers?" I ask.

"Of course, I have to explain everything to you." He lets out a heavy exhale. "Every vessel has a tether. Whether they ever connect or are even born at the same time is entirely up to fate. Yet, here we are." He motions between Silas and me. "The luckiest I have been in centuries."

I glance at Silas, and his face is filled with rage.

Malachi moves to the back of the couch and rests his hands on it above Yara.

"Oh, so you told him. Perfect." He glances at Silas. "How does it feel to be forced, forever linked to someone? To be their dog, to follow them no matter what, to love them even if you don't want to?"

"I'm not forced to do a fucking thing," Silas fumes.

"So, you think," Malachi responds. "But, your sister may not feel the same."

Silas steps forward, "What are you talking about?"

"Still haven't figured it out, have you?" He laughs. "You

Nastrondes, are something else. Although you are something much bigger, Silas." Malachi pauses. "If you ever opened your eyes."

"Keep speaking." Silas's shadows dance off him in chaos. "Right now."

Malachi pinches the bridge of his nose in annoyance. "Briar isn't the only vessel."

Silas goes rigid.

"And you aren't the only tether," I whisper, glancing at Silas.

I grimace as I put the pieces together. I open my mouth to speak again, but stop as another voice speaks.

"If this is a Nastronde thing…" Larkin cuts in. "And Silas is Briar's tether. That means..."

He trails off, and a heavy silence sits in the air, threatening to take the oxygen out of the room. Silas pans his gaze slowly in my direction as the words sink in. I don't break eye contact with him as I speak the words I'm fearful to let out.

"Then, Fenmore is Rohhit's."

"Ah. Maybe you are smarter than I thought," Malachi says.

Silas's stance shakes, and I grab his arm, steadying him.

"You are fucking lying," Silas says, letting his rage fuel him. "We would know this if it were true."

"Oh, Silas. You don't even know the half of it." He points at me. "But Briar knows. Well, at least more than you. Like always."

Silas slowly turns his head back to me and gives me a puzzled look, and guilt floods me.

Yara stirs once more on the couch and slowly opens her eyes. She sluggishly lifts her arms toward her face, rubbing her head for a moment before snapping to attention. In one smooth motion, she sits upright on the couch, her eyes widening—filled with desperation—as she sees us all standing before her.

"Finally," Malachi says, as he claps his hands together. "Now, the fun can begin."

Yara attempts to push off the couch toward us, but Malachi slaps both hands around her shoulders, stopping her.

"Silas can tell you how much I hate being disobeyed or lied to. Isn't that right?" Malachi asks.

Silas doesn't respond.

"As I mentioned, I know Yara was actively trying to betray me, which doesn't really sit well with me. It's alright, though, I was growing tired of her anyway." An unnatural grin spread across his face. "She can always be replaced."

"You are disgusting."

"Briar, are you available? Or possibly Maines?" Malachi pets Yara's head. "I know she hides just outside that door. She would work just fine, too."

"I'll fucking kill you before you could ever attempt to touch either of them," Silas rages.

"Fuck. Stop being so dramatic all the time. You know you can't stop the plans I already have in motion. But the torturous moments you three made me wait sparked new ideas in my twisted mind." Malachi raises a brow and glances toward the exit. "You'll regret coming here, Briar. I'll make sure of that. We didn't have to be enemies, but I quite like it. You've started a new war."

I disregard Malachi's hollow threats and can only imagine that Maines stiffened upon hearing her name in the hallway. I narrow my eyes at Malachi and vow to myself that if he lays a hand on Maines, he will die.

I look to Yara. Tears fall down her flushed cheeks. She was right about everything. Horror floods me, and I try to step forward once more.

Malachi clicks his tongue, and his haunting voice travels into my mind.

"If you move an inch, I will murder Silas and Larkin. It's fun having creatures you can't see at your mercy. Two Travelers are

right behind them, ready to drive their claws through their hearts. Should I give the order?"

I freeze and try to stifle a sob, cupping my hand over my mouth.

"Now, sweet Yara, should we show the Queen of Daramveer what happens when you betray me? Should we really give her a show?" Malachi walks around the couch and drags his finger down her arm.

He snaps his fingers again, and Yara stands abruptly, her body barely able to remain upright from the wobble in her legs. Her long white hair falls beside her, with a few stray strands crossing her face, and Malachi moves each piece like a predator toying with its prey.

"He's controlling her, Silas," I say in my mind. *"Don't move."*

I watch Silas barely nod out of the corner of my mind.

"You aren't going to make her fight, Malachi," Silas rages, but remains unmoved. "Don't be ridiculous. Let her go."

Silas also realizes that if either he or Larkin lunges, one of us will die, and he's right about that.

"You are correct, Silas. There won't be any fighting today. In fact, there won't be a struggle at all. I admit that takes away some of the fun."

Malachi reaches behind his back and pulls out a dagger.

Tears flow continuously down Yara's face as she stares at me, her dark eyes now bloodshot, filled with terror. I don't break my gaze from her. I rack my brain to think of a plan to get her over to us and away from Malachi, but everything I can think of puts us all in danger.

"Grab the dagger, Yara," Malachi orders.

She hesitates and grits her teeth. Even with him controlling her, she tries to resist the order, but it's too much. Her trembling hand reaches for the blade, wrapping her delicate fingers around the hilt.

Malachi lets her take the blade, and for a second, I wish more than anything that she would drive the dagger into his heart—if he even has one. Yara's arm drops to her side under the added weight, and she remains frozen, clutching the dagger.

"Good girl." Malachi pats her head and turns his gaze back to us.

His eyes convey an unsettling calmness, as if he's been plotting this for far too long.

"Malachi, what are you doing?" Larkin steps forward.

I grab his arm and squeeze my eyes shut, praying Malachi doesn't give the order for the Travelers around us to attack. Larkin freezes as an icy breath chills his neck. The invisible creature lurks close behind, revealing its presence. Larkin glances sideways, and Silas realizes that we are outnumbered and have fallen into an unfortunate trap. We are completely surrounded by death in every aspect.

"Please, Yara, drop the blade," I beg.

Yara attempts to unfurl her hand, but the hilt remains stuck to her hand.

"I can't, Briar," she cries. "I want to, but I can't."

Malachi leans in and kisses her cheek. "Oh, she's right. She won't be doing that."

Tears stream down my cheeks as Silas takes my hand to steady my shaking. He remains strong, but even through my trembling, I can feel a slight quiver in his. Silas understands that his father is insane, and he knows better than anyone right now the lengths to which he is willing to go.

"Stop this fucking show. Let her leave." Silas's shadows pulse in a dark threat. "She has nothing to do with this."

Malachi whispers something in Yara's ear, and a sob escapes her throat.

I squint my eyes to try to read any words escaping his lips, but I can't make anything out other than *dead*.

"I'm sorry, Briar. I should have never involved myself," she cries. "I was just trying to help."

"Just stay quiet," I say. "We are walking out of here, together."

"When I'm gone, look for where the light illuminates. Look where the light guided you that night. Search where you ended up."

Malachi snatches her arm, ordering her to stop speaking, "Enough."

"Don't say that, Yara. You're going to be fine." I assure her, but my words fumble out. I ignore the message, trying not to draw attention to her words. "Just drop the dagger and walk over here."

Look where the light guided you.

"How dare you lie to her right now, Briar?" Malachi huffs. "How will people ever trust you if you just continuously lie?"

He pulls Yara closer by the waist, and I clench my fists.

Malachi buries his face in the nape of her neck, and she attempts to recoil from his touch. He reacts to her dismissal with a huff of disgust, snapping his head away and loosening his grip around her waist. My heart pounds like thunder, and I realize our time is short. I glance at Larkin; his eyes are wide, filled with fury and distress.

"Alright, sweet Yara, it's time," Malachi orders. "Just like I told you."

He snaps his fingers again, and Yara slowly raises her arm, fighting with everything she has to resist the torment in her mind, and brings the dagger up to her throat. I freeze, my entire body trembling. I can hear Yara's rapid breathing from across the room.

The darkness inside me pounds against my chest, and I do everything I can to resist it. If I move, we will all die, but if I stay still, Yara will die.

A dark angelic voice snakes into my mind, *"Don't move, my vessel. He will kill us."*

The trembling blade moves to the center of Yara's throat, and she presses harder into her beautiful skin with each passing second.

"Don't be shy," Malachi whispers.

A small bead of blood moves down her neck, staining her shirt.

She mouths to me, "I'm sorry."

"Malachi, I swear to the Gods, order her to stop right now," Silas screams. "Stop!"

"This is what happens when you cross me." Malachi's voice takes on a sinister tone. "I feel no regret—no remorse—and I'd do this a hundred more times to prove a point."

I can't blink—I can't move—as I watch in horror as the blade presses harder into her skin. My feet control me, and I take a small step in her direction, desperation filling my core to stop this —to save her.

"Let this be an excruciating reminder," Malachi looks directly at me, "that I can and will continue to haunt whomever I want."

Larkin grabs my arm, and the icy breath moves my hair into my face. A low growl rattles my ear, and another tear rolls down my cheek. I quickly glance at the door and see Maines peeking through the slit. Her icy blue eye catching all the darkness and chaos pouring from the room. I shake my head for her to stay back and tucked into the hallway.

Malachi turns his head toward Yara to watch every second of what he's caused. He traces the side of her face gracefully, studying her beautiful features.

"Now, Yara."

The world around us pauses.

Uncaring this time of the creatures, uncaring of what will happen to me, I move. It doesn't matter; I need to help her. I spring forward. A desperate scream leaves my lips, but I'm too late—I'm always too late.

The sharp blade presses into her skin a final time and rips across her throat by her own hand, controlled by Malachi. The horrible sound reverberates through the room.

Flesh slices, and blood gushes down her torso like a flowing river. The familiar smell of gore stings my nose as I fly forward in an attempt to stop her.

A gurgled scream leaves her mouth, and Yara's body slumps to the ground with a thud that rattles the kingdom around us. I crash to the ground next to her, my hands desperate to grab her. I pick up her broken body and press it against mine as tightly as I can. The warmth of the bright blood swallows me, and I push harder, praying this is all another nightmare that I'll wake up from.

I frantically move her down to my legs and pray that I can somehow save her.

She begins to choke in my lap, blood spraying on my face, and I can't help the tears that fall onto her face. Her eyes flutter between open and closed, and I know she's fading. She's losing too much blood. Her hands clasp around her throat, and I pull her back into me.

"I'm so sorry," I cry. "I'm so fucking sorry, Yara."

I rock back and forth, letting my cries fill the room in an attempt to drown out the sounds of death under me. I press my hand against her neck as hard as I can in a poor attempt to stop the blood from flowing out. No matter the amount of pressure, the gash is too wide and too deep, and my hands become covered in blood as quickly as it leaks from her. Yara's eyes open one last time, and I watch the beautiful light in her dark eyes vanish.

No.

Oh, Gods.

"No. Please," I scream one last time.

"She's gone," Kalix's voice whispers in my mind. *"You must fight."*

I hear a loud crash behind me, and I know Silas and Larkin lunged with me, ready to fight to the death, but I don't care right now.

"*Get. Up*," Kalix's sinister voice demands.

Dark shadows and a blinding light fill the room in a chaotic dance of power. A strong wind whips my hair in all directions around me and Yara. Thunderous booms echo around me, but my hearing is muffled. The shouts are muted.

My world feels dull, my senses numb, and something within me fractures.

Blood once again drenches me, and my body turns a terrible shade of red—this is real. The gore I'm seeing is real.

Before I know it, her body stops twitching in my hold. I hesitantly look down, knowing I will regret what I'll see.

Her face is frozen in time, never to age again, and her eyes are forever closed. I know there's no use in asking her to open them; I know they won't.

But I still catch myself whispering, "Open your eyes."

Even covered in blood, she looks peaceful. Released from Malachi's hold, and on her way to the darkest realm, where she can dance unbothered for all eternity.

I feel the change take place. I close my swollen eyes and let the darkness bubble up into my chest, throat, and mind. I don't force the power down, I welcome it, and I swear I hear a sinister laugh in the breeze.

"*That's it*," the Great Wiitch whispers.

When I open my eyes, I feel the shift, as I realize my autumn gaze is now as lifeless as Yara, who lies beneath me.

I grasp the dagger from her cold, limp hand and hurl it as hard as I can.

Directly toward Malachi's head.

CHAPTER 27

I lift my gaze, my eyes now completely shrouded in darkness, as the blade spins through the air.

Silas moves around the room like a deadly warrior, unleashing bursts of black shadows toward the two horrifying creatures that have revealed their presence. The now-visible creatures look exactly like the one in the forest, their tall bodies towering over Silas and Larkin. Their skin shattered, gray, and dead. However, these creatures seem more desperate than the one in the clearing, their eyes brighter and wilder. Larkin assists in tandem, releasing bright shocks of light from his palms. His eyes are steady but reflect a hatred I've never witnessed.

Malachi remains rooted in the same place, with his back against the fireplace, watching the scene before him. His face shows no repentance, and a sense of pride hangs off his body.

The knife strikes just inches from his face, embedding itself deep into the wooden mantle. His gaze slowly shifts to me on the ground, and a broad smirk spreads across his aging face when he notices my state.

I slowly rise, Yara's blood dripping off my body, and narrow my eyes. Anger fuels me like a deadly serum, and I allow the darkness to envelop me in a warm, neglected hug. I widen my stance, dig my nails into my palms, and feel my skin pop under the pressure, sending a pinch of pain through my hands. My heart races, but my chest rises and falls steadily. I clench my jaw and calculate Malachi's next move.

"There she is," Malachi exclaims and smiles. "I've been so looking forward to meeting the real Briar Blackbyrne. You are quite stunning when you are mad."

Larkin pauses for a moment and looks at me.

"Fucking Gods," slips from his lips, as he strikes at the creatures surrounding him once more.

Between blows, Silas's deep voice echoes in my mind. *"Don't let the darkness overcome you too much. Stay in control and use it to guide you. I'm right here, my love."*

I glance in his direction as he moves gracefully, striking the creature with one dark blast after another, as if he said nothing to me. His power doesn't waver, nor does his endurance. The Prince of Darkness stands by my side, fighting like our lives depend on it.

I step forward and open my palms at my sides.

Shadows begin to swirl around my right hand as I sink down, concentrating all the power in my body to surge ahead. Looking down, the shadows are as black as night, creeping up my arm like a disease. I glance at my left hand, and through the fury, disbelief strikes me—a crackling, bright light shimmers in my left palm. The delicious tingle of lightning dances up my arm, and I smile at the new sensation. The powerful dance between shadows and light sends a wave of pleasure through me, and I snarl in Malachi's direction.

I fear no one at this moment, but everyone around should fucking fear me.

Malachi steps back, shocked by the surprising turn of events unfolding before him.

"You are full of surprises, aren't you?" he mutters to himself. "Just like your mother."

Larkin and Silas pause momentarily at Malachi's reaction.

Larkin's mouth hangs open in shock, and Silas glances at me, standing before his father amid my own beautiful destruction. A wide, menacing smile spreads across Silas's face.

Their gaze snaps back to the far window, which slowly opens. More deep growls slither into the room, asserting their presence. Four more Travelers crawl in from the black night. They share a quick glance, then move their backs to one another, continuing to fight. If I don't hurry, we will quickly be even more outnumbered.

Shadows and lightning swirl around my body, creating a storm of chaos fueled by my rage and sorrow. I allow the anger to continue consuming me, digging deeper into my magic. Thoughts of my father, Thatcher, and the trials surge in my mind, and the power begins to envelop me as my rage grows. My eyes start to lose focus, and the power surge becomes too much to continue holding on to.

"Keep going," Kalix's beautiful voice taunts my mind. *"Murder him."*

Malachi watches me closely, yet nothing in his expression reveals concern.

"Stay. In. Control." Silas says.

I inhale deeply, focusing my thoughts and strength only on the threat before me, not inside me.

A dark voice escapes my lips. "Do you want to know what I anticipated most about coming to Andorwood, Malachi?" I tilt my head with near feline movements. "Why I'll never regret setting foot on this soil?"

He tenses his brow but hesitates to move away, staring directly into my black eyes..

"I've thought about this very moment for weeks." I step forward, and a crackle of light sounds around the room.

I extend my left hand to my side in a snap, sending a shock of light crashing into the floor as the power surge illuminates the space. With the other, I do the same, but a darkness slaps the hard floor, sending a rolling smoke to travel around me.

Malachi's eyes widen in fear, and he steps back, his body flush against the wall.

"I fantasized about what it would be like to rip your fucking heart out, until I realized you don't have one." I take another step toward him. "So, my plans changed."

"You aren't going to do anything," Malachi teases.

I laugh. "Oh, that's where you are very wrong, *Your Majesty*," I say, mockingly.

Another clash of light and dark echoes through the room as it leaves my palms, while a surge of power makes the chandelier sway above us.

"I'm going to erase your entire presence from this realm. I know what you are. I figured it out, Malachi." I send another zap of power playfully in his direction as the light and darkness clash together in chaos. "You are a Traveler—just like those creatures behind us. You knew the Nastrondes were powerful, and you attached yourself to them like the fucking little leech that you are."

For the first time, his face reflects shock, and I smile, moving closer to him, no longer afraid. Malachi smiles, and before my eyes, his appearance changes. His skin dulls and slowly cracks across his face, like the shattered creature in the forest. I grit my teeth, holding on to the power dancing in my veins.

"How did you find out?" A hissing voice snakes from his mouth.

Out of the corner of my eye, I see Silas go rigid.

A crack of lightning shoots from my left hand and hits barely above his head. Malachi quickly ducks, and the short escape of magic feels terrific. I burrow back down, building my power once more, making sure to focus on the light more than the darkness.

"Your eyes. They are the same as the Traveler in the woods. I knew as soon as it got close enough." I grin, "And your wrist. I saw the skin discoloration at our first meeting. Your powers are slipping, old man."

"Smart," he says with a nod, and a different voice slips from his mouth. "Now you know why I keep to myself, and remain at a healthy…distance."

I move toward him and send another surge of power through the air.

"How did you get here?" I ask. "To this realm?"

"That's one thing I'll refrain from sharing," Malachi says with a smile. "We're similar, though, Briar. We can go places others can't, and I'll give you a reason to visit me someday soon—if you can find me, that is."

I hear Silas shout, followed by a pained scream from Larkin, that pulls me from my blinding hatred.

I quickly turn, focusing my attention on them, and a sense of dread fills me. One of the creatures swipes a claw across Larkin's chest. Their distress snaps me back to my right mind. I have to finish this. I glance back at Malachi, but only a trail of ink stains the area around where he stood.

He's disappeared, just like he promised he would.

Anger consumes me.

I scream into the air, still feeling the tingle of his fading presence.

"Coward."

Silas continues to battle the creatures alone, standing over Larkin as he struggles on the ground, clutching his chest in pain. I move my focus to the remaining Travelers with the pent-up magic I've collected this whole time. Nothing now will stop me from making sure these things never touch another person I love. Shadows dance alongside the lightning, and I grind my molars together. I shut my eyes and inhale, encouraging one last draw of power to come forward.

I step toward them and open both palms, extending my hands forward. The sensation of opposing magic tingles inside my body, and it is palpable.

I lower my gaze, and Larkin looks up at me through dazed eyes.

"Cover your head," I whisper to him.

Silas steps toward me, bringing the creatures closer for the release I desperately need to feel.

I shout to Silas, "Now."

He crouches, shielding Larkin from what's about to happen.

A small wall of shadows surrounds them, and I lose sight of them through the dark fog. My hair starts to float around me, my eyes are an unholy black, and I no longer care about what might happen to me. The room is charged, and it's time to put this magic to use.

I need to get us out of here.

I slam my palms together, and a blinding, chaotic black light erupts from me. A scream tears from my throat, making it raw.

The surge of magic that escapes my body sends waves of pain and euphoria through me. I close my eyes amidst the pleasure and pain, letting the magic flow out. The room bursts into light. The windows shatter, and glass flies everywhere, the fire is extinguished, and books scatter, but the small wall of shadows shielding my family remains strong. The creatures scream in agony, many attempting to flee. However, the blast is too sudden for them to react properly.

Before my eyes, the tall creatures begin to sizzle in the black light, and a glow reveals their shown and invisible forms.

Bones and ash rain down in the room as the entire kingdom

seems to go silent at the power and madness leaking from me and pouring into the air.

The breeze pauses, the air lightens, and the dust settles around me. I'm covered in blood and dirt, but the threat is gone.

I blink through the filth and see the wall of shadows vanish around the men. Silas crouches around Larkin, grabbing him in a tight embrace. A large amount of blood stains his shirt, but it's nothing that can't be healed. Relief floods me, and black dots dance in my vision. My legs quake, but I remain standing, flourishing in the power that still courses through my veins.

Silas stands and rushes to me, snapping both hands around my shoulders. "Look at me," he pleads. "Look at me, Briar."

I blink, unable to process what's happened.

My eyes revert to their normal autumn-gold, as if a veil passes over them, allowing me to see the room more clearly. Larkin stands and groans, still clutching his chest.

The door behind us slams open, and Maines rushes into the room. "Fucking Gods." Her chest heaves. "What just happened?"

"Go to Larkin," I manage to get out, pointing my bloody, quivering finger in his direction.

She glances between us, assessing quickly, and rushes to his side, recognizing he's the one in worse condition. Maines grabs his waist and guides him to the small sitting area as swiftly as she can without causing him pain. I brace myself for what I know is coming and squint my eyes.

Maines screams when she sees Yara's mangled body lying on the blood-stained carpet.

"Oh, my Gods." She slaps her hand over her mouth. "Yara?"

Her words ring in my ears, and tears begin to flood my eyes once more. The harsh reality of what's happened crashes down on me. I've been so blinded by hatred that I forgot where I am, what I'm doing, and who was just murdered.

"Speak to me, Briar." Silas wraps his arms around me.

"I'm…I'm here," I mumble, and bury my head into his chest.

His heart pounds against my ear, and doesn't slow.

"We need to get out of here before Malachi or the creatures return," he says, as he tugs on my arm.

Still in a daze, I let him pull me a few steps before I yank my arm away. Maines quickly tends to Larkin. His back rests against the large chair in front of the extinguished fire, and a black mist seeps from Maines' hands into his chest. He groans occasionally, but she continues to work with focus and precision.

"He's gone, Silas." I look up at his worried face. "He's not coming back."

Silas stares at me and quickly looks around the destroyed room. "I heard what you said to Malachi. A Traveler."

"I know," I respond.

"You knew?"

"Yes, but I haven't known long."

"I'll need you to tell me everything as soon as we're safe," he fumes. "No more secrets, Briar."

I open my mouth to speak, but stop.

"None," he snaps out, and I flinch.

"Hey," Larkin says, defending me from his position on the chair. "Cut her some slack."

"I am cutting her slack…for lying again."

"Get over it," Larkin barks.

"I wasn't lying to you," I say. "But Silas, with Malachi gone…"

"Do you realize what this means?" Larkin chimes in.

"Hush, Spiridon," Silas demands. "Let Maines work."

Maines's voice interrupts Silas's angry stare. "Keep still; I'm almost finished," she instructs. "You're a lucky one, Mr. Spiridon. A few inches to the right, and this would be a different story."

He grimaces and says, "I owe you."

"It's no problem. I know you would do the same. Horribly, I

might add, but the same." She smiles and pushes the final touches of magic from her palms.

"Did you hear him?" Larkin asks.

Maines eyes meet his. "Yes."

Larkin says, "Don't let his words scare you."

"Oh, he doesn't scare me," Maines responds.

His shirt is ruined and covered in blood, but the gash is now healed, leaving only a faded red scratch streaking along his sternum. Maines helps him to stand, and Larkin accepts the assistance. He glances in Yara's direction and grimaces before turning his gaze to me and Silas.

"We need to leave," Larkin calls.

Silas looks at me. "He's right. We need to go right now."

"I won't leave Yara like this," I respond, the words painfully leaving my lips.

I turn my head, unable to look at her lifeless body on the ground. Maines scans the room and finds a blanket near the couch. She rushes over to grab the fabric and unfolds the dark blanket. She drapes the soft material over Yara's body. I stare at the cloaked figure beneath the blanket and fight back the urge to sob. This could have been avoided if I had stopped her. The plan would never have worked, but I didn't object. I let her do this because my own desires blinded me.

Silas nods, knowing my wishes, and glances at Larkin. They exchange a quick, understanding nod. Silas takes my hand and pulls me closer to the door, and I try to jerk my hand away, but he holds tight.

"Let go of my hand, Silas," I snap.

"Please, just listen." His glare pierces my eyes. "Warrick will ensure Yara is taken care of."

"Take Larkin to my house," Silas orders, looking to Maines. "There should be more tonics to accelerate his healing. Fen will show you where they are."

Maines and Larkin move toward us, ready to take their leave, but hesitant to leave us behind.

"Taken care of? No. I'm not just leaving her here alone. She deserves respect." I snap.

"And she will have it, Briar. But we can't stay here another minute." Silas's eyes are serious and carry a look of anger; this time, I know it's aimed at me. "Warrick is going to notify her family. They are going to honor her." Silas's voice is harsh as he turns to speak to Larkin and Maines. "You two, go."

She gives me one last look of sorrow and grabs Larkin's hand. They turn to mist before my eyes, leaving me alone with Silas and Yara's body. Grief overwhelms me, and I feel as if I'm a second away from spiraling.

"You are being heartless." I rip my hand from his hold.

Silas glances at Yara's body lying beneath the fabric. "Do you truly think I'm heartless? After everything?" He releases a long exhale. "I'm trying to ensure your safety. I'm trying to keep us all safe."

I flinch.

"They will have a ceremony for her. I will do whatever I can to ease this pain. I swear it to the Gods, my love." His voice rises nearly to a shout. "But you must stop lying to me."

"I didn't lie to you," I whisper, and the guilt layered on top of my grief nearly pushes me over the edge. "I just didn't know how to tell you."

He cradles my face in his trembling hands. "I'm trying to keep someone I love from being the next to die, but you're making it impossible when you withhold vital information."

Silas releases his grip and turns away from me.

The distance between us feels icy, and I can't stop my hands from shaking. He gazes across the expansive room, and I realize he's focused on the family portrait on the wall. He examines each face, frozen in time.

His sister is so small compared to the others in the painting. Her long black hair falls messily around her, and she smiles. She is so young and naïve compared to the pain the others experience.

His mother, her beautiful face both regal and troubled, hands resting on both of her children, and I know she's doing all she can in every moment to shield them from the monster next to them. Even from the gentle touch the photo portrays, I see now, she is protecting them… from him.

Even in the portrait, Malachi's hauntingly aged visage seems to pierce through you. No kindness is evident behind his eyes, and even in the delicate paint strokes, a bright flicker of green dances within them. His irises glow unnaturally, as if even they are desperate to show the real him.

And there's Silas— the fresh wound above his eye, the bruising, and such sadness in his young eyes—forever marked on canvas in a mockery of his actions. He's not even a teenager yet, but his demeanor feels much older. I hadn't noticed it before, but both of his fists are clenched tightly.

Silas turns back to me, meeting my gaze, and I notice something shift in his eyes that I can't quite place. For a brief moment, I could swear I saw a tear that quickly vanished. Silas stands taller, his shoulders broader, and he tucks his hands into his pockets.

"Our royal bloodline comes from my mother's side," he explains. "We have to tell her what's happened."

"I understand."

"Malachi is gone?" he asks.

"I think so." I nod. "Yes."

"Where?" He snaps.

"I'm not sure."

He grabs my hand and pulls me through the door into the long hallway leading back to the central part of the castle. The air feels lighter out here, and I am thankful we left the room. It was too heavy in there, and with each passing second that I stayed there with Yara's body, I felt myself slipping away. Silas remains at a distance from me, giving me time to protest, but I don't. I stare at him, watching the wheels turn in his mind.

"I'm going to make sure that we give our respects to Yara. She deserves to be at rest, and Warrick will take care of it. I'm sorry, Briar. I'm so fucking sorry." Silas lowers his head. "Malachi is a monster, and I didn't stop him."

I blink in surprise at his apology. "He would have killed us all, Silas. If anyone is to blame, it's me."

"It's not your fault, and don't say that again. You did what we all thought was right. You were risking more than just Yara by going through with that; I hope you understand that."

I nod.

"Yara wanted to help. She was brave, braver than any of us could have been. She will be recognized as such, I promise." Silas stops and turns to face me. "One day, things are going to change. Andorwood is going to change, and I'm going to do everything in my power to ensure that."

I nod, knowing everything he speaks is true.

"It's an intense weight to carry," Silas says.

"I know the feeling."

"Do you also know the feeling of constantly trying to keep you safe?"

I don't respond.

"I nearly fucking break every single day, worried about your life."

"Stop worrying so much, then," I say.

"I can't," he says. "And I'll never stop keeping you safe. I won't rest until I know this is over—all of it—and I know for a fact that it's only us. Just me and you."

He closes the distance between us, cupping my face once more with intensity.

"Tell me you are okay," he rasps. "Please, look me in the eyes and tell me the truth."

I hesitate and stare into his eyes.

"I deserve the truth," he whispers.

"I'm not okay."

He nods. "Let me help."

"I don't know how you can."

"I'm tethered to you, Briar," he says. "Let me carry some of this load with you. Lean on me—use me—and when you are feeling weak, take my strength. Take fucking all of it, because I'll give it to you willingly."

A tear falls down my cheek.

"I'll give you anything," Silas whispers.

"What do you need?" I ask. "This isn't a one-way street. I can help you, too, Silas."

He doesn't respond at first. Instead, he looks at me—truly looks at me—and my breath hitches.

"To be honest," Silas says. "I need you right now, or I'll fucking fall apart."

I'm taken aback when he crashes his lips against mine. Lost in the moment, the realization hits me, and I understand why Silas is stunned—speechless, and overwhelmed. It's not only death that lingers around us. It's about what just changed. Changed with him, our future, and Andorwood.

He pulls away and gently traces my profile with his finger.

I stare into his intense green eyes.

Silas, my Silas. I watch as shadows begin to swirl around him, as if a new surge of power has entered his veins. His shadows seem darker, like something just snapped into place.

Andorwood is going to change from here on out. Everything we've feared has just opened up for us: a new beginning, a new future, and a new power in charge.

"My love," he whispers, his forehead pressed to mine. "My queen."

"King," I reply. "You are the king, Silas. King of Andorwood."

CHAPTER 28

The cliff surrounding Silas's house is silent, with the exception of the crashing waves below. We land, hand in hand, facing the flickering lanterns on the shadowy porch. Silas takes a moment to catch his breath and admire his house before us. I'll never get over the quaint, deceptive façade of this house, and I make a mental note to burn this image in my mind. I'll never tire of its small beauty. The front door opens, and Warrick steps out of the shadows. Even in the darkness of night, his light hair shines, and an unmistakable Lumor aura floats around him.

His tall figure looms larger as he approaches, and his footsteps are almost silent in the late-night air. His expression is typically stern, but it softens when he sees Silas, because he knows. He knows that he now looks upon someone different. His friend, his commander, his new king.

"Larkin told us what happened." Warrick's voice remains steady and calm. "I'm really sorry, Briar."

"Thank you," I say, as I force a smile.

"Let me know what I can do to help," he smiles. "I'm here for you."

Warrick's eyes shift to Silas.

"And for you."

Silas stands tall, our hands still intertwined, waiting for the words to leave Warrick's lips regarding the new status of the kingdom. Warrick starts to bow, and Silas extends his hand, his palm pushing against his leaning shoulder, halting him.

"Please," Silas says. "Don't."

Warrick stands upright from the push. "All right. No bowing, then. But my Gods, I never thought I'd live to see the day. Silas Nastronde, King of Andorwood."

"Things are going to change." Silas slaps Warrick's shoulder with a smile. "But, we have much to do before that happens."

Warrick's smile fades, and he glances over his shoulder toward the house in the distance. I look around him, half expecting someone to be standing there, but only darkness greets my stare.

Warrick moves away from the contact and says, "You need to know something, Silas."

"Can it please wait?" Silas asks, defeated.

Warrick shakes his head and glances toward me. I make a pained face, and nod for him to keep going.

"Hux is gone."

"What do you mean, gone?" Silas questions.

"No one can find him." Warrick lowers his head. "We think he left."

My stomach drops.

"With Malachi."

Silas runs his hands through his hair and pauses to massage his temples. "Find out. Immediately." He shoots a look in my direction, and I immediately look at the ground.

"I told you," I say, privately.

"Absolutely the wrong time for gloating," he snaps.

"Where is Fen?" Silas demands, speaking to Warrick.

Warrick almost recoils and tosses a look over his shoulder toward the house. "In there, waiting on you."

Silas nods.

"She's pretty shaken up." Warrick fidgets.

I hadn't even considered Fen and her reaction to everything. Not only has Silas's world just changed, but so has Fen's. Silas had months to come to terms with everything outside of his father's truth, while she had been thrown into turmoil in a matter of minutes. I can't imagine how she's feeling. She needs her brother right now.

"Are you alright?" Silas asks Warrick.

He sighs, and his lips form a thin line. "She's a tether? Like you?"

Silas responds, "Yes."

"She's linked to someone else, whether she accepts it or not, for the rest of her life?" Warrick glances back at the house, as if he can see her.

"She is," I answer, giving Silas a break.

"What if she doesn't want this? What if *I* don't want this?" he asks, and I can't help but notice the pain in his voice.

I shake my head. "I'm not sure, Warrick, but it doesn't always mean what you think. Fen can be a tether without having any romantic feelings. It doesn't have to be like ours."

Warrick stares at me. "And you know this for a fact?"

I don't respond.

He shifts his gaze back to Silas. "Could you do what you do for Briar and not feel anything more?"

Silas winces. "No..." He pauses before adding, "I don't think so."

His hand tightens around mine.

"That's what I thought." Warrick shakes his head. "I'm going to do what you've asked of me, Silas. I'll return by midmorning."

"Warrick." Silas tries to stop him. "We can figure out another plan if you need a moment."

"You are my king now. I will obey your orders, Your Majesty. It's my job."

"This isn't about work right now, Warrick," Silas says.

Warrick shrugs.

"Come on," I say, also attempting to stop him. "Just take some time, please."

His gaze finds mine, and such sadness sits behind his dark eyes—as if the devastation is trying to break free.

"Just take a second," I repeat.

"I will," Warrick says. "Alone."

Warrick shifts, a trail of light following him as he heads toward the castle to attend to Yara. The thought of her pains me, and I fear I'll never get over the events that transpired tonight. The image of her slitting her own throat plays over and over in my mind, and I wish I could erase it from my memories. I feel broken and defeated, but I know the others need me right now. I can't crumble just yet, even though I feel seconds from bubbling over.

Her family will know of her bravery, and they will make sure she is laid to rest. It's only fair they get to say their goodbyes. My stomach drops, thinking of Warrick having to tell them. A mother getting a house call like that makes me want to spill my guts on the ground.

Silas squeezes my hand, realizing I'm lost in the shadows of my mind, and plants a kiss on the top of my head.

"She won't be forgotten," Silas whispers. "And he will be okay. Warrick's the strongest man I've ever met."

I nod. "I know."

He gazes toward the house, and I know the shadows of his own mind start to haunt him.

"Will you speak to Fen with me?" Silas asks.

I glance up at him. "Don't you think it would be better to talk to her privately? I wouldn't want to intrude."

"I want you there. She respects you. Also, she will have questions, and you can help me answer them. I want her to have as much information as she can handle."

"Then, let's go."

Silas smiles softly, and we walk toward the house.

When we enter the small upstairs area, the house is silent. I can only imagine what time the others went to sleep, and I'm grateful they are getting rest. Exhaustion hangs over my body, and I, too, am desperate for sleep. We all need it right now, but that can wait—it always does.

The stairs creak under our weight as we descend into the darkness below, into the heart of the house. The sound of crackling fire hits my ears, followed by its warmth, and I almost groan from the safety this house always seems to offer. The living area opens up, and I scan the room looking for signs of Fenmore. A muffled cry sounds from the sitting area, and I look up at Silas, who spots her first.

Fen sits in the large antique chair, her arms wrapped tightly around her legs—as if she's trying to cave in on herself. Her face is buried in her knees, and I can hear faint sniffles coming from her. I glance to the left, where Larkin is sleeping in a chair near the hallway. His broad chest rises and falls peacefully, but his positioning looks miserable. His large body barely fits in the chair, but I can't help but feel thankful he stayed by her side.

As our presence makes itself known, she slowly lifts her head in our direction.

She stands from the chair and runs toward us. Tears stream down her cheeks like fresh rain, and her eyes are swollen. She wraps her arms around both of us and squeezes tightly. Silas returns the embrace, encircling us, and I feel a sense of relief wash over us all.

Silas pulls away from the embrace and ushers Fen back to her chair to take a seat. I move toward Larkin and gently pat his shoulder. The touch startles him, and he jolts awake.

"Shit," Larkin yelps.

"Go to bed," I whisper. "We're going to talk to Fen."

Larkin looks around the room, spotting Silas, and gives me a sleepy nod. His gaze settles on Fen. He stays fixated on her, as if he can't trust that she's okay.

"Did Warrick already leave?" Larkin whispers.

"Yes." I lean closer, not wanting to draw attention to us. "He's going to…" I pause.

"You don't have to say it, I know where he went."

He looks back at Fenmore. "I didn't know what to say to help."

"Sometimes you can't help."

He nods.

"She's going to be alright." I pat his shoulder and smile. "Now, go."

His expression softens as he rubs his eyes. "Wake me if you need me. I'll be down the hall."

Larkin rises with a groan, his healing wound still tender, and shuffles down the long hallway, vanishing into the darkness.

I join Silas and Fen, sitting cross-legged on the floor around the warm fire, and pull a blanket around me. The chill from the night seems to have settled in my bones. Fen merely stares, her eyes darting between us, and as always, she clutches her necklace, using her finger to trace the smooth parts of the beautiful stone.

Silas starts, "First, what do you know?"

Fen slowly meets his stare. "I think everything?"

I stay quiet, giving them time to speak and work things out as siblings. My chest aches thinking about Barlowe and how I wish we had more time to discuss things. We were too stubborn and impatient. There are many things I regret about our relationship. I think of Maines's offer of a ritual for closure, but I quickly shake the temptation from my mind.

"Alright, I'll go ahead and start," Silas responds into the silence. "Everything went terribly wrong tonight, Fen. Malachi killed Yara."

She nods, and tears well up in her eyes again. A pang of pain strikes my chest at the sound of her name.

"Warrick is at the castle now, cleaning everything up. We are going to make sure she is laid to rest by her family."

Fen responds, "I know that much. Warrick talked to me about that."

Silas sighs and continues, "Malachi isn't our father, and I'm grateful to have learned that. Although it's about thirty years too late. He's a real monster, just as we've known our whole lives, a Traveler—a leech that latched onto our family years ago—and now he's gone."

A sob leaves her throat. "Silas, you are the King of Andorwood now."

"Yes."

"Thank Gods." She leans forward, hugging him once more.

"I know you know there is more," Silas says, leaning away again.

The conversation falls silent, and Fen buries her head in her lap again. She hugs her legs tightly, allowing the words racing through her mind to sink in.

"I'm like you," she replies, lifting her head.

"Yes."

"I am a tether."

He offers her a soft smile. "You are."

Fen looks at me, and a tear rolls down her cheek. She glances back at Silas, silently trying to process what she's learned, and accepting something I believe she already knew. I extend my hand and grasp hers. I hold on tight, feeling her tremors take hold.

"That's who has been calling to me."

Silas shifts in his seat. "It's odd at first, like a whisper of a breath, but you get used to it."

I attempt to understand how this may feel for them, but I'll never know.

"Do you know…" I try to speak, but she cuts me off.

"Rohhit," she whispers.

I can't help the shock that crosses my face, and I see Silas stiffen from the corner of my eye.

"I'm Rohhit Harte's tether," she says aloud, and I can feel the fear and relief she experiences as those words come into the open.

"Yes, you are," I respond, giving Silas time to also process this.

He grabs my hand.

"It's going to be okay, though. Silas and I can help you through this."

"I hear him sometimes, screaming. It's horrible, Briar. He sounds so far away, so desperate for help. I didn't realize that was happening, but it started about three weeks before you came home."

When Rohhit was possessed.

I think to myself.

That's when the tethers snap into place.

"What?" Silas snaps.

"I didn't want to worry you, and I was confused. I knew about your dreams and Briar's, but I never thought the same thing would happen to me. They started blurry—as if watching the events unfold through a haze—yet they began to build, and the devastation of the dreams started to take over." Fen chokes up. "They are using him, Silas. They are making him do horrible things that he doesn't want to do. He's fighting, I can feel it, but he's losing."

"Is that why you've been having headaches?" I question.

"I believe so, yes." She wipes her eyes. "I want to go to him. I need to go to him; it's difficult to ignore."

Silas straightens. "You need to ignore it."

I snap my attention to him. "What? Are you out of your mind?"

"It's too risky, Briar. I can't let her wander off searching for Rohhit."

I narrow my eyes at him. "And what would you have said if she told you to ignore the pull you felt toward me?"

He doesn't respond.

"Fen, resisting this is going to be impossible. Do you think you can help? Do you think you could pull him back?" I ask.

"I'm not sure. He doesn't even know me, although I feel like I know him deeply." She furrows her brow. "Why would he listen to me?"

"Oh, he'll listen," I add. "It's impossible to ignore, believe me, and hopefully, this means he isn't too far gone, and we can still save him."

Silas looks at me, his jaw tightening. I know he's reeling, thinking about when he experienced this exact situation. He felt deeply for me long before he ever knew me, the intense pull of the tether constantly tugging at him to find me. He's horrified watching Fen go insane over someone he's disliked for a long time. He hates this, and I know he feels her pain. I can't blame him. Asking Fen to do this is dangerous, and there's no way to know what she's walking into. She'll have to face this alone.

Silas sighs. "Then we will come up with a plan, Fen."

"He needs me," she whispers. "And somehow, I feel like I need him, too."

"It's the pull," Silas says, understanding exactly what she means.

"It hurts," she admits, as another tear falls down her cheek.

Silas studies her, and grief settles into his core.

"I'll help you get stronger with this, and after that, you will help Rohhit," he announces, understanding her pain. "I'll help you get to him."

She looks up with swollen eyes. "Really?"

"Yes," Silas breathes. "I can't imagine someone telling me to ignore what I felt for Briar. The pain I would have endured by burying that natural instinct, and the desperation I felt to protect her, would have consumed me. It would have destroyed me, and I'll never let you experience that."

A broad smile brightens her face as she leaps forward to hug both Silas and me. Her bright green eyes shine in the crackling fireplace, and a sense of familiarity washes over me when I see them. After letting us go, she settles back into the large chair, snuggling up to a nearby pillow.

"I'm worried about Warrick," Fen confesses. "He's such an amazing guy."

Silas makes a face, and I nudge him.

"You two will figure this out, I promise." I smile.

She tilts her head to the side, resting in the chair, and closes her eyes.

Silas takes my hand and pulls me to my feet. We're all worn out, and nothing sounds better to me than resting my head on a pillow beside Silas. We tiptoe toward the hallway, keeping quiet to let Fen get some much-needed sleep.

"Silas?"

We hear her voice calling from the chair. We both turn around and see her sitting back up, a look of concern painted across her beautiful face.

"Yeah?" Silas asks.

She hesitates, as if the question is too painful to ask, and Silas angles his head, waiting for her to continue.

"If Malachi isn't our father, who is?"

Even the breeze seems to freeze around us. His body goes rigid against mine as he's asked a question he never thought he would face in his life.

"I don't know, but I'm going to find out."

CHAPTER 29

"*ake up!*" A hissing voice wakes me from my sleep. I sit straight up and scan the dark room before me, trying to calm my pounding heart. Beads of sweat line my brow as I throw the covers back, seeking some air. The window is open, and for a moment, I swear I see the tail of a long black cloak moving through the window into the dark sky from the familiar dark creature that I think enjoys haunting me these days.

I rub my sleep-filled eyes and see the room mostly shrouded in darkness. The faint outline of the antique furniture fills the space, and through the crack in the heavy curtains, I can see a subtle glow indicating that dawn is near but not yet here.

Gods, this creature is going to fucking age me.

I slip out of bed and wrap a blanket around my shoulders to guard from the cool morning air. I tiptoe across the cold floor and open the door that leads to the spacious sitting area in the main part of the house. The house is silent, and I push my way through the door and into the darkness of the narrow hallway.

The hall ends, revealing the vast living room before me. The brightness of the new day is still about an hour from reaching us, so it's dim, but my eyes adjust quickly. I walk toward the long table and pull out a chair to sit for a moment, when a figure on the balcony catches my eye. I jump in shock at the sight of someone else being awake.

I creep toward the balcony and instantly recognize the person standing before me, holding a hot cup of tea. The scent of thyme and lavender reaches my nose in the crisp morning air, calming my racing heart.

Rose stands on the balcony, wrapped in a blanket and sipping freshly made tea. She turns as she hears me approach, and a bright grin spreads across her, lighting up the area around us.

"Good morning, my little shadow," she greets, smiling. "Always creeping in the darkness, aren't you?"

"I didn't think anyone was awake."

I step further onto the balcony and join her, resting my hands on the railing, and wrapping the blanket around me tighter. She looks at me and studies me for a moment. I wish more than anything that things were back to normal and we were in the kitchen in Daramveer with Lang grumbling to himself about something. But, things weren't normal then; we just pretended they were for the sake of sanity.

"I'm old, Briar," she chuckles. "You know I don't sleep much anymore."

I let the silence of the early morning fill the vast space once more. She places the cup in her left hand and slides her right across the railing to grasp mine. The darkness of the morning begins to fade, and I know the dawn of a new day is approaching. Today will be challenging, and I can't help but let the dread filling my chest bubble up.

"You alright, kid?" she asks.

"Things have gone horribly wrong," I respond. "And someone died because of me."

Rose angles her head and says, "It wasn't your fault, Briar, and I need you to know that."

"That's easy for you to say," I say, with a heavy sigh.

"Do you think if you were able to speak to Yara right now, she would blame you?"

I shake my head. "No, she wouldn't blame me."

"I don't think so, either. Her blood is not on your hands; that is not a mark you have to bear."

"I feel as if I'm somehow stained," I add. "Like the constant blood will mark me permanently after a while."

"It will."

I snap my gaze to hers.

"You will always feel the weight of what's happened in your past," she says. "But, that weight doesn't have to pull you down."

I listen to her intently.

"You need to use that as a driving force to stop this. To make sure the evil is stopped. Don't get over what happened; get angry. And then, get angrier."

"And then what?"

"Then, you can start living the life you are meant to have." She smiles, adding, "With that handsome boy of yours."

I laugh, letting her words crash upon me like the waves below.

That's a thought.

After this is over, what will my life be like?

What is the life I'm meant to be living?

I sigh and turn to her. "I need to ask you something."

She nods, giving me time to find the courage to speak again.

"My mother…"

"Go ahead," she replies. "Don't let mere words make you nervous."

"Was my mother a Dusk Wielder?"

She smiles and turns her gaze back to the sea before us. Her dark eyes reflect in the water, and I watch her, this time allowing her the space to process the question.

"She was, yes."

I nod, having already assumed the answer to my question.

"A gifted one at that," Rose continues. "She kept her magic extremely private. Very few people knew of her wielding abilities," she replies.

"Not even me."

"Why did you think to ask this?"

I only gaze at her before taking a second to look at my stained hands.

She knows the answer to that question, and I make a puzzled expression.

"I see," she says. "You have the same ability, don't you?"

"I had no idea. I was scared and desperate, and I prayed for light in such a dark time. I felt like I was drowning."

"And?" she pushes, not allowing time for the words to catch in my throat.

"Before I realized it, light burst from my body, saving me, and Yara helped me escape."

"Fear has a strange way of making us act. I'm not surprised, though." She shakes her head. "You resemble your mother so much, and when you stopped using magic, I knew your powers would only be postponed."

"You knew?"

"Call it a hunch," she says, and smiles.

She turns to face me fully and grabs both of my hands.

"Your eyes brighten more each day. Have you noticed?"

"I don't look at myself in the mirror much," I admit.

"Well, you should. You're stunning. I'd look at myself all day, every day, if I looked like you," she replies, with a smile.

"Oh, please."

She huffs a laugh.

"You know, there's a way to change your eyes, to hide your abilities from those around you. It's how your mother managed to conceal her powers from the outside world."

"But, I always knew my mother had these autumn eyes." I attempt to pull my hands away, but she holds firm. "I suppose I never thought to ask. I feel foolish remembering the things I always swept under the rug."

"She wanted you to see them, Briar." She squeezes my hand. "And you were young. No one thinks about things too deeply when you're young. We all have things we regret, my shadow."

I furrow my brow and fight back the urge to blame myself for everything once again.

I was naïve and only thought of myself. My mother tried to warn me and tell me many things, but I ignored her advice. My thoughts start to spiral, but I choke down the overwhelming feeling.

"I don't want to hide my eyes. I want people to see who and what I am."

"Then don't. Give the people someone to fear." She winks, nudging my shoulder. "Give them a reason to look at you, not away from you."

I smile at her support and continuous understanding.

"Things are going to fall into place one day. You're going to make it out of this."

"And if I don't?" I ask.

Rose chuckles. "Briar Blackbyrne, you would never let that happen. You're too stubborn for that." She glances over her shoulder, looking into the dark house. "We often try to talk ourselves out of showing our greatness. It's easier to hide because it's comfortable. We pretend we don't want more in our lives, but we all do. We all want to achieve great things, yet some never get the chance."

I look into the dark house with her, but nothing catches my eye.

"You have that chance," she says, returning her gaze to me. "Don't waste it."

A tear sits heavy in the corner of my eye. "But, I've already failed so much."

"My shadow, we all fail. But, those who choose to view their failures as new beginnings are the ones who emerge from this life feeling fulfilled."

I let the tear roll down my cheek, and like so many times before, Rose is there to wipe it away.

"Don't fear your future or the things that lie beyond the horizon. Face them directly and tell them that you are Briar Black-byrne, and you don't give a fuck."

Her cursing surprises me, and a laugh escapes my throat. She joins in on the laughter and tilts her head to the sky. Her long white hair flows beautifully beside her. She resembles my mother so much, and even through the grief, worry, and devastation, she's stunning. I gaze at her, memorizing her silhouette, and I remind myself that no matter what happens, I have someone in this cruel world who loves me as much as my mother did.

"Get going," she orders. "You have a big day today, and you have a beautiful man asleep in your bed. If I were you, I would never get up."

"Oh Gods, Rose." I nudge her arm and chuckle. "You need to stop spending so much time with Maines."

Rose pulls me into an embrace. "I love you, shadow."

I squeeze her tightly and inhale deeply, savoring her wonder-fully familiar scent. "I love you, too."

I peek my head back into our dim room and see Silas on his side, still fast asleep. Dark amber hues fill the room with the first light of day, and I climb back into bed next to him, closing my eyes. The sheets are warm, and the room is silent except for Silas's calm breathing. I giggle to myself, and think—*this man could sleep through a hurricane.*

I look out the window, gazing at the vast ocean stretching endlessly before us, the water as black as the previous night, but somewhat reflective in the morning light. The waves crashing against the cliff wall have quickly become one of my favorite sounds. It's peaceful, yet forever churning. I feel I resemble the ocean, always restless and moving. I lie here in this moment, wishing that the days ahead wouldn't come and I could stay here forever, warm and calm next to Silas. Rose's words replay over and over in my mind, and she's right. I'm going to stop fearing what's coming and get prepared.

Silas begins to wake, and I hear a soft groan leave his throat. He rustles in the dark sheets, and I feel a hand move closer to my body under the covers. He pushes his arm under the small of my back and pulls me toward his body. His shirtless chest pushes against my back, and Silas buries his head into the crook of my neck. As quickly as he stirs, he falls back asleep, his breath steadying once more with the knowledge I'm there.

I look down at his arms locked around me. Small, aged scars from fighting line them, and I trace each one with my fingers, thinking about what he has endured in this life. I roll onto my back, still held in his embrace, and stare at the ceiling. The room quickly fills with a bright glow from the rising sun, and my surroundings come into sharper focus. I continue to caress his arms, trying to remain this relaxed for as long as possible. Thoughts of what's coming start to intrude, and I close my eyes.

Stop, Briar. Relax.

I can't stop moving restlessly.

Silas stirs again, inching closer to the nape of my neck, and I shift my hand from his arm to the side of his face. He leans into my touch but keeps his eyes closed.

"Do you ever sleep?" he mumbles.

"Not like you," I respond. "You sleep like a bear...or a corpse."

He chuckles and cuddles closer, kissing the back of my neck. "And I thought I was the grumpy morning person."

I turn to face him fully, and he opens his eyes. His familiar green eyes gaze into mine, and I relax. His face is handsome, and his eyes are drowsy, still filled with sleep. Silas smiles softly and moves his hand to my cheek. He doesn't speak, only stares, and I think he's memorizing my face, studying me so he never forgets this simple moment between us.

"I'm not grumpy, by the way." I grin.

"Oh, sure," he teases, and tickles my side. "And I'm the resident funny guy."

I squirm and yelp from his touch, but quickly snuggle back into him.

"More like the resident chronic worrier."

He laughs at that.

Silas leans in and kisses me, slow and gentle. His hand wraps around and cups my ass, pulling me even closer to his hot body. His chest presses against mine, and I change the pace. I move my hips against his and deepen our kiss. My hand moves to the back of his neck, and his tongue moves around my mouth, tasting how perfect we are together. A low groan leaves his throat as I continue to push my hips even closer to his. Silas's hand squeezes my ass while his other becomes tangled in my messy hair.

I move my hand from his neck and slowly trace my fingers down his chest, his abs, and his hips, grabbing exactly what I want at this moment. My core quickly becomes molten at the feel of his hard length in my hand, and an exciting tingle moves through my system. He jerks against my hold, and I smile against his mouth.

"Good morning to you, too," he laughs.

Silas returns the favor and slowly guides his hands down my torso, but not before cupping my breast for a second. His large hands trace each curve of my body and slide into the waistband of my pants.

Before I have time to react, two fingers plunge inside of me, and a moan escapes my throat.

Silas presses his mouth against mine once more, muffling the sound, and he begins to pump his soaked fingers in and out of me. I hold tight to his hardened cock and slowly move my hand up and down. His lips break from mine, and he kisses the side of my mouth and jaw before he moves to my neck, slowly kissing and licking as his hand continues to work. I grind my hips against his touch, allowing his fingers to move deeper inside of me.

I close my eyes and allow the pleasure to build. Silas moves from my side and positions his body over mine. His fingers leave me, and I immediately feel empty and huff in protest. His eyes pierce into mine, and there's nothing of the earlier softness in his gaze. A hunger lies behind them, and my mouth waters. Silas slowly removes my pants and orders me to remove my shirt, leaving me completely bare before him.

With his knee, he spreads my legs further, allowing space for his body to lie on top of me. I feel him lower his pants, and a thrill runs through me, already intensifying the heat in my core.

He pauses and looks at me.

"I've been dying to fuck you."

His fingers tease around my clit, sending a jolt through me.

"Just looking at you drives me mad," Silas groans, glancing up and down my body. "I've been dying to shove my cock deep inside of you, Briar.

I feel him remove his dick from his pants.

"Ever since our night in the woods. You left me craving you, and I've been desperate to worship you ever since."

My mouth parts slightly, and I swear I'm seconds away from losing it from just those words.

"Then worship me, Silas."

I grab his dick and move him toward the middle of my thighs.

"Show me how well you can fuck me."

He hums.

"Remind me how perfect we are together," I encourage.

A grin spreads across his face as shadows pulse around him. A wall of dark shadows swiftly surrounds us, providing all the privacy we need in this house. Silas winks at me, assuring me that his shadows will hold, and I respond with a dazed smile.

Silas thrusts his hips against mine, and I feel his hardened length slam into my core. A cry leaves my lips, and I arch my back against the warm sheets. Silas moves his arm under my lower back, propping my hips higher, allowing him to thrust deeper.

"Scream my name, Briar. No one can hear you except the Gods. Let them know who fucks you right now, who you belong to."

I grasp his back and claw into his skin, letting myself completely give in to him. I slowly move my hands lower and cup his ass, encouraging him to slam into me harder.

"Silas," I moan.

He buries his head into the nape of my neck and bites, sending a wave of pain to mix with pleasure. His breathing is rapid and hard, and I forget everything around me. He thrusts in and out of me, making my eyes roll back in utter bliss.

I lift my knee and push with everything I have to flip on top of him.

The abrupt movement causes a look of shock and excitement to shoot across his face as we land with me straddling him. I position myself back over him and lower onto his length once more, taking my time to feel every inch.

A deep guttural moan leaves his throat as he slowly slides into my core. My legs work to lift me up and down over him, and I watch his eyes change from hungry to absolutely drunk with lust. His hands dig into my sides, helping me rock back and forth, and I tip my head back, allowing him a great view of my undulating body.

I lean forward to grab his hands and pin them over his head.

I gaze into his eyes and smile.

"Eyes on me, Silas," I say. "I want you to watch only me."

Silas Nastronde, the King of Andorwood, is completely helpless under my weight. I kiss him slowly, biting his lower lip as I pull away. Shadows and light dance around my body, and I feel myself seconds away from losing control.

His piercing green eyes bore into mine as I ride his cock, feeling every delicious inch of him moving inside me. I lower my gaze, slowly sliding up to his tip, and hover there for a moment.

"Turns out, I want you to scream my name, Silas. The Gods can't hear you, because I am your only God. You belong to me."

His eyes widen with excitement, and I slam my hips down, going as deep as I can handle.

"And don't ever fucking forget that."

Pleasure explodes through us both, and my body tingles with lightning from the inside out. I arch my back, and Silas rips his hands from my hold, grasping onto my hips once more. His strong fingers dig into my skin. Silas groans deep and wild, throwing his head back and slamming his hips upward. The world pauses, my worries don't exist, and I allow pleasure to slam through me.

I collapse forward, our chests resting together. He heaves under me and moves his hands into my dark hair that pools around us. We remain this way for a moment, lost in pleasure and one another.

Silas moves, flipping me back onto the bed, and props his elbow near my head. His hands trace alongside my profile as I work to catch my breath, before he drops his head onto my chest.

"Fuck, Briar."

I smile proudly.

The dark shadows around us start to fade, and the sounds of the outside world fill the space once more. The crashing waves hit the cliff wall, the morning sun shines through the open windows, and the sound of movement echoes down the long hallway.

I close my eyes, and my body relaxes into the warm bed. I want to stay this way forever, in peace—in the stillness of a new day—and near Silas.

As much as I try to ignore our reality, the weight of the day slowly begins to press against my chest, and I look at Silas, turning to face him.

"I wish we could stay this way forever," I say, as I cup his face.

He presses a kiss to my lips and smiles, but it doesn't reach his eyes.

"You always ask me, but I never ask you. Are you okay?" I sigh. "Last night was…a lot."

I regret the words as soon as they leave my mouth. I should have allowed more time for us to remain in peace and together, uncaring of the troubles that constantly surround us.

Silas stares at me for a moment, his eyes hardening. "I'm fine."

"Now who is lying?" I cut my eyes toward him.

"That man was never a father to me. He won't be missed."

The room is filled with a morning glow, and a burst of white light brightens the dark space. Silas squints against the glare, and I glance out the window once more. I wrap the sheets around me and prop on my elbows. The cherry hues of the sunrise remind me, and I sit straight up. Silas throws both hands behind his head, stretching his chest, and yawns.

"Tonight is the crimson moon," I state, matter-of-factly.

"It is," Silas responds, casually.

"The Archives will be the easiest to enter tonight." I turn back to look at him, still lying shirtless on the bed. "We have to find a way to get in there."

He rubs his eyes and sits up next to me, propping his elbow on his knee. "My mother is going to meet us mid-afternoon in her wing of the castle. We have a lot to discuss with her."

I raise my brows at him.

"No," he laughs.

"You should…"

"I'm not asking about my father. As far as she knows, we have no clue Malachi disclosed this to us."

"Fine," I sigh.

He moves off the side of the bed, and the sheets wrap around his hips, exposing his strong back. Silas walks to the window, pushing open the curtains and then the shutters. He turns to me, clearly considering holding something back from me.

"Today is going to be interesting," Silas admits, throwing a shirt over his head.

"That's an understatement."

He chuckles. "Every day has been interesting since I met you."

"That doesn't sound like a good thing."

He smiles and narrows his eyes. "It's a good thing. I know I'll never be bored."

"Were you concerned about growing bored with me?"

"Not even for a second."

The memories of last night flood my mind. Malachi, the Travelers, the book, and Yara. A flash of her lifeless body covered in blood hits my mind, and I flinch. Silas moves closer to me, noticing that I'm lost in thought. I look into his eyes, unable to stop the tears from forming. He cups my face and brings his forehead to mine.

"When all this has settled, I will take you to meet Yara's family if you would like. They would appreciate hearing about her bravery," he says. "And, I think it may help you."

"I don't know. I don't think I could face them, and I doubt they would want to meet me," I respond.

Silas smiles gently. "I think you would be surprised, Briar. Just think about it. Promise me?"

"I promise."

He walks toward the door, running his hands through his messy hair. "Get dressed; we have a big day ahead."

"Can't we just stay in bed and hide?" I ask, refusing to put my feet on the floor.

He glances over his shoulder. "There is nothing I'd rather do than stay in bed with you all day."

I pat the bed next to me, and before I look back up at him, Silas races toward me with a smile spread across his whole face. His large body crashes against mine, and he falls on top of me, pressing my back against the silk sheets. I let out a startled giggle as his hands move to both sides of my head, and he leans forward, pressing his lips against mine.

"Don't tempt me, Briar."

I kiss him again. "What's on the agenda, Your Majesty? Since we can't stay like this all day."

He rolls his eyes at my snark before saying, "I'm heading to the castle shortly with Fenmore to ensure everything is in order. I'll see you shortly before we meet my mother."

"Wait." I angle my head. "What am I going to do until then?"

"Someone wants to see you near the cliff's edge in thirty minutes."

CHAPTER 30

After dressing and grabbing a quick bite to eat, I rush onto the grounds, eager to see who awaits me outside. I round the edge of the house and pause in my tracks when I see Larkin, Maines, and Oak standing near the cliff.

This can't be good.

The sun sits high in the sky, gracing us with a bit of warmth. The fresh air feels light, and the day is becoming beautiful compared to the gloomy days we've experienced so far in Andorwood. I look behind me and glimpse the city limits. The kingdom seems to have a veil hanging over it, with dark clouds swirling only around the center. I can now understand why Silas moved away from the city; the air feels cleaner and more appealing out here, away from the castle.

Maines waves as I approach, and Oak has a broad grin on his face that instantly indicates I'm in for something I won't enjoy. Larkin stands with his back to the others and looks out over the sea. Being head of the ocean operations for Andorwood, it's no surprise that he always has an eye on the sea. Silas mentioned once that he spends a lot of time on this cliff, as it's a great vantage point for incoming ships.

"Good morning, Dusk Wielder," Oak snarks. "So happy you could join us today."

I roll my eyes. "What is this about?"

Larkin turns to face us, and my stomach drops at the sight of him. He looks worried, and my senses immediately perk up. He brushes off the concern and quickly shifts his expression to a casual calm as soon as he realizes I'm watching.

"Hey," he says, joining in with Oak. "Good morning."

I continue forward and am met with a tight embrace from Maines.

"This was Silas's idea," she encourages. "Oak is so excited, though."

"Excited about what?" I ask.

Larkin claps his hands together to get our attention and walks to the center of the drawn circle. "So, Briar is going to show us her Lumor magic this morning."

"I'm what?" I respond in shock.

"I'm so fucking excited," Oak says.

Larkin clears his throat.

"With what sails toward Andorwood, if we can improve your abilities further, we have a chance to send these bastards back to where they came from," Larkin says. "This will also benefit us in future battles. Even though I don't think it's wise to use much of our magic right now, Silas insisted we train."

"And we do what Silas says," Oak laughs. "I also enjoy imagining Nolan and Calia's faces when they see what you can do."

Larkin huffs a laugh. "Oak and I are going to assist with the Lumor side of things, and Maines is here to fight you."

"Again, what?" I snap.

She laughs, "I'm not going to fight you. They have asked me to simply throw some magic your way for you to deflect. Plus, I believe this will be a wonderful stress reliever for you." Maines leans in closer. "I honestly think they have me here in case one of you gets hurt."

"She's not wrong," Larkin says.

"I don't even know how to do this. It was completely accidental both times."

"We thought you might say that," Oak adds. "Elements and emotion fuel our natural tap of magic. We have both of those with us right now. The earth is our element, and Larkin is here for the emotion. We know he's good at pissing you off."

"Happy to help," Larkin snarks, returning to prep a few things within the training circle.

Hearing Calia and Nolan's names evokes a memory: her hateful face deep within Daramveer's castle, taunting and tormenting me as she tried to resurrect Carobon. I don't think it would have changed the outcome, but being more powerful would never be a bad thing. I don't know how, but we need to learn more to stop the Great Wiitch when we return to the mainland. Each day that passes increases my fear of what's changed there. The potential for destruction and devastation sends me into a panic.

I break my blank stare and walk toward the edge of the cliff, and Larkin attempts to stop me.

"Give her a second," Maines snaps.

The slapping waves below fill my ears, and I close my eyes, letting the strong breeze rush around my body.

Rohhit, tell me you are okay, I say in my mind.

Silence.

Rohhit, please. If you are there, speak to me.

I'm met with nothing, and a wave of dread crashes against me like the waves below. The longer we wait, the more I fear Rohhit will be pulled away from his physical body. I need to do whatever it takes to be as strong as possible. If mastering this magic gets me one step closer to destroying Carobon, I'll do whatever it takes to do that while protecting those around me.

"Alright," I say determinedly, as I turn around. "Where do we start?"

"Fuck yeah." Oak smiles. "We're going to start with the basics."

"Fine."

"Come into the circle. We've charged several crystals placed around the edge. I want you to focus all your energy on the elements surrounding you." Oak points into the dirt, drawing on the ground.

"I know how to do basic magic, Oak," I reply.

"As far as we are concerned, you are starting from the beginning, so no, you don't know how to do basic Lumor magic," he responds, and I narrow my eyes at him.

Larkin steps forward. "Your Lumor ability is weak, Briar. We're going to have to build it from the ground up. You can call your shadows at any given time, but not your light. You have to figure out how to pull that from within."

"Okay, then. What do I do?" I ask.

"Allow your instincts to guide you. Push aside your shadows and focus on the light. You need to feel calm and confident. Try to lessen the darkness of your shadows, and in a little bit, we'll move on to incorporating emotion."

I close my eyes and widen my stance, feeling lost and embarrassed.

The wind around me seems to pick up, and I let the glow of the sun warm my face. I place both palms outward at my side and focus on my breathing. Steady breaths expand my lungs. The world around me goes quiet, and the crashing waves become a muffled noise in the background. I delve into my own mind, feeling myself travel farther and farther.

With each passing second, I go further into the depths of the darkness.

Focus, Briar. Lessen your shadows.

An image of my mother comes into my mind. Her smiling face pains my chest. Her long, flowing hair blows in the wind before me, and her eyes dazzle in the sun. I don't open my eyes, but I want to in hopes that she is truly standing before me. Without thinking, I reach my hand forward, trying to get closer to her.

A pained expression moves across her face, and she snaps her head behind her. My mother's shadowy figure behind me fades, and I feel the darkness begin to creep up inside of me.

Bury it.

Focus on her. Focus on your mother.

But her beautiful silhouette vanishes, replaced by a haunting image of a large figure before me.

I squeeze my eyes shut even tighter.

"Briar, shadows are coming forward. Try to focus on the breeze, the warmth of the sun, and the grass under your feet." I hear Larkin coaching from beside me. "Look for light."

I move my feet, pushing them deeper into the soft ground, but the figure draws nearer, as if something in the distance is trying to reach me. I feel the darkness beginning to tingle around my fingertips. With each passing second, the figure inches nearer. Fear floods me, and I sense myself losing control.

No. No.

Open your eyes.

I attempt to crack them open, but they remain shut.

"Briar," I hear Larkin call. "You're going the wrong way. Your shadows are taking over."

I feel the wind shift, and my hair starts to whip around my face. My chest begins to rise and fall quickly as the figure comes into focus. A haunting smile glimmers in the darkness, and a face swiftly comes into view.

Kalix.

Her haunting face isn't hidden this time, hoping to fool me and pull me closer. Her true form is now entirely on display. Black hair clings to her face, and a desperate look paints it. She reaches for me, her hands now replaced by the claws of a creature of darkness.

"*Back so soon?*" she hisses.

Fear consumes me as I watch her approach. I'm frozen, unable to pull myself away from her gaze. She hoped this would happen, waiting for the chance for me to dive deep without direction. I open my mouth to scream, but nothing escapes my throat.

I won't be trapped again.

Light. I need light.

I slowly push away the fear and whisper *light*, repeating it over and over in an attempt to fool myself into believing that I can do this. Her expression shifts to one of confusion, and I feel the mist of shadows swirling around my hands quickly transform into small bursts of light, but it's not enough. My Lumor Wielding is too weak to challenge her.

I hear Maines's muffled voice say, "Briar, open your eyes."

The image of Kalix still exists in my mind. She continues to move forward, reaching for me.

"Open your eyes," Larkin shouts. "Now."

I feel a surge of magic zap into my body, sending a shock-wave through my limbs.

For a moment, I believe it was my own doing, pain I've caused myself—or possibly a claw from Kalix finally ripping into me—but my body instantly flies backward, away from the talon reaching for me. Tingles rush through my system, and I land on my back with a thud outside the charged circle.

My eyes snap open, and the sunlight sears them.

I look within the circle, and Maines stands there with her hand over her mouth. Oak bears a shocked expression, and Larkin's large frame towers over me, already by my side. His eyes are filled with concern, and his palms hang limply at his sides. Pain travels through my back, and I reach behind me, feeling a tiny wet spot on my shirt. I move my hand in front of me to look and see blood coating my fingertips.

"Sorry." Larkin extends his hand for me to take. "You wouldn't snap out of it so…I sent a surge of light your way."

My mouth drops open. "Are you insane?"

"Tell me I was incorrect for doing that?" He leans closer.

Kalix disappears, and I inhale the fresh sea air.

"Something went wrong, and I'm not letting you go back toward her. That blast snapped you back into reality, my friend."

"Thank you."

"I told you I have your back, and I wasn't lying, but I've unfortunately made you bleed in this situation."

He smirks, proud of his reaction. I roll my eyes.

I grab his hand, letting him pull me off the ground. Maines rushes over and lifts my shirt, exposing a cut on my lower back. After a quick examination, she lowers my shirt again.

"You'll be okay. It's a superficial wound. Nothing that will scar. I'll save my healing magic for when you kick Larkin's ass for doing that."

Larkin smiles broadly and walks back to the circle.

I brush my clothes off and tame my messy hair. Oak dusts my upper back as I join them again in the training circle.

"Well, that went horribly wrong," Oak says with a shrug. "Let's try another route before Silas shows up and murders us all."

Larkin nods. "We're going to have to try to get it to come up organically. Deep diving isn't an option right now until you have more control."

"I don't have much control, Larkin."

"Yes, you do."

"Not from *her*," I respond.

A rush of breeze moves through me, and I swear I hear a vicious laugh echo in my ears. I shake off the fear. I'm here, and I'm alright. I widen my stance once more and prepare for the next portion of this miserable training. Although my back stings, I'll be fine, and I can't wait for Silas to find out that Larkin hit me.

"So, since I just blasted Briar, Oak, it's your turn." Larkin motions Oak to come forward.

Oak looks around and says, "I'm not trying to get Silas Nastronde on my bad side. After all, he's my best friend."

Maines throws her hands in the air, exasperated. "Again, everyone is your best friend but me."

"I have to tell them all that." Oak winks and whispers, "Don't worry."

Larkin rubs his head and snaps his gaze at me. I shrug, as if to signal that this happens constantly.

"Oak, get in the circle," Larkin warns.

"Wait, I thought Maines was going to do this," Oak responds.

Larkin turns to Maines. "Given how this is already going, we will need her to heal, not fight."

Maines lets out a relieved breath, and Oak moves slowly into the center of the circle and sighs. I smile, watching the drama leak from him, and return my gaze to Larkin, waiting for the next orders.

"Briar, go face Oak."

I drag my feet and center myself, facing Oak. He lifts his brows twice, teasing me, and I can't help but grin. He's utterly ridiculous.

"Oak, please begin to zap Briar gently," Larkin instructs. "We want to get her emotions going to see if we can evoke her Lumor ability to present itself."

Oak smiles. "Alright. This could be fun."

Before I have time to react, small zaps of light begin to erupt from his palms, crashing into my sides, legs, and arms. It stings, but it's a pain I can handle. I move aside, attempting to dodge as many as possible, but they keep coming. Instincts kick in, and I feel my shadows wanting to retaliate.

"Don't think about your shadows," Larkin shouts. "Only focus on your light. Use that to defend yourself."

I continue to jump and shuffle around the circle, unable to coax any light to come forward. Oak continues to send small bursts of lightning my way, and frustration builds in my chest.

"Stop! It's not working," I shout to Oak.

He ignores my request and continues to tease me with his wielding ability. Larkin and Maines watch from the sidelines and don't come to my defense to tell him to stop. The frustration builds stronger, and the shadows begin to swell around my palms.

"Wrong direction," Larkin bites.

That doesn't alleviate my frustration, which is quickly bubbling into anger. Control seems to slip away from me, replaced by my fury, and shadows pulse around me.

"Wrong," Larkin calls again. "Way."

I lower my gaze, narrowing my eyes, and Oak's eyes widen as he notices the anger building in my chaotic shadows.

"Shit," Oak mouths, knowing what's coming. "Maybe I should stop?"

"Don't," Larkin barks.

A surge of darkness rushes from my palms, striking Oak and sending him sprawling outside the training circle. He lands with a thud as his back hits the ground, releasing a pained breath.

Maines rushes to his side, and Oak supports himself on his elbows. He shakes his head and allows Maines to assist him in standing.

"Gods, you knocked the fucking… breath out of me," he huffs, clutching his chest.

"I'm sorry," I say, grimacing. "That was more of a reaction than a conscious decision."

"This isn't working." Larkin steps toward us. "We are going to have to try something else."

"Or, we could just stop," I add.

"Silas told us to get you to use your dusk abilities, and I'm not leaving until that happens." Larkin runs his hands through his white hair. "Briar, go back to the circle."

"Can I have a second?"

"No. You can't. You are charged right now, and we need to keep this going."

I shake my hands and move back to the center of the circle. The breeze seems to pick up, and I glance at the few charged crystals that line the border. They pulse as my magic enters and dance with excitement. Maines and Oak stay outside of the line and watch intently.

Larkin dusts off his hands and steps across the line. A surge of power illuminates the crystals, and my brows shoot up. He stands opposite me and stares intensely into my eyes. The direct eye contact is distracting, so I break my stare and look at the ground for a second.

"You are being weak," Larkin's voice travels across the space. "Scared."

I snap my gaze up. "What?"

"You aren't trying. You're comfortable remaining in the shadows. You choose to linger there," he taunts. "Because you want to be there."

"You are joking."

"Then prove me wrong," he snaps.

"You think I chose this? You think I wanted this path for my life?" I furrow my brow.

Larkin begins to pace. "I believe you have forgotten that there is light in this world."

"That isn't true."

"It seems that you are so accustomed to the darkness that being consumed by it feels effortless—easy—and you are being lazy."

"You're insane," I hiss.

Larkin huffs, "And you are being a pain in my ass."

"Then leave," I snap.

"Nope."

"Then, shut the fuck up."

"Again," he says, narrowing his gaze. "No."

We begin to slowly step in a circle, never allowing our backs to turn to one another. I know he's taunting me, trying to provoke a reaction, but I'm determined to resist. I won't let his words triumph.

"I believe you forget who inhabits this body, who resides deep within me." I narrow my gaze and feel the anger crawling up. "I could easily kill you."

"Oh, are you threatening me now?" Larkin smirks. "Awesome."

"A threat and a reminder."

"I didn't forget. I choose not to let it cloud my judgment when it comes to you. I can separate you from the darkness," Larkin scoffs. "Unlike yourself."

I harden my steps. "I am not Kalix."

"Then stop allowing the darkness to control you, Briar. It will consume you. Let the light guide you," Larkin begs. "Let it counter what lives within you."

I freeze in my tracks, his words sparking something in my memory.

Yara.

She said something during her last moments in Malachi's

office: *"When I'm gone, look for where the light illuminated. Look to where the light guided you."*

That was a message, a clue to something. I didn't realize it at the time, due to the chaos of the moment.

It was her bedroom. I have to go to her bedroom.

"Larkin, we have to stop." I turn my back to him and bound forward to cross over the circle. "I need to go somewhere."

Another breeze moves around me, and I slow my steps, feeling the crackling of lightning dancing around me as Larkin draws into his own powers.

"What would your brother think?"

"What?" I snap, keeping my gaze forward.

"Wouldn't he want you to run from the darkness?" Larkin's power grows in his palms. "Would he be proud of you right now?"

My body comes to a halt, and I turn slowly to face Larkin once more. He knows exactly which cord to strike.

"Don't fucking say a word about him," I seethe.

"Why?"

I nearly growl.

"Prove it, Briar. Show me what you can do."

I drop my gaze and bound toward him. I dive into my magic, but this time, I ignore the call of the darkness. Anger fuels me, and I allow my instinct to guide me. My brother's words flow into my mind the night he died. He told me I was strong, stronger than him. Emotion floods me, and I race forward, my feet slapping the ground. If Larkin wants me to prove it to him, I'll give a show.

I look over the cliff toward the sun rising in the bright sky.

Light.

I need light.

A brilliant tingle moves into my palms as I approach Larkin, and a grin spreads across his face.

"That's it," Larkin calls. "Push."

I ignore his praise and thunder forward. Lightning zaps my open palms. Maines and Oak watch with wide eyes beside us, and out of the corner of my eye, I see Oak pull Maines slightly behind him in case there is fallout.

I stand inches from Larkin's face, allowing the light to charge within my body and soul. His words become a driving force as I concentrate the light, urging it to come forward. For a moment, the sun appears to shine brighter, and I realize the light is coming from me.

"Do it," Larkin whispers. "Let it out."

I grind my teeth together.

"Show me," he says.

I slam my palms together, allowing the surge of light to flow through me. I strain every muscle against the unfamiliar surge of burning power, but I don't hold back.

"You are too close to him," Maines screams from the side. "Back up!"

I glare into his dark eyes, intoxicated by the power coursing through my system. Larkin remains still, prepared to endure any blow I see fit. I could kill him right now at this distance, and I grit my teeth, fighting back the urge.

The memories of what he said about my brother, what he sold him, and the danger he placed Barlowe in swirl in my mind. I am furious with him, so furious, but I don't want to kill him.

Yet here Larkin stands, unmoving and ready to accept the fate he believes he deserves.

A sadness spreads through me, and the shock of the need for the power to exit my body takes over. I push my palms down, away from him, facing the ground, and the flow of my light stings as it leaves my body. I scream, and a bright light of power erupts, letting the magic, anger, and sadness leave my body. The blinding light explodes, and we both go flying backward.

We crash against the ground in opposite directions, and my

vision blurs as I hit the grass, my head slamming against the earth. Maines rushes to my side, and Oak goes to Larkin.

"Gods." I hear Maines scream as she kneels next to me.

I groan from the hit and roll to my side, glancing toward Larkin. I do a quick survey of pain and don't feel anything other than the ache in my lower back and shoulder. I lift my hand and feel against my face, and a scratch sits high on my cheek under my eye.

"I'm okay." I sit up.

I look across the circle and see Larkin sitting up as well, rubbing his head. Relief washes over me seeing that he's okay, but regret hits me harder. I thought about killing him; it was short-lived, but it crossed my mind. Maybe I'm destined to thrive in darkness, as my thoughts seem to wander there every time the anger creeps in.

Oak brings Larkin to his feet, and although my vision is still a bit blurry, I see him smiling widely. His shirt is ripped, his hair a mess, and a long scratch on his face matches mine, along with a few others peppering his neck and chest.

He looks worse than I do.

"She's fine," Maines shouts across the circle.

Oak nods while Larkin limps toward me. Maines gives him some space, and Larkin extends a hand for me to rise. I grasp it, and he pulls me up. A flash of pain courses through me, but I ignore it. I stand before him, bracing for my reprimand for losing control yet again. He towers over me, and his stare sears into mine.

Larkin lifts his arms, and I flinch, ready for a blow back.

Surprise hits me as he tightly wraps both arms around me, pulling me into the tightest hug. I stay in shock for a moment, and then he hugs me even tighter. I look at Maines through his arms, and she smiles. I return the embrace and wrap my arms around him, squeezing as tightly as he does. A calmness moves through me, and I can't help but imagine I'm hugging my brother. I feel safe, happy, and a tad guilty for almost hurting him, but I bury my head into his chest nonetheless.

He pulls away and slaps both hands around my shoulder. "That was fucking awesome."

"I could have killed you."

"Yeah, but you didn't," he responds, casually. "I wasn't worried."

"Liar."

"You're right," he laughs. "I was seconds from panicking."

I crook a smile.

"I'm sorry I mentioned your brother. I didn't mean anything I said."

"I know."

"I wanted to see if emotions would motivate you, since the elements didn't, and boy was I right." Larkin shakes my shoulders.

I can't quite pinpoint him, but he's proud. So proud of me, and I can't help but laugh.

Oak walks up. "You two look like you've been in a tavern fight."

"Gods, an ale sounds great right now," Larkin says, and releases my shoulders on a laugh.

I watch him and angle my head.

"Yeah, it does," Maines agrees.

"I'd say that's enough for today," Oak says, grasping Maines hand to lead her back to the house. "We will head to the castle in about an hour. You two should definitely clean up."

They continue forward, leaving Larkin and me standing in our small ruin.

"Thank you," I say to him.

"For what?" he asks.

"For pushing me, for challenging me, and for being there for me."

He nods. "Always."

My heart swells. I may have lost my older brother, but I feel as if I've gained another. I glance down at my hands and can't hide the shock on my face when I see that one of my fingertips is no longer covered in darkness. It's normal and pale. I tuck my hands into my pants and ignore the urge to stare.

"I need to do something before we meet with Aerona," I say, as I walk toward the house.

Larkin follows behind me with a limp. "Alright. What can I help with?"

I pause and stare at him. "We need to get Silas and go to Yara's bedroom."

CHAPTER 31

The castle walls are filled with a thick, musty air. Somehow, the hallways seem darker than before, and I quietly make my way down the corridor toward Yara's bedroom. My senses are on high alert, and every noise sends me into a panic. At any moment, I feel as if Malachi could return, or I might encounter one of the Travelers head-on, just like the last time I was in this hallway.

Even though we were exhausted and beaten up, Larkin and I shifted here shortly after returning to the house for a quick freshen-up. However, it didn't do anything to hide the dark bruises forming on both of our faces. Her words continuously play in my mind, and I know for certain she left something here.

Look to where the light guided you.

The first night my Lumor abilities manifested, my light guided me directly to her room. She used that as a code, knowing Malachi would have no idea what she meant at the time. I struggle against the flashes of memories in my mind and try to focus on something else, but it's impossible. The image of her standing there, so scared, dragging the blade across her throat, will forever be burned into my mind.

I fear I'll never be able to cleanse it.

I close my eyes and pull on the tether, keeping Silas and me together.

"*Silas*," I call in my mind.

"*Hey*," he responds. "*You alright?*"

"*We are in the castle.*"

"*Who?*"

"*Larkin and I. We are going to Yara's bedroom.*"

"*I'm with Fenmore*," he says. "*Need me?*"

"*Are you done?*"

"*I am now.*"

We round the last corner down the hallway, and anxiety floods me. I genuinely have no idea what I'm about to find or if I'm making the whole thing up and will be let down when I find nothing. I shrug off the doubts and come to the final room on the left.

Yara's bedroom.

Like all other doors, this one also has a snake embedded in it. Clear, jeweled eyes watch me as I warily move my hand to the knob to push open the door. My fingers graze the cold metal handle when I feel a presence growing—his presence.

Silas shifts into the hallway.

His eyes find mine, and I smile, forgetting how I look after the fight on the cliff. Silas's face contorts, and he looks me up and down, as he walks our way.

He storms forward, cradling my face. "What the fuck happened?"

I smile, thankful to see him again after being apart. "I'm fine, you insane worrywart."

He presses a kiss to my lips, then angles my head to check the scratch. "You are scratched and bruised. I take it training either went really well, or someone is dead."

"Yeah, you should see the other guy," I laugh and wink at Larkin.

Larkin chuckles, extending his hand. "Hi, I am the other guy."

Silas casts a warning glance his way, but the faintest sign of a smile twitches his lip.

"I asked them to train you. I didn't think it would result in you all trying to kill each other." Silas places his hands into his pockets and gives me a look.

I laugh. "It was hardly that."

I stand on my tiptoes and give him another kiss.

"To be fair, *I* didn't try to kill anyone," Larkin says, smiling, as we move toward the door.

"Explain what we are doing," Silas insists. "How can I help?"

"I think Yara left me something in her room. Right before… you know what happened, she mentioned something. At the time, I didn't understand what she meant, but it finally hit me."

"Alright," Silas replies. "What are we looking for?"

I shrug. "Since Malachi threw the book into the fire that contained the Rigil, we needed to enter the Forgotten Archives. I'm not sure what we are looking for."

I turn the knob and push against the thick wooden door. The room is filled with an impenetrable darkness, and my senses are on high alert. Silas walks ahead of me toward the small sitting area and throws open the heavy curtains. Dust fills the air, and the room is instantly brightened by the sunlight streaming in from outside. Even in the glow, the room remains dim, musty, and aged. This definitely isn't like the other rooms I've encountered in this castle.

A few things catch my eye that I didn't notice before when I was in here. Books of all kinds—romance, history, and fiction— are scattered around the room along with beautiful paintings. A pang hits my chest, and I move deeper into the room. No one has been in here since Yara, and everything sits untouched. Larkin and Silas split up and begin looking through things that may be able to assist us.

"Wait," I stop them. "I feel bad going through her things."

They both pause, their hands almost touching her belongings, and exchange a glance.

"I don't think she would have led you here if she didn't expect you to look through her stuff. We will be able to cover more ground if we search together," Silas responds.

He's right. Our time is limited, so looking together will only help. I replay our brief conversation in my mind, but nothing stands out. Frustration bubbles in my chest as I move toward the window, trying to think of something, anything.

The city center below is dark, yet people travel to and from various places. I can't help but think about how different Andorwood is from what I imagined. Yes, it's dark and full of various deadly rebels, but it's a kingdom. It's people who want to live their lives away from the mainland, indifferent to the rumors that travel across the seas.

The men continue to shuffle through various papers and drawers in the room, but are unsuccessful at finding anything of importance. I peel my gaze away from the kingdom and scan the surroundings.

My eyes slide to the many books that scatter around the room. Outside of furniture, there aren't many places that something could be hidden, so I take that as a sign to start there.

I move swiftly and crash to my knees in front of the books, beginning to flip through the pages. At this rate, it will take hours to sort through all these books. Silas and Larkin turn their attention to me.

"What are you doing?" Larkin questions.

"Maybe she hid something in the pages?" I respond. "I mean, I would hide something here."

They join me, each grabbing a book. Larkin makes a huff, closing the spine, and I look in his direction.

"Not your style of reading?" I ask.

"I've read my fair share of romances, but this one isn't a favorite of mine, is all."

I bust out laughing.

"I'm serious, the ending made me so mad."

Silas looks at Larkin and laughs. "You are something else, my friend."

Focus silences our conversation as we continue flipping through numerous books. Silas concentrates on the history books, while Larkin and I browse through all the romance novels. Pages filled with tales of great adventures and even greater love catch my eye, and I mentally note to read a few of them when things calm down. If they ever do calm down, I remind myself. Time feels like it's passing at warp speed, and I know each second that ticks by is another moment lost in our search for something.

Larkin stands, shakes his hand, and gives his back a good pop, taking only a second's rest.

"How can someone have so many books?" Larkin crouches back down and returns to flipping through the worn pages.

"It's easy," I shrug.

Each completed book makes my heart ache more, knowing we've found nothing. I know she wanted me to come here, and this has to be where a clue lies. Frustration begins to overwhelm me, and even though I know the others feel the same, the men continue to help me search.

After finishing flipping through the last book before us, I drop mine and head back to the window, letting the cool night air calm my frustration. We are missing something—I know it, but I can't figure out what. Under the window is a small sitting area covered with worn pillows and a few blankets. This must be where she spent many hours reading these books.

I lower my hands to move a few pillows when a book falls from behind one and hits the ground, echoing throughout the room. Larkin and Silas glance in my direction, making puzzled faces. My heart begins to thunder, and a sense of hope sparks within me.

I lean down, grasping the book's old leather spine. The thick red hardback weighs down my arm as I lift it to get a better look. I flip the book over and see the title, *The Huntress*.

This isn't a romance but more a haunting fiction book that tells the tale of a brave woman who sets out to travel to the darkest realm to fight death itself. I shudder at the thought of the story I was told as a young child, remembering it vividly. The woman in the story always believed she was the hunter, but in fact, she was being hunted her entire life, driven there by fate. In the end, she never makes it out. This story used to give me nightmares as a child. Even though this book haunted me, I hold it closer and bring it over toward Silas and Larkin.

"I remember that book," Larkin says, pointing at it as I set it on the table. "Fucked up is what that book is."

"I'm surprised that book is even in this castle," Silas adds. "My father hated that book."

As I flip through the pages, terrifying drawings of someone clawing their way from the depths of darkness fill the pages. I can't help but think of the similarities between myself and this book. As I move toward the back of the book, the images become increasingly disturbing and haunting, but I keep my eyes fixed on the pages.

The book comes to an end, and that's when I spot it and gasp. A thin piece of paper is wedged into the fold of the book, and had I not been looking, I would have never noticed anything else within the thickness of the spine.

Larkin and Silas's eyes widen as I carefully remove the folded page from the book. I set the book down and allow my mind a moment to grasp what's happening. The paper is worn—yellowed and so thin—that I fear a strong gust of wind could rip it in half.

I slowly unfold the paper. Silas and Larkin remain on my

sides, hovering over me and watching intensely. I try to steady my trembling hands and take my time making sure I'm as careful as possible.

With the document fully open, I pause for a moment to look at the paper. It's blank—no words, no Rigils, and nothing that can help us. I hear Silas sigh from behind me, and Larkin places his hand on my shoulder in defeat.

"Maybe she was just speaking out of panic, Briar. Maybe it didn't mean anything." Larkin says.

I stare at the paper, hoping something will appear, that something will change, and that this entire thing wasn't a waste.

"She wouldn't have said that if she didn't intend for us to find something, Larkin. I'm not making this up," I bite back.

Larkin withdraws his hand, allowing me some space. "I don't believe you are fabricating anything, but perhaps it simply isn't what we expected."

Silas moves to the large window and opens the curtains more, allowing more light to shine into the room. I stand with my back to the light and focus on the shadow of my body on the page, unwilling to accept defeat right now.

Think, Briar.

I scan the room with the page still in my hand, but I can't think. Nothing comes to mind, leaving me back at square one. With a slight shift in my stance, a corner of the paper catches the sun, revealing a subtle change. I squint my eyes, unable to process what I'm seeing. The page starts to glimmer where the sun hits it, so subtly that if you weren't looking, you would miss it.

Yup, I've gone insane.

Silas walks back across the room and comes to my side. He towers over my shoulder and looks down at the slight shimmer in the corner of the paper.

"What the fuck?" he whispers. "Move it into the sun."

I slowly turn, moving the page completely into the sun

spilling into the room. The entire sheet begins to shimmer like thousands of diamonds dancing on water.

My jaw drops open, and the page turns the brightest, glowing gold. I grab it with both hands and slowly lift it toward the window, giving the sun a chance to fully drench it in its golden rays.

Before my eyes, the shape begins to darken in the middle, and small words develop with the help of the sun.

"Gods," I hear Larkin mumble. "It was warded."

The words become clearer the longer they're placed in the sun, and I wait impatiently for everything to develop before reading what it says. An ancient Rigil forms at the center of the page, and excitement floods me. I can't help but squeal when I see we've found it. Yara got the page from the book. I don't know how, and I probably never will, but she managed to do it.

"That's the Rigil," Silas rasps, coming to the same conclusion. "Yara ripped it from the book."

A large circle accompanied by two others fills the page. Lines and markings fill the space, creating a Rigil unlike anything I've ever seen. It's a work of art, and I'm in awe of its beauty. There are words written within the largest circle, but it's nothing I can read. We will need Oak for that.

A few other words begin to appear, and they're in a language I can read—our language. I quickly realize that it's from Yara. Written on the glowing page is:

Briar,

This symbol is essential for entering the Archives with care. However, the Rigil can only be used once on a single person. Utilize it to acquire the information you seek. If you are reading this, I apologize that things did not go as planned. I look forward to seeing you again one day, my friend.

Yara.

My chest aches, but a sense of calm washes over me. It wasn't for nothing; this wasn't all a waste. She did it; she left this world a hero, and I'll do everything I can to ensure that she is honored once this is over.

"We need Oak to translate what this text says." I turn to Silas and Larkin.

They nod.

I move the page from the sunlight back into the shadows of our bodies. Before me, the page begins to fade, and the words slowly vanish, revealing a completely blank sheet. I carefully fold it back and secure it in the middle of the book.

I tuck the book under my arm and look toward Silas and Larkin. Silas stands with his hands tucked into his pockets, a sense of pride showing behind his eyes. Larkin looks distressed as usual, and I fear he'll never get over the antics we seem to encounter daily.

"Should we go see Aerona?" I ask.

Silas clicks his tongue. "We should indeed."

We walk toward the threshold, ready to move toward the far east wing of the castle, where Aerona's quarters are. It's a part of the castle I've never been to, so excitement and nerves dance in my stomach.

"You're taking that book with you?" Larkin asks.

"I am." I smile. "I think I'm going to read it."

He shivers. "Don't you think you should pick up something happier?"

I shrug. "Not my style."

Silas takes the lead as we move into the castle halls, knowing exactly where he is going after making trips there his whole life. I reflect on my childhood in Daramveer Castle. To many, the hallways were a maze, but I knew each turn and crevice like the back of my hand. The memories of the many times Barlowe and I played games throughout the halls send a wave of sadness mixed with happiness through me. We would spend hours running through the halls, desperately trying not to get caught by one of my father's many useless guards.

I watch Silas turn with purpose around each corner, and I quickly catch up to wrap my hand around his. A heavy exhale escapes his chest from my touch, and he cuts his eyes toward mine. A soft smile curls on his lips, and he squeezes my hand twice in return. Larkin follows closely behind us, glancing over his shoulder every so often to ensure we are making this journey alone.

As we move through the long hallways, further away from the center of the castle where Malachi spent most of his time, the air seems lighter. This wing has more windows, allowing more light to shine through, illuminating the halls with a sense of hope. It's easy to get lost in the gloom near where we stayed, tucked into the center of the castle. I understand why Aerona chooses to stay in this wing instead of the others, but I can't for the life of me understand why Silas and Fen decided to remain in those rooms.

I glance out a passing window and see that we've traveled quite high near one of the castle's points. The distance between us and the ground makes my palms tingle, and I subconsciously move further to the inside wall.

Silas notices my flinch and chuckles. "I forgot your fear of heights, my love."

"For the hundredth time, I'm not afraid of heights, but the thought of falling isn't my favorite."

He laughs again and lets us move further away from the passing windows.

We round the last corner and come to a large wooden door embellished with a snake, just like the others.

"I will start us off with my mother," Silas says. "She will want to hear from me what happened with Malachi."

Larkin nods, and Silas looks directly at me. "I would like you to chime in as well. Since you are going to enter the Forgotten Archives, I want you to ask the questions you need answering."

Shock paints my face. "I'm entering the Archives? I didn't think you would let me do that alone."

He smiles. "Believe me, I want to argue with you, but I know that would be useless, and I would lose just like every time before. Everything within me tells me that you are the person who needs to do this, no matter how scared it makes me."

"But, what if I don't want to?" I ask.

Silas laughs. "Wow, the one time I don't argue, you would have listened to my persuasion. That seems about right. If you choose not to, then I will go, but please know that the decision is ultimately yours."

"Thank you," I mutter.

He steps closer, his large presence looming above me. "Briar, there are creatures in Andorwood that have existed here long before the Great Wiitches. I'm going to let you enter the Archives, but not before you are prepared. If the Archives contains documents this important, I can only imagine the creature that haunts the space. I fear we are facing something truly terrifying."

Fear runs through my veins like icy water.

"I don't know, I feel like I've had my dose of terror from the Traveler in the woods," I say.

"That will seem childish compared to what's in the Archives."

Silas raises his hand and drives his fist into the heavy wooden door. The knock echoes down the long hallway behind us, and I can't help but listen to the nerves that fill me. Light footsteps sound behind the door, and I brace myself for another awkward meeting with Silas's mother.

The door swings open, and to my surprise, Fen is standing there. I wasn't aware she would be joining us today.

"Come in," she says with a smile, but a heaviness still weighs her down. She moves for us to enter.

Silas strides in, followed by Larkin, and I have to convince my feet to move into the room. The air is light, the sun is bright, and the room is drenched in an emerald green that makes it seem as if the forest and her room are the same. It's stunning and a room I could only dream of having one day. Vines cover most of the walls, and the real forest peeks into the windows from behind the castle. The room is vast and seems to stretch for miles longer than the other rooms.

The room has several seating areas, but the main one features a few grand chairs and a dark couch that looks divine. Fen walks back toward the large fireplace, settling into what I assume is her assigned chair. Silas joins Fen in a nearby chair, followed by Larkin, and my eyes catch sight of Aerona. Her back is to me, but I can already sense her piercing gaze.

"Come sit, Briar," her strong voice calls.

My senses urge me to stay alert as I cross the room and find the last available chair, directly across from Aerona, and tuck the book behind my back. From our few meetings, I can't help but have a guard up around her. I sit down, and her gaze locks onto mine. A broad grin spreads across her face.

"Welcome," Aerona says.

CHAPTER 32

"Hello, Aerona," I respond.

Silas shuffles his chair near me, and I see worry flash across his face.

"I'm sure you have heard, Mother, but it was dire we spoke with you today," Silas cuts in.

Aerona peels her gaze away from me and settles back into the large couch. Her emerald green dress flows to the floor, and her long, straight hair is perfectly tamed. The pendant she wore the night of the dinner hangs delicately around her neck, and the dark stone glimmers in the light.

Silas and Fenmore clearly inherit their looks from her. I allow myself to relax for a moment, knowing that Silas is taking over the conversation. The room seems to pulse from the anticipation that fills it, and no one truly knows how to act.

I look at Larkin, who sits perfectly still and poised in his chair. I sometimes forget that he is before royalty in these situations and must act with respect—not to me, but certainly toward Aerona. He winks, noticing my gaze, and my cheeks turn a light shade of pink.

Fen remains stone-faced in her chair, not fully listening or aware of what's going on. After learning everything about her ability and potential future, I know that she is deep in thought.

"Fenmore and I are tethered to the vessels of the Great Wiitches, Rohhit Harte and Briar," Silas says, his words strong and concise. Not a hint of doubt escapes his lips. "I'm sure this is no shock concerning me; however, I was not aware that we both had this ability."

Aerona stills.

"I will ask you this only once," Silas threatens. "Your family passes this down, yes?"

She looks at Fen, and a wave of sadness washes over her eyes. "Yes, my grandmother was a tether. I don't know much, but I am aware of the ability. I never dreamed it would happen to both you and Fenmore."

"I thought so," he bites back. "Anything else you would like to share with me and Fen before I continue?"

He's testing her.

Giving her an opportunity to come clean about Malachi, and I hold my breath, waiting for her response.

"*Silas*," I say in my mind.

"*She will lie to me*," he responds.

"*Be careful asking things if you aren't prepared to know the answers*."

He doesn't look toward me, but instead keeps his gaze glued to his mother's, waiting for her answer. Silas's jaw tenses as Aerona takes a breath.

"No," she shakes her head. "There is nothing else I'm with-holding."

"Very well," Silas responds, casually, even though I know he just took a strike to the heart.

I exhale sharply and look at Fen. She's gone pale, knowing that her mother just directly lied to her face about something so huge.

"Malachi is gone," Aerona speaks, and Fen flinches. "Isn't he?"

Silas sits taller. "Yes, to our understanding, he is gone."

"I see," she whispers.

I watch her intently, trying to see if I can spot any sense of relief or grief, but her face is as hard as Silas's. No emotion shows behind her eyes, and that scares me, because the one thing I was hoping for was shock, which did not emerge from behind her eyes.

"Tell me what happened," Aerona speaks again, her tone much harsher this time.

Silas stands and walks to the fireplace, momentarily lost in thought. I can't blame him for taking a second. How could anyone comfortably explain this?

"He disappeared shortly after murdering Yara," Silas blurts out.

Gods, so much for taking it easy.

Silas cuts his eyes to mine as Aerona pales.

"As you know, Mother, Malachi is a monster. How you've managed to deal with him for so long is something I will never understand. I am not here to sugarcoat things for you. I know you are also aware of Yara and her relationship with him."

Aerona fidgets, making me think it's due to embarrassment. "Your father had many suitors during our marriage. Their names blur together after a while."

"It's nothing to be ashamed of, Mother," Silas says, turning to face her directly. "I don't blame you for making sure he was well entertained to give you a break."

She lowers her head, as if the weight of the memories forces her gaze down.

"I want you to know what he did. You need to know. I need you to understand who we are dealing with."

Aerona lifts her gaze, and a pain moves through my chest.

This is her life, and these are her children. She may not be perfect, but she is still their mother.

"Malachi made Yara slit her own throat, and we were there."

Aerona pales, but her gaze doesn't drop. "Stop, Silas."

Silas pushes to continue, "We witnessed the entire thing."

"Stop," she repeats.

"He believed Yara betrayed him, and being who he is, he reacted the only way he knew how, which was by murdering someone he claimed to care about."

Aerona abruptly stands. "He didn't care for her, and I know who we're dealing with, Silas."

"Mom," he rasps. "I just…"

"I am your mother. Don't speak to me as if I've been blind my entire life."

This is going great.

"I don't think you are blind. I know you've witnessed his horrors. But so has Fen, and so have I. Malachi is gone, and I pray to every God listening that he never fucking returns."

She huffs and turns her back for a moment, placing her trembling hands out of sight. Even though I hate this man, I can't help but feel sorry for Aerona. Malachi, believe it or not, was her husband, someone she spent many years with, and I would guess at one point, she thought he loved her. It's heartbreak and betrayal all in one.

"Did Malachi say anything to you before he left?" Aerona asks, with a shaky breath.

Silas glances at Larkin, Fen, and me, as if silently telling us to keep quiet. It isn't my news to tell so, I sit back further in my chair. She notices my expression and gives me a cautious side-eye.

"No, nothing of importance. He was frantic," Silas sharply responds.

"Did he speak of me?"

Silas hesitates and whispers, "No."

She sighs. "Where is the girl?"

Silas stands and steps toward her. "Warrick made sure that her body was given to her family."

"Gods damnit, Silas," she swears under her breath. "Do you know how this looks?"

"I know exactly how this looks. I want Andorwood to know."

Aerona snaps her head toward him.

"Malachi got away with this countless times before, but never with a true innocent. I hope this spreads like a disease throughout the town. I hope they hate him more than ever before, because I need them to."

She looks at him through hard eyes. "Why?"

"Because, I don't think you realize that I am now the King of Andorwood. I have a kingdom to protect, I have people to protect, and I need every single fucking rebel on my side to fight what's coming—to fight for our future, the entire realm, and for what's right. The time of evil is over, and I'll do whatever it takes to end it."

Her eyes widen as she processes the volume of Malachi's departure. Silas is king and will start acting as such. He only needs to tell her to put it into motion.

"Oh, Silas," her hands fall to her sides.

"I am prepared."

I glance at Silas, and see nothing but determination settling behind his green eyes.

Aerona takes a long breath. "Tomorrow, you will meet with the kingdom. You will be introduced as the king. Whether they decide to fight with you is up to them. They are not easily controlled, royalty or not, Silas. You know this."

Silas nods.

"Prepare for everything." She walks back over to the sitting area and sits down again. "Including disappointment."

"I can absolutely handle them." Silas follows her with his stare. "Briar and I will stand together tomorrow and convince them to join us in the fight. I am not concerned."

Aerona's eyes shift to mine. "You— I can't help but think this chain of events has absolutely everything to do with your arrival."

Silas steps closer to where I sit. "Careful, mother."

I lean forward. "I do believe that some of these events were because of me, Aerona. I will not sit here and pretend that I am not to blame for some of this."

Silas snaps his head to me. "Briar!"

"She is right, Silas." I stand next to him. "Many things have brought me here, have led us all here, so I don't think it benefits anyone to ignore the obvious. I came to Andorwood desperate for help. The events that have unfolded are horrific, and I'm here to stop a war from happening, if possible. Carobon has fully possessed the Prince of Eddris, Rohhit Harte. Every day that passes, Rohhit becomes more lost. Anything we can have against them is going to help us."

Aerona watches me as I begin to pace. I can't help but look at Fen, who looks as if she's in pain hearing the name and state of her vessel.

"Calia Thornfield and Nolan Harte brought Carobon forward after the final trial was complete with the resurrection stone. She and my father had these plans in motion for many years, although she made a fool of him in the end. Nolan is their child, my half-brother."

Her brows shoot up, and I continue.

"They plan to rid the realms of all Shadow Wielders if we don't stop them. I know you are aware of the tales about what the world was like when the Great Wiitches freely walked the realms, and I know you don't want that to happen."

She toys with the necklace around her throat.

I lean forward. "I believe we can stop them, but I'm here to ask you about what you know regarding the Forgotten Archives."

She flinches at the name, and for the first time, I see panic flood her. She doesn't want to talk about the Archives, her experiences there, or what she was doing.

"I need you all to leave." Aerona stands, nearly tipping over the furniture.

Silas laughs. "We are not leaving, mother. You need to tell us what you know, because believe it or not, we have the Rigil to enter tonight during the crimson moon, and we are going to do it with or without your help."

Fear drenches her, and I notice a slight tremor move through her.

"Everyone out," she shouts. "I am still queen of this kingdom for another day, and I demand you leave."

Aerona points to the door, and Fen quickly stands, urging Silas to leave the room. He hesitates but eventually responds to his mother, encouraging Larkin to stand and head toward the door. I follow close behind them, hiding the book containing the Rigil under my shirt. I move across the room, unable to hide my irritation that this has gone horribly wrong again.

They cross through the door, and I hear her voice once more. "Briar can stay."

Silas whips around. "What?"

"Briar," Aerona repeats. "I would like to speak with you alone."

I look at Silas, whose face is hard and filled with frustration. I slip the book into his hands and give him a reassuring smile.

"We have things to prepare, so don't take too long," Silas replies. "I'll be outside."

"I will let her leave in one piece, don't worry."

"Oh, I'm not."

I slowly turn, having not yet fully exited the room, and face her. I steady my racing heart when I hear the latch sound from the door closing behind me. Aerona walks to the large window and looks toward the forest.

"I don't blame you, Briar," she says without turning to me. "Not for what happened with Malachi, or for anything that's occurred."

I slowly move behind her, waiting for her to face me again, but she doesn't. She keeps her gaze fixated on the forest.

"Can Kalix hear us?" she asks, and the question catches me off guard.

"To an extent, I believe she can. But she is not present right now." I pause, finding myself doing a quick check. "I've mastered keeping her at bay over the years. It's difficult, but it's doable," I explain. "But, to be honest, it's not manageable forever. Each day gets harder, and one day, I know my time will run out."

She turns to me and studies me. "Does Silas know?"

"He knows a lot." I shake my head. "But I haven't told him the extent of how hard it is."

"I know you keep it from him to protect him, to keep him from worrying, but don't. He would burn this world to the ground for you and rebuild it using the bones of the fallen."

My heart thunders. "That's exactly why I keep it from him, Aerona. I fear he would destroy himself to protect me, and right now, I can't put that on him. It's an impossible weight to carry."

"Nothing is impossible." She moves toward me. "But, I understand your fear. There are many things I've kept a secret to protect those around me. It's hard—it eats at me daily—and I fear every second that the truth will come forward."

I know exactly what she is speaking about, but I remain quiet to allow her to ponder her own words.

Aerona fidgets with her necklace, moving the jewel in and out of her hands. The dark jewel gleams in the light. It's distracting, even amid the beauty of this bedroom. I can't help but stare at it.

"I've entered the Forgotten Archives a few times, and would you believe me if I told you each time was an accident? A gravitational pull for me to enter it."

"I believe you," I respond.

"I have always searched for something, knowledge regarding something, and each time I was lost in thought, desperate for answers, it would appear. I had family members go mad searching for the Archives, but it opened each time for me."

Aerona moves back to the couch and plops down, like a weight sits heavily on her shoulders. I remain standing, watching her for a moment.

The queen lets out a shaky breath, recounting the memories. "Without knowing, I entered the Archives and was quickly turned away by the darkness that haunts there."

I move to sit back down near her. "Is that the answer you were looking for? Haunting creatures that aren't from this realm?"

She slowly pans her gaze to me. "Yes."

"Why?"

A tear sits heavy in the corner of her eye. "I think you know why, Briar."

I don't respond, but I watch a tear roll down her cheek. I can't imagine the weight she feels from having lied to her children their whole lives about their father. As much as I want to dislike her, I pity her. A woman faced with an impossible choice will often do desperate things, especially for the sake of her children. I now know why she wanted to speak about that alone. She couldn't tell Silas why she was in the Archives without having to come clean about Malachi.

"Are the answers we seek in the Archives?" I ask.

"Yes," she whispers.

"How can we safely get in there? How does this Rigil protect me?" I lean forward, and I can feel the desperation rolling off my tongue.

She exhales and dives deep into her own mind for a moment. "When you enter, immediately hide. There is a desk in the middle; don't go to it. That's what the creature wants. There is a large bookcase to the left. Rush behind that and gather yourself." She swallows as if remembering the fear she experienced. "The creature will feel your presence and prepare. Draw the Rigil as quickly and accurately as you can on your hand. You can't draw it before entering, or the wards won't move into place. The Rigil will make you invisible for a short while. Use it wisely and go after what you want."

"And if that goes wrong?" I reply, making mental notes of everything she said.

"Then you need to run as if your life depends on it—because it does."

I swallow hard, and she stares at me even harder.

"What's in there, Aerona? What is everyone so desperate to find out?"

She squirms in her seat and fiddles with the jewel resting low on her chest. "After the Great Battle, many tried to destroy all documents related to the Great Wiitches. People were ashamed and afraid and wanted no records of their magic or stories. A few individuals saw this as wrong and sought to preserve history, which is why the Forgotten Archives were established. The Great Wiitches, the stones, even the Gods, have weaknesses, and those weaknesses lie within the Archives."

I nod, allowing the words to sink in as I prepare to stand up to take my leave. I don't believe there is anything else she is willing to discuss.

She sighs. "There is one thing that won't be in the Archives."

She once again clutches her jewel, and I drop my gaze, not wanting to stare continuously.

"This has been passed down through my family for many

generations. I only recently learned more about what I have possessed all these years."

I freeze, anticipation taking over me. She removes her necklace and extends her hand for me to take it. I don't move.

"Take it," she offers.

"I don't believe that's necessary, Aerona," I respond, retracting my hand behind my back.

"Please." She extends her hand further. "There are many things I regret in my life, and I don't want to make this one of them. It will be of better use to you."

I angle my head and study the jewel perfectly crafted into the necklace. The light dances off the stone, casting dark green and black colors into the room.

"You will learn more in the Archives, but it's yours, Briar. Wield it, use it, and wipe those fuckers off the face of this realm."

I slip out of Aerona's room and back into the narrow hallway leading down to the main part of the castle. Her words rush through my mind. Entering the Archives tonight will be challenging, but nothing I can't handle. I'm ready, but even in the back of my mind, what dwells within makes my stomach roll. I've seen my fair share of haunting creatures before, but something tells me this one is where the rumors started in Andorwood.

I glance in all directions, looking for my worrywart of a man, but I don't see or feel his presence.

I continue my stroll, trying my best to ignore the height staring back at me through the large open windows. I feel my palms become sweaty, so I move to the farthest stone wall, dragging my hand along the rough surface. Aerona's necklace sits heavily in my pocket, and I reach in, messing with the thick chain holding the jewel. My fingers tingle against the smooth texture of the stone, and I can't help but feel as if I'm back in the forest from so many months ago, finding the resurrection stone. However, this time is different. My magic isn't pulsing, and this stone feels dead.

I understand this signifies something important, and I'm eager to learn why.

My senses perk, and something in my chest tightens. A smile spreads across my face as I round a corner, leading me down into the castle. Silas leans against the stone wall with his arms crossed, his back to me, impatiently waiting for me to arrive.

Without even turning, his voice sounds around the hall. "Hello, my queen."

"Hello, my stalker. I'm having flashbacks of you at Daramveer Castle, always lurking around the narrow halls." I grin and grab his arm, turning him to face me. "Are you always this desperate for my attention?"

"I'm desperate for anything concerning you," he says with a smirk.

"Come on," I tug on his arm, pulling him to follow me.

"You know I want to ask," he says, his steps falling in line with mine.

"Oh, I'm sure you are dying to know what I talked about with your mother."

"I am," he bites back.

"She loves me," I say, sarcastically.

"Who wouldn't?"

I huff. "A lot of people, apparently."

He chuckles.

I pause, planting my feet, and Silas runs into the back of me.

The abrupt stop causes him to trip, nearly taking us both to the ground. Turning to stare at him, his face is laced with confusion. I reach into my pocket and pull out his mother's necklace. His eyes widen, but he doesn't speak.

"Aerona gave me this." I extend my hand for him to take it if he wishes, but his hands remain at his side. "She told me I would find out what this is within the Archives."

He gazes at the stone, his eyes widening slightly. "I can't believe she gave you that. She's had that for as long as I can remember."

"She provided me with information about the Archives, and I trust her regarding the documents. She also informed me about how to use the Rigil to our advantage and where I should hide once I enter."

"Alright," Silas replies. "That sounds great, but I sense you're not happy about something?"

I nod. "She told me to go to the left and hide, but what she doesn't realize is that I've been in the Archives, and there is no bookshelf to the left."

He angles his head, still confused.

"There is a tunnel in that direction, but there is nothing there for me to hide behind. She's lying, and I don't know why."

"Maybe she just got confused, Briar. I don't think my mother would lie about this," Silas defends.

"I thought you might say that," I shake my head. "Then, tell me why she gave me a fake stone as well."

"What?" he unintentionally shouts.

I clutch the stone and close my eyes, allowing my magic to react. Once again, nothing happens. Silas watches me, his eyes intensely focused on me and the stone.

"Your mother has the stone Yara referred to, not Malachi, and I think it's similar to the resurrection stone. She acted like she wanted me to have it, but this is a fake, and I know it for certain."

"Wait," Silas snaps, understanding exactly where I'm going with this.

"Your mother doesn't have the real stone. Fenmore does."

CHAPTER 33

S ilas's mouth drops open, and he stares blankly at the jewel. "This entire time, Fen has had the stone," I finally speak.

Silas stutters, "I…I had no idea."

"I never realized it, either. I'm also not sure what it does exactly, but I'm going to find out. Tonight."

Silas rubs his face, stopping at his temples to apply pressure. His eyes close, and I allow him a moment to process this information. He leans to the side, propping his shoulder against the stone wall once more.

"I gave Larkin the book to return to the house. He was going to tell Oak to start translating the text on the Rigil."

"Thank you."

"Do you think this is a good idea? You are making it harder and harder for me to let you do this alone," he mutters.

"Nope," I respond.

Surprise dances on Silas's expression for a moment before he tilts his head back and laughs.

"Well, alright then," he says. "Just really driving a knife in my heart, aren't you?"

"I think this is a horrible idea, but what other choice do we have?" I respond and hug him.

"I don't think we have many choices here," he responds.

"We don't have long before the ship arrives. We will do this, then focus on what's ahead. I know the others have been preparing for days. We will be ready as well."

I stand on my tiptoes to nuzzle my face into his neck. We stay this way momentarily before I pull away, cupping his face.

"I can do this."

"I know you can," Silas sighs, before kissing me softly. "We need to return to my house to update the others. Nightfall will arrive before we know it, and the crimson moon will rise. We must be prepared, but you, above all, must be ready."

"Have you talked to Fen anymore?" I ask.

"Not really," he says. "She is still processing everything."

"Do you think she will be able to handle all of this?"

"I do," he says. "She is strong like you."

I smile. "Try to talk to her again. She needs you."

Silas nods and grabs my hand as we shift together out of the stuffy castle walls and toward his house on the cliff. The world blurs as we move swiftly through the shadows. Even though my body doesn't feel like my own, I continue to grip Silas's hand tightly.

My mind races faster than our bodies. Aerona is lying for some reason. Fen has had the stone this entire time, and I believe we possess something akin to the resurrection stone, though I have no idea what gifts or curses this stone could bring. I know that we are one step closer to discovering everything we need to fight this battle, yet my nerves don't ease. The truth being so close only makes me more anxious. I say a silent prayer to the Gods that what we seek is truly in the Archives and can help us.

Our bodies reappear outside the small house on the wooden porch that covers most of the front. Silas smiles and squeezes my hand, opening the door that will lead us down into the main part of the house, in the open living area.

As we enter the house, I can hear the muffled bickering of Maines, Oak, and Larkin below. The translation must have already begun, and they are arguing over who is correct. We descend into the central part of the house and find them all sitting around the large wooden table, the unfolded sheet of paper before them.

Oak holds his head in his hands while Maines paces around the room. Her usually perfect hair is a tangled mess, and Larkin sits back with both feet propped on the table. I glance around the room for Fen and Warrick and can barely see their silhouettes on the balcony, alone. The paper illuminates in the sun but quickly fades as a shadow of a cloud crosses the low-hanging sun.

Larkin sees us first and quickly drops his feet to the ground.

He notices my stare toward the balcony and says, "They need a minute alone."

Silas moves toward the table and sits down in his usual spot at the head. I follow suit and sit between him and Larkin. Oak raises his head, his tired eyes filled with confusion and worry. Maines returns to her seat and forcefully sits down beside Oak.

Silas clears his throat. "I see the translation is progressing well."

"Oh, shut up, Nastronde," Oak snaps back, placing his glasses back on his face. "It's going terribly. None of this makes sense."

Maines rubs his hand, offering him some comfort and support.

"What does it say, Oak?" I ask.

He wipes his brow and places both hands on the table, trying to calm himself. "I told you it doesn't make sense, and the same text is written three times."

Oak slides a piece of paper in my direction with many different scribbles, written text, and practiced Rigils in Oak's handwriting.

I study the page and read:

Shadow and light must coexist in harmony. The blood of the panicked must be bled for the answers to be obtained.

I glance at Oak, and his hair is even more disheveled than before, and I read the last sentence.

Invisible darkness cannot fight the undetectable.

My thoughts run wild, and I lift my gaze once more, finding Oak practically falling out of his chair as the anticipation fills him. I find it hilarious, I must say. A loud bubble of nervous laughter escapes my throat, and his face turns puzzled.

"This is funny to you?" Oak sits straight up. "I'm over here about to go cross-eyed, and you are laughing?"

"I'm sorry." I laugh again. "How the hell did we wind up here?"

I glance around the room, and the others watch me, clearly believing I've gone insane.

"A year ago, we would have all thought someone was insane if they told us where we would end up."

Maines smiles. "I agree."

"I wouldn't want to be here with anyone else, though. I'm going to fix this for us."

Fen and Warrick walk back into the room, hearing our conversation, and Fen sits at the table beside Maines. Her face is pale, and I can tell she hasn't slept well. The stone around her neck is distracting, but I do all I can to ignore the jewel after discovering what I think is a second stone. It's been safe this long with her, so I'm going to let it remain that way until we know more. Warrick remains cold as ice, and for the first time, his face looks gaunt and tired.

Larkin shuffles in his chair. "You speak as if you are doing this alone, Briar. You aren't alone."

"Agreed. We are doing this together or not at all," Silas speaks.

"You all may proceed without me, because if I endure any more of this, I'm likely to die from stress," Oak says, clearly having regained some of his humor.

"No, you aren't," Fen says. " You are stuck with us all, Hombern, whether you like it or not."

We chuckle briefly until silence falls back over us. The page before me burns into my memory, and I take a moment to mentally prepare for what's to come.

"I'm assuming you all know what the message means within the Rigil? I'm the only one feeling left out?" Oak asks.

"You aren't left out, Oak," Maines replies. "I just know that Silas and Briar already have a plan, like always."

We exchange a quick look, and I give him the go-ahead to fill them all in.

Silas clears his throat. "Tonight, Briar will enter the Forgotten Archives. We will take the information that we have and pray that it's enough for her to find the answers we seek. Many documents in there pertain to the Great Wiitches, and possibly what we need to destroy them, or at least save our vessels."

Fen flinches at that word, like the link between her and Rohhit is painful.

Silas continues, "I have no idea how long Briar has in the Archives, but we will wait outside the door. Should anything go wrong, I'm prepared to enter, protected or not."

"I'm prepared, too," Larkin says.

"So are we," Maines says, along with Oak.

I snap my gaze to them. "No way. If you're not protected, then there's no way you can come in after me."

"Like we said," Larkin interjects. "You aren't alone in this, so stop trying to be."

I smile, and a rush of gratitude fills me.

"Then it's settled. We will prepare for tonight." Silas stands.

"Tomorrow morning, I will declare myself King of Andorwood before the entire kingdom. I will give them the option to choose their own paths or fight alongside us. Andorwood has kept the true state of this kingdom a secret all these years. However, we are still a band of rebels. Whatever happens, our plan remains unchanged."

"I agree," I say, standing alongside him. "We have our plans in motion and are prepared for when the ship gets closer. We will stick to the plan we established together."

The rest of the group stands and dismisses themselves. Silas and the men move toward the sitting area to discuss the upcoming events, while Maines heads to her bedroom to gather a few healing properties we may need should things go wrong tonight. Fen remains alone, and I watch her sluggishly return to the balcony, desperate to be in a wide-open space.

I give her a second to settle in, and I follow behind her. The open air tickles my nose, and I take a deep breath as I walk up beside her at the railing.

"Are you alright?" I ask, hesitating because I already know the answer.

Her beautiful face turns in my direction. Her long black hair moves in the wind, and her piercing eyes seem dull, like she's lost.

She huffs an uncomfortable laugh. "I don't even know anymore."

"Do you want to talk about it?"

"How do you cope with everything that's happened? I feel like I'm constantly falling into a deep hole, and the deeper I go, the harder it will be to come back up for air." Tears form on her eyelids. "He's consuming me."

"Who?" I ask, but know the answer.

"All my waking thoughts revolve around Rohhit. It's an itch I can't scratch—a need—a desperate desire to find him. If this is anything like how Silas felt for five whole years, I don't know how he endured the pain without ending it all."

Her words take me aback, and I watch her chest rise and fall rapidly, trying to catch a proper breath. I wrap my arm around her shoulders and pull her close, trying to provide her with warmth and comfort in this moment.

"Warrick tries to help. He says everything he can to soothe my pain, but it doesn't work, and it makes me want to push him away because he's not him. The only person who can help is…" She trails off.

"Rohhit," I answer.

She turns to me, and her eyes are now overwhelmed with tears. They rapidly fall down her cheeks, and my heart shatters.

"Did it hurt this bad for you? When Silas wasn't around?"

My lips form a thin line. "I think it's different for us. I felt like I was missing something, like someone was always whispering my name, but I couldn't reach them. It was daunting."

"It's awful," she whispers.

"I think it hurts because you know Rohhit is in pain," I say, hesitantly.

A tear rolls down her cheek.

"We will save him," I say. "I'll do anything to make sure neither of you is in pain."

She sighs, glancing toward where Warrick stood earlier. "I think I'll always be in pain."

My heart slams against my ribs, and I watch as her face contorts into pain. Fenmore lowers her gaze, and I fully turn toward her.

"The first time I saw your brother, he had broken into my bedroom, and I tried to slit his throat."

She chuckles, and more tears fall. "Sounds about right. What did Silas do?"

"Flirted."

She laughs again.

I continue, "But, when I got close to him, I felt it—a cord snapping in my chest. From that moment, thoughts of him consumed me. As much as I couldn't stand his unbearable hovering, I craved his attention and closeness. I pushed it away as long as I could, but it was nearly impossible. Rohhit knows you are out there, Fenmore, and he's waiting on you to wake him up."

She lets out a muffled sob and buries her head in my shoulder. I wrap her tightly and let her cry.

"He's lost, so fucking lost, and I fear I may never find him. I can't go on with this pain," she sobs.

"Then we will do everything in our power to find him. Just keep holding on to that feeling. Listen to your instinct and keep the cord vibrating for him. He can feel it, I promise."

She wipes her tears and stands up straight. "Thank you, Briar."

I give her shoulder another squeeze before dropping my hand against the railing once more. Her sniffles begin to quiet, and her chest moves at a steady pace once more.

"Can I ask you something?"

"Of course. Anything," Fen responds.

"Since being in Andorwood, all I've seen are different variations of serpents. What do they mean?"

She smiles. "Ah, yes. All over the castle and streets. I'm surprised it's taken you this long to ask."

I huff a laugh, "Been a bit busy."

"For as long as I can remember, serpents have been everywhere in Andorwood. They symbolize so much to all of us here. She pauses before continuing, "Andorwood is known for housing rebels—the forgotten, the criminals—but truly, Andorwood is a place where you can be who you want without judgment. Serpents are celebrated here because they not only represent our kingdom but also embody all of us."

I narrow my eyes, waiting for her to continue.

"The snakes symbolize many different things: healing, rebirth, temptation, life, wisdom, evil, and unity. We use serpents as our symbol because it allows everyone to feel included, regardless of their reasons."

I nod.

"When you leave here, I hope you recognize that the people here aren't the monsters you should fear." She points a trembling hand toward the mainland, where all our problems began. "Those monsters reside over there."

"I plan to get rid of those monsters," I respond.

"I like to think about the positive aspects the serpent represents." Fen smiles but hesitates to continue, and I assume it's because her mind goes dark.

"Legend has it that a creature larger than the mountain once lived on the isle of Andorwood, long before the Great Wiitches roamed this realm. Legend states that the God of Darkness, Raddnoke, created this beast."

"Silas mentioned something about that long ago," I reply. "We've heard those stories on the mainland. Do you believe it?"

"I don't know." She shrugs. "Aren't legends created by drunk men sitting around a fire? I don't pay them much attention."

I laugh, and silence falls over us.

"Things are going to change with Silas in charge," she says, as she looks at me.

"Yes, they are, but it's going to be for the better."

"Can I ask you something now?" she asks, hesitantly.

"Anything."

"Have you thought about when this is over, and you have to rule Daramveer, and Silas must rule Andorwood, what you are going to do?"

Her question surprises me.

No, I've never considered that, because honestly, I'm not sure we will ever reach that point. A wave of emotions washes over me, and I struggle to maintain a calm expression.

Why the fuck would she ask that?

"If it's worth anything, I think you should come here," Fenmore whispers. "Permanently, when all this is over."

I feel my chest tighten. "You know I can't leave Daramveer, Fen."

"You can," she argues. "If the reason was enough."

I blink at her, unable to process what she's saying.

Give up my reign over Daramveer and return to Andorwood to rule alongside Silas?

"I guess we'll see what happens," I reply, sharply.

"I can live with that answer." Fen turns to enter the house once more. "Come on, let's get you ready for the Archives. I have some armor that your ass is going to look amazing in."

I boom a laugh and follow her into the house, but I can't shake her question.

When this is over, what happens to Silas and me?

CHAPTER 34

The sky is aflame with the deepest shades of auburn and red as the sun sits low, barely peeking over the horizon in the fresh night sky. On the opposite side of the world, an unforgettable crimson moon rises, sending a chill up my spine. We exit Silas's house together, as prepared as we possibly can be for tonight's events. We spent the rest of the afternoon devising plans for various scenarios that usually ended with something going wrong, the plan failing, or not finding the Archives at all.

Despite preparing as much as I could, I feel like I have no clue what I'm up against.

We move across the vast grounds, and I revel in the open air. We take turns shifting toward the kingdom, but never all together so we don't attract unwanted attention from the surges of magic. Something about being here has deepened my love for nature, despite the threat from the creatures in the woods.

That's one thing I fear I'll never get over.

I gaze up at the sky and think of all the past moons I experienced in Daramveer. Many times, I would venture out to the roof of the castle to watch the moon rise and fall after my birthday had passed. I never got over the beauty of the different moons marking each new season. However, this moon is filled with an ominous calm that does nothing to settle our nerves as we head toward the castle in the night.

The moon's eerie red glow illuminates our surroundings, and the air feels thick—as if holding its breath in anticipation. The clouds above swirl in violent chaos, with tinges of a blood-red glow casting a beautiful yet unsettling feeling through my bones. This is the night, and I swallow down all the fear desperate to break loose.

Silas walks beside me, his towering body calm, steady, and filled with a lethal focus. He's dressed in fine armor that perfectly contours over each of his finely toned muscles. The armor resembles what he wore upon our arrival, featuring a deadly serpent on the front and sturdy sections of thin metal that protect him from external threats. The other men are similarly attired, and I couldn't help but feel surprised when I saw Oak clad in such darkness.

Fen lent me and Maines some of her finest armor—also adorned with serpents—allowing us to wear similar fittings to the men. Ours differs slightly, as our snake is bright gold, flashy, and a bit excessive, which perfectly describes Fenmore in most settings. I begged Silas to let me bring my axes, but he assured me that they would do nothing to protect us from the creature that dwells inside the Archives. I protested, but finally agreed to leave them behind. They would have looked perfect against the gold snake on my chest.

We walk together as a united force, outmatching the chaos that swirls above us in the sky. No one dares to come near, aware that it would be a deadly mistake, as we move closer to the castle. The castle grounds are quiet, and I can't help but glance around every corner for something unseen. Anxiety about Malachi's return gnaws at me, but I push the feeling down.

We enter the castle from the back instead of the usual front door. Hours earlier, we decided that shifting to Silas's room would be an obvious choice. Since we don't know where the Archives will open and can't afford any mistakes, we opted for a secret back passage that Fen knows about. That girl is sneaky, and I absolutely love her for it.

Moonlight shines through the castle's windows, making it appear as if blood is smeared across the stone walls. Our steps are soundless across the hard stone floors, and each noise has us all on edge. As we move deeper into the castle, the air becomes impossibly thick, and a bead of sweat forms on my brow—from the armor and nerves. Silas leads the way as we move through each winding hallway, always looking over his shoulder to make sure I'm close behind him. The others cover us with Warrick at the very back.

The lit torches compete with the brightness of the moon, and for the first time in a long while, I wish the darkness concealed us more. Being this exposed makes me uncomfortable, especially when we want to avoid any unwanted visitors. Silas comes to a stop and turns to face us all.

"Do you have the page with the Rigil?" he asks, looking at me.

I nod, patting my breast pocket. "Yup."

"Any clue where this thing will open up?" Larkin asks.

"Unfortunately, no. I'm not aware of that. The last time I genuinely encountered it. A Traveler was pursuing me, so I was panicked and desperately searching for a place to hide."

"So, emotions played a role in finding it," Silas thinks aloud.

Oak steps forward and says, "There's no way you'll find another Traveler to chase her."

Silas rolls his eyes. "No, Hombern. I'm not having that happen. However," he says, clearly thinking. "Briar does have another creature that seems to help her."

I snap my eyes at him. "Not an option. Plus, that thing comes when it wants, not when I call it."

"Have you ever tried?" Larkin asks.

"Well, no," I respond. "What do you suggest, Larkin? Just shout, 'Come here, creature. Come help me, please.'"

Larkin huffs, "Alright, sheesh. I was just asking."

I lean forward to nudge him, but he bats me away.

Silas sighs, obviously tired of us already. "Well, if that isn't an option, we have to think of something and fast. We need to look for any signs that this is going to open up for us."

I look at Fen, who stands closest to Warrick. As usual, her hand is wrapped around the jewel that hangs low on her neck, outside of her armor.

If this stone is important and similar to the resurrection stone, then perhaps it can assist us now. I push through the others and walk before her. She jolts back at my presence, and I gently remove her hand from the jewel.

"Can I see that?" I ask quietly.

I can tell from her reaction that she did not see this coming, so I allow her some time to think. She glances down at her hand wrapped around the stone and unfurls her fingers. She slides her thumb across the smooth crystal and hesitates to respond.

"I believe what you have is something special. Your mother gave me hers, but it isn't the right stone." I take her mother's necklace from my breast pocket and show it to Fen. "When I first realized the stone was fake, I accused your mother of lying. But now that I think about it, I don't believe she knew. I think all along she believed she had the real stone."

I hear Silas exhale with relief, hoping that his mother may not have betrayed us. Although, I can't shake her telling me to go toward the bookshelf on the left. There isn't a bookshelf on the left if my memory serves me correctly.

"May I hold the stone? I know it's important to you, so I'll do my best to be as careful as possible." I give her a kind smile and make sure to keep my voice low and gentle.

She hesitates but motions for Warrick to unclasp the chain from around her neck. He slowly reaches up to her neck and works for a second to release the necklace. The jewel falls in her hand, and she stares at it for a moment, lost in thought. She raises her gaze to mine and extends her hand for me to take the pendant. I move my head toward the shining jewel, and my magic dances excitedly.

This is the right stone.

She drops the jewel in my hand, and a shock travels up my arm, similar to the resurrection stone. The weight of the stone is surprising.

How could anyone wear this daily around their neck without developing neck problems?

I turn to face Silas once more. "This is going to help us. Don't ask why; I know. I'm following my instincts."

"Lead the way, my love." He beams with pride.

I push past the others and make my way down the winding halls deep within the castle walls. With each step forward, the passage darkens, making it harder for the moonlight to seep through the stone cracks. The air grows musty and hot, accompanied by a faint trickle of water echoing in the darkness. I don't tell the others, but I have no clue where I'm going. I push forward, faking my confidence with each step, and pray the others can't tell I'm completely lost.

I continuously look down at the stone, hoping that something will give me a sign.

I hear Fen whisper to Silas behind me. "Do you have any idea where we are?"

He doesn't reply, so I know his answer must be no.

Frustration begins to grow in my chest, and I know the others are starting to tire of mindlessly wandering around the castle backrooms. I close my eyes and focus forward. Even within the depths of the stone walls, I swear I can hear a faint breeze. I pause, causing the others to stop abruptly behind me, and I hear Oak curse softly after slamming into Maines.

I keep my eyes closed and tune them out, focusing on what my surroundings are trying to convey. My magic starts to simmer within my veins, and I release control, allowing my shadows and light to guide me. I need to know the truth that the Archives holds. The jewel in my hand responds to the small bouts of magic dancing around me, and I glance at my palm.

The dark green stone begins to illuminate, causing my hand to tremble under its weight. Silas leans over my shoulder for a better look, and I feel his body tense beside me. I hold my palm forward, allowing the stone to brighten the way, only to be met with a stone wall a few yards ahead in the darkness. Defeat spreads through me.

A dead end.

"Well, this is unexpected," Oak chimes in through the darkness, followed by a loud *"shhh"* from Maines.

Silas places his hand on my shoulder. "Is this what happened the first time?"

I stare forward. "Yes, but it almost immediately showed itself. I didn't have to do anything."

"Close your eyes. What are you feeling?" he coaches me.

"To move toward the wall, even though it's solid," I respond.

"Then go for it," Silas says, kissing the top of my head. "Be careful."

He gives me a gentle nudge, and I move forward with the stone trembling in my palm. He stops the others from advancing, allowing me time to listen to what my body is screaming at me to do. The wall before me is solid, cold, and dense. I feel foolish for standing in front of this dead-end while the others watch.

I place my hand against the stone and dive into my magic.

This is the place, and I don't know how, but I can feel it in my bones. I place my other hand, holding the jewel against the wall, along with my forehead.

I breathe in deeply and whisper, "I need to know the truth. I just need answers."

The wall remains solid stone, and defeat spreads through me once more. This is impossible. How do you find something that wants to remain hidden? I push off the wall and stare at it, hoping my anger will force it open. The others remain silent behind me, watching with wide eyes. I'm sure they are either waiting for me to explode or for the wall to yield.

I know this is the place.

I clutch the jewel hard in my hands, and I can feel the edges dig into my clenched fist. I refuse to accept defeat or consider an alternative path.

Show me the truth.

I push my free palm against the stone wall once more, not caring that I look insane to the others, and pray that this will somehow work. Crazier things have happened, right? But once again, I'm met with nothing. My shoulders slacken, and I turn around to face the others, even though I'm filled with embarrassment. Maines and Larkin offer me reassuring smiles.

"We will try another route," Silas says.

"I'm sorry," I respond. "I thought this was it."

Warrick spins on his heels to file out of the thin hallway, but I remain frozen in my spot.

The wall, stone, and hallway around me begin to tremble, and the stone sends a painful zap shooting up my arm. My dark veins start to pulse, and I jerk my head toward the wall and step back a few paces, only to stop against Silas's strong chest. The others watch in awe as the once-stone wall begins to shift into a shimmer of brightness, nearly blinding us from the blast of light.

Just like before, the wall shimmers like diamonds floating underneath dark water.

"This is it. It worked." I mumble to Silas.

"Are you sure?" he asks.

"Trust me."

I step forward, feeling vibrations all around me, throbbing as I make my way to enter the Forgotten Archives once more. Fear pulses in my veins, and I attempt to calm my racing heart. I move forward with confidence, but I wish I weren't doing this alone right now. I pat my pocket to make sure the perfectly folded piece of paper remains there, and I quickly clasp the necklace around my neck.

I place my hand against the stone wall and let the familiar crushing feeling envelop me as I move through the wall and into the Archives. Once again, I pray that I haven't just walked to my death, and for some reason, I fear I have. I hold my breath as the walls constrict around me, pushing me further into the depths of what feels like another realm. I try to turn my head to watch the others disappear behind me, but the pull of the Archives keeps me focused ahead. Every second I remain in this limbo, I feel my limbs begin to stretch, and a searing pain travels from my core to the tips of my fingers. I grind my molars, and with one final push, I move forward into complete darkness.

I keep my eyes closed, and my body feels like it's piecing itself back together. Minutes, seconds, or hours pass—I'm not sure—but the familiar smell of aged paper fills my nose. I move my feet, feeling the firm ground under me, and slowly open my eyes.

Just like before, the sconces on the wall ignite with flames, acknowledging the presence of someone entering the library. The candle, just as the last time, sits on the nearby reading table, and I grab it and light the wick from the sconce of the nearby wall. The room is silent, except for my heavy breathing, and to my surprise, no other small serpents slither at my feet, as if they have vanished since I was last here. I'm alone for now, and that doesn't make me feel any more at ease.

I force myself not to think of the fear I felt the last time I entered this place, but I fail to steady the rhythm of my heart. I exhale a shaky breath and step one foot further into the space.

I quickly survey my surroundings, and my mouth slightly parts in shock when I turn to my left and see towering bookshelves stretching for miles before me. I snap my gaze to the right, where a dark tunnel tucked in the corner gives me nothing but bad vibes. The large wooden table in the middle remains the same, but it's as if the room has flipped. Everything that was on the left is now on the right, and vice versa.

What the fuck?

Aerona somehow knew that the room would change, and I can't make sense of how. She wasn't lying; she was preparing me for the confusion I currently feel. I don't allow myself to dwell on the change for long, because I know there are still moments left before the creature I hoped never to see again makes its appearance. I glance behind me at the exit, and it looks like an impenetrable wall again. I fight the urge to move forward and instead rush behind the bookshelf to my left. Only silence fills the library, and I wonder how much time I truly have.

My footsteps are nearly soundless as I rush to the side and crouch behind the towering bookshelf. Thousands of books rest toward my back and above my head, concealing me from the library's depths.

So far, so good.

I fumble to reach for my pocket, housing the folded piece of paper that contains the Rigil I will need to draw on myself to shield me from whatever creature haunts the library. As soon as Oak read what the ancient text said, I immediately knew I had to enter the library alone and use my own blood to draw the Rigil on my body three times.

I remove the paper and unfold what Oak gave me with the text and the Rigil. I somewhat remember the exact lines, but he thought it would be beneficial for me to have a guide should I need it, and I did not argue with him about that. I stare at the Rigil before me, and the color drains from my face. The ink is smudged, and I can't fully make out the exact lines. If the Rigils aren't completed to perfection, the ritual won't work. I squint my eyes to better focus, but the lines are too smudged for me to have an exact replica.

My hands begin to tremble, and I dive into my memory, making sure I can remember the marking as well as possible. A fuzzy image of the Rigil comes to mind, and I have one shot to get this right. I unsheath the dagger from my side and take a deep breath. I will have to cut myself deeply to get all the blood needed for three intricate Rigils. I pull up my sleeve and prepare for the pain.

I place the blade across my upper forearm and press into my skin. Painful memories flash across my mind. Barlowe and his lifeless body lying below me, moments from death, and Yara, slicing her own neck.

Not now. Don't panic now.

I hesitate to swipe the blade across my arm when I hear it—a low growl that drains me of all happiness, as it sounds through the library. I jolt and drop the blade, sending it crashing to the ground.

CHAPTER 35

I press my back against the bookshelf and try to calm my breathing. The dagger is a few feet in front of me, so I lean forward to reach for the blade, but it's too far away. My mind freezes, and for a second, I can't think of the Rigil that I need to draw on my body. I use my foot to reach for the blade and successfully snag it, pulling it back within arm's reach.

I bring the trembling blade to my forearm once more and press it into my skin. A dull pain begins to travel up my arm as the dagger slowly cuts into my arm. Another low growl reverberates around the library, and I hear books start to fall from the shelves. Whatever this thing is, it's large enough to barely fit through the vast spaces between each towering shelf. Through the growls, I can hear something sliding, like someone is pushing something large across the floor, but I don't let myself think about the sounds until I finish this task. The smudged paper lies beside me, and I close my eyes.

I swipe the blade across my left arm, feeling the searing pain move up my arm and down to my fingertips. A hushed whimper leaves my throat, and tears well in my eyes as I drop the blade once more. The blade clinks against the floor, and I regret not holding on to it. That sound just told whatever lives in here where I'm hiding, again. Warm liquid begins to run down my arm, and I open my eyes to see blood pouring from the cut.

I look at the paper, my vision blurred from the tears, and dip my finger in the thick crimson liquid. On the back of my right hand, I move my leather back as far as possible and begin to draw the Rigil as best I can remember. My hands tremble so much that each circle is warped, but it will do. Three circles overlapping with a line through the middle, followed by exactly three dots, and a few more markings, complete the first Rigil. The drawing illuminates with a white light, and it dries in place. My arm bleeds, and I take a second to assess the cut. It's not too deep, and even in my panicked state, I swiped the blade precisely. Gratitude fills me for my previous training in wielding a blade.

I dip my shaking finger back into my own blood, now covering most of my arm, and move on to the second Rigil. I flip my hand over, beginning to work on the second one. More books continue to fall behind me, and I can't help but flinch at the loud sounds that move around the typically silent library. With each passing second, the creature moves closer, and I can feel a slight breeze coming from behind me. A hissing noise makes me move faster, and I draw each overlapping circle once more and complete the second to last Rigil.

An overwhelming stinging sensation moves through my arm, and I grit my teeth to stay focused.

One more time.

With most of my body covered, I lift my quaking arm covered in blood and begin to repeat the marking on my forehead. The liquid is hot, and I attempt to keep it from running into my eyes, already blurry from tears. My chest heaves, and a breeze moves through the Archives, bringing a stench with it, and that's when panic fills me to the core. The breeze isn't from the wind; it's breath. The creature's breath gets closer each second I take to protect myself.

A growl sounds so close that everything within me tells me to run, but I stay still, making sure the last Rigil illuminates and dries quickly into place. Should all three work, I will be undetectable from the beast that haunts this library. We have no clue how long the wards work on my body, but I pray it's long enough to find what I need.

My arm continues to bleed heavily, and I begin to wobble from the blood loss. I grab a cloth from my pocket and begin working on the cut by applying pressure and wrapping it tightly. I move my leathers over the cut for extra pressure and stay as still as possible with my back flush against the shelf. I blink through the fear and nausea, waiting for the marking on my forehead to snap into place.

The hissing grows louder, and I know it's right behind me. The creature slips one bookshelf behind me, and a terror I've never felt rushes through me. My eyes blur.

No. Gods, no.

I feel myself begin to slip. Maybe I didn't cut myself with precision, and I, in fact, went too deep, causing too much blood to leak from my body quickly. I slowly put both hands on the ground and grind my teeth as I push myself to stand. I squint my eyes and can still see the sconce marking the exit. I may get out before the creature sees me if I can run. I don't think the last Rigil worked, and I have to run. Right now.

I feel a tingle in my forehead as blood drips into my eyes, blurring my vision further. I take a step forward, and a book directly behind the shelf I was hiding behind crashes to the ground—a sound I fear I'll never forget. Fear and pain course through me as I move one foot toward the exit. My entire body sways, and my head throbs. I look toward the exit, and my vision begins to show small dots darting around like black stars.

Don't pass out.

Keep fucking moving.

Another step slowly moves me forward, and the bookshelf no longer shields me. I'm completely exposed, and I hear the slithering of the beast closer than ever. I sway side to side. My left arm slumps to my side, and I extend my right, hoping it will push me forward. My forehead continues to throb, and in the darkness ahead, I see a spark of light shine before a hot stench surrounds me. My hair blows forward, and I desperately take one more step before my legs give out and my world goes black.

"Get up."

"Get up, Briar."

"If you don't get up, this will all be a waste."

I can't open my eyes.

My body feels like it's floating, but I feel no pain. In fact, I feel nothing at all.

"*I swear to the Gods,*" the voice booms. "*Now.*"

Rohhit. That's Rohhit's voice.

"*Open your fucking eyes, Briar, and look for the red book.*"

A gasp escapes my throat, and I sit straight up.

I snap my gaze in every direction, realizing I'm still in the Forgotten Archives. I look down at my arm, where the two Rigils remain perfectly dried, and a small pool of blood has leaked through the bandage and leather, but it's stopped. I lift my unsteady arm to my forehead and feel the liquid hardened on my face. I remain silent, realizing I'm out in the open, no bookshelves surround me, and I'm near the exit, but not close enough to slip through. I don't hear any sounds near me, but I can hear a muffled sound deep in the library. It knew I was here, but it left. The Rigils worked, and the creature couldn't see me. I'm invisible to its sight.

Rohhit's voice. He screamed at me to get up. The short memory comes crashing back into my mind.

Red book.

Find the red book.

I slowly turn, and the library behind me remains silent. A few books lie scattered from the creature moving through the aisles, but it's nowhere to be found. The table in the center of the room is tipped over, and dark shadows move across the floor like a dense black fog.

I stand on unsteady legs and move toward the middle of the room.

The bookshelves loom above me, and I scan the ones I can clearly see. I spot a candle on the ground, so I lean over to grab it. The deeper you go into the library, the darker it gets, so any light will be needed to find the book. A nearby sconce is still lit with a flame, so I place the wick in the fire to illuminate the candle. Thousands of books fill the shelves, and I widen my eyes. How am I supposed to find one book in the sea before me?

Without knowing how long I have until this wears off and remembering that time passes differently here, I begin to walk down the aisle to my right, scanning the books as I go.

Ancient text fills the space, some spines I can read, others take me a minute to translate, and others are in a language forgotten by time that I'm not convinced even Oak could read. I drag my hand against the books and feel the aged spines. Dust covers my fingertips, and I continue down the dark library.

My senses remain alert, but my fear and the sounds of movement throughout the library fade. Wherever the creature is, it is far away, so I allow myself to steady my racing heart and continue down the dark paths.

Minutes, perhaps hours, pass, and I feel as though I've been walking for miles; however, the candle I'm holding hasn't appeared to change. It remains as tall as it was when I first lit it, so knowing how much time has passed is meaningless. My aching feet keep moving forward, yet I haven't seen a red book once. All the books lining the walls are dull, brown, and aged leather. None display an ounce of color, and I feel as if I've temporarily lost the ability to see color.

A sound startles me in the distance, and I quickly press my back against the bookshelf. The muffled sliding noise begins to echo again, and I cover my mouth with my hand, trying to quiet my breathing. Books fall in the distance, and the sound grows closer. I quickly extinguish the candle, and faraway sconces still shine a bit of light around me. I move farther into the shadows, trying to get as close to the shelf as possible.

"I know you are here, little one. I can smell your blood."

A voice slithers into my mind, and the color drains from my face.

"Why do you hide?"

A concealed sob escapes my throat, and I squirm, trying to rid my mind of the hissing voice.

"Come out into the light. Let me see you. You smell delightfully dark like the God himself marks you."

I scale the shelves and move deeper into the aisle, maintaining my focus on the opening ahead. My back brushes against the books as I use my hands to guide myself backward. I see a shadow approaching from the left, moving toward me through the darkness. I keep my hand clasped over my mouth, and a tear rolls down my cheek.

A creature larger than the mountains comes into view and slowly slithers across the opening. Black scales cover its impossibly large body, and spikes as tall as small trees rise from its back. Eyes as orange as a burning forest rest upon its head, and a long tongue flicks out of its mouth, tasting the air—searching for me.

The creature's large body moves past the opening where I am hidden, and I watch in shock as it glides before me. Its serpent-like form continues to flow by the shelf, and my jaw drops when I realize that not only is the creature a serpent, but also that two long claws line its body, tucked in like wings poised to spread and strike when needed.

"Smart one you are, little one. Hiding in plain sight."

The words crash into my mind, evoking fear I've never felt before.

"I won't hurt you. Let me see you."

Even a heavy breath could reveal my location, so I remain as still as possible, though my quivering only increases out of fear. I keep my thoughts silenced, refusing to respond, even in my mind. I continue moving backward when a book, sticking out farther than the others, strikes my arm and crashes to the ground. The creature's tail finally sweeps across the end of the corridor and disappears around the corner.

I continue to backpedal down the long passage, stepping over long-forgotten fallen books and various scrolls, but keeping my gaze focused ahead of me. The slithering sound pauses, and so do I, too afraid to make any noise. The darkness clouds my vision, so I focus on any flickering candlelight I can find along the walls.

I remove my hand from my mouth and exhale, hoping the creature has vanished once more. Ice billows into the open air from my breath, and I quickly realize how cold I am, wrapping my arms around myself.

A low, ancient voice slithers into my mind again.

"I may not be able to see you, but I can hear you. I can smell your fear, feel your quivering, and your fumbling around. I make you nervous."

A book catches my foot, and I stumble backward, unable to steady myself. I clumsily crash to the ground, landing flat on my back.

"Very nervous."

The bookshelves on both sides of me tower above, and I freeze. I see the creature high above, gaining a better vantage point in hopes of spotting me somehow. Its long, slick body moves in unison from head to tail, revealing its underbelly for the first time.

Orange and red scales illuminate the creature's belly as it breathes in and out. The beast pauses high above, and I scoot against the shelf once more, concealing my body in the darkness. I can't move, and even though I'm invisible, I'm frozen in fear. Its large head scans around the room, looking into the aisle next to me before it trains its gaze on the aisle I'm hiding in. The creature's long face cascades lower to the floor, and I press my back as hard as I can against the shelf. Its tongue flicks out of its mouth as its head gets closer and closer to my body.

"I smell you."

I slap my hand over my mouth and move my opposite hand up my leathers toward the cut, blood staining the bandage.

"I hear you."

I slowly unwrap the gauze from around my cut, placing the blood-soaked fabric in my hand.

"And I want to see you so badly."

The creature's head moves close enough for me to reach out and touch it.

I grasp the fabric in my trembling hand and throw it with all my might in the opposite direction. The wet fabric, filled with my scent, slaps against the end of the bookshelf, prompting the creature to hiss and whip its giant head around before quickly moving in that direction.

"I'm coming, little one. There's nowhere you can run in my domain that I won't find you."

I push myself from the shelf and sprint in the opposite direction. I crash through a few books in a panic, but I don't slow my speed as I round the corner, doubling back to race down the next bookshelf. My legs bark in protest, but I never slow my pace. Maybe if I can twist between these shelves, I can lose it.

I hear the creature hiss loudly, discovering the bloody cloth with no body attached.

"Devious little thing. You won't fool me again."

The slithering becomes so loud that my instinct is to cover my ears. As I sprint past each bookshelf, I scan the walls, desperately praying that I'll see worn, red leather. I check my hands, thankful to see each Rigil still pronounced and dark on my skin.

Each bookshelf looks the same, and I start to feel hopeless thoughts creep into my mind, but I press on. Each winding shelf pulls me deeper into the library, making me fear I may never escape this place alive.

This was a very bad idea.

I hear the slithering a few aisles over, maintaining an even pace with me. I turn left out of the passage and feel a similar icy breeze cover my body. The creature is behind me.

I turn right into another long hallway filled with books and see it: a bright red book glowing over twenty shelves up in the dim lighting around us. The necklace around my neck begins to vibrate and warm. My senses flare, and I grab the jewel, as if it's tempting me to move forward—to keep going in that direction—

so I listen. With all I have, I know that is the book. That's what I need to escape with if we want information.

I rush under the glowing leather book and look up. There is no way I can reach the book, so my only option is to begin climbing. I grasp onto the bottom shelf and carefully lift myself. My arm throbs against the weight, but I climb higher and higher, making sure each hand and foot placement is perfectly balanced on the old shelves.

I'm close, but not close enough to grab the book I'm so desperate to reach. The air in the passage shifts, and a strong, cold wind makes my body sway on the bookshelf. I look before me and pause. The creature's long, serpentine body snakes below me, its black tongue tasting the air. I don't let fear overtake me, and I move. Only a few rows separate me from the book. Maybe I can continue to climb up and use the tops of the shelves to rush back to the entrance.

I extend my arm and stretch my body toward the red book. My fingers barely graze the book's spine, so I plant my right foot and lift my opposite leg to lean toward the ancient text. Beads of sweat cover my brow, and horror fills my core. My lifted leg bumps into another book, causing it to leave the shelf and tumble to the ground. I watch the book descend into the darkness below me, and my world freezes.

The giant below me pauses and lifts its head using its wide, sharp claws at its side. The beast's face becomes eye-level with me, invisible and frozen on the bookshelf. I'm trapped. If I move, it'll know I'm here, and if I fall, it's likely to do more damage to my body than good.

My chest heaves as I reassure myself that it can't see me. It doesn't know I'm here. Its long tongue flicks in and out, tasting the air.

I swallow and reach for the book, but I'm still not close enough.

The creature gazes directly into my eyes, and it smiles, revealing rows of razor-sharp teeth.

"Hello, little one."

CHAPTER 36

'm too shocked to speak, and I'm too terrified to open my mouth.

The creature can't possibly see me. The Rigils still show on my hands, gripping the shelves. I should be invisible; I should be undetected. This can't be happening.

I stare into its hopeless eyes. My heart races, my legs feel numb, and I can't blink. The markings are dry and sealed to my body.

Realization travels through me.

My face is covered in sweat, and my forehead is soaked. It's not sweat that's dripping down, it's blood. The blood that is supposed to be guarding me from the creature staring directly into my eyes.

I open my mouth to speak, but words don't come out.

"Whom do I have the pleasure of meeting?" The words echo in my mind.

The creature's mouth doesn't open. It only stares, and I realize it's speaking only into my mind, not into the open. My hands tremble, and sweat now pools around my palms. I won't be able to hold on much longer. I cut my eyes to the book, still glowing in the darkness around us.

"I…I'm Briar," I say, failing to keep my voice steady.

Its tongue flicks out, taking in my scent even more.

"And what are you doing here?" it asks, its voice rumbling in my head.

"Seeking answers," I force out.

"As many come here to do and fail." The creature angles its scaled face.

"What are you?" I ask.

The massive serpent lowers its head, creating just enough space for its sizable body to move closer. A large claw glides over the shelves, lightly brushing the leather spines of numerous ancient books.

"I am the protector, the guardian. I am Eldursyth, the creation of the God of Darkness himself. I am death and destruction."

My face pales, but I remain as calm as possible, even though that feels pointless.

"Nice to meet you," I squeak out.

I start to move, the uncomfortable position beginning to weigh on my aching body. The creature notices my flinch.

"Allow me to assist you down so we can converse better," the creature hisses.

The beast's face shifts downward, creating room for its large claw to grip my body, lifting me momentarily toward the red book. I scan above the towering bookshelves and see the table in the middle of the room. I'm not far from the exit. I quickly extend my hand and grasp the worn leather, snapping it to my side while praying that the creature didn't notice. The sharp talons bring me to the ground, but don't release me.

"Thank you," I say politely, as my feet touch the solid ground again, and I smile.

Eldursyth shifts his massive body to get a better view of me. I stand face-to-face with a creature larger than anything I've ever encountered. Its tongue flicks out again, almost making contact with me, prompting me to step back.

"You don't smell like the others. You smell odd and ancient yourself," Eldursyth says. *"The better question is, what are you, little one?"*

I step back again. "I am a Dusk Wielder. That is what you smell. I possess powers of both Gods."

Eldursyth hisses. *"That is not all you possess."*

"It definitely is."

"You have a rider deep within you, a leech. A creation of the Gods, like me."

I continue to move backward, each step small and nearly motionless. If I can get to the passage's end, I can run again. I need to keep the creature speaking so the distraction will grant me more time.

"Nothing possesses me," I lie. "I am merely a Dusk Wielder seeking answers on this crimson moon."

He slithers closer, and I hold my breath.

"Do you take me for a fool?"

"Gods, no! Only sheltered," I respond, regretting the words as soon as they leave my mouth.

The snake only stares for a second, and sweat beads on my forehead.

"I've been guarding the Archives for many centuries, preventing those who have questions from ever finding answers. What is written here should remain forgotten, Briar."

I squeeze the book behind my back and nod. "And you've clearly done a great job."

The serpent moves closer and raises its head, ensuring I remember its size. I awkwardly grin and feign calmness. The true size of this creature is unlike anything I've ever seen. The legends are true; a beast of this magnitude exists, and I'm somehow standing in front of it, trying to steal a book from its ancient collection.

Eldursyth's head slithers forward. "*Are you frightened?*"

"Nope," I lie.

"*Brave or foolish?*"

I shrug. "A little of both, I suppose. Depends on who you ask."

"*Foolish.*"

"I do think I'll be going now," I say, taking another step back. "It was extremely nice to meet you."

I glance behind me and find that I'm only a few feet away from the edge of the bookshelf. I begin to tap into my magic, praying for a blast of light to momentarily blind the creature of darkness, allowing me time to rush around the corner toward the entrance.

"*You won't save him,*" Eldursyth whispers, stopping me in my tracks.

I narrow my eyes. "Save who?"

"*The one like you who also carries a rider. Except, he isn't in control anymore, is he?*"

"How do you know anything about that?" I grow defensive, knowing exactly who he refers to.

"*I know everything—past, present, and future—little one,*" he speaks into my mind. "*I also know what hangs around your neck, but you don't, do you?*"

I instantly touch Fen's necklace and grab it in my hand. "Will you tell me?"

The snake smiles, again. "*If you return the book.*"

I think for only a second, knowing his offer and my life may expire at any moment. I place the book on the ground in front of me, slightly kicking it in his direction. "Fine. Tell me."

"*Impatient,*" it hisses.

"I've heard that before."

A dark laugh coils into my mind, and I shudder at the sound. The serpent looks at the book, and back at me before speaking.

"The resurrection stone isn't the only powerful crystal in these realms," Eldursyth begins. *"The Gods created a stone for each kingdom centuries ago, which was given to the kings at that time. The resurrection stone was bestowed upon your family, while stones with other gifts went to the others."*

I feel the tingle of the stone against me.

"You currently possess the stone of Andorwood."

"What does this stone do?" I press, but can't hide the panic I feel. The others have the resurrection stone, and what if they obtain more?

"You possess a powerful one, but it is not as powerful as some others." Eldursyth slithers closer. *"Andorwood was bestowed with the Stone of Truth. Many seek answers when they journey to Andorwood, desperate for the truths of the realms, but few ever acquire that knowledge."*

I move backward, nearly outside the passage and into the open space, but I keep my gaze on the book. I can't leave without it.

"What is the most powerful stone?" I ask.

Eldursyth grins. *"That is up to the Wielders in possession, I would say. Each is powerful and deadly if you are creative."*

"How are they destroyed?" I dive into my magic again and think of light—only light.

"Oh, little one, only a God can destroy the stones," the serpent hisses. *"A war is coming—one like none other. I will be here long after the war ends, but you won't be. There is no use in trying."* Eldursyth rises higher in the air over my small body. *"There is no use in praying for a God for help. They abandoned you all long ago."*

My magic simmers within me, and I can feel the painful need for it to escape.

"What does this stone do? How can I wield it to help us?" I ask, attempting to hide the desperation in my voice.

The creature ponders me before answering, *"The stone you possess is the most interesting of all the stones, but telling you upfront would be giving away too much. Information costs you; I hope you know."*

I cut my eyes toward the book. "What is your price?"

"Nothing you would be able to give me," the serpent hisses. *"What I want is freedom. I grow so tired of being in here alone."*

"I understand, but you do such an amazing job at guarding these books," I say, creating distance between us again. "And I don't want to interrupt you any longer."

"Oh, little one, you've provided me with such entertainment today. I'll think of our encounter for centuries to come, but I'm also growing tired of your pestering. I believe our conversation is coming to an end." Eldursyth opens his wide mouth, revealing thousands of teeth.

"We aren't the only ones that the Gods may have abandoned, Eldursyth." I open my palms, letting a bit of light dance on my hands.

The serpent angles its large head.

"You've been trapped in this library for centuries, guarding books day in and day out. A creation of the God of Darkness, Raddnoke. The Gods may have abandoned us, but they abandoned you, too."

"I will wait for him to return for me."

"And if he doesn't come?"

"He's already here."

Panic surges through me, and I step backward one final time.

I extend my palms forward, allowing a blast of light to fill the dark space with a blinding glow. Eldursyth hisses in pain, turning its enormous frame into a bookshelf. The large shelf tips sideways, barely staying upright from the force of the beast. I lunge forward, wrapping my hands around the spine of the book, and watch in terror as the creature tries to see from its glowing orange eyes.

The creature's chest begins to turn the same shade of orange as its eyes, and that's when I notice it. A spark of fire ignites in its chest, and it's willing to burn down the library completely rather than let a book leave. I bound around the corner toward the front of the library. Nothing will slow me down in this moment. I propel my body forward, running faster than I ever have.

Hissing screams fill the air. *"You foolish thing. You will never leave this library. Fire will rain down upon you. You will die. I will kill you."*

I see the final corner standing between me and the center of the library. Just a few feet beyond that lies the exit. I can do this. I'm going to make it.

"I will burn the world around you."

I round the corner, and the library opens back up into the vast space. The book stays tucked under my arm, and despite the pain in my arm, I push myself into a dead sprint.

I look toward the exit, the shimmering doorway to my safety, and dread fills my already-pounding heart.

No. No, this can't be happening, I think to myself.

Silas, Larkin, and Maines stand at the entrance and exit from the library. Their eyes land on me and widen at my state.

Silas steps forward while Larkin steps toward Maines.

"Run!" I scream at them. "Get out."

"I see you have company, Briar. This must be my lucky day," the serpent's raspy voice shouts from behind me. *"Let me introduce myself."*

They remain frozen, and that's when I realize Eldursyth is behind me, ready to breathe fire upon me and the entire Forgotten Archives. I race forward, unwilling to drop the book to move faster across the vast space.

I can't stop. I have to keep moving.

Silas screams, "Don't look. Keep your eyes forward."

The heat of Eldursyth's breath begins to warm the air around us, but I keep moving, my feet slapping the smooth floor. I look at Silas and know my face reflects the same terror that he feels.

"Eyes on me," he shouts.

Silas watches in horror as my feet can't move fast enough, and I fight the thoughts that swirl in my head that we've done this before. He pushes Larkin and Maines closer to the exit and starts sprinting in my direction—the opposite way I wish he would go.

Larkin lunges for him, but Maines slaps her hand around his forearm, stopping him from entering further. Silas charges toward me and the serpent.

Eldursyth locks eyes with Maines, Larkin, and Silas, and speaks, *"A beautiful female Shadow Wielder, a warrior Lumor Wielder, and you...a man... a Shadow Wielder, but not."* The snake halts, and the entire library vibrates. *"It can't be."*

Silas doesn't stop.

He moves toward me, and we collide. A sob escapes my throat, and my chest heaves with desperation for rest.

"Almost there, my love," Silas says, grabbing my arm and pulling me into another dead sprint toward the exit.

Eldursyth breathes in once more, collecting fire in its throat. *"Liars! You two are deceitful liars. Show your true selves!"*

We are a few steps from Larkin and Maines when fear floods their eyes.

"Liars!"

A whoosh of fire bursts from the serpent's mouth, and we dive through the wall. The library around us fades, along with the heat of the flames. The walls collapse around us, and we move through time, back into the castle of Andorwood. The pressure takes my breath away, and I close my eyes, allowing the wall to crush me once more.

Through the wall, I hear a scream that could shatter a mountain of glass. It's not Silas or Larkin. We materialize on the opposite side of the wall, collapsing and gasping for air. Without thinking, I open my eyes and desperately crawl in Maines' direction, hoping what I heard wasn't real. It can't be real. My nails dig into the stone, but I push.

My body screams at me to stop, but I can't.

Maines.

What happened?

She lies face down, her clothes almost melted away, with fresh, deep burns covering most of her legs.

"She's not moving," Fen shouts, covering her mouth. "No. no."

Warrick shouts, "Get her to Silas's house now!"

Oak pushes from behind Warrick, nearly clawing his way forward, and a bone-chilling sob escapes his throat. He crashes to the ground next to her, his knees ripping against the stone. Without hesitation, he picks up her burned body and shifts into a million bright lights.

CHAPTER 37

We all stare in shock for a moment as I remain on the ground. I can't lift my gaze or feel my body; I zone out somewhere else—somewhere quiet and far away from the chaos—unable to process my thoughts, emotions, or the events that have unfolded. I hear the others speaking around me, but their words don't register. I only hear Maines's scream. The echo reverberates in my mind, and her burned body flashes before me. I squeeze my eyes shut as panic rises, bile surges, and I'm seconds away from spilling my stomach onto the ground.

"I... I know a healer. I'll bring her to Silas's house. I'll be there as soon as I can." Fen shoots a glance at Warrick. Their hands clasp together as they shift from the depths of the Andorwood castle.

Silas closes the distance between us and lifts me from the ground.

"Briar, I need to know if you are all right?" He pats up and down my body, checking for the slightest injury. "Please speak to me."

I can only stare through him.

He snaps his head at Larkin and says, "She's in shock. I'm going to get supplies to assist with the healing. I have to help."

My jaw slacks, and I try desperately to take a breath.

"We have to act now, or this is going to turn quickly. I don't want to leave her, but she can't shift right now. Larkin, get her to my house, and don't you let a fucking thing happen to her."

I slowly scan my eyes in his direction, still in a daze.

He cups my face and gently kisses my lips. His voice is raspy, and a desperation fills his tone. "You are going to be okay, my love, and so is Maines. I promise. I'm going to help save her."

I nod, barely blinking. "O…okay," I manage to get out.

"I'm going to save her," he repeats, in an attempt to convince himself as much as me.

Silas clings to our touch for as long as possible, and before me, he turns into a shadowy mist, but not before I notice his eyes filled with tears. I immediately feel his presence fade, and my chest constricts.

Terror, confusion, and anger begin to bubble in my chest, and I blink back into myself. The events of the library and Maines crash into my mind, and I look to Larkin. He remains frozen, horrified by the events, and unsure of what to say to me or how to help.

"We should go," Larkin says gently, as he steps toward me. "We can help."

I feel my anger rising, and I can't control it. It becomes so unbearable that I feel like my body is going to rip in two.

"Idiots!"

I bound toward him, stopping inches from his face, and narrow my eyes.

"Why did you let her come with you? Why did you let her enter the fucking library?" I slam my fist against his chest and cry. "You knew the risks, and you let her anyway. This is all your fault."

I hear the words leave my lips, and I know they aren't true, but I can't stop. Anger fills me, and I need a desperate escape. Larkin is the only one around to receive the blows. I can't stop myself, and I don't try. I can only see blood, burnt flesh, and death.

"She wanted to help," he rasps.

I swing my fist against his chest.

"Stop talking," I weep.

"You know Maines would do anything for you," he whispers.

I hit him again, slamming my fist into his hard body, and he watches my outburst in shock.

"Why did you let her enter the fucking library?" I cry as I continue to drive my fist into his chest, letting the tears roll down my cheeks like falling rain.

Larkin doesn't move.

He stands steady and unwavering against each of my blows, letting me take out every ounce of anger and sadness that over-whelms me. My vision blurs through the tears, and I look at his face. It's stone cold, and he refuses to meet my stare, but he remains.

"She could die. The only person who has loved me through everything might die." I slam my fist into his body again, weep-ing, and my knuckles ache. "Die. She could die!"

"Stop, Briar," Larkin orders.

"No."

Larkin remains calm, but catches my fist as I try to drive it toward his cheek. His fingers wrap tightly around my wrist.

I try to pull my arm away, but he holds on, keeping his gaze fixed beyond me.

"I can't lose her." I begin to sob uncontrollably and try to throw my other fist toward him.

He catches my other wrist and grips them both tight before I can pull from his hold.

"Please, stop," Larkin begs, and I hear how desperate his ask is.

"I'm going to be alone in this world," I cry, feeling my legs give out. "I can't lose her. I can't fucking lose her."

"You aren't alone."

"I am," I sob, my cries filling the narrow hallway around us. "I am so alone."

"You aren't," he snaps. "Silas is here. Oak is here. You aren't alone in this world."

"Everyone left," I sob. "I have no one."

"Look at me." He grips my wrists, forcing my gaze to find his. "I am here. I am real."

Tears streak down my cheeks.

"I'm here, Briar."

Larkin pulls me against his chest, wrapping both arms around me as tightly as he can with my hands by my side. I try to move back, but his hold prevents me from doing so.

"Let go of me," I snap.

He doesn't speak; he stands there, applying pressure around my trembling body. He rests his chin on my head and embraces me, keeping me from swinging at him or crumbling. I feel my body calm and bury my face in his chest, letting the tears soak his shirt. I weep and can't stop, but Larkin doesn't move. He holds me steadily, allowing me to cry for as long as I need.

I cry for Maines and Yara, for my brother, my mother, and all the people who have been hurt along the way. I cry for our past, our uncertain future, and for right now. My present seems impossible to endure, and Larkin holds me just like Barlowe would have, just like he did when our mother died.

Tears streak down my face, mingling with the dust, sweat, and blood coating me, yet Larkin remains steadfast. He holds me firmly, gripping my back. I stay still with my head against his strong chest.

Bursts of sobs escape my throat, and I feel my anger fading.

I gradually pull back from his grip and glance up at his face. Larkin has tears rolling down his cheeks, and he lets me step back a few paces to catch my breath.

I simply stare at him, feeling something within my chest expand, even as my heart crumbles. He uses his thumb to wipe a tear from his eye quickly and stares back at me.

"Larkin," I say, and shake my head. "I…I'm so sorry."

"She's going to be alright," he replies.

"No, you. I'm sorry."

He lowers his gaze.

"Why?" I step forward. "Why did you let me hit you?"

Larkin doesn't respond.

I grab his hand. "Why did you just stand there?"

"Because… you needed me to."

I'm surprised I still have tears left to shed, but they continue falling from my red eyes.

"I told you I would spend the rest of my life ensuring you are okay, Briar." He pauses. "I owe that to Barlowe, and I owe it to you, now." He wipes another tear from his eye.

"I shouldn't have done that."

His face softens. "You didn't do anything I couldn't handle."

"Will you take me to her?"

He nods. "Of course."

"Thank you," I reply.

Larkin extends his hand, and I take it, stepping closer to him. I pick up the red book that may have cost me everything and tuck it under my arm. He burrows down into his magic, and light begins to fill the dark space around us. He glances at me one last time, and a gentleness I've never seen settles into his dark gaze. I feel my body turn to light, and a weightlessness takes over. He shifts us toward Silas's house faster than I've ever shifted before, and I know for sure that Larkin will protect me until we reach the darkest realms and beyond—just like Barlowe did until his very last breath.

Silas's house is quiet—too quiet—as we arrive. I pull my hand away from Larkin's and race down the stairs, ignoring my sore body that screams for rest. The sun rises slowly in the distance, signaling a new day ahead of us—the day Silas will be announced as king, and hopefully the day I won't lose my best friend.

I race down the hallway leading to Maines and Oak's bedroom and freeze when I see Fenmore slumped against the wall with her hands in her lap. Silas and Warrick stand next to her, leaning against the wall, and Silas runs his hands through his hair. They whisper in a quiet conversation, not noticing our arrival.

"Silas?" I question.

He jerks his gaze to mine and rushes toward me, pulling me into a tight embrace. He pulls me back and studies my face, coated in blood and tears. Fen lifts her head and gives Larkin a nod.

"She's alive," Silas whispers.

Relief floods me, and I feel my body sag against him. I squeeze him back, wrapping my throbbing arms around his body.

"What happened?" I ask.

Silas looks at Fen and Warrick. "They were able to get three of Andorwood's top healers here faster than I expected. I gathered supplies and prepared the room for their arrival. They nearly arrived before me."

I shake my head. "How is she?"

"Asleep. They will work for many more hours to heal the damage and minimize scarring, although it seemed that might not be possible. She will be alright, but they asked us to remain outside, except for Oak. He refused to leave her side."

"How is he?" I ask, looking toward the closed door.

Silas looks at Fen and Warrick. "He's calmed down, but just barely. I've… I've never seen him so scared and so angry, and I hope I never witness that again."

"Thank you." I feel the tears welling once again. "Thank you all so much."

"We would do that for any of us standing here. We're family, after all," Fen says, standing and smiling.

Warrick stands alongside Fen. "Can I get you anything, Briar?" he asks in his usual, gentle tone.

I attempt to steady the tremors coursing through my body from adrenaline, exhaustion, and fear. "No, I'm alright."

Fen observes my mental and physical state, then indicates my bedroom down the hall. "Go take a bath and rest. When she wakes up, you will be the first person I come to get. I won't leave this door."

I look down at myself, and I'm filthy, coated in my own blood and dust from the library. "I don't think I should leave," I reply.

"Well, do what you want, but I know the healers won't let you near Maines while you're coated in blood. The cleaner you are, the better," Fen replies.

She's right, I need to get out of these clothes and cleaned up. I reek of sweat and blood, and this is no way to see Maines.

"Come on," Silas urges, as he grabs my hand. "I'll run you a bath."

I nod and let him guide me down the hallway toward our bedroom. The door opens, and fresh morning air fills my senses from the open windows. The sea I've grown so accustomed to hearing crashes below us, and I feel my body relax—something I never thought possible again. Silas lets go of my hand and disappears into the bathing chambers to run the bath for me.

I walk over to the large open window and glance across the sparkling ocean. Right now, it's calm and quiet. But, I can't shake the feeling that something is off, and I know it's what heads toward us. Every day it gets closer, growing more restless to put its feet on the ground. We are prepared for this fight, but with all the recent events, I know exhaustion hangs over us like a shroud.

On the horizon, I swear I see something, but it quickly vanishes behind the glow of the light. I push away from the window and turn to see Silas standing at the threshold, his hands tucked in his pockets, watching me.

"What?" I ask.

"You are filthy," he huffs, indignantly.

"That's all you have to say?" I reply.

"Oh, no. I have a lot to say." Silas tilts his head, looking at me. "But first, I'm worried about getting all the blood off of you. The water is running, so come on."

"Impossible worrywart," I mumble, as I walk past him into the room.

The bathing chamber is filled with warm, steamy air. I almost groan at the sight of the hot, running water pooling in the tub, and the space is filled with the scents of various soaps. The drain isn't latched, so I can ensure the water runs clear before plugging it. I slowly remove my pants, letting them hit the ground with a thud and make my way to my shirt. My body screams as I lift my arms over my head, and my injury barks in protest.

Silas stands behind me, helping me remove the blood-soaked shirt while paying close attention to the cut across my forearm. He tosses the shirt across the room, and my arms dangle at my sides. Silas carefully unbraids my hair and assists me in stepping into the warm water.

I slowly lower myself into the warm water and close my eyes. I never thought a bath could feel so wonderful. Silas grabs a pitcher and a rag and sits beside me on the ground.

"Sit back," he instructs.

I don't argue.

I lean my head against the hard porcelain tub and close my eyes. Warm water flushes around me as Silas works to clean the dried blood from my body. He slowly takes the rag to my cheeks and forehead to rid my body of the Rigils, both completed and broken. I know he sees that and is burning to ask me questions.

I crack open my eye and see his gaze burning through me.

"Go ahead," I say. "Ask."

He chuckles. "You can't relax for five minutes, can you?"

"Hardly," I reply, closing my eyes again.

"The Rigil on your forehead was broken when we entered the library, so the ward didn't work."

"It worked for a while," I answer. "I found the book in time for it to smudge, and that's when I was seen."

"I see," he says, and quiets.

"Is that the monster you all speak of?" I ask.

"Yes," he says, dipping the towel back into the water.

The warmth of the water surrounds me, and I watch Silas's face intently.

"I had no idea until I saw him myself. The God of Darkness created the creature as a protector. Legend has it that this island was his home before the Wielders came into existence. It lived freely, which, as you saw, isn't the case anymore. It hates all kinds of Wielders now and only obeys Raddnoke."

I nod, opening my eyes. "He told me his name is Eldursyth."

"You might be the only person who has been told that creature's name and lived to tell the tale."

"Lucky me."

"You, my love, are destined to become the stuff of legends." He leans in and kisses my forehead.

"Eldursyth told me something regarding the stone," I confess.

Silas attempts to remain steady, but his posture straightens. "And?"

"A stone was created for every kingdom. Daramveer, Andorwood, Eddris, Cammon, and Brinkym. All different, and all deadly. Whoever is in possession of the stone decides how it should be wielded based on its magic. Andorwood's is the Stone of Truth."

Silas remains silent, and I can tell from his eyes that he is battling his own swirling thoughts.

"We need to find the other stones before Calia and Nolan do," I add. "They already have the resurrection stone. If the others are that powerful…" My mouth goes dry at the thought.

Silas looks at me. "Do you think Oak has any idea about Brinkym's stone?"

"No." I shake my head. "I don't think so."

"Now isn't the right time to ask. He's consumed with Maines —understandably so. We will talk to him when we have the time."

I give an agreeable nod and settle back into the warm water.

Silas picks up the small towel and starts to wash my arms, being careful of the cut on my forearm. He moves toward my head, taking a small cup, and running the water through my dark hair. I close my eyes, and sit forward for him to continue bathing me.

I hear his sigh and cut my eyes toward him, questioningly.

"Today is a big day. I'd be lying if I said I didn't have my doubts."

"Doubts about what?" I sit up further in the tub and plug the drain.

"These people are scarred from Malachi. They will be excited to hear of his disappearance, but acceptance is what I fear. Acceptance of me, and acceptance that Malachi won't return one day."

I lean my arms against the side of the tub, looking into his eyes. "You are going to be an amazing king, Silas."

Silas runs the towel up my back. "Will you stand with me today?"

"You want me too?" I move into his touch.

"Of course."

"Then I will," I say, with a smile.

We fall into silence as he continues to run the towel over my body and finishes washing my hair.

"I can only hope that I lead these people with fairness and grace."

"You will," I smile.

"With you by my side?"

I look at him and cup his face. "I'm not going anywhere."

He presses his forehead against mine, closes his eyes, and inhales deeply. He then brings his lips to mine, and we lock into a kiss—slow and steady, but filled with passion and amplified by the fear still coursing through our veins.

His hand drops the towel and travels up my body, becoming tangled in my hair. He presses my face closer, and I lean nearer to the edge of the tub.

I feel momentarily lost, only here with Silas, and the connection between us appears to sing in from our closeness. I press myself to the tub's edge again, wanting to be as close to him as possible—as safe as possible—and I know I have that when I'm near him. His hand moves through my hair, never breaking our connection, and our kiss deepens. I move my arm over his shoulder and press my bare chest against his.

He pulls away. "I love you."

I gaze into his green eyes. "And I love you."

A knock on the door echoes through the room, and Silas glances at the door. He swiftly grabs a towel for me and shouts, "Yeah?"

I hear Fen's voice, and I quickly stand from the water and wrap the towel around my body.

"She's stirring. They think she may wake up."

CHAPTER 38

I dress, throwing the dark green stone into my pocket, and move out of my bedroom faster than I ever have in my life. I rush down the hallway, my hair still soaking wet, and pause outside Oak and Maine's bedroom. Fen and Warrick still wait outside the door while Silas stands behind me.

"You can head inside, Briar," Warrick instructs, stepping to the side. "I told the healers you'd be coming in."

I smile in his direction, and he nods back.

"I'll be right outside. You go in first," Silas says. "I'll come in a bit later."

I push open the thick wooden door and step inside, hearing the latch slowly close behind me. The windows are open, and the brilliant morning sun spills in, making the room bright and airy. A few healers move around the room with bowls and various instruments, and the scent of incense fills the air. Their room is dark like Silas's, but something different lingers here.

Oak sits beside the bed, his head hung low, and one hand rests against Maines. A bright halo of light appears to pulse around him. Maines lies on a small bed, and her eyes are closed. Oak slowly lifts his head, and his eyes are red, swollen, and filled with a sadness I've never seen them harbor before.

My heart splinters.

I cross the room, keeping my eyes fixed on Maines. As I approach the bed, she gently opens her beautiful blue eyes. A soft smile curls her lips, and I sit next to Oak, placing my hand on his leg to assure him that I'm here. He grabs my hand, and I feel the warmth of his light.

"You look like a wet rat," Maines rasps.

I let out a sob mixed with a laugh, and Oak squeezes my hand. He moves closer to the bed, helping her sit up higher on a few pillows. Maines groans in pain, and Oak gently traces her cheek with his thumb. Her eyes are exhausted, but she's here. She's alive and receiving care. She's going to be okay.

"How are you?" I ask.

"As you would expect me to be after being barbecued by a giant serpent," she replies.

Even after everything, she is still trying to crack a joke. Even though she can laugh, I glance at Oak, and he isn't smiling. He's still horrified, and I know how he feels.

Once you see someone you love go through something like that, it changes you, and not for the better. He refuses to let his eyes leave hers—as if he's waiting for something else to happen.

I squeeze his hand, and he slowly glances at me, but doesn't say anything. I almost flinch under his gaze, but he doesn't release my hand, only squeezes harder—like he can't imagine losing us. I believe that in this moment, he needs to sense that this is real, that she is truly here with us.

"I can't believe you came into the library with them," I whisper. "It was too dangerous, Maines."

She attempts to lift herself higher but winces and leans back on the bed. "You were gone for hours. I don't regret my decision at all, because even knowing for a moment that you were okay was worth it."

She coughs, and Oak stands, getting her a sip of water.

"I got the book," I fill her in. "I achieved what I set out to find. I'm not sure what happened once you all entered the library, but it caused Eldursyth to halt in his tracks like he was startled. I believe you all coming in is why I'm sitting here right now."

"It has a name?" she asks, and closes her eyes, exhaustion weighing on her. "Great."

"I'll tell you more about it later. You rest right now."

"So bossy," she rasps.

"Rest."

She cracks open her eyes, staring at Oak, and extends her hand. He immediately takes it.

"Don't leave until I fall asleep," she tells him. "Please."

"I'm not leaving," he responds, planting a kiss on the back of her hand.

She snuggles back into bed, and within seconds, she's asleep again. The magic flowing into the body during an intense healing overwhelms both the healer and the person being healed. I'm thankful that they managed to get three healers to assist, given the severity of the injury.

We fall back into silence, and I glance at Oak. He kisses her hand once more and places it gently beside her body.

He stands, grabs my hand, and pulls me to the corner of the room, wanting to speak privately.

"Are you alright?" I ask, as we get to the farthest corner of the room from Maines.

He shakes his head. "I'm alright because she is."

I lean forward and embrace him. He rests his head on top of mine, but his body remains tense.

"What are the healers saying?" I sigh, looking back at Maines resting.

"What you would expect." He shrugs. "They are surprised she is even awake and speaking. They said any more time, and she would be dead."

The door creaks open slightly, and I see Silas peeking through, hesitant to disturb us. I wave him over, and he slips through the opening, joining us on the far side of the room. He rushes to Oak and pulls him into a hug. I smile, watching their sweet, awkward embrace.

"I don't think I've ever hugged you," Oak says, pushing Silas away.

"It was a good one, wasn't it?" Silas chuckles.

A healer shushes us, and we all flinch.

I glance toward the healer, but she shields her face, making it impossible to see past her flowing white hair. I ignore the urge to walk toward her and return my gaze to the men.

"Should we let her rest and take this somewhere else?" I ask.

"I'm not leaving her," Oak says.

Silas nods. "We understand."

Oak's face hardens. "Did you bring the book here?"

"Yes." Silas looks to me, but answers, "We have it with us."

"I don't think we should mess with what's in that book," Oak says. "You need to hide it. If anyone finds out we have it, we will have a bigger target on our backs than before."

"We know." I give a nod in agreement.

Silas leans in. "We are going to need your help with this, Oak. It's in a language we can't read. You will need to translate every-thing," Silas explains.

"The entire book?"

We nod.

"Gods, as if I'm not busy enough," Oak says, as he rolls his shoulders. "I'm not starting right now. Maines needs me. And honestly, if the book is as old as we think, there will be parts I can't translate. Even the newer items aren't very translatable."

"That's fine," I chime in. "We aren't asking you to do it right now, but we will need to start soon. Silas has to make an announcement to Andorwood shortly, so perhaps we could begin after that?" I offer him a smile. "Or whenever you are ready."

He glances back at Maines, sleeping peacefully in bed. "The healers say she will be bedridden for days and will move slowly after that for weeks. What are we going to do about the ship that travels here?"

"We will do what we can without her. We have talented healers in Andorwood who were involved in the plans when Maines met with them. They are ready, and she will stay here with Rose. She'll be safe." Silas places his hand on Oak's shoulder. "But we really need you, Oak."

Oak looks back at us, tears forming in his dark eyes. I reflect on how it felt when I first lost my mother—the first death I faced —and the deep impact it had on me. Maines didn't die, but it was close, and for Oak, that's the closest he's come to losing someone more important to him than all the realms combined.

"I know you're shaken up, Oak—we all are—but she's okay. She is the strongest person I know. Maines will pull through this and still be her wonderful, sarcastic self," I try to remind him.

A tear rolls down his cheek, and I can't help but feel the urge to cry with him.

"I have to tell you both something," he whispers, and acts as if he's scared to speak the words aloud. "I can't shake the feeling that there's something more. She seems to be her normal self, but there's something else—a darkness I've never felt from her."

I furrow my brow. "Maybe it's just the effects of being so deep within the castle around Eldursyth."

Concern laces his entire expression. "I felt it before that."

"What does it feel like?" Silas asks, sharply.

"I can't exactly tell, but it's like a dark veil hangs over her— like something else is with her."

We swap glances, and a chill runs up my spine.

"Let us know if you need anything or when she wakes up. We'll keep an eye on her, Oak. Keep your light around." I glance toward Maines. Her chest rises and falls steadily.

"She's going to be okay. I promise." I lean back in and give him one more squeeze.

Silas places a hand on Oak's shoulder. "Let me know what you need. Anything at all."

He nods.

Before Silas and I head out the door, I watch Oak settle back at her side. She remains asleep as he places his hand on hers. A halo of light begins to illuminate around him, casting a subtle golden glow that fills the room. No darkness lingers over Maines, and nothing makes my senses scream, but Oak's words replay in my mind. All I see is Maines, my best friend, surrounded by someone who would willingly give his life to protect her. She's safe and will be safe for the rest of her life in Oak's arms.

We enter the hallway and hear hushed conversations in the main part of the house. Silas cuts his eyes in my direction, and I follow him toward the vast living space. As we approach, female voices fill the air, and a bead of anxiety sits on my chest, knowing exactly who speaks.

Aerona sits in the living area next to Fen, with Rose filling the space across from them. We round the corner, and they all turn their heads in our direction. Silas strides forward as his mother stands and quickly embraces her in a hug. Rose stands, grabbing my hand to pull me next to her, and Silas settles in next to Fen and his mother.

"You never venture this far," Silas says, directing his gaze toward his mother.

"Not every day is my son going to make an announcement to the entire kingdom. I came to offer my support." She smiles in return.

"I appreciate you being here," he responds. "Your support will be much needed when the time comes."

"I forgot how amazing your house is out here. It's so airy, yet moody—just like you. You know how suffocating the castle can be," Aerona says.

"You should come out here more."

Aerona smiles, looking at me. "Briar, I'm so sorry to hear about Maines. Fen was telling me she will recover, but it was close," she says.

I nod. "Yes, she has a long road ahead of her, but the healers say she will recover."

"That's great," Aerona says, before her eyes darken. "And the Archives?"

I shudder.

"Did you get what you were after?"

I hesitate to respond. The fewer people who know I brought something ancient out of there, the better.

"The trip wasn't wasted. However, I don't think Maines's injury would ever be worth it," I say.

She leans forward, and I notice Silas tense. I sit further back in my chair, creating distance between us.

"Did you see him?" she whispers. "The serpent."

"Yes," I reply. "I did."

"And did he see you?" Aerona's eyes widen.

"Yes."

She leans back, settling into her chair and diving into her own thoughts. Her dark hair pools around her sides as she smooths out her dress. Out of habit, she reaches for the jewel around her neck that no longer rests there. She looks at Fen, noticing that hers is gone, then glances back at me.

"You are quite impressive, Briar."

"Yes," Silas says. "She is."

Rose chimes in, "You have no idea."

I'm grateful for Rose now, and I can't help but think that some of this was a test for Aerona's approval. Seeing her reaction, I know I've earned it.

"Oh, I think I'm starting to get an idea." Aerona smiles in Rose's direction.

The weight of the Andorwood stone drags me down, and I can feel its smooth edges in my pocket. I slide my hand into the soft fabric of my pants and fidget with the stone. I need to learn more about what I now possess and what the other kings have.

I take the stone from my pocket and open my hand, pointing it directly at Aerona. "I assume you knew what you were possessing when you handed me this—or at least thought you did."

Aerona tenses, and I see Fen do the same out of the corner of my eye.

"I am aware that I had something of importance, yes," Aerona responds, sitting up a bit straighter. "However, it wasn't in my possession, was it?"

Fen angles her head at her mother. "It was my stone that possessed the powers. It has been hidden in plain sight all this time, and you wore a fake. Why?"

"I created a fake to protect you, Fenmore. If someone realized we still had the stone after all these years, they would likely assume I had it and come after me. If word got out, I always intended to tell you to keep you safe." She reaches for Fen, but she retreats.

Silas stands and begins to pace. "So what does this stone do?"

"That is something I have tried to uncover for years. The stone reacts uniquely to each Wielder. For me, the stone revealed ancient, hidden, and forgotten things. For others, it could reveal different things."

"Like the Archives," I chime in.

She nods. "Exactly."

"The stone had a similar effect when I had it as well. It revealed something I was looking for," I explain.

"The stone can do more, but you must know how to wield it," Aerona adds. "But, I can't help, because honestly, I don't know how."

Silas walks over to where I sit. "What can you tell us about the others?"

"The other stones?" Aerona asks.

"Those were given to the kings at the time of creation," he responds, his tone sharper.

"Very little." She stands as well. "These are old and seldom discussed. Many consider them to be mere legends, but they aren't. Whoever could possess them all would be unstoppable."

Silas looks at me and says, "We will need to gather more information about what each kingdom possesses and whether the person in power actually has it."

I nod and stand to join the others as Aerona walks across the living space with feline grace. Her long gown travels behind her like a serpent's tail, and I can't help but perk up my senses around her.

"I have a bad feeling about these stones," I whisper, as I peel my gaze away from Aerona's back.

Silas leans in. "So do I."

Fen and Rose remain on the couch, talking in hushed tones, allowing us privacy to speak.

"Silas," Aerona calls from the bottom of the stairs. "It's time to go. Andorwood is expecting you."

CHAPTER 39

We shift to the outskirts of town to allow ourselves a moment of privacy before addressing the kingdom. The Kingdom of Andorwood is quiet as the shadows dominate the sun's midday glow. The dark buildings tower over us, and I move closer to Silas as the thick air swirls around me. The salty sea breeze mists our faces, and I hear footsteps in the distance as we make our way through the back roads.

The oppressive black castle looms over us, its tall points shooting into the sky like jagged teeth. A dense fog begins to roll in as we make our way close to town, and an unsettling feeling washes over me. I glance in all directions—searching for signs of life beyond Silas, Fenmore, and Aerona—but the haze filling the air blurs my vision.

The weight of my axes feels familiar on my back, and the clink of metal echoes around us. It was Silas's idea for me to bring my axes—he mentioned earlier that the more prepared we are, the better. Fen had argued that it conveyed a negative sentiment, but Aerona had the final say, determining that we all should be armed. I didn't disagree and felt thankful that I could have something of my own to protect us if needed.

I look toward Fen, who moves calmly. It's obvious that she has done this countless times, so even though this is a significant announcement, it's nothing new to her. A sword rests across her back, and she is dressed in tight clothes, perfect for running or fighting if needed. Aerona stays close to her children, but her eyes are always forward, never worrying about what lurks in each dark alleyway. She wears a jeweled dagger at her waist, and I realize this is the first time I've seen her armed. Silas's face is like stone, and he also keeps his gaze fixed ahead. He grasps my hand, pulling me closer to his side, as we move together. He wears his familiar armor, but he stands taller and exudes power as we move closer with each step.

Without glancing in my direction, he whispers, "Keep your eyes forward. It isn't our business what hides in the alleys. I wouldn't want you to witness something you'd regret."

"Alright," I respond.

Silas leans down as we continue to walk. "Larkin and Warrick are close by. They will remain hidden and cloaked, but they're watching in case someone should try anything."

Nerves envelop me, and I turn my gaze to the road ahead. Even with Larkin and Warrick watching our backs, I can't shake the feeling of unease. We move forward as a unified force, silently heading toward the heart of what appears to be an abandoned kingdom.

We near the end of the street, and Aerona stops, turning to face us. "I will go first, should anything or anyone come forward. Fenmore will come forward next, followed by you two."

We all nod and move around the corner, the street opening up into a vast space filled with people and various vendors. Even in the open, the air feels dark and thick, filled with a mix of defiance and chaos that hangs heavy around us. Smoke permeates the air from cooking fires and the dimly lit torches that illuminate the center. Hushed voices echo around us, and even though people wander while shopping, everyone moves with a purpose—to get what they need and then get out.

I attempt to study the faces we pass by, but most of the civilians are cloaked, and their faces are barely visible. I try to spot Larkin and Warrick in the crowd, but I fail—everyone looks the same in the crowd. Although I feel as if thousands of eyes are upon us, most keep to themselves and their daily shopping, while others slightly raise their heads as we pass. They all separate and huff as we pass by, giving us space to walk toward the center of the square. I can't help but think my presence causes their disdain. I hesitate, but I look toward the alleyways to find numerous cloaked figures staying back, shielded by the smog, dust, and darkness that the narrow entrance offers.

As the last few people part, allowing us to step into the center of town, the color drains from my face. Before us sits a wooden platform, built so that the crowd has visibility to whatever is happening on the stage. Stains of old blood and various other liquids taint the ground, and worn ropes line the platform. I glance at Silas, and his expression remains the same—focused, steady, and unafraid—though I know he feels my stare. His jawline tenses slightly as he realizes I know exactly what this platform was used for.

Before me is the place where Silas—among many others— would fight for his life publicly. Royalty or not, Silas was humiliated here—he was made a man here—and now, he will declare his reign in the place that nearly broke him.

Aerona steps onto the platform first, giving the people the chance to stop what they are doing and give her their full attention. A silence sweeps across the crowd, and a chill runs through me. Everyone's cloaked faces slowly turn toward us as Fen hops onto the platform next. Her swift movement is graceful, her long black hair flowing in the wind, and she smiles, but nothing in her eyes shows kindness.

Silas turns to me, his jaw tight, and extends his hand to help me step onto the platform. I follow his lead and try to step onto the wooden surface. I place one foot on the step and begin to move when a large hand wraps around my shoulder, stopping me. The action catches me off guard, causing me to stumble backward a few steps away from Silas's grip, nearly crashing to the ground. Before I have time to react, Silas lunges forward with his sword drawn, pointing at the man's throat.

"Get your fucking hand off her," Silas's voice booms through the square.

The crowd grows quiet, and everyone steps back. The old man's voice whispers in my ear, and he doesn't release my shoulder—as if this is the only time he has to speak to me.

"Your Majesty," the old man's voice trembles. "Don't let your guard down. They are closer than you think."

I study the old man's face, aged by time and hardships.

"What do you mean?" I whisper back.

The sword remains poised at his throat, but Silas's startled rage dissolves as he permits the man to keep speaking. The crowd hangs back, and Fen widens her stance, utterly aware of the situation unfolding.

"Th…the creatures," the man stutters.

I angle my head, and Silas lowers his sword. "What do you know about the ship?"

The old man narrows his eyes. "Your Majesty, I'm not sure what ship you are referring to."

"But you said creatures. Which creatures, then?" I ask.

Aerona's voice shouts above us, "Enough!"

The man jolts.

Silas leans close enough to whisper in the man's ear. "There are better ways to get our attention. Next time, I suggest speaking to us privately instead of nearly knocking down the Queen of Daramveer in such a public space."

"I'm sorry," the old man rasps.

Silas's eyes dart to the crowd and back to the man. "Go and hide before things get bad here. Take your loved ones."

"Bad, Your Highness?"

I watch Silas, and he speaks gently to the old man. "Protect yourself. Go to the mountains. Trust me."

I grab Silas's arm, and the man nods, backing into the whispering crowd. I watch his figure disappear into a sea of cloaked civilians, and fear bubbles up into my chest.

If he wasn't talking about the ship, what did he mean?

I move back toward Silas and hop onto the platform, shaking the old man's words from my mind. I join Fen and Aerona, turning to face the crowd. Their eyes shift to me, and I give them a reassuring nod. Silas follows me, hopping onto the platform with a warrior's grace. Even though this isn't much higher than the ground, I feel miles above those standing below, and a wave of nausea hits me as I stare at the cloaked figures. Hushed whispers move through the crowd, and I hear grumbles of curses flowing in our direction—my direction.

Silas steps forward with his sword still drawn, facing the people of Andorwood. Many figures before us remove their hoods, and I study their faces. Shadow and Lumor Wielders stand in front of us, each looking unique except for their hair color. Rebels, criminals, and travelers fill the crowd, and I know that everyone before us came to Andorwood with a common goal—to start a new life in a kingdom that had hope. I can only pray that one day faith can be restored.

Children, adults, and elderly Wielders stand before us, and even though looks of caution, concern, and hatred shine back at me, I'm filled with anticipation that they will unite to help us defeat a common enemy.

Silas wastes no time. "Andorwood!" His deep voice carries

through the crowd. "I stand before you today to announce change, hope, and a new future free of fear, doubt, and hiding."

The crowd falls deathly quiet and still. I stand beside Silas, in awe of his steadiness and his ability to speak before an audience. The last time I declared something to a crowd, I almost spilled my guts in front of everyone. Anxiety fills me, and I will my hands to steady themselves at my sides.

"Malachi is gone," Silas shouts.

Hushed whispers fill the crowd, and Fen steps forward, shushing them. Her presence commands attention, causing them to quiet once more.

"He fled, abandoning Andorwood without a second thought. Your king has left, and he won't be returning," Silas continues, stepping closer to the crowd. "Malachi lied to you all. He ruled this domain with fear by haunting us in the shadows of this kingdom and our minds. He tormented and tortured all..." He pauses. "Myself included."

Someone from the crowd shouts, "Good fucking riddance."

A few laughs travel over the crowd like a disease, and something twists within my gut.

"I thought you might all feel that way," Silas says, as he dips his head in agreement. "And I know you all understand what that means for this kingdom."

Silence falls over the crowd, and Aerona steps forward to stand beside Silas while Fenmore stays back.

"Silas Nastronde is now King of Andorwood," she shouts. "He will reign with fairness and understanding, and no longer will fear spread across this kingdom. Silas will restore Andorwood to what it once was—a kingdom of peace, equality, and freedom— and we will rise once more. No one will have to hide any longer. We will no longer be outsiders, but will band together as a king- dom. A new Andorwood is coming, and I hope you all will stand behind the Nastrondes as you once did before Malachi."

Whispers sweep across the crowd, and a bead of sweat forms on my brow. I scan the area, still desperate to lay eyes on Larkin and Warrick. Knowing they are nearby will calm me, but I'm only met with dark stares from unfamiliar faces. Anxiety floods me, and I feel as though I'm back on display in Daramveer, my life easily being handed over by my father.

My memories crash into my mind, and I appear before a crowd of people cheering and clapping, even though my brother had died mere days ago. I'm before a crowd, sobbing over Silas's motionless body on the cold ground during the fourth trial. I'm before them, screaming at my father, declaring that his ritual worked, and letting the world know that Kalix lives within me.

Panic swirls like gloomy clouds above my head, and I feel my legs wobble. How can I rule a kingdom when standing before a crowd haunts me? That's when it hits me—I can't. I'll never rule like Silas. I don't *want* to rule in my state, and I fight the urge to flee this platform to disappear into the crowd of people before us. My hands tremble, and my palms are soaked with sweat. I attempt to steady my breath, but the panic continuously rises.

My wide eyes scan the crowd while Silas continues to speak. I hear his words, but they don't register in my mind. Each unfamiliar face intensifies my panic. Something is wrong. Something is about to go wrong. My darkness begins to simmer under the surface, like a near-boiling pot of water, and I close my eyes.

Breathe.

Swallow the feeling down.

In the back of the crowd, I catch sight of a figure that stands a head taller than the rest. A cloaked face stares back at me, and my chest rapidly rises and falls. The figure slowly lifts the hood covering his face, and I see him—Larkin.

His brows furrow, and I know he can see the panic on my face.

"Are you alright?" he mouths, and I return the slightest shake of my head. *"Breathe, Briar."*

The hood returns over his face, and he begins to make his way toward the platform, staying on the outskirts of the crowd. His growing presence helps steady my wobbling body.

I'm okay.

We are okay.

I slowly come back into my surroundings and hear the crowd growing louder.

"The Nastrondes are the reason we are in this position to begin with," a civilian shouts.

"Why should we allow another to take over? What if he turns out to be just like his father? We can't trust them so easily."

"Malachi killed a castle worker," a woman shouts, and my blood runs cold. "A poor girl that didn't deserve death, and they let her die."

I slowly turn my gaze to Silas; his face is hard, but I know he's struggling. How can you rally people who have hated your family for so long? Silas may be possessive and harsh, but he's fair. He would never risk our safety standing here right now to argue with the crowd. He needs them, and he will take every blow if it means winning us allies for what's coming. His eyes show me that he is calculating every word that enters his mind and will only speak when the right words come.

A raspy voice escapes Silas's lips, demanding attention. "I am nothing like Malachi. Haven't I proven myself to be different? For years, I fought alongside all of you for my own life. I'm not asking for your immediate trust, but I am asking for time. Only then can I prove myself as your king."

The crowd grows restless.

"Malachi is a monster, and you share the same blood," a man shouts from the back of the crowd.

Silas tenses, and shadows begin to pulse around his body. I

step toward him, as if to protect him from the words of the crowd below us. The crowd seems to step back as I move forward. They fear me, and for the first time, I wish that weren't true.

"She is going to bring us all to ruin," someone else shouts, and many others chime in, agreeing.

Silas's shadows intensify, and Fen positions herself on the opposite side of me, realizing that the crowd is becoming increasingly out of control. She glances toward Silas, whose gaze remains fixed ahead. His shadows loom larger, and I watch as his palms curl into tight fists. Silas contorts his face in pain, and I know his internal struggle is tearing him apart. He wouldn't expose his mother by revealing that Malachi isn't his father unless it was essential.

"Calm down," I whisper, placing my hand on his forearm. "They are processing all of this, just as we did."

He turns his head, angling it away from the crowd, and his words flow into my mind. *"This is escalating, and they will attack if they see fit. The people of Andorwood are hard to control. If they touch you, I will kill them. I will fight this battle alone if I must."*

"Just calm down, Silas," I say, aloud.

Rage fills his eyes, and I squeeze his arm, praying that things de-escalate.

"If Silas is with her, we are against him," another voice sounds, and the crowd explodes into an uproar of chatter, shouts, and curses directed toward me.

Larkin's tall figure reappears in my view, this time accompanied by another cloaked figure of similar stature—Warrick.

Fenmore signals something, and they split up, making sure they are on either side of the platform should things continue to go very wrong.

Silas steps forward, spreading his shadows across the wooden stage like deadly black wings. "Quiet!" His voice vibrates around the square. "Speaking ill of Briar won't bring about the fairness I've been discussing."

I tighten my grip on his arm, feeling the connection between us grow stronger.

"Damnit, calm down. That won't help," I think, and Silas shoots me a look. *"Don't fucking threaten them."*

"See?" a man shouts. "There are his true colors. Willing to hurt us for speaking ill of Kalix's bitch."

The words hit me harder than a blow to the face, and I stagger backward on the platform. Silas quakes with rage. He steps forward, causing the crowd to pause. Shadows rise behind him like a tidal wave of darkness, and I immediately forget the man's words, focusing instead on Silas. He will kill these people—his people—and someone has to stop this. I quickly move back in front of him, ignoring the raging crowd at my back, and place both hands on his arms to hold them down, gazing into his nearly glowing green eyes.

"Breathe," I snap. "His words can't hurt us, but you can hurt them. Everything will be for nothing if you lose control."

His eyes slowly meet mine, and instead of the piercing, steady gaze I've grown accustomed to, they are ablaze with anger—green flames swirling chaotically. His eyes almost look as if they are vertical slits.

"You need to calm down," I whisper. "Don't let them see you like this. Fear isn't going to make them come together. It will only pit them against us."

His chest rises and falls rapidly, and darkness seeps from him like I've never witnessed before. Not even in the depths of Daramveer Castle did I encounter such anger and darkness emanating from Silas, but I know it isn't solely anger; he's as panicked as I am, and that's fueling his magic. I'm taken aback, yet I remain steady, knowing that the recent events—the fear, the death, the betrayals—are drowning him.

The crowd's shouts become muffled as I pull him in, our chests pressed together, tugging on the connection between us with everything I have. In this moment, I have to be the one to keep him grounded.

A woman from the crowd steps forward, the unruly people around her allowing her to advance. Her long white hair—a result of her Lumor abilities and age—shines against the overcast sky above us, catching our attention through the corners of our eyes. The woman moves closer to the platform—as near as she can get without climbing up—and turns to face the crowd. She is the only person in Andorwood who has looked familiar thus far, and it's because she bears the same face as someone I once knew.

My hand slides down Silas's arm, and I grip it harder than before, driven by shock and the need to remain upright. The woman gracefully waits for the crowd to simmer down, and I stare at her. I know she feels my gaze burning into the back of her head, but I can't stop. My heart rages like an animal in a cage, and I suck in a breath.

Everyone, including the sea breeze, seems to pause, and my heart drops.

I am sure that this woman will either make or break our desperate pleas for unity. She holds an envelope in her hand, and I glance at the familiar writing on the paper stained with ink.

I know the writing; I had a similar note.

My heart sinks, and my hands shake against Silas's.

Yara's mother steps forward and prepares to address the crowd.

CHAPTER 40

The woman stands tall and firm, not concerned with facing us, but focused solely on the raging crowd before her. I glance over the edge of the platform as the woman slowly opens the letter. The paper shakes in her grip, and she clears her throat to speak. My mouth slightly parts, and I look toward Larkin. His eyes are as wide as mine.

"Malachi killed my daughter."

The crowd grows quiet, giving the woman the chance to speak.

"Oh Gods," I hear Aerona whisper from behind me, and the color leaves her face.

"Yara was an amazing young woman with so much life ahead of her, but she was not perfect—none of us are. Yara made decisions that put her in impossible situations, many of which you will never experience, and I hope it stays that way." She clears her throat once more, fighting back the tears that are desperate to escape her grieving heart.

The crowd remains deathly quiet, also grieving her loss.

"When news of Yara's passing reached me, I was angry, confused, and desperate for answers. Warrick Pierce arrived at my house carrying Yara's body and explained to me what happened. He detailed how Malachi was to blame, and how Silas Nastronde, Briar Blackbyrne, and Larkin Spiridon risked their lives to save her, and when they were unsuccessful, they risked their lives to give her the final respects she deserved."

The crowd gasps, and I cut my eyes toward the cloaked figure I know shields Warrick. He defended us. Even when he was hurting, he made sure our names were cleared, and for that, I'm forever grateful.

"I didn't believe him. In fact, I kicked him out of my house and refused to listen to anything else the man had to say. I regretted that decision when this showed up."

The aged woman extends her hand, showing the crowd the trembling letter. Yara prepped for this, just like she did by leaving my note. She knew Malachi was going to kill her, so she did everything she could in the time she had left to warn and take care of the ones around her.

"Mother,

If you are reading this, please know that I love you.

However, I have left this realm to embark on a new adventure, one that we will someday have the pleasure of experiencing together. But I can honestly say that my greatest honor is leaving this world trying to help those in need. Briar Blackbyrne and Silas Nastronde need our help. Even in peril, Briar promised me things: a better life, opportunities to grow, and more. They, too, are facing an impossible task, and please know I died helping them because I believe in them and a better future.

If I can ask you for anything, please help them.

Please convince Andorwood to assist them. She is good. They are good, and they are trying to rid this world of the evil that haunts us all.

All my love,

Yara."

The woman wipes the tears from her eyes while the crowd remains silent, watching in shock. I can only stare at her, feeling a growing hole in my heart that can never be healed.

With a weak voice, the woman speaks again. "I'm not asking you to trust them, but I am asking you to listen and give them the time Silas Nastronde requests. They aren't speaking to us today to waste our time. Our time is limited, and without us—without our help—it's even shorter than we think."

A tear falls from my eyes, and I face the crowd, stepping forward.

"A ship sails toward us. I know that most of you have heard the rumors, and I regret to inform you that they are true," I warn. "Our time is as limited as this woman indicates. Calia Thornfield and Nolan Harte have resurrected the dead, transforming them into horrifying creatures, and they travel toward Andorwood to uncover forgotten information to aid in Carobon's quest to rule over all the lands once more."

The crowd erupts in hushed chatter, their eyes wide, and they begin to fidget at the news.

"We are asking for help." Silas steps beside me. "We are *begging* for help."

I look toward him and reach for his hand as he continues.

"We seek your strength, power, resilience, and ability to come together as the forgotten—as the rebels of Andorwood. Andorwood will be known as a kingdom that unites through fighting, just as the rumors have echoed across this realm for centuries."

The crowd stills, and a growing sense of pride explodes in my chest.

"This is a kingdom that will send a message: 'never fucking mess with us.' We will lead you." Silas glances at me and back to the crowd. "We will guide you, and I swear to the Gods that I will protect you."

I look to the crowd—their faces hard as stone, but the chatter has faded and the pulsing tension begins to ease.

Silas pauses, taking a breath. "But, I will not force you. This is your decision alone. In a few days, the ship will arrive, and we will be there, ready to fight. I hope you all will choose to do the same."

Slight nods of approval begin to appear among the crowd of rebels in front of us, and no one speaks, rejects, or tries to argue. Concerned expressions flash across the faces of the civilians, and the silence is deafening. Without waiting to hear anything further, I leap down from the platform, leaving Silas to speak with his family, and stand before the woman who changed everything for us—just like Yara.

"Thank you," I whisper.

"That was for my daughter," the woman replies. "She asked that of me, and as her mother, I would do anything for her."

"Just like Yara, you've changed everything." I smile.

The woman extends her hand. Her dark eyes sparkle like black diamonds, and her face is beautiful, yet harbors a sadness I have unfortunately known many times before. The woman's skin is smooth, yet shows signs of graceful aging.

"I'm Pia Herst, Yara's mother. I helped heal your friend, Maines."

My mouth falls open, and my stomach flips.

The woman in the room refused to turn fully to me. She knew who we were and what had happened to us. Even in the midst of her own grief and hurt, she helped save Maines.

Without thinking, I wrap both arms around the woman, and I feel her shock from my touch, but she returns the embrace.

"Thank you," I say, pulling back. "I see now where Yara got her heart. You have done more than I can ever repay."

Two men walk up behind me and remove their hoods. Larkin and Warrick stand around us while Pia glances at both of them.

Warrick speaks, "Good afternoon, Mrs. Herst."

"Hello, boys," Pia says. "It's nice to see you, Warrick."

He smiles. "You as well."

She returns her gaze to mine and offers me a soft smile. Her face is so similar to Yara's that I can't help but feel sadness, knowing that in years to come, Yara's face would have looked the same—beautiful, aged, and soft.

"When the ship arrives, if you would like to seek shelter in Silas's house, you are welcome," I offer.

"I have been asked to assist with healing the wounded near the pier. I will do what I have been asked, and I will fight. Even if I am the only civilian who shows up, I will be there. Yara would have done the same," she replies, sternly.

I know there is no arguing with her.

"Very well." I smile. "I will be happy to fight alongside you, and I will feel safe knowing that you are there, healing."

Pia points to the axes on my back. "I would love to have a weapon like that," she says with a wink. "Just in case."

I chuckle, softly. "I'll see what I can do for you."

"Thank you," she replies. "I am heading back to the king's cliff house momentarily. I came to town only to gather a few more supplies for your friend's healing. She is lucky, Your Majesty. She has many months ahead of her for healing, but with my help, she will be just fine."

"Is there anything I can do to help?" I ask.

She shakes her head and turns away to take her leave. "Just fight like hell. We need you to win this war."

"We will."

She smiles, and Warrick steps forward. "Would you like me to walk you home?"

Pia shakes her head. "That's okay, boy. I can make it on my own."

Warrick dips his head in respect.

"Please be careful," Pia says.

"Always," Warrick responds.

The woman moves gracefully through the crowd, and they don't hesitate to part for her. The civilians treat her with respect, and I can tell that she has been a long-time advocate for them. They trust her, and they listen to her words. Without her, I fear this would have gone terribly wrong. Some of the crowd stay in tight circles, likely deciding what they will do, while others return to their daily chores.

I glance toward the dark alleyways, and tucked beneath the shadows, the prominent, cloaked figures remain.

Larkin moves closer. "You okay?"

I nod. "I'm okay now that things have died down. We owe a lot to Yara and Pia."

"We will repay her one day."

I angle my head toward the shadowed alleyways, trying not to be too obvious about whom I'm speaking about.

"Who are they?"

Warrick and Larkin merely cast their eyes toward the darkness that the sun seems to overlook. The fog continues to spill out of the alleyway, as if the shadows are so thick that they have nowhere else to go but billow out.

"Did you think the rebels and criminals were referred to figuratively?" Larkin asks.

I shrug. "I thought it was more of a group name for Andorwood."

Warrick laughs, and I turn my head sharply in his direction.

"Those are the ones we speak of," Warrick says. "They keep to themselves, hide in the shadows, and to our knowledge, they are an army in themselves."

"Did Malachi know about them? How were they not punished?" I ask.

"Of course, he knew, but not even Malachi could figure out

their plans. It's hard to find someone who is rarely seen," Larkin whispers.

"Will they fight with us?" I ask.

"I doubt it," Larkin replies. "But, they've been eager for Silas to join them for years. He would never risk it with Malachi around."

Warrick chimes in, "What he means is, Silas had too much to lose. Having him as king now could change everything."

Larkin flashes a grin at Warrick and says, "And, we have someone who may be able to persuade them."

"Who?"

"The leader is Cyrus Pierce," Larkin says.

Pierce.

Larkin smiles as I put the pieces together. "Warrick's father."

My jaw snaps open, and I look at Warrick. "What?"

His gaze goes down the alleyway toward the tall figure that remains barely visible. The cloaked man slips just out of sight, and Warrick slowly turns his head back in our direction.

"Can I speak with him?" I ask.

Larkin laughs. "You wouldn't be able to find him to do so. Their showing up will be a gamble that I'd never bet money on. Though he would probably love to speak with the Queen of Daramveer."

"I like a challenge," I add.

"Yeah, right. You're delusional if you think Silas is going to let you find Cyrus alone." Larkin nudges my shoulder.

I huff. "I never said anything about doing that alone."

Silas hops down from the platform, joining us. "Why is it you all always talk about me?"

"Our favorite troublemaker wants to speak with Cyrus Pierce," Larkin teases.

Silas's lips form a thin line, and he glances at Warrick. "And who is the one who told her about Mr. Pierce?" Silas angles his head.

Warrick places both hands in his pockets and returns his gaze to us. "It's hard to ignore his looming presence in the alleyways, Nastronde." He tosses a look over his shoulder. "He heard every-thing. I noticed my father and a few others hidden in the shadows —listening—almost immediately."

"Can't say I'm surprised," Silas replies.

Warrick nods, "They are still close."

"I see," Silas says.

"Maybe it's time you finally speak to him, Silas," Larkin says. "There's no way he won't expect you two wanting to talk privately."

Silas remains quiet, and he dives into his own thoughts for a second. With what is coming, we could use anyone and everyone to assist, and having the army of Andorwood rebels could change everything.

"C'mon, you know we need them," I think in my mind, and Silas cuts his eyes toward me.

"You are right," he replies.

"Say that again."

"You're right," he repeats.

"Music to my ears," I smile.

Silas shakes his head and glances toward Warrick and Larkin.

"Are you going to come, Warrick?" Silas asks.

I fight back the urge to jump with excitement.

"I don't think I'm ready for a family affair," he replies. "You two can do this alone."

"Very well," Silas agrees. "You two head back to the house and take Fen and my mother. Check on Maines, then fill Oak in."

They nod.

"Start prepping for what's to come. From this day forward,

every day will count. Gather numbers on how many we will have at our side and help those willing to fight."

Warrick waves Fenmore over, along with Aerona.

"Where are you going?" Larkin asks.

Silas locks his fingers around mine as we move across the stone streets of the square. He glances down a few alleyways, deciding which one is the right one to explore. He calls over his shoulder to Warrick and Larkin, who are watching us intently.

"We're going to have a drink."

Larkin laughs, and we move through the square, ignoring the passing glances we receive. It must seem odd to them, the Queen of Daramveer, hand in hand with their new king. Even more bizarre to me is that Silas just announced we were off to have a drink.

We walk in silence through the crowd, turning a corner that leads down a narrower walkway. The crowd thins out, and soon it's just Silas and me walking toward a tucked-in door halfway down the alleyway.

"Thirsty, are you?" I finally ask, once we are away from the prying ears of the civilians.

"After that? I'm dying for an ale." He looks down at me and smiles.

Our pace slows as he takes his time passing the few store-fronts in the alleyway. Fabric stores, pottery shops, and other random stands fill the spaces, while the owners either wave at us or quickly turn their heads away.

"You did great up there," I say. "I'm proud of you for calming down like that. I know it wasn't easy to control your anger."

"Thank you."

"I understand how it feels to have your entire kingdom turning its back on you. I believe we are going to be okay—Andorwood will come around."

"I don't feel like I did well," he responds. "I almost lost it, Briar. How can I rule if I can't control my anger?"

"But you did control it, Silas."

"Barely." He lowers his head and continues to stroll forward. "I considered wiping them all out. I thought they would come for you, and I wanted to destroy them—my own kingdom—for you."

"But you didn't."

"That's not the point," he says, looking at me. "I would burn this isle to the ground for you in an instant. If anyone tries to cross me, fine, I can handle it. But if anyone crosses you? I fear that for the rest of my life, I will struggle with wanting to murder any poor soul who dares to speak ill of you."

"Then, you will have to work on controlling that. You can think what you'd like, but we must control our actions. I can handle myself; you know that," I reply. "I haven't felt that rage before over something so small. What was that?"

"I don't know," he says. "I've never felt this angry."

"Then, tell me when you are feeling close to losing it, and I'll help you."

He nods, and the conversation quiets, giving him some space to think and breathe, even in the confined space of the alleyway. Soon, we come upon a wooden sign that hangs from a stone building: *Ophidian's Den.*

"Why are we coming here? It can't be because you want a drink this badly," I inquire.

"First off, yes, I do need a drink badly. And second, you wanted to meet Cyrus, didn't you?" Silas smiles.

"Well, yes. I think it would be prudent," I respond.

"Alright, well then, we're having a drink." Silas pulls me toward the door. "Or three."

"How do you know he's here?" I question, planting my feet, and not letting him pull me any closer to the bar.

"Because he asked me to meet him here two days ago."

CHAPTER 41

Inside, the light is dim, casting shadows in every corner, and the air smells of stale ale and something far more unpleasant—like a mix of sweat, mold, and musty wood paneling. The floorboards creak with every step beneath our weight, and Silas keeps a firm grip on my hand. The person behind the bar raises a drink at Silas's entrance, and he returns the smile, signaling to bring over two drinks once we are seated. The bartender is aged, with deep lines etched into his forehead and gray hair shining against the darkness of the bar. A few scattered tables line the front of the space, but we continue deeper through the bar toward the back. Various maps and photos line the walls in no organized fashion.

The place is empty except for a few men who sit alone in the shadows. Their comfort tells me that they are here often, and I can't help but think of the few bars in Daramveer. When the ports were thriving, I could hear shouts and laughter from the drunks leaving the bar at all hours of the night during the summer months. Even though this place makes me feel sorry for those who are here constantly, an unexpected thrill runs through me.

As we walk deeper into the space, the light becomes even

more scarce, providing a level of concealment that I assume Cyrus prefers. The hushed chatter fades, and a door appears before us that I didn't notice when we entered the bar. Silas turns his head toward me and flashes a bright smile in the darkness.

"Come here often?" I ask.

"Larkin and I used to close this place down," he says, as he chuckles. "I met him here for the first time. I punched him in the face, then tried to kill him."

"I heard," I respond and chuckle.

"I knew we would be friends as soon as my knuckles touched his cheek," Silas says.

"You did?"

"Fuck no," Silas laughs. "I hated him."

Silas pushes open the heavy door, and whatever lies inside is completely covered by darkness. Nerves twist in my gut, but I follow Silas inside, closing the door behind me.

As we move further into the room, my eyes quickly adjust, and I see a single cigar burning in the darkness. The smell causes my nose to tingle, and behind the glow, I see the face of a white-haired man—Cyrus Pierce.

His deep, raspy voice speaks into the darkness. "I didn't think you would show."

Silas pulls out a chair for me, and I sit down as he joins me. I remove my axes and place them within reach on the floor next to me.

"Things have changed," Silas replies.

Cyrus chuckles darkly. "I'm aware."

"Are you?" Silas bites back.

"And you brought Briar Blackbyrne, the Queen of Daramveer," Cyrus hums. "This must be my lucky day."

"Where she goes, I go," Silas says, with a shrug. "She thought it was in our best interest to speak."

"She's smart."

"Indeed."

"Is she trustworthy?" Cyrus continues.

Silas leans forward, and I shift in my chair, clearing my throat.

"Hello, Cyrus," I say. "I won't say it's nice to see you. The darkness conceals too much of your face for that."

"I prefer it that way," he says, his deep voice turning in my direction.

"Yeah," I say, leaning closer to get a better look. "I heard you are a fan of the shadows. Are you shy or just embarrassed by your looks?"

A deep, thunderous laugh blows the cigar smoke in our direction, and I use my hand to swat away the aroma of stout tobacco, sweet spices, and leather.

"And she's a smartass," he continues, laughing wildly. "Even better."

"That is for certain," Silas adds.

A whoosh of light erupts from his palm, illuminating the room with a bright glow. The sconces on the walls ignite, and the candles on the few tables surrounding us flicker. My eyes adjust to the light, focusing my gaze on his face.

He's older, around my father's age, and his eyes are as dark as the bottom of the ocean. His hair is white and gray, yet his face remains hard, and his features resemble Warrick's handsome ones.

"That's better," I say, observing his expression.

"I prefer the shadows, Queen, because they're quiet." His aged eyes meet mine. "Less sarcasm. The light can be…blinding at times."

I smile, propping my elbows on the table. "We need to talk."

Cyrus settles back in his chair as the door creaks open. Without turning around, I see him wave the man inside. The bartender rushes in, carrying three cups filled with brown liquid, and he sets them on the table. The smell of dark ale hits my nose, making my mouth water. It's been ages since I had a drink, and after today, I agree with Silas. A drink—or three—sounds delicious.

"I've closed the bar until your meeting is over, sir," the man whispers. "You will not be disturbed."

"No, need Kipp, this won't take long," Cyrus replies, putting out his cigar. "Right?"

I meet his gaze, and I smile sarcastically, dipping my chin.

The man bows. "Either way, sir, the entire bar is yours. Take your time."

As quickly as the barkeep entered the room, he exits, leaving us alone once more. I can tell that Cyrus is a man of power, based on the way people interact with him. Even sitting before the King of Andorwood, he shows no nerves—no hesitation—and oozes confidence. Apparently, Cyrus has been asking Silas to join the rebels for years, and I can't help but think of what those conversations looked like. I would have paid to be a fly on the wall for those meetings.

Silas stirs in his chair. "I'm assuming you saw the uproar we caused today?"

"I wouldn't have missed it for the world," Cyrus says. "Although I didn't expect Briar to jump in like she did. You were seconds away from losing your mind, Nastronde. That wasn't a good look."

"I don't respond well to threats against someone I love." Silas adjusts his shirt. "I know you don't understand what I mean, though."

"Can you elaborate?" Cyrus furrows his brow. "Or do you want to continue being passive-aggressive?"

I huff a laugh.

"Have you ever loved anyone, Cyrus?" Silas replies. "Other than yourself?"

Cyrus huffs a laugh. "Always bringing up my family matters whenever you can, Silas."

"Just calling it like I see it."

"It gets old," Cyrus responds. "Warrick is grown. He can fight his own battles and choose to speak to me should he see fit."

"Bullshit," Silas spits.

"I'm always available."

"You know that isn't the truth, Pierce." Silas goes still, placing both hands on the table. "Available isn't a word I would ever use in a sentence regarding you."

I roll my eyes at their bickering.

"What word would you use to describe me, then?" Cyrus's anger grows.

Silas opens his mouth to speak, and I clear my throat, punching him under the table.

"Are we going to discuss what the true threat is?" I scoff, taking a long drink of my ale. "Or are you two going to throw digs the entire time?"

They glance at me.

"If so," I prop my legs on a nearby chair, "I can gladly order a second ale and get comfortable."

Cyrus tips his head back and laughs. The sound travels through the room, and I keep my gaze focused solely on him.

"I like her, Silas," Cyrus says, continuing to laugh. "She's going to ruin you in the best way."

Silas cuts his eyes toward me. "She already has."

I place my hands around the chilled cup, lowering my legs. "A ship is days away from docking. It's filled with the resurrected. Calia Thornfield and Nolan Harte have been working to raise an unstoppable army to assist Carobon in taking full control, as he tried centuries ago. We need your help now, and again in the future when we confront the Great Wiitch."

Cyrus goes quiet and traces small circles around the frost on his cup.

"And what are we supposed to do when the other Great Wiitch—Kalix—comes forward?" Cyrus questions. "Will she attempt to eliminate all Lumor Wielders to ensure the darkness regains full power once more?"

I tense. "That won't happen."

He studies me. "And how do you plan to stop her?"

I narrow my eyes. "Kalix has lived within me for nearly six years, and she has yet to step forward fully. I've mastered controlling her, and every day I'm one step closer to destroying her. But," I pause, glancing at Silas, "I plan to ensure that those around me have a strategy to handle her if it happens. Whatever that means for my own being."

He furrows his brow, and Silas slowly travels his gaze toward me.

"*What*?" His voice snaps in my mind.

"*Later*," I respond.

"*Briar*."

That's the first time I've said that aloud, and I know he wants to object. However, he remains quiet and lets me speak.

"I seek peace and fairness. I want all Wielders to coexist in harmony, without fear of power or death. I plan to cleanse this realm of both Great Wiitches, as others have attempted before, and quite frankly, I'm tired of power-hungry assholes ruining everything."

He huffs, nodding his head.

I take a deep breath. "I can't do it without allies."

Cyrus looks at Silas and back at me. "And if you fail?"

"Then you're dead anyway," I answer. "We all are."

Cyrus takes a drink of his ale.

"Help us, so we can ensure that neither of those options comes to fruition."

He nods his head, listening to my words. He takes another long sip of his drink, and the foam clings to the stubble dusting his upper lip. He wipes it away and stares at me, dark eyes piercing into mine, but I remain firm and steady.

"What of Daramveer?" Cyrus asks.

I look at Silas; his gaze could ignite this bar. I follow in Cyrus's footsteps and take a sip of my own ale before me.

"First on my list of things to do when I return to the mainland is reclaiming my kingdom and ensuring Eden suffers for the pain and torment she inflicted." I lean forward. "Daramveer is mine, and I owe those people a safe home. I plan to do whatever is necessary to achieve that."

Cyrus hums in response, then continues, "The people of Daramveer fled when they learned the truth of who lives within you, and today, Silas almost lost Andorwood. Why would I consider joining you when you have nothing to offer me? You two can't even rule your own kingdoms."

"We can," I snap. "And we will."

Cyrus sounds a sarcastic huff.

"When this is over, you can guarantee that you have safety in Daramveer. You are free to travel to my kingdom as you wish." I remove the dark green stone from my pocket and set it on the table in front of us.

Cyrus freezes, along with Silas.

"And, I have this."

The green stone shines in the dim lighting and demands attention. Its beauty surprises me each time, and I swear the table warps under its weight.

"The stone of Andorwood. We are going to gather all the stones from the kingdoms. Once we learn how to control them, or at least this one, you can have it. I'm offering you power."

Cyrus's face contorts as he thinks.

"Can I trust you?" he asks.

"Yes."

He smiles as he takes the cup in his hand and finishes the ale.

"Can I trust you?" I question back.

"You'll just have to see, won't you?" A sinister smile spreads across his aged face.

He slams the cup down and stands up. The sudden movement takes me aback, and I notice that Silas is, too.

"Cyrus," Silas nearly growls.

"I don't say this often, but meeting you, Miss Blackbyrne, was a pleasure. I most enjoyed our drink together." Cyrus walks toward the door, placing the cloak back over his head. "We should meet for drinks more often."

"And your decision?" I question.

His hand pauses before reaching the rusty doorknob. "I have things to discuss with my people before I agree to anything. If we move forward with what you have suggested, you will know. If we decide not to, you will know." Cyrus flashes a look toward Silas. "Give my regards to Warrick."

"Cyrus," I call.

He slowly turns. "What?"

"If you have, in fact, ever loved someone in your life, I think I know who it is."

His body goes rigid.

"And he also needs your help."

Cyrus doesn't turn to meet my words. Instead, he swiftly exits the room, leaving a trail of light behind him. The room's glow dims as his magic moves further away, but the candle continues to burn, casting a shadowy light around us.

Silas sits back in his chair and sips the dark liquid in his cup. "I may need a second drink after that."

I look at him, taking my cup in hand as well. "I kind of like him."

Silas laughs. "There is no surprise there. He is almost as big of a smartass as you are, my love."

I laugh, taking another drink.

"No way are you giving him that stone." Silas looks at me.

I smirk, unable to hide the pride on my face. "We have an exact duplicate, remember?"

Silas laughs. "He'll likely kill us on the spot if he finds out."

"Good thing he won't. Well, not until we are long gone."

"This is going to end very badly," he says, giving me a warning look.

"Then, we'd better come up with a plan once we get to that step."

"I can't wait to see the look on his face," Silas chuckles.

Silas and I both take drinks of our ale, taking a moment to let our thoughts swirl in our heads.

"I thought that went well," I say, breaking the silence.

"Oh, it definitely went well, but Cyrus is unpredictable. His choice will come just moments before we need them. He may assist us in a few days, but he can't be relied upon."

I take another sip of the ale. "Why doesn't Warrick speak to his father?"

Silas takes a long breath.

"Warrick is second in command of the Andorwood army. He is a rule follower, loyal, and has always been. How he came from Cyrus Pierce, I'll never know." Silas sets his cup down. "If your father led a group of rebels, would you join him? Even if it went against everything you fought for and believed in?"

"I don't know," I respond.

"Their relationship is complicated," Silas says. "Always has been."

"And his mother?"

Silas shifts in his chair. "Died shortly after he was born."

I don't respond; instead, I think of everything that's happened.

My heart races, and I feel like it hasn't slowed since we arrived here. Nothing about this has been easy, and I fear the challenging parts have yet to arrive. I enjoy the silence for a moment and continue to sip my drink. The strong scent of hops fills my nose with each sip, and I think back to us on the ship before we arrived. The night of my birthday was so normal and fun. Things have changed significantly since then, but I always knew it would.

"Silas," I say, as I glance toward him to find he is already staring at me. "You are the king and Commander of the Andorwood army. Why don't you make them fight? You could do that, you know."

He exhales. "Yes, I could. But my father forced them to do so many things for years. The pain I see in their eyes haunts me. And yes, I could compel them, but I want my kingdom to stand behind me willingly. I want them to choose to be a united force of chaos. I want them to accept me, and if I force their loyalty and we fail, what future would I have as their king then?"

"They would see you no differently than Malachi," I whisper.

"Exactly, and that is my biggest fear." His eyes drop. "So, when the day comes that I must stand and fight against the resurrected, I will do so, even if I stand alone on that pier. I will prove to them that I will protect them or die trying."

I turn in my chair to face him fully, cupping his strong jaw. "Look at me, Silas."

I apply pressure, forcing his eyes to find mine.

"You will not be alone on that pier. We will be beside you—we will fight—and when the day comes that peace has filled these lands once more, I will stand beside you until the darkest realms take us."

He tries to avert his gaze, but I hold firm and continue.

"You, Silas Nastronde, will earn their trust and rule Andorwood as it should always have been. You are destined to be great.

The people of Andorwood will bow to you, only with acceptance and grace."

His hand travels to my face and tucks a fallen strand of hair behind my ears.

"They will bow to you because you are good and deserving."

"And I will bow only to you, my love."

Silas's eyes burn into mine, and he leans forward, planting a soft kiss on my lips. I place both hands on his muscular thighs, running my hands up his legs. Silas pulls away, and his hard stare is replaced with a look of pure darkness.

I slowly stand and walk toward the exit, flicking the lock across the wooden door, and smile. Silas stands, watching me slowly turn to face him once more.

I narrow my eyes and bore my gaze into his.

He smiles. "Those eyes."

I step closer.

"Those deadly eyes."

I watch him gaze at me with a desperate hunger.

"Keep up that stare, and I'll fucking die."

A devious smile spreads across my face.

"Kipp said he was closing the bar until we left," I say, closing the final distance between me and Silas.

I stand on my tiptoes and kiss him deeply. My tongue teases the entrance of his mouth, and I smile at his reaction. A low growl leaves his throat, and I pull away, waiting for him to respond.

"Indeed, he did," Silas responds, and his hands trail up and down my spine, sending a tingle of excitement straight to my core.

"We have some time before we have to head back to the house," I say, slowly raising my hands to pull him closer.

"Indeed, we do." His eyes flare.

Silas glances at the table behind us, the surface littered with cups. He looks at me before taking his arm to rake it across the surface, causing the cups to crash to the ground with an echoing clang.

His strong hands wrap around my waist, and he picks me up and sits me on the freshly cleared table. Silas leans in and kisses my mouth, my jaw, and travels to my neck. While he works, he slowly begins to undo the bow keeping my shirt together, exposing my collarbone and shoulders. He plants a kiss there and continues down my chest as my shirt slips to the table.

Silas pauses right above my breasts and steps back to admire my nakedness. He slowly unclips the sword at his belt, and the metal drops to the ground. He lifts his shirt over his head, joining me in being topless. His toned stomach shines in the dim lighting, and the shadows complement each muscular groove of his tan skin. Silas stalks forward and uses his hips to spread my legs open, allowing his bare chest to mold against mine completely.

He places a finger under my chin, tilting my face up to meet his gaze. "Do you want me to fuck you right here? On this table?"

"Yes," I breathe.

His hands slowly glide up my sides and around my breasts, stirring a growing need between my legs.

"Then tell me," he commands.

I can barely get the words out. "Please."

"Say it," he demands.

"Fuck me, Silas. Right now." I reach for him, desperate for his touch. "On this table."

Silas Nastronde, King of Andorwood, stands before me and grabs the waistband of my pants. His shadows ripple from his back, and they spread like black wings in the candlelight. The room around us seems to pulse as our darkness swirls in tandem. He slowly lifts me to pull my pants lower, putting my naked body on full display for him. He studies me like I'm a work of art, then slowly lowers to his knees.

Silas leans in, teasing me with every second of torturous anticipation.

"A king," he rasps.

I suck in a breath as I feel his warm breath so close to my center.

"Bowing only to his queen."

He kisses the inside of my thighs, and shocks of electricity move through my body. I tip my head back and close my eyes, focusing my attention on every single one of his touches. He uses his hands to spread my legs further, his fingers digging into my thighs, and I use my arms to prop myself further on the wooden table.

"Let me show you that I will always praise you; let me prove how perfect you are." He slowly pulls back and gazes up at me through his lashes. "And, let this serve as a reminder of what I can do to you whenever you think about us."

His tongue does a full sweep of my center, and a sharp hiss leaves my mouth as I dig my nails into the table. Silas lowers down further and wraps my thighs around his shoulders, giving himself a better angle to devour me. His mouth works as he licks and sucks, causing my vision to blur, every ounce of my body trembling from his touch. He is complete darkness—chaos and completely wicked—between my thighs. The connection between us hums in pleasure as his tongue pumps in and out of me.

"Fuck," I whine, as I claw against the table, overwhelmed with pleasure.

I feel his smile against my core, and he responds snarkily, "Only once I'm finished."

I move my hands into his hair and grind my hips against his face, desperate for more.

"Please, more," I plead in my mind.

"For you?" he responds. *"Anything."*

He removes his hand from my thigh and pushes his fingers into my soaking core without warning.

I gasp, and an eager moan leaves my lips.

His hand and tongue work in perfect unison, and I feel the pleasure building inside me. My body feels like it's becoming lighter, and I welcome the feeling of my orgasm building. I arch my back, feeling it rise higher and higher.

Close. I'm so close.

My core trembles, and with one more swipe of his perfect tongue, I completely unravel against him. He wraps his hands around my thighs once more to keep me steady, as the pleasure makes me grind and thrust my hips in all directions.

"My Gods," I scream, grasping his head still between my throbbing thighs, holding him in place while simultaneously pushing him away.

He remains sturdy, working me as I ride my pleasure to the highest peak and back into my shaking body. My arms give out, and I lie backward against the wooden table.

Silas slowly stands, wearing a cocky smile on his lips. He wipes his mouth and pulls at his own pants, dropping them to the ground. He stands bare before me, and even through the exhaustion of the pleasure, my mouth waters at the sight of him. His body is perfect, and the dim candlelight shows off every groove, every scar, and everything I'm desperate to have deep within me.

"Now, my love," he says, as he toys with me, crawling upon the thick wooden table like a hunter after his prey. "Now, I will fuck you."

My eyes widen as he reaches me, and with one swift thrust, he drives his hardened length into my throbbing core. I tip my head back and scream as he pumps into me. His lips find my neck, kissing and licking my soft skin, biting softly, and sending a mix of pain with the blinding pleasure. I wrap my arms around his neck to pull him closer and crash my lips against his. His kiss consumes me while he thrusts harder each time. I continue to moan against his touch, and he swallows each one as our connection never breaks.

I slide my hands down his toned back and dig my nails into his beautiful skin, feeling the scars beneath my touch. I use my arms to slam his hips against mine even harder.

"Silas," I gasp.

Each thrust brings us both one step closer to absolute bliss, and I bite at his collarbone. Silas pauses and stares at me for a moment, still buried deep inside me. I move my hands up his body and cup his face, looking into his stunning green eyes. I know he's savoring this moment, knowing what's coming and not knowing what the near future will bring. He holds his gaze, and lustful darkness swirls within his eyes.

Silas slowly glides his hand down, brushing my sensitive clit. A gasp leaves my mouth, and he thrusts hard back into me once more with a smile across his devilishly handsome face.

His lips slowly find mine again, and his kiss is deep, filled with a desperate need to always be near me—to keep me safe.

Even in this moment, I know that can't always happen.

Before I can react, he pulls out of me and flips me on my hands and knees. I feel his hands wrap around my hips as he drives his cock deep inside me once more. Unable to control the sensations moving through me, I dig my hands into the table and cry out in pleasure, allowing my grip to keep me steady while enjoying the feeling of Silas's hips crashing against mine.

He slams his pelvis against mine again, and my arms nearly give out. A white heat spreads through my body like an all-consuming light, filling me from head to toe, and I grind my ass against his hard body to create more friction. Silas leans forward, burying his face between my shoulder blades, and a deep guttural groan leaves his throat. I move my hands forward, falling to my stomach, and let the moans escape my lips like nothing else matters.

We ride the high together, still working and moving in perfect harmony. Silas falls on top of me as he spills his warm arousal into my body, and the deep groans that leave his lips from his own pleasure make me wet all over again.

My body relaxes as my pleasure fades, and Silas moves from behind me to my side on the table. I trace my fingers up his strong arms and turn my head to kiss each wrist. His scars glimmer in the dim light. Silas grins, making my heart pound, and I can feel its rapid pulse through my body.

"This may be my new favorite bar," he smirks.

I laugh and push against his arm. He leans over and kisses me once more, taking his time to climb down from the large wooden table. I turn and prop myself up on my elbows, and he gathers my clothes, making sure I'm covered. He slips into his pants and scans the room momentarily.

"I'm sure Kipp would like to reopen his place now," I say, regaining his attention.

Silas turns to me, slipping his shirt back over his head. "I'll pay that man whatever it fucking costs to keep it closed if we can do that again someday."

I huff a laugh and pull my clothes back on. "Consider it a date."

He extends his hand for me to take, and I do so, walking toward the exit and ensuring that we are both properly dressed and armed, including our weapons. Even though I know Silas has zero shame, he would waltz out of this bar completely bare if needed.

"We should head back to my house to tell the others about Cyrus," he says, unlocking the door before kissing my neck. "Back to reality, I guess."

"Back to reality," I respond.

CHAPTER 42

When we return to the house, the others are sitting in the living room discussing recent events. To my surprise, Oak is sitting among the group. Heavy purple circles sit under his eyes, and his typically bright hair appears dull.

Fen sits next to Warrick as always, while Larkin is closest to the blazing fire, sitting beside Rose who is holding a cup of tea. As we descend the carpeted staircase, Oak lifts his gaze, and a smile appears on his face that doesn't reach his eyes. I can't help but notice how Warrick always keeps an eye on Fen, as if she's seconds away from disappearing from his grasp.

"There you two are," Fen says as she stands. "I thought I was going to have to come pull you two out of Ophidian's."

"Have you both been speaking to Cyrus this entire time?" Larkin asks.

"Doubtful," Warrick mumbles. "He's never stayed anywhere for that long."

Silas shoots me a smirk.

I respond before he can embarrass me. "Something like that."

"Well, come join us." Fen waves us over as she tucks back into Warrick.

We stride across the vast living space, and I marvel at my surroundings—I don't think this house will ever cease to amaze me. Each time I descend the stairs, I find myself awestruck by the beauty of this home and its stunning views. My eyes linger on the large windows, looking out at the sun, which hangs low in the sky, casting shades of pink and red across the horizon like a mix of melted flowers. I watch it dip lower with each passing second, the crimson hues quickly overtaking the pink—brighter than I've ever seen a sunset—reminding me of dripping blood inking the sky. I tear my gaze away and shake off the unsettling feeling.

Warrick and Rose begin a new conversation, likely talking about their travels, while Larkin and Fenmore spat about who will drink more ale at Ophidian's when this is all over.

I move immediately to Oak and sit before him. "How is she?"

"She's asleep right now," Oak replies, with a heavy sigh. "That's about all she does currently, but the healers assure me it's how the body will heal itself faster. She should wake up more in the coming days."

"Those healers know what they are doing," I assure him. "Trust them."

"How was your day?" he asks.

"Gods, we don't have the time to cover everything that happened in our day."

"Everything went okay, though?" he pushes, looking for more information.

I don't want to burden him further with the uncertainties of what the next few days will bring, but I can't bring myself to lie to him, either. He deserves to be included like everyone else, and keeping him informed will only make us more prepared and united when the time comes.

I shake my head. "I don't really know, to be honest. I know

you heard we spoke with Cyrus. The conversation went well, in that he listened, but I'm not sure I did a good enough job convincing him. As far as Silas announcing he is now the King of Andorwood…" I pause. "It could have gone better."

I feel the stares from the others after hearing Cyrus's name, and I can't help but look directly at Warrick. His brows tighten, and he fidgets with a piece of fuzz on his thigh.

"It will be a gamble if he helps us take down the ship, and it will be an even bigger gamble if we can rely on him in the future," I say.

"He won't help," Warrick grumbles. "He looks out for one person and one person only. He'll leave us on that pier to fight alone."

"Maybe he won't," Larkin adds.

Warrick furrows his brows. "He will, and when we win, I plan to make sure everyone knows that the rebels are cowards."

Fen jerks her head in his direction. "Warrick, no, you won't."

"I won't?" he asks, annoyance flashing in his eyes. "Why wouldn't I?"

The rest of us remain quiet, watching.

Warrick continues, "He is a piece of shit. I should expose him for what he is."

"How would that be helpful for our future goals?" she bites back, narrowing her eyes.

"And what are our future goals, Fenmore?" Warrick's anger rises.

"To save—" she starts, but he cuts her off.

"To save Rohhit? To put you in danger so you can drag him back from the Gods know where?"

I can see how quickly resentment begins to fuel his words. He's hurt that Fenmore is tethered to another, and it's been evident for days.

"Yes, Warrick," she says, lowering her voice. "That is the plan."

"Amazing," he responds, sarcastically.

"Warrick," she snaps.

"What?" he bites back.

"I'm choosing to save someone's life because they are good, and they don't deserve the fate they have been given."

"You don't even know him." Warrick stands. "He doesn't know you, and you are so willing to risk everything for him already."

Her face reddens. "I do know him."

"No, you fucking don't," Warrick shouts, and from his expression, I can see he instantly regrets his harsh words.

"Please, Warrick," Fen whispers, letting every crushing word pull her deeper into her guilt. "Just calm down."

Silas stands. "Warrick, sit down and lower your voice."

"Take it easy, buddy," Larkin adds.

"Is it true?" Warrick steps toward Silas, curling his fist. "What she says?"

"About Rohhit?" Silas responds.

"Yes," Warrick snaps. "The connection."

Silas glances at Fen, who remains motionless, watching with wide eyes—as if wishing he wouldn't ask. I can't help but feel for her. It's a sensation that feels so natural with the tether clicked into place, yet so terrible as she witnesses Warrick's heart shatter before her eyes.

"It's true," Silas says.

Warrick huffs, tossing his hands in the air.

"It's a connection I can never fully describe to someone who can't feel it. It's raw, powerful, and all-consuming." Silas acts as if he doesn't want to speak the following words. "She claims to know him because, with everything that she is, she truly does—deeper than he may know himself."

Warrick blinks slowly and brushes his hands through his blonde hair, striding to the open balcony doors.

"I can't do this anymore, Fen."

"Do what?" Tears well in her eyes.

He turns to her. "Love you while you love someone else."

She lets out a sob. "It's not like that; I don't love him."

"Yet," Warrick snaps. "Right?"

"Please," she begs.

"Fine. Then I will not stick around to witness you fall in love with someone else."

"Warrick!" she weeps.

"I'm going to get some air."

"Please, don't leave," she begs, standing as if she wants to follow him.

He glances over his shoulder. "With Hux gone, someone needs to patrol the island. I'm going to check on the men stationed around."

"*Warrick*," she pleads, stepping closer in an attempt to reach him.

"I'll be back later."

"No," she snaps.

Warrick's gaze remains glued to her for a moment. He slowly pans his head toward the open air, and shifts—a trail of white light lingers in his wake. Fen watches the empty space—as if she expects him to return at any moment and apologize—but only the fading daylight and sea breeze drift through that door.

A tear rolls down her cheek, and she slowly returns to her seat, crumbling into the cushions.

Larkin stands. "I'll go after him."

Silas nods, watching the balcony.

Larkin walks directly to Fen before heading to the open balcony doors. "You two will be okay."

"No," she whispers. "We won't."

"Just give him some space to breathe," Larkin replies, and he leans in and kisses her cheek before striding to the balcony to shift.

Even with two people gone, the room feels cramped—unable to hold the swirling emotions that we all feel. My heart breaks for Warrick and Fenmore, and I dive into my own thoughts, trying to think of anything that can help.

Silas watches Larkin leave in silence, then turns back to Fen. "He is just confused. He doesn't understand, but this isn't your fault, Fen."

"I don't even understand this, Silas." She turns to glare at her brother. "And yes, this is my fault—I'm the reason he's hurting."

"You aren't doing anything wrong," he says, and tries to take a step toward her.

"Oh, I'm just doing exactly what I was designed to do. Well, what if I don't want this?" Fen sits forward in the chair. "It's not real—the feelings aren't real—they are forced. You couldn't ignore them, but maybe I can. I don't want to hurt Warrick anymore. He doesn't deserve this pain."

Her words swirl in my mind because I have had the same thoughts.

"You can't blame her for thinking that." I say to Silas in my mind, then ask, *"Are these feelings real?"*

Silas snaps his head in my direction and snaps, "Don't you fucking think that."

The others go rigid, knowing something just happened that isn't group knowledge.

I grimace but keep my gaze strong. "Fen is just trying to figure this out like we all are, Silas. It's normal to have doubts. You know exactly what our first few meetings were like. Give her time to sort this out."

Fenmore rubs her temples, and I can see how tense her body is from across the sitting area. Her nails dig into her scalp. "I can ignore this. I think I can ignore this if I try."

Dread crashes into me.

We can't save Rohhit without her, but I keep my mouth shut. I can't bombard her right now.

"You can't, Fen. Even if you wanted to," Silas warns. "Stop acting this way."

"I can."

"How?" Silas steps toward her, and I grab his arm to keep him at a distance. "How can you ignore something like that?"

"Because I haven't felt his tug or heard him in almost three days."

My legs go numb, and I try not to show the panic on my face. Oak keeps his head low, not wanting to interject, and Rose shuffles to the kitchen, likely to pretend to make something.

"Why didn't you say anything, Fenmore? This isn't a game." Silas furrows his brow. "I know this is unfortunate for you, and you feel torn, but this is serious. Keeping things from us can result in our loss."

"This is my life, Silas."

"It can lead to our realm turning to shit. This also affects all our lives."

She doesn't respond.

I walk toward her and pause. "Can you try to speak to him now?"

She shakes her head. "No."

"Why?"

"It's like there's nothing there for me to search for. I've tried, but it's dimmed so low that in the darkness I can't find him—I can't hear him."

"I refuse to believe he's gone." I turn to Silas and Oak. "He is stronger than that. I know he is."

Oak stands. "What do you suggest we do?"

I turn and race down the hallway leading to Silas's room. I cross the threshold and crash to my knees before the small table in the sitting area, where the large red book sits like a beacon in the night. I flip open the book, and a shudder runs up my spine. The thick, worn pages of the ancient book feel heavy against my fingers, and even though my senses scream, I turn each page, desperate to see anything that might help.

I hear footsteps behind me and turn to see Oak and Silas race around the corner after me.

"I can't read any of this," I rage.

"We can try," Oak says.

Ancient texts, markings, and pictures cover each page, yet none of them make sense to me. Oak stands over my shoulder, trying to glance through the leather book as I do, hoping he might decipher something. My fingers can't move fast enough, flipping through each page, and a sharp pain shoots through my finger. I wince and jerk my hand back, watching a drop of blood fall to the ground beside me.

"Ouch," I hiss, putting my finger in my mouth to stop the bleeding.

The pages come to a halt, and I freeze, staring at a page written in a language I can't understand. Oak leans in closer and squints his eyes. He retrieves his glasses from his breast pocket and places them low on his nose.

"Hang on," he whispers, and leans in closer to the text.

Fen enters the room and joins us, plopping down in one of the nearby chairs. I offer her a soft smile, despite my system being on fire with anxiety. She watches Oak with a burning intensity as he studies the page.

She leans forward. "What does it say?"

"This is the first time I'm seeing this book, and my Gods it's fucking old," he says, and places his glasses on his head as he looks up from the text.

My heart thunders in my chest, and anticipation creeps up into my throat.

Oak shakes his head. "I can't read this. I had just begun studying this ancient text when we left for the trials in Daramveer. I'm not skilled enough to read anything in this book, to my knowledge."

My shoulders slacken, and Fen sits back against the tall cushions.

"But, I know someone who can," Oak says cheerfully, trying to give us an ounce of hope.

"Who?" I ask.

"My grandfather," Oak replies. "He was the one who taught me when we were in Brinkym. He should be able to read most of this book."

Silas leans against the mantle while the roaring fire makes shadows dance across his face. "How does that help us now, Hombern?"

Oak grimaces. "It doesn't, but at least we know someone can read this. We just need to get this book to Brinkym."

I push against the table and get to my feet. "Amazing. Let's add this to the list of impossible shit we have to do."

"It's doable, Briar," Silas chimes in, and turns to Oak. "Would your grandfather be willing to help?"

Oak nods. "I would think so, yeah."

"Then, when we head back to the mainland, Brinkym will be our first stop," Silas commands.

"And Daramveer?" I add.

"Calia and Nolan will expect us to return to Daramveer. We need to be strategic when the time comes to go back. They will have spies everywhere—watching for our return—so reaching anywhere safely will be the ultimate challenge. We will need to remain unseen when we return."

I remain quiet because I don't disagree. They will definitely expect us to return at some point, and Daramveer is the first place I want to visit. So even though it pains me, I understand that we can't go there right away. They know we can't stay here forever. But a thought flickers in my mind, and a broad smile spreads across my face.

Oak looks at me. "Either she has a plan, or she's finally lost her mind."

"Both, I think at this point," I respond. "Especially when you hear what I'm going to say."

They all wait with bated breath.

"We can be invisible."

Silas laughs, and I know he knows exactly what I'm referring to.

"You are a genius, my love."

"We have a specific Rigil on our side that offers a degree of invisibility. When we return, we can be unseen. We can set foot on the mainland again, and for a moment, no one will ever see us."

Oak claps his hands together. "You are right. That, at least, seems like a plan we can set in motion. Now, we just need to cross off the other hundred things on our list, and we're golden."

I turn to Fen. "Rohhit will be okay, but please don't give up on him. Keep listening and continue tugging on the tether. Maybe he felt you pulling back and stopped searching for you as well. Please, Fen. Don't give him another reason to give up."

She nods. "Alright."

"*Please*," I whisper.

"I'll keep trying."

"Thank you," I breathe, placing my hand on her arm. "Warrick is also going to be alright. He cares about you deeply, Fen, and this doesn't mean you care about him any less, either."

"It just means I have to care about Rohhit more," she replies.

I squeeze her arm. "That's up to you to decide."

She wipes a tear from her eye and stands, heading to the threshold of the room. "I'm going to bed. Please wake me if any other revelations occur, but please, Gods, I would like one night of good sleep."

Silas moves forward. "I'm going to walk you to your room."

She nods, and they move into the hallway, leaving Oak and me alone for a moment. He stands and walks to the open window in Silas's room. The heavy curtains sway in the breeze, and the sun has completely disappeared from the sky for the evening, gracing us with the largest white moon I've seen in ages.

I join him, and we gaze upon the vast black sea before us. The waves crash against the cliff's edge, and the water churns like a storm is coming.

"Maines feels lighter," Oak says. "I've been obsessing over the darkness I felt attached to her, but today, it seems to have lifted a bit."

"Any clue what it could be?" I ask.

He shakes his head. "No. It was dark, as if a shadowy hand was constantly resting on her shoulder. When it was there—I won't lie, Briar—I was afraid to even touch her."

A shiver runs up my spine. "Have you asked her about it?"

He turns, facing the door where Maines rests. "Before this happened, no, I never did, and I regret it. But, now isn't the right time to push her. Resting is her main priority."

I fidget with the ends of my hair and press my back against the wooden windowsill to look toward her room, too. "Do you remember when you first felt it?"

He stills, and his blinking slows. "Yes."

I angle my head toward him and await his answer.

"It was right after Malachi killed Yara."

I remain steady, even as I fight the urge to let my legs wobble. I think back to that night—the pain, the suffering, and the blood that filled the room like a rushing red river. Malachi's words, promises, and threats echo in my mind. I brace my hands against the ledge and glance at Oak. His eyes stay fixated on the closed door where Maines sleeps peacefully, unaware of the terror I feel right now.

"Do you want me to stay with you until Silas gets done speaking with Fen?" Oak looks at me.

"No, you go check on Maines and get some rest. Tomorrow, we can make a plan and see if Silas knows anything about this darkness."

He moves toward the door. "You should rest too, Briar."

I smile as he exits, closing the door behind him. I wait for a few moments before striding across the room to the bathing chambers, taking Oak's advice. I splash some water on my exhausted face and remove my worn clothes. I slip into something lighter and more comfortable before moving back toward the large, dark bed in the room. The silk sheets are cold and so soft that I can barely feel them as I slide under the thick duvet. A soft groan leaves my lips as I settle my head against the feathery pillow.

With the sun behind the horizon, the moon shines into the room as I extinguish all the candles, wrapping the space in darkness. I pull the covers high and feel myself slipping into the nothingness that sleep has recently graced me with. Out of the corner of my eye, I see a spot deep in the curve of the room that somehow looks darker than the black of the room, but my eyes are too heavy to stop me from drifting to sleep. I tell myself that Silas will be back soon, and my eyes close.

The world around me is dark and familiar, yet not home. My eyes adjust to the suffocating darkness, and through the smog, I see the city center of Andorwood. This time, though, there are no bustling civilians, no vendors, no scents of cooked food or delicious spices, and none of the pleasant chatter of people discussing their daily lives.

The center of Andorwood lies in ruin, and ash falls from the sky like dusty gray rain. I turn my head in all directions, but I'm alone. Fear creeps over me, and I force myself to look down each dark alleyway, each leading only to despair and misfortune. The chilled breeze whips my hair about, and my surroundings are bleak. The air is thick and reeks of the burning memories of what this kingdom once was. The bodies of the civilians lie in a scattered mess around me.

Growls in the distance snap me to attention, and I rush toward a building that is barely standing from the destruction. I press my back against the cold stone and steady my trembling hands.

This isn't real.

This isn't real.

The growling intensifies, and the sound of barely audible footsteps sends a wave of terror through my veins. My shadows pulse, and something within me screams to run, but I don't know where to go.

An angelic voice sounds through the air and into my mind, "My sweet Briar. Where are you?"

I slap my hand over my mouth to muffle the sob that escapes my throat.

No.

Gods, no.

"You were exhausted tonight. Oh, so exhausted. It was quite easy to come forward when your guard is low." Her voice floats into my mind like a disease. "Do you know where we are?"

I move my hands to cover my ears and crouch down, my back scraping down the stone building.

"Briar, I wanted to show you this, and you willingly followed me here—a realm where Andorwood loses the battle that's ahead. This is what you will bring to those people. This kingdom will cease to exist."

"Get out of my head," I scream into the open air.

A haunting laugh that holds only threats reverberates around the fallen stones.

"I'm not in your head, sweet girl. I'm here, and I'm very much real. You know your present realm is the only one I can't travel to—without your help, of course. Let me take over, and I can save them. Let me travel back with you, and you can end this faster than it will begin."

I rise slowly, my legs still trembling from fear. "And after it's over, what then?"

"There is more to be done after that." Her voice gets closer. "So much more."

"I can save them without you," I shout.

Kalix laughs again, and the sound of the breeze transforms into the flapping of wings. It's the crows, getting closer to where I stand with every passing second.

"That seems almost impossible when everyone is so quick to turn their backs on you and that exasperating tether. The odds aren't looking great for you, and unfortunately, if you fail, I'll be out of a vessel for quite a while."

"I can save them," I repeat.

Kalix's voice whispers, "You can't, and your constant attempts are getting tiring."

"I'll never give up. I'll leave you in these shadowy realms until I can discover how to destroy you, and when I do, I'll proclaim from the mountaintops how you have failed. Kalix, the Great Wiitch of Darkness, was defeated by her own vessel." I move further down the alleyway but continue speaking, "You are nothing but a leech—a desperate ghost of the past, a miserable bitch, and, quite frankly, a huge pain in my ass."

Her growls turn feral.

"Let…"

The wings flap closer.

"…me…"

They move closer.

"…in."

Her voice screams in my ears, and I take off down the dark alleyway in a full sprint. I jump over fallen stones and round the corners faster than I've ever moved. The breeze picks up, and gusts of wind try to knock me off balance, but I keep moving. The sound of my feet slapping the stone streets resembles thousands of horses charging against an enemy.

"Silas!"

The scream rattles in my throat. I turn left, trying to run farther away from the center of the kingdom, and bound down a narrower alleyway. Filthy water splashes as I move past the large gutters, and I continue forward, covering my nose from the smell. A tug of the connection pulls me down the stone street, and I hear him.

"Briar," his voice calls. "Wake up."

I sprint forward, and his shadowy figure comes into view. His eyes are wide, and he sprints toward me with his hand extended.

"Fucking run," he screams.

I hear Kalix's thundering footsteps and her army of the sky just inches from my back. The talons of the large birds swipe at my hair, whipping behind me, but I don't stop.

Kalix's voice begins to fade, and she stops, knowing she won't catch me.

"Briar, you will be in this realm again sooner than you think. You will have to come searching for something you hold dear. I will see you soon, my vessel, and I can't wait to dig my claws into your beautiful body and rip your mind to shreds."

My chest collides with Silas's, and he wraps his arms around my body.

"Hang on," he whispers, and the ruin, the burning, and the thick air vanish.

Chaos surrounds me, yet I know I'm back in my body in Silas's room. The rustling of clothes and the loud clang of weapons fill the air. I become aware of my surroundings before my eyes open.

"Briar, get up right now," Silas orders.

I open my eyes, and it's still dark outside, the moon barely hanging in the middle of the sky. I sit up in bed and hear other people in the house moving around, their loud chatter echoing down the hallways.

"You had to do that right now?"

"What do you mean?"

"We don't have time for this," he snaps. "Stop searching for her."

"I'm not."

He freezes and stares into my eyes.

"What's going on?" I remove the blankets and find myself covered in sweat.

Silas pauses from across the room, then storms toward the

edge of the bed and grabs my face, trying to pull me entirely from sleep. I notice he's completely dressed with weapons strapped to his back, and his familiar sword rests just above his shoulder. His face is hard, his eyes are dark, and his chest heaves.

"They are here. The ships are here," his voice spits out.

"Ships?" I respond, unable to process his words.

"They are early, and it's not just one ship. It's two."

CHAPTER 43

I leap out of bed and start to dress. I pull on the armor that Fen had previously lent to me for the Archives, the jeweled snake eyes shining in the moonlight, and begin to strap on my axes. Silas works quickly, keeping to himself to prepare as best he can for what's ahead.

"How far are they?" I ask, my voice trembling.

"They will be in the harbor within the hour," he bites back.

"How…how did we find this out?"

Silas pauses. "Larkin and Warrick were out patrolling after his fight with Fen and saw the ships over the horizon." He takes a long breath. "They came back here immediately after seeing it and alerted me."

"Fuck," I whisper.

"Then, I had to come after you. You can't let yourself get so exhausted anymore, and you have to stop thinking about her."

"I wasn't thinking about her," I snap back.

He glares at me. "All you do is think about her. I know it. I can feel it."

"Silas," I extend my hand, and he takes it, placing it against his heart.

"It's okay," he says, defeat lacing his tone.

I focus on his rapidly beating heart. "I'm serious."

"We don't have time for this, my love. We need to go. We need to fight." He turns his gaze toward the chaotic sea. "Now."

"Maines," I exclaim. "Will she and Rose be safe?"

"Warrick is placing another ward around the house now. He is skilled, so I'm confident they will stay safe and hidden. He taught Rose the Rigil of invisibility should things go wrong." He cups my jaw. "She's prepared to hide with Maines if the time comes."

I feel panic rising in my throat, and Silas steps toward me, cupping my face once more.

"You need to focus; you can't let fear take over." His lips crash against mine for a moment. "Don't let your guard down. Stay calm and fight, Briar. We don't have any more time; we need to leave."

I nod, my head barely moving.

"Larkin. Where is Larkin?" I ask.

"He's preparing the ship to go out toward them, just like we planned. Do you still want to go with him?"

My chest heaves.

"Do you still want to join him on the front lines?"

I think for a moment, knowing how limited our time is, and swallow down the fear banging on my chest like a caged animal.

"Yes."

He sighs, his gaze boring into mine, and a deep conflict dancing in his green eyes like flames. "Okay. Let's go."

Silas grabs my hand, and we dash out of the room. Oak and Fen are in the center of the house, gathering weapons they can carry without being weighed down. They glance in our direction and give us concerned looks before hurrying to finalize their preparations. Rose stands in the kitchen, her hands firmly clutching a hot cup of tea. The dark, steaming liquid in the mug trembles as I storm toward her.

"Hey, my shadow," she says.

"Are you going to be alright?" I ask.

She smiles, setting her cup down on a nearby counter. "Of course, you are worried about me right now. We are going to be fine. I trust that big man to protect this house, and we have a backup should I notice anyone getting too close to the wards."

I dip my head and wrap my arms around her. She nuzzles into my embrace and takes a second to stay in this moment.

Rose pulls back. "I need you to promise me that you'll be okay."

I stare into her dark eyes and her beautifully aged face, quickly memorizing her features, so similar to my mother's. I tuck a stray strand of hair behind her ear and lean in to kiss her cheek.

I don't respond, and she understands why. She knows I can never make that kind of promise to her, especially one that I may not be able to keep.

"You ready?" I hear Silas shout from across the room. "It's time."

The others walk toward him, draped in armor, and I hesitate to leave the house. So much beyond those balcony doors is uncertain. The howling wind rips into the room, and I close my eyes and steady my breath. I move to take a step forward when I hear a weak voice speak behind me.

"Briar?"

I whip around and see Maines standing just beyond the shadows of the hallway. Her trembling legs barely keep her upright, her under-eyes are a deep purple, and you can tell from a distance how weak she is. She leans against the wall, and my mouth drops open.

"My Gods." I rush to her side, holding her upright as I wrap my arms around her slender waist.

A second later, Fen, Oak, and Silas are there, gawking at her presence as if we've all just seen a ghost.

Her lips curl into a faint smile. "Can you all stop looking at me as if I'm a creature of the night?"

"What the fuck are you doing out of bed?" Oak snaps.

She huffs. "I'm offended you all think you can leave without saying goodbye to me."

Oak moves to her other side, wrapping his arm around her. "I said goodbye, darling. Now, please go lie down." He kisses her temple. "Rose is staying to watch over you and the house."

She stares at Fen, Silas, and me, and her eyes hold such sadness—such worry—that my heart shatters from her gaze.

"We will see you again very soon, Maines," Silas says. "All of us."

"Don't say that," she snaps. "Do not say things you don't know are certain."

"Go rest, and when you wake up, all of us will be back, and I mean all of us," Fen says cheerfully, but it's clearly faked.

"Don't," Maines whispers. "Don't pretend."

Fen and Silas drop their gazes, understanding the weight of her words and the gravity of the situation.

Her eyes shift to mine. "Promise me, Briar, that you will return."

They all wait for my response, and I inhale deeply.

"I will come back, Maines. I promise."

Oak moves her toward the hallway. "I'm going to lay her down, and I'll shift to the pier to meet you all shortly."

Maines keeps her gaze fixed on me while Oak gently guides her down the hallway toward the bedroom. I will keep my promise and return to this house, but I am uncertain if I will come back alive or dead after all this is over, and I know we all feel that way.

We move quickly across the living space and out into the open air of the balcony. Even from this distance, I can hear the chaos on the pier. Without hesitating, Fen shifts into the night, going to assist with prepping the kingdom as best we can for their arrival. But, I know she moves quickly for one person—Warrick.

Silas wraps his hand around mine, and we both delve into our magic, drawing it forward to shift us there faster than we've ever traveled through the shadows.

We land on the wooden pier with a thud, and immediately I'm overwhelmed by the bustle of Wielders everywhere. It may not be two ships' worth of people, but I'm stunned by the civilians of Andorwood who are ready to help right now. Silas also takes a moment to look around, slowly blinking in awe. I glance toward him and watch him absorb the surroundings. His people have come to help.

Seconds later, a growing presence compels us to turn around to see Oak land on the pier in a bright white light. Fen stands nearby as well, and she scans the crowd, looking for one person and one person only.

"She's not going to sleep anytime soon," Oak says, walking toward us. "She is worried sick."

"I can't say I'm surprised," Silas responds. "Or blame her."

Fen continues to scan the crowd, stepping toward a looming figure. A sigh leaves her lips, and she lowers her gaze in defeat.

"He's coming," Silas says, stepping forward.

Fen glances at her brother. "I don't have time to wait."

"You do," Silas says.

"Tell him that I went to prepare the others," Fen says. "Tell him I'm sorry for everything. Tell Warrick I choose him, and always will."

Silas nudges her forward. "You tell him."

Through the chaos, Fen goes rigid as she spots a large figure nearing us with intense purpose. Warrick approaches, his wild hair contrasting with the dark weapons strapped all over his body.

His expression is both hard and panicked, and his gaze is fixed solely on Fenmore amid the distracting turmoil. No one else matters to him right now but her.

I see Fen suck in a breath as he reaches us.

She doesn't move and waits for him to make the first move, whatever that may be, after their last exchange.

Warrick bounds forward, not slowing his steps, and without a second thought, crashes against Fenmore. Her chest heaves as he pulls her in, placing his head in the nape of her neck. His arms wrap around her petite body, first around her waist, and then one hand slowly travels to the back of her head, pulling her in as close as possible. She melts into his chest, and without words, I know they're apologizing for the fight.

In this moment, their previous words don't matter. What matters is making sure they know the love they have for one another before everything could change.

Silas turns his head, not wanting to watch the exchange between his best friend and sister, and for the first time, I see their lips meet. Warrick's massive body looms over her, and she tilts her head as his lips crash into hers. His hand tangles in her hair as she slings both arms around his neck.

It's passionate and messy.

It's understanding and raw.

It's *them*.

They pull apart, and his hand slowly traces her jaw. His gaze is steady, but neither speaks. They don't need to.

His lips press against hers for a final kiss.

"I'm sorry," Fen whispers.

"Me too," he replies.

Fenmore smiles, but dips her head. "Everything is fucked, Warrick."

He quickly lifts her head with the tip of his finger. "That's life, baby, but I'm here to live in this fucked up world with you."

She smiles as wide as her face allows, and he tucks a piece of fallen hair behind her ear. She inhales deeply, reveling in his proximity, and even on the brink of battle, she relaxes for a second.

"I choose you, Warrick," she says, as she cups his face. "The rest we can figure out."

He nods, pressing his forehead against hers, and smiles. "No matter the outcome of my life, my choices, needs, and wants are always you."

"Always," she whispers.

He throws his arm over her shoulder, pulling her in, and they turn to us.

Silas clears his throat, and Fen flashes a quick smile up to Warrick as he plants another kiss atop her head.

Silas steps forward, clasping his hand around Warrick's. "Without you, brother, we would have been blindsided. Thank you."

Warrick nods. "Just keeping those I love safe."

Silas turns to me, and the others follow his lead.

"Does everyone remember the plan and their positions?" I ask.

"I'll remain closer to the center of the kingdom to assist any stragglers. I'm sure it will take people some time to reach the mountain for safety," Fen says. "If you need me nearer to the pier, just shout, and I can make sure my post is covered. If the center is breached, I'll be there to fight."

Warrick speaks next, "I'll stay between the pier and the city center. This way, if things go wrong, I can get to Fen, alerting her to get those people to safety as quickly as possible." He glances at Silas. "I can monitor how the pier holds and prepare for whatever is needed, but leaving Fen completely alone isn't an option."

I shoot him an understanding glance along with Silas, who I know appreciates Warrick in thousands of different ways right now.

"I'll be on the pier with Oak near the water. Once the Andorwood ships enter our waters, I'm going to create a wall of shadows to shield us and the civilians for as long as I can," Silas says. "This will give you time, Fen, to get the remaining women, children, and men who don't want to fight out of the city and give the people fighting time to prepare," Silas finishes, and Oak nods in agreement.

"And I'll be here," Oak chimes in. "Trying not to shit my pants."

Silas slaps his shoulder and smiles, appreciating the bit of laughter breaking the tension that fills the air.

They all pause and turn to me, waiting for my orders.

The sea around us is furious, and the waves crash together in a chaotic, dark rage. Black storm clouds fill the night sky, obscuring all signs of light and stars. I open my mouth to speak, but stop when I feel two solid hands clasp around my shoulders and squeeze. I peer up through my lashes to see the familiar chiseled face dusted with facial hair.

Larkin stands above me.

"Briar and I will be on the ship." He squeezes my shoulders again with a sly grin. "We have two ships filled with strong warriors ready to confront the resurrected. We will hold them off as long as possible and take out as many as we can." Larkin's voice demands attention. "I need all of you to be ready and prepared, but understand that we will fight. We will fight fiercely to keep those on the shore safe. If we can, we will return to the pier and fight on land alongside all of you."

I feel a sense of relief knowing Larkin will be with me, and I won't be on the ship alone, but this is my fight, and I plan to take on those creatures headfirst. But his choice of words lingers.

If.

"We should move to our positions immediately," I command. "We don't need to waste any more time."

Fen races toward Silas and wraps her arms around her brother, pulling him in so tight he groans.

I hear her whisper, "Fight hard. I love you," before releasing him so she and Warrick can venture deeper into the city. She shoots Larkin a quick glance and winks before turning away and stepping off the pier onto the streets of Andorwood.

Warrick slaps Larkin's shoulder and pulls him into a quick embrace. "Love you, brother."

"Don't be sappy," Larkin says. "You are too big for that."

Warrick booms a laugh and turns, following Fen into the alleyways.

Larkin takes a second to watch them move into the distance, and shouts, "Love you too, buddy."

I watch Fen and Warrick for a moment. Even on the brink of battle, Warrick is gentle with Fen—almost tender—as he leads her into the dark alley. He places a hand on the small of her back, and she doesn't recoil; instead, she steps into his touch, and their hands wrap together.

They disappear, and I think to myself that Warrick would follow Fenmore almost anywhere.

"He would," I hear Silas say back as he watches them vanish into the darkness, too.

I give him a weary smile.

"They will be alright."

"I'm worried," I respond.

"Fenmore is strong, and Warrick won't let anything happen to her, just as she won't let anything happen to him. They will protect each other," Silas hums into my mind.

"I know," I respond.

Oak lets out a heavy sigh, "Can you two stop speaking without me? Let's do this."

Silas, Larkin, Oak, and I walk toward the edge of the pier, and in this moment, I feel as if we are on the world's edge with only darkness below and before us. The howling wind rips in all directions, making it hard to hear anything else. The large ships beside us rock in the angry water, and many warriors on board prepare the masts, ensuring the boat is in perfect condition before we set sail.

Captain Darcy leans over the side of the first ship. "Spiridon, we will push off in a few minutes. Get on board the second ship or stay back."

He nods and turns toward Oak and Silas. Their faces are resolute and tense, showing no signs of fear in their eyes—only strength and determination to emerge victorious. Larkin reaches toward Silas and pulls him into an embrace.

"Fight like the Gods are watching," Larkin says, releasing him, and gently taps his cheek with his palm.

"Good thing they are," Silas responds, pulling Larkin's forehead to his. "Keep her safe."

They quickly part, and Larkin turns. He squeezes Oak's shoulders and climbs onto the rocking ship from the bridge.

Oak rushes toward me, and I open my arms, expecting a massive hug from the smiling Lumor Wielder.

He grabs both my shoulders and looks in my eyes with fury. I flinch, waiting for the statement to burst from his lips.

"If you die," he says, frantically, "can I have your axes?"

"Fucking Gods," Silas mumbles under his breath.

I punch him in the chest and laugh. "Yes. Yes, you can, my friend."

Oak smiles and quickly hugs me tight. He steps back a few paces before getting into position. I turn to Silas and gaze at his handsome face. He inches closer and rests his forehead against mine.

"Are you sure you want to go out there?" he whispers.

I nod against him. "I can do this; I can stop some of them from docking."

"I know you can, my love."

I hear a shout from the ship's edge. "Blackbyrne, either board the ship now or stay back," Larkin's voice travels through the dark. "It's time."

"Don't let down that wall, Nastronde. Keep it strong and high. I will see you soon." I kiss him, and he kisses me back, hard, wrapping his strong arms around my waist and pulling me in tight. "I promise."

The weight of the world sits upon us, but I kiss him deeper, knowing this could be the last time.

"*I love you*," I say in my mind.

"*My soul belongs to you*," he responds. "*It's yours*."

We part, and I turn, stepping up the wooden bridge onto the ship.

Each step feels like a weight trying to hold me back, but I push forward. From this height, the vast sky appears darker before us. I look over the edge as the large boat moves ahead and see Silas in the same position. His gaze burns into me as I watch his figure shrink in the distance. As the second ship leaves the dock, my heart fractures.

I watch him turn, taking a few steps away from the edge of the pier. His hands drop to his sides, and his palms open, but he hesitates. For a second, I swear he is going to bound for the ship, but he stops himself, focusing on the plan.

The plan I created.

The darkest shadows begin to paint his hands as he dives into his magic, building a wall of darkness from pure fear and rage. The memory of leaving Daramveer hits me as I see the wall rise, the shadows being stacked brick by brick, and obscuring my view of the shore, my friends, and Silas. This feels familiar because I've seen it before, except this time, I'm the one sailing into danger while Silas remains on the pier—safe for now. The wall rises higher and higher until the only thing visible is the faint flicker of torches through the thick shadows.

I turn away as Shadow and Lumor Wielders rush around the deck. I scan each one to see if Larkin is nearby, but I don't spot him.

The water around us heaves and swells, while the roaring wind seems to pulse with tension, anticipating the impending battle that is about to begin. A flash of white catches my eye in the crow's nest, and I see Larkin standing there, surveying our surroundings. I ensure my axes are properly positioned and begin to climb up the shrouds toward the highest mast, where Larkin perches.

My arms burn as I reach the top and climb onto the small surface that seems miles above the ground. My heart races, and my palms are slick with sweat as I observe my surroundings.

Gods, I fucking hate heights.

Larkin huffs a laugh as I grasp onto the rail, as if any moment I'm going to fly over the edge. My legs wobble, and a tingle starts in my hands.

"I forget your insane fear of heights," he laughs, as he turns to me. "Oh, I'd better say 'falling from heights' before you yell at me."

"Thank you for correcting yourself," I say, and quickly catch my breath, refusing to look down as I hear the groan of the ship below.

"See anything?" I ask.

"Look," he responds, and points.

I look across the sea, and that's when I see them—the two ships in the near distance. They are not ones I recognize, and they bear no indication of which kingdom they come from. Their sails are torn to pieces, the wood nearly as black as the sea, and I can hear a thundering coming from the ship—a steady drumbeat preparing them to fight. I can barely make out the heads standing on the boat, but from what I can see, the entire deck is filled with horrifying creatures. Nerves settle into my core like buzzing bricks, and I grab the railing to keep my hands from shaking.

Larkin looks ahead. "Remember when we first met up here?"

"I wouldn't call that a meeting, Larkin." I turn to him. "You wouldn't even look at me, similar to now."

He smiles and peels his gaze to mine. "Are you ready?"

"I think so," I respond. "I'd be lying if I said I wasn't scared."

"Battle is ugly, Briar. It's so ugly, but whatever happens, you can't stop." He looks back toward our uncertain future. "You need to swing those axes until the last creature falls. No matter how tired you are, keep moving, because once you stop, they will take advantage of any weak spots. Use your magic, but sparingly—you can't run out."

I nod.

"Don't worry about anyone around you. Focus on the creatures and fight."

My stomach rolls, and I can't help but grab his hand to keep my nerves steady.

"I will worry about you," I admit.

"Don't."

I narrow my gaze. "Too bad."

He smiles.

"Are you ready?" I ask.

"To wipe these fucking creatures from this realm? Absolutely."

"Aim for the nape of their necks," I advise. "They are weakest there and go down easily if you can injure them enough with the first blow. Hitting their arms or legs does nothing, so don't waste your time trying to aim there."

"What do they look like?" he asks.

I flinch at my memories. "Awful. They look familiar, but haunting—alive, but dead—and something about how they resemble who they once were is more frightening than the creatures that stalk these woods."

"Do you think we will know any of them?"

I look into his dark eyes. "I hope not."

"Same." He squeezes my hand. "I've got you, Briar. Thank you for being out here with me. I wouldn't want anyone else by my side." His eyes fill with pride. "Your brother would be so proud of you for your bravery, your resilience, and your…"

Larkin trails off and looks past me.

His eyes widen, and before I have time to turn, Larkin wraps his whole body around mine, becoming a shield of strength, and pulls me to the floor of the crow's nest.

"Fuck!" Larkin screams.

Two boats sail toward us, while a third lingers in the shadows.

The two boats ahead kept us focused and ignorant of the looming presence of the third ship, and as we approached the impending doom that awaited us, they struck.

A loud crash fills my ears, and the wood of the crow's nest splinters into a million pieces as the ship nearly rips in half. The warriors below us scream in horror. Larkin's large body presses against mine, and our eyes meet. Terror floods his dark eyes, and I know.

It's starting.

The drop makes my stomach roll, and I scream as my fear finally comes to life, and we fall from the height I've always dreaded.

CHAPTER 44

My ears ring as I regain consciousness on the deck of the ship.

I stand, fighting to stay conscious, and my vision blurs. A throbbing pain shoots through my head, and I lift a shaky arm to my face, feeling the blood. Luckily, there's only a small scratch across my cheek, and the rest of me seems to be untouched. Chaos comes into view as my vision clears, Wielders and creatures clashing in a tangled, gory mess.

I hear Larkin screaming my name to move, but I can't process what's happening. The clang of weapons and blasts of magic rattle my ears, and I stumble backward, unsure of which way to go.

Two hands wrap around my shoulders, and Larkin shakes me as his face comes into view.

"Briar," he screams in my face. "You need to fight."

He turns with a warrior's grace, his sword drawn, and the long metal clashes against a creature's armor. Larkin is already covered in blood, and my jaw slacks as I watch him rip out a piece of wood that protrudes from his upper thigh. He grits his teeth, but acts as if nothing pains him in this moment. I slowly blink back into my body, and my vision steadies, allowing me to see clearly for the first time.

Snarling creatures claw at the wooden surface as they crawl from their mangled boat to ours, and dozens of resurrected beings move across the splintered wood, not caring that it digs into their dead skin. I realize that this ship isn't as full as the others, but it is still overwhelming.

I stand in disbelief as I watch a creature approach me, noticing my shocked state. Its semi-human face gnashes its rotting teeth in my direction, snapping at me like a rabid animal. Long arms and legs propel it forward at an unnatural speed. This poor soul races toward me, resurrected against their will and forced to fight, and I can't move.

The creature nears me, and I realize I have neither axe drawn for my protection, and I am completely defenseless. It raises its long black claw to strike me down when Larkin jumps before me and drives his sword into the creature's neck. The creature screams and scratches at its open throat.

The resurrected being falls to the ground, twitching before it becomes lifeless once more. Its body shrivels into a grey knot, and I step back in horror. I snap back into my body, realizing our time is limited before this ship goes under due to the amount of damage done to it, and I have to help.

Now.

"If you don't move, I'm going to kick your fucking ass," Larkin hisses and pushes me forward. "Move, or you are going to get us both killed."

I quickly grab both axes and clutch them in my hands.

"Larkin," I breathe. "It's worse than I thought."

"I know," he responds.

The familiar weight of the weapons feels good, and I gaze at the shining gold blades. Fear has left me, and the only thing that remains is rage. I step forward, swinging one axe after the other, showing no signs of slowing down. I work in tandem with the surrounding Wielders, bringing my axes down upon every resurrected being that comes into view while Larkin remains at my back. When my arms scream at me to stop, I quickly lower one axe and send a surge of magic toward the crowd of creatures. Shock ripples through me when I realize I wielded light instead of shadows.

My body screams in pain as I force myself to continue forward, striking creatures down one by one. The wind rips around us, the howling unable to drown out the growls and screams of those being taken down either by Wielder or creature. Blood sprays in all directions, and I have to work twice as hard to keep the hot liquid from getting in my eyes. I move carefully over each fallen body, twisting with my weapons as we race against the sinking ship around us.

"The ships are going ahead," Larkin shouts, through the clangs of weapons and blasts of magic. "The second ship is coming to stop one of the others from reaching the pier."

I quickly glance over the ship's edge to see Andorwood's second ship passing us, Darcy instructing the crew. The large, dark wooden vessel heads in the direction of the two resurrected ships like a beast of the sea.

I close my eyes and push against the connection to Silas on the pier.

"*Silas*," I think. "*Can you hear me?*"

The connection is dark, and I can't feel his presence nearby. I glance toward the wall. His magic must be blocking more than just the looming ships sailing their way.

"*Silas, Gods damnit*," I yell into my mind. "*There are more than two ships.*"

No response.

"We have to get off this ship," I shout back to Larkin. "Silas can't hear me."

Larkin moves to the opposite side of the ship, swinging the sword, as if he had done this his entire life. He fights with such ease that I can't help but admire his stamina and precision. With each creature he strikes down, he moves on to the next one, occasionally taking on two at a time. Larkin swings his sword and slashes through the ropes that keep the lifeboats anchored to the ship's side. The small boats crash into the churning water, and some of the Wielders begin to abandon ship. The creatures scream as the water rises around the boat, recoiling with every drop that touches their cracking skin.

Are they afraid of water?

I watch a creature miss the dock's landing and plunge into the choppy water below. A brutal scream escapes the creature's mouth as it claws against the current, desperate to grab onto anything. Its long arms slap against the waves, and the resurrected begin to vanish beneath the black water. I watch in horror as the once-human face disappears into the darkness.

"Silas, they can't swim. The creatures can't swim," I scream, praying he can hear me.

Larkin races back to where I fight, just in time for me to drive my axe into the neck of a resurrected being. Blood peppers my face, and we have a moment of reprieve while the others continue fighting, and I use my magic to rest my aching arms.

"Good shot," he cheers.

I stop to catch my breath, my chest heaving. "Thank you."

"We have a decision to make right now," he says, his chest also rising and falling rapidly.

"You aren't supposed to make decisions under pressure," I respond, wiping my eyes.

I pause for a moment and expel another surge of magic toward a creature stalking us. The blast throws the resurrected being back, taking out two more in its path, allowing us a moment to speak.

"This ship is sinking, and we have limited time to get off. We can shift as close as possible to the pier, or we can shift to the other ship and help them fight."

I glance toward the pier and see the wall standing tall, still intact, without even a flicker of light escaping through the darkness. Then, I turn my head toward the ship, racing to cut off the other two containing the resurrected.

I consider both sides: one houses the people I care about the most in this world, and the other is filled with warriors who are risking their lives to fight for their kingdom.

I glance back at Larkin, and through the blood, his dark eyes shine with adrenaline, and his hair is no longer blonde; instead, it's dark and coated with dark red blood.

"I don't think the resurrected can swim," I rasp. "I believe they crashed into this boat to bring down an entire ship of ours to limit our numbers. They were willing to sacrifice these creatures so the other two ships could sail toward land."

"I think you are right," he agrees.

"We need to head to the second ship and assist those Wielders. If they realize the creatures can't swim, it gives us an advantage being in the water."

"Alright," Larkin says, turning to race to the front of the ship. "Hurry."

I follow closely behind, swinging my axe at every creature that moves in my view. The screams fill the air, and even amidst the battle, I can't help but think of those on the shore. The anxiety, the fear of what awaits them. If we can control this from the water, we stand a chance, but I'm not sure how to stop both ships from docking.

My vision snaps around the deck, and I notice a Wielder wearing different clothing than ours, with Rigils scarred into his body. I narrow my eyes, realizing several people are steering the ships on the long journey across the sea. I hit Larkin, and his gaze immediately finds the Wielder scrambling on the ground near a fallen resurrected creature. Larkin rushes over to the man and lifts his sword. The enemy raises his arms, and I can see he mouths something to Larkin, begging for mercy. Larkin's eyes turn dark, and I flinch as he drives his sword through the man's chest. The opposing Wielder slumps on the wooden deck.

I turn to face the Wielders still fighting for their lives and attempt to ignore the ones that have fallen so soon. Brave women and men lay motionless on the sinking ship, and it pangs my heart.

This battle has just begun, and our numbers are already down.

"Abandon ship. The creatures can't swim; shift as far as you can to the shore, or get on the lifeboats." I begin to wave my arms to get their attention. "Warn the others. Do not keep fighting. Go!" I scream, my throat becoming raw as my shouts struggle to compete with the howling wind.

Some of the Wielders vanish into the shadows or bright light, while others continue to swing their weapons desperately, aiming to bring them all down before the job is done.

I scream again, "Shift. Go to the shore. They will drown on their own."

The water rises higher, and the last remaining Wielders abandon the ship, leaving a few creatures screaming as the darkness below drags them to their watery graves.

We both quickly holster our weapons.

Larkin extends his hand, and I struggle to hold onto it against the dark liquid covering most of our exposed skin and clothes.

"Hang on," he instructs.

We shift together, both using our magic to propel ourselves toward the Andorwood ship—still intact and waiting to fight the next ship of the resurrected beings.

Faster than a shooting star, we land on the ship's deck, startling a few Wielders who wait with anticipation and weapons drawn. Upon seeing Commander Spiridon and the Queen of Daramveer in this state, several gasps rise into the thick air, and I hear hushed prayers offered to the Gods of Light and Darkness. I push through the tight crowd of waiting warriors and make my way to Captain Darcy, who is steering the ship.

"My Gods," he says, as we walk up the wooden stairs to the command deck.

"Captain," Larkin says, with a dip of his head. "I'm sure we are a sight to see."

"You two look as horrifying as the creatures aboard those ships," he says with a flinch. "Your Majesty, are you alright?"

"I'm fine for now," I say. "Our surviving Wielders are headed back to the land to prepare the others. The creatures can't swim."

His eyes widen. "Blessed, a fleet of ships traveling with weapons that can't swim."

"Exactly," I respond. "They have a plan, and it's in action. The first ship was designed to take one of our ships down; I believe the second one will be an attempt to wipe us out, while the third will contain their strongest heads to shore." I wipe my blood-soaked eyes. "They have Wielders steering the ships, and they have Rigils everywhere on their bodies, like scars. If we can take out the Wielders, we can stop them from moving forward."

Darcy shoots Larkin a look and raises his brows.

"She's impressive, I know," Larkin says, responding to their silent conversation.

I narrow my eyes. "If you agree, I think we should sink the strongest ship."

"And how do you suggest we do that?" he asks.

"Well," I say. "Like their ship did to ours."

Larkin sighs, "Briar."

"What do you mean?" Darcy says with a weary look in his eyes.

"We will ram it."

"Oh, blessed Gods." Captain Darcy shakes his head. "You can't be serious."

My lips form a thin line. "I am."

He pauses and looks toward the two ships heading in our direction. Both appear identical, with what seems to be the same number of creatures lining the decks. Distinguishing which one is which will be nearly impossible and a gamble. The violent winds rip around us, and our time is running out as the angry waves continuously push us closer. I glance toward the shore, and that familiar shadowy wall stands tall.

"Or, we try to take them both down instead of risking it with choosing one," Larkin says.

I snap my head in his direction. "How?"

"We split up," he says.

"No," I say, with a furrowed brow. "Absolutely not."

"I can take a few of our strongest warriors and shift to the boat. You stay back with Darcy and the masses and take down one of the ships entirely," Larkin explains. "Killing even a few of the creatures will help us if they get to land. Once we can limit their numbers or kill the Wielders in charge, we will shift to the shore to prepare Silas."

I roll my head around my shoulders and weigh the options. "I don't like this, and he's going to kill you for leaving me."

"I'll be okay, and from what I've seen, you are perfectly capable of fighting." Larkin nudges me and bounds toward the front deck, gathering a few men of his choosing to join him at the front of the boat.

Larkin shouts over his shoulder, "Just yell which boat I should go to when we're ready."

"Larkin," I shout.

He turns his head toward me.

"Just fight, Briar, and don't stop."

My heart pounds against my ribs, and I clench my teeth.

The black ships sail toward us faster than the raging sea. The hollow sails whip in the whistling storm, and the growling grows in intensity, causing my senses to scream louder than the wind. Darcy angles the ship to fit right in the middle of both the haunting ships, giving Larkin and the men a straight shot to shift directly onto either deck, taking the creatures by surprise, while we quickly steer the boat directly into the other ship's side. Choosing which way we go will be a quick call at the last second.

"Steady," Darcy chants, holding the helm firm and gritting his teeth. "Steady."

We approach the black ships, and I nod to Larkin at the front of the vessel. I whip my head between both boats, unsure which one holds the most dangerous resurrected beings. The waves from all three ships crash together—like a storm of chaos—and sweat beads on my brow.

The resurrected beings aboard the ship stand motionless, like ghostly soldiers waiting for the bloodshed to begin.

I glance at the ship to the right and see numerous rotting heads —almost human, but altered. Their hollow eyes stare forward, uncaring about the ship close to them. They gaze only at the shore. I look at the ship to the left and see a nearly identical situation. Nothing about either boat stands out, and I can't shake the unsettling feeling that courses through my system.

Darcy looks at me. "Queen, it's time to make your call. Which boat?"

My heart thunders like the raging storm around us, and I can't decide. I can't choose, because something doesn't feel right. I place my hand in my pocket and feel the stone's vibration shoot through my veins in hopes it can point me in the right direction. In the turmoil surrounding us, I can't decipher the feelings, as if my system and the stone are filled with madness.

"If he's going, yell now, Briar," Darcy's hoarse voice shouts.

My hands tremble, and even the seconds seem to creep by. I suck in a breath.

"Left!" I scream toward Larkin, praying that wasn't the wrong choice for either of us.

As soon as the words leave my mouth, he glances at me, a reassuring look painting his expression, and smiles wildly, vanishes with the group of warriors. I watch the white light turn to mist as it moves toward the left ship. My vision shifts right as Darcy turns the wheel as sharply as the ship will allow. The edge of the boat dips low into the water, and I brace myself against the side to avoid falling as the waves nearly crash onto the ship. Captain Darcy maintains a firm grip on the wheel, and I can hear the strain in his voice as he shouts orders to the men around him.

I keep my gaze fixed on the right ship, focusing my mind, body, and strength to keep fighting—to persevere—and to do whatever I can to save those around me. The ship of the resurrected beings comes into clear view, and I inhale sharply, preparing for the two ships to crash together.

"Prepare for the impact," Darcy screams, and all the Wielders scramble to take cover—moving away from the edge, and grabbing hold of something—as we brace for the collision. I widen my stance and take the last deep breath I fear I may ever get.

The bow of the ship slams against the side of the enemy ship, and just like before, the wood splinters into pieces. Resurrected creatures scream into the night air and scramble to keep the water from reaching them. The crash jolts me, and I fly forward, landing on my chest against the deck. I slowly stand, catching my breath, and look back to ensure Darcy is alright after the blow. He gives me a shaky thumbs-up and unsheathes his sword. A look of madness alters his expression as he races forward, screaming into the air.

"Fight!" the Wielders yell in unison, and I grab both axes, moving forward through the rubble connecting the two ships.

I duck, spin, and sprint past the creatures, swiping my axe through their legs, arms, and abdomens—anywhere to slow them down for the Wielders coming up behind me. The coppery smell of blood fills my nose, and during my small breaks, I wipe my eyes coated with hot, dark liquid. I look at each passing being, desperate to find the Wielders steering the ship. The creatures are similar to the others on the ship—no difference in size, rage, or people—and I realize this isn't the strongest ship.

I pause and glance toward the other ship, still moving toward the shore at a rapid pace. Screams echo into the night, and I know the others fight for their lives on that ship, severely outnumbered against resurrected Wielders and creatures.

For the first time, I say a prayer to Raddnoke that he protects Larkin from those beasts, and another surge of power leaves my body as I push all I have toward the creatures racing toward me. The Wielders work perfectly together around me, like an army of trained assassins.

A creature comes before me, and I pause, widening my stance. It is large, and I immediately know it was never originally human. It looks familiar, and I realize it's a resurrected Figgawen—larger and more menacing than ever before.

The lanky beast drops to all fours and sizes me up. A wicked smile spreads across my face as I drop both arms beside me, wanting the creature to feel victorious in its perceived triumph over me. The creature lowers even further and licks its cracked, bleeding lips. Its hollow eyes stare into my soul, and I want nothing more than to send this resurrected fiend back to the darkest realm.

I step forward, and the creature freezes, lowering its head to the ground, as if bowing in respect to something else. Even without eyes, it seems to look at something or someone beyond me. My senses flare, and my veins bubble with darkness. Even in my loud surroundings, a voice snakes into my mind, sending me into a flood of panic.

"*Turn around, Briar*," Kalix says, her voice sounding in my head—as if helping me in this moment. "*Hurry*."

I keep one eye on the bowed creature and slowly turn amidst the chaos. My mouth drops open, and one of my axes clangs to the ground from the shock that rattles my very soul.

Nolan Harte stands a few feet behind me.

The same Nolan I once knew, yet changed—more insane and angry—with scars of Rigils covering his entire body.

A feral grin, filled with madness, sits on his face.

"Hello, sis," Nolan says.

CHAPTER 45

I step backward, uncaring of the resurrected that remains frozen in the face of Nolan and his burning gaze. The creature growls at my closeness, and I pause.

"It's nice to see you again," Nolan says.

"Can't say the same."

"You look awful." He tilts his head.

I don't respond; I can only stare at his condition. Deep white scars mar his face and trail down his neck. His once-white hair has dulled to gray, and his eyes are darker than the night swirling around us.

"No," I bite back. "Actually, you look like shit."

His vicious laugh bursts into the air, and I create distance between us.

"You look surprised to see me. I can't imagine why," he says, as he takes a step forward.

The creature hisses once more, and I spin, dragging my golden axe along with me. The sharp blade finds its mark directly across the throat of the creature. The beast screams and claws at its neck before falling to the ground with a heavy thud.

"Someone's been practicing," he exclaims, clapping before stepping even closer to me.

I narrow my eyes. "What the fuck are you doing here? Calia let you out of your cage for an outing?"

"Still with that sarcastic fucking mouth," Nolan laughs. "I'm glad the trauma hasn't changed you."

"It has."

"It's not killed you."

I step forward, picking up my second axe, and clutch my fists around the cold metal. "A lot of things have changed, Nolan."

The battle rages around me as the water quickly rises once more on the ship. The creatures hiss, and Wielders swing their weapons through the night sky, like shooting stars of death. When the timing allows, some of the warriors tap into their powers, flaring shadows or light across the ship in chaotic blasts. I need to lower the lifeboats soon for any Wielders too weak to shift, then I must work on getting myself toward the pier.

However, both of those options seem impossible right now with Nolan before me.

"Where is your tether?" Nolan asks, as he angles his head.

I glance toward the shore to see the third ship nearly arriving. Fear drenches me, and I snap my gaze back to Nolan. The screams pouring from the nearly docked ship die down, and my heart races as the nerves settle in that something has happened.

He smiles. "Oh, good, they are almost there. The real fun can begin."

"You are fucking awful," I spit out, growling in his direction.

He shrugs. "I do hope your friend is okay."

Larkin.

Oh, Gods.

"He is fine," I bite back, moving toward the dangling lifeboats.

"I wouldn't be so sure."

Nolan stalks forward with each step I take backward.

"We are here for something. Well, you could say many things," he laughs, wickedly. "I know you are aware of that, though. We came for the book I'm assuming you took from the Archives, for the stone that weighs down your pocket, and that other tether."

Shock rattles my core. "Fen?"

Nolan nods. "Indeed."

"Good fucking luck getting near her," I snap.

Nolan glances toward the shore. "I don't think we'll need any luck."

Carobon.

Rohhit.

"Is Rohhit here?" I shudder at the thought.

"Rohhit? He's long gone, and we want to make sure it stays that way, which is why we need Fenmore."

"I won't let you touch her."

He laughs wildly.

"As for Carobon," Nolan pauses, and my heart thumps. "He is here. And there. And over there. He's wherever he wants to be, Briar." He looks back at me, and continues, "I'm merely here to set the plans in action. Then, you won't see me again until it's time."

He's here.

Rohhit is here.

The water rises around my ankles, and I lunge backward, slamming my axe against the ropes holding the lifeboats in place. The wood caves in from the force, and the ropes spiral out of control. They barely fall into the water before floating next to the sinking ship. The creatures continue to hiss as water pools around them. They claw at their skin, as if the liquid burns them to the very core, and I cut the other ropes.

"Go," I scream. "Wielders, leave the ship. Head for the pier or board the lifeboats. Warn the others while you still can."

I turn, watching the third ship grow closer to the shadowy black wall with each passing second.

"The third resurrected ship is about to dock," I shout again. "Hurry."

The Wielders scramble as I keep a close eye on Nolan, who continues to study me from a few feet away. His hands remain in his pockets, and I realize he bears no weapon for defense.

"I don't want to hurt you, Briar. Not yet, at least. Too much is in the works for that part of the plan to unfold yet." He remains still. "Plus, what would be fun about that? I will most enjoy watching you suffer from afar."

"Afar?" I step forward, gripping my axes so hard my knuckles whiten. "You stand right in front of me. You are so close that I could swipe this blade across your fucking throat."

My eyes catch sight of movement behind Nolan.

I see Captain Darcy creeping up behind him with his sword drawn. I try to remain calm, not to signal his presence, and as badly as I want to stop him, I remain motionless.

"Wrong again, sis," Nolan teases. "Gods, you should really stop being so cocky all the time."

Nolan lifts his hand and snaps his fingers, the click rattling into my mind.

A blood-curdling scream leaves Captain Darcy's throat, and I watch his leg break at his shin, his bone splintering as it protrudes from his leg. He falls to the ground, and I slap my hand across my mouth, muffling my scream. I start to race toward him, but Nolan raises his hand.

"Not yet."

I pause, frozen in fear and sorrow.

Darcy lies on the ground, clutching his leg. If I can get to him, he'll be fine, but if I can't, he will likely go down with this sinking ship.

"I need that stone in your pocket," Nolan says, as he steps forward. "Now, or I'll make sure every single person on that island dies."

"Just let me go to him," I plead.

"I don't think so."

"Please," I beg.

Darcy lifts his head, and the pain that sits behind his aged eyes shakes me to the core. Our time is running out, and I need to get to him.

"Nolan, I swear to the Gods," I snap, and point my axe in his direction.

I step forward, but am stopped by an invisible force that keeps my feet rooted in place. I attempt to lift my leg, but it's as if a weight keeps it pinned to the ground.

"Give me the stone," Nolan barks.

"No."

"Then he will die," Nolan says. "And his blood will be on your hands because you couldn't fucking listen."

Nolan lifts his hand again, and I watch in horror as time slows and he moves his fingers to snap again, likely to bring down another injury to Darcy, lying helpless on the ground.

"Stop!"

Nolan pauses, and a sinister dazzle fills his eyes.

"I'll do whatever you want," I whisper. "I'll give you the stone."

Nolan smiles. "Amazing choice."

The invisible force keeping me still lessens, and I sprint toward Darcy, crashing to the ground beside him, turning my back to Nolan. His pained, aged eyes stare into mine, and I prop his head in my lap.

"You're going to be fine," I whisper. "I'm getting us out of here."

"Don't give him the stone," Darcy deeply rasps.

"Trust me," I squeeze his hand, and shake my head that nothing of the sort will happen.

I wink at him, and while Nolan turns toward the shore, I put the shining green jewel in Darcy's jacket pocket and pull out the fake stone. Nolan snaps his gaze back to us and taps his foot on the soaked wooden deck.

"Hurry up," he barks.

I extend my hand containing the dark green jewel. Nolan studies it for a second before smiling and reaching for the stone.

"If you weren't so weak, Briar, you'd come to realize the actual powers you had from the Great Wiitch. Carobon has done many things for me."

"Clearly," I snap. "He's a talented tattoo artist, I see."

"He's changed me for the better, you sarcastic bitch, and I can't wait to watch you suffer. It's coming, sis, and I'll smile through every scream that rattles your throat."

"Do you ever shut the fuck up?"

He huffs a laugh, and stares into my eyes. A shiver runs up my spine, but I don't back down. Instead, I think of driving my axe into his chest.

"He's here," Nolan whispers.

Nolan begins to tap into his power, and a bright light shines around him, brighter than the sun. I watch him intently, staring through the blinding light. A large hand snakes up to Nolan's shoulder, and through the blaze, I see his face.

Rohhit.

Now, wholly possessed by Carobon.

His face is the same, yet different. He appears aged, but still just as beautiful as I remember, if not more. His dazzling dark eyes gaze into mine, and tears begin to fall from my face, pooling like the sinking ship around us. I don't break my gaze as they fade into the light, and for a moment, I swear to the Gods that Carobon blinks, revealing Rohhit's true face shining through.

"Rohhit?" I cry. "Oh, fuck. What has he done to you?"

He's neither lost nor gone, and I must ensure we bring him back.

"Wait," I say, in an attempt to move forward. "Rohhit."

A sob escapes my throat as they disappear, and I look down at Darcy. His eyes are shut, and I quickly assess the damage to his leg. I glance toward the pier and see the shadowy wall still standing tall. Silas has warded the wall so that only civilians of Andorwood can pass through while it remains standing.

"*Silas?*" I plead in my mind. "*Can you hear me?*"

No response.

"*He is here*," I weep. "*Rohhit is here.*"

Defeat churns in my system, and I know time is running out as the water continuously rises around us like a darkness.

"This is going to hurt, Captain, but hold on," I speak to him.

I burrow into my magic, letting sadness and fear pull me toward the shore. I dive deeper than I have before, thinking of my people on the pier, and praying the one who stayed with me has made it.

Larkin.

Oh fuck.

I shift and pull Darcy with me, letting the shadows and light propel us forward through the wind, chaos, and churning sea below. We move like a bolt of lightning engulfed in darkness. The wall tries to keep us out, but I push, grinding my teeth together, letting out a vicious scream. Even being mist, my muscles strain with the weight of Darcy with me, and I push one last time through the wall and toward the people who still need protection.

We crash land a few hundred yards from the pier and are

immediately surrounded by civilians of Andorwood. I release Darcy's hand and roll to the side, making sure he's alright.

"Help him," I shout. "Where is a healer?"

The civilians freeze, and a few shuffle away to get someone to assist. Blood drips from my body along with water, and quickly pools around the dry ground.

"Please take him away from the danger. He needs healing."

Darcy groans beside me, and I get to my knees, placing my hand on his forehead.

"Now."

A woman parts the crowd, just like she did during our time in the city square. Pia Herst sprints toward us, landing beside Darcy to begin assessing his leg. With a shaky hand, Darcy removes the stone from his pocket and places it in my hands, closing my fist around it. I offer a soft smile, and tuck the jewel into my pants, feeling the vibration of power once more.

"Thank you," Darcy whispers.

I glance at Pia, and her eyes are wide but focused, ready to do what needs to be done.

"Can you help him?"

"He will be okay," she says. "But I need to take him, now."

I nod, moving out of her way, while a few others rush from the crowd to assist her in lifting him and carrying him through the kingdom to the primary healing base. A few civilians dressed in armor gasp as I stand on wobbly legs, but I ignore them, pushing my body to move back toward the pier.

"Prepare to fight," I shout as I move along the cobblestone streets toward the Wielders, yelling at anyone who looks in my direction. My legs carry me forward, and I'm unsure how I'm still going.

"They are coming." I race forward toward the dock.

The howling wind rips around me, pushing my soaking wet hair in my face, and I continue toward the pull I feel in my chest.

Toward Silas.

"*I'm here*," I scream in my mind. "*Silas, I'm here.*"

The crowd parts for me, and I glance at their horrified faces. Many of them are ready but fearful of what the near future brings. I offer any reassuring looks I can, but in my state, the shock settles in like the night around us.

"*Where are you?*" Silas's frantic voice echoes in my mind. "*Where the fuck are you?*"

I stumble forward, not letting the exhaustion slow me.

The crowd lessens, and I move as quickly as I can. Tripping, I catch myself and look up to stare directly into Silas's eyes across the short distance as he pushes against the flow of the crowd. Panic contorts his beautiful eyes, but he charges toward me. Relief overtakes me, and I race forward, crashing into his strong chest. His hands wrap into my tangled hair and pull me into him.

"Thank the fucking Gods," he whispers.

"I'm okay," I say, burrowing into his chest.

Silas pulls me back, his eyes moving up and down my sore body. He grimaces and cups my face. "You don't look okay," he says.

I glance down at my armor—gashes and blood cover most of the fabric now, exposing my hip and various parts of my arm. My skin is already bruising, and blood trickles from my split lip. Silas remains untouched, still in perfect condition, and compared to the other people on the pier, I look horrifying.

I pull away and shake my head. "We need to prepare for them to collide with the pier, and fast."

"Catch your breath," he says.

"They are almost here, Silas. We are outnumbered, even with one of their ships. This one is the strongest, and it doesn't just carry resurrected Wielders. There are creatures on that ship."

"I heard you, Briar."

"You did?"

"The creatures can't swim. I prepared the pier with the information I was able to get from you. It felt like our connection was hazy, but I heard you in pieces."

"Oh, thank Gods," I say, still sucking in deep breaths.

"They are ready," Silas says.

"That isn't all."

He hesitates before speaking, so I continue, desperate to get everything out.

"Silas," I grab his arm. "They are after Fen. We have to get her to the house and hidden, right now."

"They?"

"Rohhit," I say, struggling to get my words out. "He's here."

Silas pales. "I didn't fucking hear that."

I feel like I may vomit. "For her."

"That isn't Rohhit." Silas's eyes go dark. "You know that."

Without another second passing, Silas spins to a man standing near him, whom I've seen a few times, but can't remember his name.

Silas grips his shirt. "Where is Warrick Pierce?"

The man points toward a dimly lit alleyway. "Last time I saw him, he was there with Captain Nastronde."

Silas takes a step forward, and I stop him.

He spins, his face contorted with concern and rage.

"You can't go, Silas. We need to stay on the pier until the wall breaks."

He looks at me and hesitates, but slowly accepts the truth of my words.

Silas shoves the man, releasing his grip on the shirt. "Go find Warrick immediately and tell him to get Fenmore to the cliff house."

The man nods, but hesitates.

"Now," Silas orders, and a deep voice rattles from his throat that shocks me. "Run."

Without another word, the man sprints toward the town in search of Warrick.

I clasp my hand around Silas's arm. "He will keep her safe."

Silas nods, but I know he doesn't trust anyone but himself in this moment.

His eyes grow wild, but he stays focused. Silas turns, screaming at the warriors around him to get into position and draw their weapons. Metal clinks into the air, and everyone faces the dark wall of shadows, waiting for the creatures to crash through at any second.

Oak stands near the front lines and smiles when we make eye contact. He runs to Silas and me, wrapping his arms around me.

"I've never been so happy to see you, Briar," Oak says.

"We did the best we could," I respond, quickly.

Oak smiles. "You are incredible. Disgusting at the moment, but incredible."

I huff a laugh, wiping the creature's blood from my face as best I can.

"Where's Larkin?"

I pause and look to Silas.

His eyes grow hard and worried.

"He should be here by now. He left before me and shifted to the third boat with a few men," I respond, catching my breath.

"Third boat?" Silas snaps.

"They attacked us, sinking one of our ships. Darcy and I sank the second one." I push past them and run closer to the edge.

"Gods," I hear Oak whisper.

Silas steps forward, "Briar."

"He should be here." I snap back.

"We…" Oak hesitates, "We haven't seen him."

Dread fills me like rising water.

The shadow wall begins to pulse, and from behind me, I can hear Silas grit his teeth against the power surging through his body with a heavy groan. How he's been able to hold this amount of magic for this long, I'll never know.

The King of Darkness is unlike anything I've ever seen.

In the corner of my eye, toward the small beach, the pulse continues against the wall. Anticipation floods me as I wait for the creatures to slither through at any moment. Before my eyes, hands begin to claw through the shadowy barrier, and a few men tumble through as Silas opens up his magic, allowing those of Andorwood to cross over, desperate for a moment of reprieve.

Men I don't recognize fall on our side of the wall, and I realize these are some of the men who went with Larkin to the second ship. The waves push them onto shore, and they crawl as fast as they can across the shadowy wall.

My world pauses as I wait to see one last hand come through the opening.

"Come on, Larkin," I whisper, my eyes focused only on the beach.

He doesn't move through the wall.

"I need to close it back up," Silas says. "I can't keep it open if someone else isn't coming through."

"Wait," I plead. "He's coming."

"Briar, I don't want to, but I have to," Silas warns, and I can tell he's struggling with this decision.

"Wait!" I scream at him this time.

"I have to close it…or I risk the entire wall falling."

In this moment, seconds feel like hours as I wait for him to pass through the wall, but only the crashing waves come through. My anxiety churns like the sea, and a dread I've never felt before washes over me as my hands tremble.

"I can't hold it with the tear, it's too much for me," Silas admits, as his face contorts in sheer pain.

"We will find him, Briar," Oak calls.

I close my eyes and feel hopelessness seeping into my soul. The small hole fills once more with a thick shadow.

I begin to cry.

He should be here.

The small opening begins to close fully, but I feel as if a new wound in my heart begins to open. The wall pulses once more, and I gaze at the obscure fog, tilting my head.

"Silas!" I scream, and he grits his teeth against the hesitation. "Wait."

I narrow my eyes, watching the shadow wall flicker like a lit candle, and time slows. I suck in my breath, and attempt to steady my pounding heart. I step closer, the slapping waves drown out all sounds, and my body vibrates with anticipation.

Come on.

A bloody hand punches through the wall, and I step closer, not breathing.

Come on, Spiridon.

Silas curses under his breath, and I watch in disbelief, ignoring everything else around me.

Please, Gods.

Another bloody hand grips the sand, turning the white beach a shade of red around it. The two arms drag its body toward the shore, and my eyes widen. A few of the surrounding Wielders pause, waiting for the figure to fully emerge. The shadow wall seals shut as the figure appears on the beach, coated in blood, sweat, and desperation.

Larkin Spiridon slumps to the ground on our side of the wall.

Relief strikes me harder than any blow I've ever endured, and I take off in a dead sprint toward him, shifting in small bouts to get there faster.

He rolls onto his back, and his chest heaves with exhaustion as his hands fall to his side. The waves nearly obscure his body, and the sand conceals his torn armor, but he's here. I reach him as he struggles to lift his weary form.

"Larkin," I exclaim, and feel as if my legs can't move fast enough.

He lifts his head, and a tired smile appears on his sand-coated face. He gives us a shaky thumbs-up.

Larkin rises on his elbows, allowing the waves to crash against his body, before rolling to stand on shaky legs. He begins to limp up the shore as quickly as possible, trying to create distance between himself and the ship. Silas follows behind me, along with Oak, as I slam into Larkin's body. He staggers back a few steps as I wrap my arms tightly around his neck before his unsteady hands wrap around my back, returning the squeeze.

He groans against my hold, but I squeeze tighter.

"We took out as many as we could," he says, breathlessly.

"That doesn't matter right now." I let go and examine his body. "Are you hurt?"

"I've been worse," he responds. "I'm fucking tired, to be honest."

Silas and Oak laugh, but my gaze doesn't relax.

"I'm okay, Briar. I promise."

I push Larkin's chest. "You fucking scared me to death."

"Sorry, I'm late." He straightens up, dusting the sand off his body. "But, we need to get ready."

"We are," Silas says.

"It's bad, Silas. That boat is covered with the resurrected beings. With everyone I killed, I felt like I was surrounded by three more."

"We're outnumbered," Oak says.

"There is something beneath the ship. Growls I've never heard before were coming from below, and it made my skin crawl." Larkin's gaze shifts toward the dark barrier that separates us from the ship.

"It's Figgawen and other creatures. Not just Wielders," I begin to explain, but before I can continue, the wall pulses forward.

Silas widens his stance and glares at his forcefield. The wall pushes inward, causing it to curve. He grinds his molars, keeping his magic focused forward. Screams and growls that could fuel nightmares begin to seep from the other side of the wall, and my stomach rolls.

I glance at Silas, and he's not speaking. His face is pained, and I know he's barely keeping that wall up with everything he has.

"It's like they are all pushing against it," Silas whispers. "I can't keep this up much longer."

We all nod and draw our weapons. I turn to the Kingdom of Andorwood. The civilians before me look as horrified as the men on the ship.

"Fight," I yell over the crowd. "Fight for your family, your honor, and your kingdom. We can take them. We will rest when the last one dies."

The crowd screams into the air as I turn back to my friends, waiting for the dam to break.

"I can't hold it," Silas rasps.

I touch his shoulder, and he peels his gaze from the wall to mine.

"Let go," I whisper. "It's okay."

For the first time, fear fills his bright green eyes, and we stay locked in this moment for a second longer.

"Don't go far from me," he pleads, groaning against the power being drained.

I nod, and smile. "Silas, let go. We're ready."

Silas inhales deeply, letting the magic swirl around us for a second longer before it fizzles out, like a candle in the breeze. The shadowy wall falls like a curtain being torn down, and my eyes widen. Hundreds of creatures and resurrected Wielders stand on the opposite side. Their razor-sharp teeth gnash together, and they all lower their heads, like hunters poised to pounce on their prey.

"Don't stop for anything," Larkin tells me, Oak, and Silas. "Tonight is a test of what's to come."

The world pauses.

Silas whispers, "Tonight, we will genuinely fight for our lives."

"Together," I whisper, and Silas cuts his eyes to mine.

"See you bastards when this is over," Oak says, as we all take off into a sprint toward the resurrected.

CHAPTER 46

Wielders—both alive and resurrected—crash together in an epic battle of bloodshed and desperation.

The sound of metal clangs into the air, and sparks fly, like thousands of bolts of lightning striking the ground. I stay close to Silas, wielding my magic and axes as if they were an extension of me. The exhaustion I once felt has vanished, and I tear down every creature that steps in my path, but they keep coming. I glance over my shoulder to see Oak and Larkin remaining close. One always has the other's back, fighting like trained warriors.

The warriors of Andorwood swarm the pier, attempting to push any creatures into the choppy sea below. Screams echo into the night sky, and I lose myself in rage. My darkness swells, and I can feel magic leaking from everyone around me—as if the masses are drunk on power and fury—seeping into the air like a dense fog that clouds over the moon.

I feel like I'm moving in slow motion as I turn and swirl my axes around me. I continue to move, never stopping, as I've been instructed. I don't dare look at the faces of the once-living Wielders I strike down.

From the beginning, there's been a fear that I may recognize one of the resurrected Wielders, and I know that would cause everything in my system to beg me to stop—to try to save them, knowing they can't be saved. I take a break from my axes, sending a surge of power forward that knocks three to the ground in a tangled mess. Oak takes the opportunity to drive his jeweled sword into the necks of the fallen.

As many as we kill, more continue to pour off the ship, like a disease spreading across the land. The creatures push with all their power to get past us on the pier, and with every passing second, our line of Wielders weakens.

Rotting teeth snap in my face as I'm pushed backward toward the cobblestone street. A few creatures race past me on all fours, disappearing into the alleyways of the kingdom.

"They are too strong," I shout toward Silas.

"Has anyone seen Cyrus?" Larkin shouts over the chaos.

Silas spins, taking down one of the creatures, narrowly missing its long claw.

"No, no one's seen him," he responds, and continues to slash through the grey, rotting creatures that cover the land.

"Fucking coward," Larkin shouts as he sends a blast of light into the chest of a creature.

Silas and Oak's faces now look similar to mine—coated in blood and sweat—but they continue to fight, exhaustion not an option. Silas slices a creature in two and turns to sprint in my direction, never allowing too much distance to separate us. He quickly fills the gap, assisting me in taking down anything that steps in our path. Oak and Larkin continue to fight alongside the Andorwood civilians.

The ground is scattered with bodies, and I blink past the horrors that fill my eyes. Images of creatures, Wielders, and resurrected Wielders burn once more into my mind, and I fight back the urge to spill my stomach. A loud scream pulls my gaze, and I see creatures begin to climb over the heads of Wielders, their swords no match for the deadly things recently released from the depths of the ship.

"Tighten up," Silas commands.

The people of Andorwood come together in a human wall, attempting to keep the creatures from passing and disappearing into the alleyways.

"We need to go into the city and fight the ones that have made it past; we can't let them overrun the streets," Silas yells to Larkin and Oak. "Dozens have gone by already."

They nod, signaling for someone to cover their spots quickly, and race toward us.

We unite as a front and dash down the cobblestone streets, deeper into the heart of the kingdom. Screams echo through each alleyway, and as I round each corner, I flinch in anticipation of what lurks in the darkness.

Claws scrape against the stones, and I hear feet shuffling in every direction. The narrow passages grow disorienting as I continue to follow closely behind Silas, Oak, and Larkin, bringing up the rear.

"They are looking for Fen," I shout ahead, and Silas turns left into a thin pocket of shadows, allowing us to rest for a moment.

We huddle close, each of us gasping for air, and Oak rests his hand on his knees momentarily. My lungs burn as they expand, desperate for a deep breath in this thick, musty air.

"I haven't seen Warrick," I say.

"He took Fen to the house," Silas breathes.

"So, she's safe?" Oak asks.

The color drains from my face when the thought hits me. I turn to Silas, and his brows narrow.

"What?" Silas snaps. "What is that face for?"

"Carobon will feel her pull. She may not be able to resist Rohhit since he's this close." I gasp for breath before continuing. "She may not be strong enough to control the pull, yet."

"Fuck," Silas shouts, and drives his fist into a nearby stone wall.

The rock shatters under his hand as if it were made of glass, and the heavy rubble falls to the ground in a dusty mess. Silas stills and looks at his hand, the rage taking over his body completely.

He swings his other fist, crumbling the wall further.

"Nastronde," Oak says, stepping back. "How the fuck did you do that?"

"Is your hand alright?" I reach for him, and he pulls his hand back.

"He's going to go to the house," Silas says, stumbling away from the crushed stone. "You're right. She won't be able to resist him, Briar. She will go to Rohhit." His eyes fill with rage and tears, but shine the brightest green I've ever seen. "I know that feeling, the pull. She won't be able to stay hidden. She will go willingly."

My legs quake, and I hold onto the nearby wall. My heart pounds so hard I can feel it in my temples.

"We have to go," Silas says.

"What about the creatures? We'll lead them directly there," I demand.

"They all have one common goal, and it's to find the book and Fen," he says. "They will eventually go to the house, anyway."

"Alright," I agree, apprehensively.

"Stay close," Silas orders.

He peers around the corner of the alleyway where we stand and motions for us to move forward. He takes off in a sprint, and we follow behind him, our footsteps pounding on the stone streets. The kingdom is still intact, but many buildings are damaged, with either their windows blown out, their doors ripped off the hinges, or both. From what I can tell, the creatures received orders to ransack every shop in search of the book and Fenmore.

My legs sting from the continuous movement, but we don't slow down. Silas leads the pack, followed by Oak, then me, and finally Larkin. From behind, Larkin continues to speak to me, urging me to keep moving, keep my head up, and not to worry about the alleyways.

I do my best to listen, but the urge to scan the fallen Wielders and creatures for anyone familiar tugs at me. We leap over bodies, blood kicking up behind us as we move faster than we ever have toward Silas's house. I burrow deeper into my magic and sense a slight simmer of darkness mixing with the remaining light. Still, the overwhelming feeling of exhaustion makes shifting nearly impossible, and I can only imagine the others feel the same.

Each step brings us closer to the edge of the kingdom, allowing us to head toward the house. Nerves twist in my gut at the thought of the open space that awaits us, the narrow alleyways no longer able to conceal us. We will be fully exposed to the elements, and I pray that we can muster up some magic by then to make the final distance.

In the area surrounding us, I hear footsteps followed by the sound of claws scraping against the stone ground. I stay close behind Oak and Silas, catching their glances occasionally to ensure Larkin and I are still with them. I glance over my shoulder and see that Larkin has fallen back a bit, but he wields a new sword that he grabbed from a fallen Wielder. The beautiful piece of metal is gripped tightly in his left hand—the hilt black and decorated with bright auburn jewels—the handle molding perfectly to his large hand.

I roll my eyes and push forward.

He'll catch up.

As we near the last few alleyways, Silas continues forward, like a black streak of lightning leading the pack. I can't help but glance down the narrow passageway ahead, and my entire body tingles with fear. At least six creatures—taller than small trees—stand hunched over something in the darkness—a young female Wielder with dark black hair, fallen and motionless on the ground.

The creatures snap their heads up at the sound of our approach, and I hear Silas curse from ahead.

"Don't stop," Silas shouts.

Their terrifying growls echo as they prepare to chase us by widening their long stances. Fear propels me forward, and we clear the passage, our feet sounding like an army of horses barreling down the street. I glance back over my shoulder and see that Larkin is further behind, not yet past the passage. Terror causes my body to freeze as one of the creatures peers its long neck around the corner to spot Larkin, the lone Wielder, rushing in their direction. My feet dig into the stone as my body comes to a complete stop. I immediately clutch my axe tighter and try motioning to Larkin without too much attention being drawn to us.

It doesn't take long for Silas and Oak to realize something has happened and come to a stop ahead. Larkin races forward, unaware of what lurks in the upcoming passage. I lift my axe in the air and wave it in his direction. His eyes hit mine, understanding dawning that something that requires his full attention is coming up.

His fist wraps tightly around the hilt as he slows his pace. If he continues forward at that speed, they will likely all jump him faster than he can move. I remain still, tucking myself into a small pocket of shadows while Larkin remains completely visible. The only thing separating me from Larkin is the alleyway filled with deadly creatures.

The streets around us are silent, and all I can hear is the shaky breaths escaping my burning lungs. Larkin's eyes are wide, yet he's patient and calm, no fear showing behind his dark eyes— only determination. I know we will have to fight these creatures to get him across the path, but from what I've seen, Larkin can take these beasts out alone if he has to.

Two of the beings crane their necks around the passage, and Larkin smiles, waving at them sarcastically to make it painfully clear that their cover is blown. A scream rattles the air around us, and they barrel out from the passage toward Larkin. Their long claws grip the cobblestones, and through the distance, I can hear their teeth smashing together. Fear grips my chest, and I sprint in his direction.

Just keep moving, I tell myself. *If you stop fighting, they will strike*.

Larkin's sword collides with a claw as all six of the resurrected creatures begin to surround him. I hear Silas and Oak racing behind me, but they won't reach Larkin as fast as I will. I pull my axe upward, slashing through one of the creatures blocking me from Larkin. A hissing scream rattles my ears, but I charge forward. His sword clangs against the massive claws as he fights them off.

In the near distance, I hear more claws tearing at the ground, and I know we will soon be outnumbered, as we have been for most of the night. I strike down another creature and can finally see Larkin's face. He's focused and steady but covered in dark blood. I turn my gaze to the creature on my left and move my axe around me, an extension of my arm. I work in perfect unison with my weapon, and I no longer feel the weight of the beautiful metal, only the determination to get us past this final stretch alive.

More resurrected beings and creatures round the corner as Silas and Oak join me on the opposite side of Larkin.

Finally, I think in my mind.

"Sorry," Silas says, never fully pausing.

They both immediately begin fighting, and in that moment, I feel triumph. We are going to mow these things down and continue on our way to save Fen.

I slash through another beast and raise my gaze to see Larkin doing the same. Our eyes meet, and he shoots me a quick smile through the smeared blood.

A tall creature steps between us, facing Larkin, and I see his body go unnaturally still. As the additional creatures surround us, it makes it increasingly difficult to fight and keep my eyes on Larkin, but he's not moving.

Why isn't he moving?

"Spiridon," I hear Silas scream.

I spin and duck the claws of the beasts, doing everything in my power to get to Larkin. A new motivation drives me, and I have to see what he's doing. Silas moves beside me and strikes the creature down, allowing me time to peer through the chaos.

"Go," Silas shouts to me. "Get to him."

Larkin stands completely still, gazing into the eyes of the creature before him. I can tell from the back of the creature that it was once a Wielder—a Lumor Wielder from the white hair that still peppers its head in various places. The color has completely drained from his face, and the brilliant sword trembles in his hand.

Fuck.

That resurrected creature is someone he knew.

I grind my teeth and push forward. "Larkin," I yell, trying to penetrate his frozen state. "Don't stop moving."

But he remains still.

I'm closing the distance between us, but it's not fast enough.

If he doesn't move… I shake the thought from my mind and snarl like the beasts around me. My legs threaten to give out, and my lungs burn, but that doesn't stop me. I move like a creature of the night, desperate to aid my friend.

Behind Larkin, I see a creature step out from a nearby pocket of shadows. Dread fills me as Larkin remains planted, unmoving, only staring at the creature that hisses and stalks in his direction.

"Larkin, behind you," I scream, causing my lungs to burn more.

He acts as if he can't hear me.

It's as if he is completely numb right now, and I can't imagine the horrors he's experiencing.

I remember how it felt the first time I saw Barlowe: his altered yet familiar face, the way he moved, the way he growled. But mostly, it was that he didn't recognize me. My brother looked into my eyes and was willing to kill me without a second thought. That hurt me more than any physical blows he could have landed. It was horrifying and has been burned into my memories, haunting me every time I close my eyes.

I refuse to stand by and let Larkin die.

With one swipe of my axe, I take down another creature, splitting it in two at the waist. I ignore the twitching body beneath me and leap over it, taking one step closer to Larkin. I send a surge of power toward them and push myself faster.

"Move," I continue to scream. "Please, Larkin. Move."

A new threat looms before me, and my vision blurs with the panic and tears streaming from my eyes. Through the creature's lanky arms, I spot Larkin, only staring forward, while the monster behind him raises a claw, poised to drive it into the back of Larkin's head. The black nail glints in the moonlight like a blade, and a sob escapes my throat.

I hear Silas and Oak behind me, fighting fiercely to push forward, but just as I feared, we are outnumbered. My axe clangs against the creature's claw before me, and I don't dare send another surge of power their way for fear I would hit Larkin.

No.

No.

I momentarily stun the creature with a blow to its long, gray leg, just as I see the threat behind Larkin beginning to lower its claw toward his head. My entire world moves in slow motion as the claw slices through the air, and a scream that rattles the mountains around us escapes my throat.

CHAPTER 47

"Larkin," I cry.

I see him blink slowly as he snaps back into his body.

From the shadows, a figure moves toward Larkin so quickly my eyes can barely register it. The towering figure tackles the creature and the talon just misses Larkin's head and instead strikes his left arm.

Cyrus Pierce fights the resurrected, driving his sword into the creature's throat. I glance in all directions, watching concealed Wielders rush down all alleyways, like a deadly curse to their enemies. I hear footsteps in the distance, and relief floods me— the rebels. I slash down the creature before me and sprint toward Larkin, who clutches his arm in pain.

Blood pours from the back of his arm, yet he's alive.

He will survive this. The creature he knows still stands before him, stalking closer with every passing second. I reach Larkin and position myself between the creature and his injured body.

"I'm so sorry," he winces.

"It's okay." I throw a look over my shoulder.

He doesn't respond.

"I have to kill this creature," I say, focusing back on the threat. "Alright?"

Silence.

It crawls closer, and I widen my stance, gripping both axes so tightly my knuckles turn white. I glance past the creature and see Silas and Oak relentlessly fighting, steadily reducing the number of creatures surrounding us. Cyrus stands and whistles into the night sky. Rebels fill the alleyways, taking down creatures one by one. They fight as one—a united force that runs deep and true. We need them for what's coming, and I can only pray that Cyrus didn't settle any debts by saving Larkin's life.

"Larkin," I respond again. "It has to die."

He staggers forward, grimacing from the movement, and steps in between me and the creature.

"Let me do it."

He steps forward, and I extend my hand, offering him one of my golden axes. His gaze finds mine, and determination and sadness settle behind his dark eyes.

The creature growls and lowers its head, preparing to lunge. Within a second, Larkin moves forward and they collide. Screams from the beast rattle my ears as I watch in awe and terror.

Larkin slices the blade across the creature's chest, stumbling backward, before driving it straight into the creature's thick neck. The creature pauses, and death paints its horrific face. It thuds to the ground, and the axe crashes along with it. Larkin's chest heaves, and I race to his side, wrapping my arms around his waist.

"Can you keep moving?" I ask.

He nods.

I lean down, grab my axe, and push us forward away from the chaos in time for Silas and Oak to finish off their creatures. The area around us is a pool of blood, bodies lining every available space.

"Are you two alright?" Silas asks, wiping the blood from his forehead.

"His arm is bad," I respond. "He'll be okay if we can get him to the house."

Silas looks ahead. "We need to hurry."

"What about Cyrus and the rebels?" I ask.

"They will be perfectly fine."

"Are you sure?"

"Absolutely," Silas replies.

I keep a tight grip around Larkin, barely able to pull his large body forward, but our steps begin again as we head down the last alleyway toward the open space of the outskirts of the Andorwood. Our steps become soundless on the soft blades of grass as we cross the last street.

"We need to be fast but aware," Silas shouts over his shoulder. "Oak, get behind Briar and Larkin."

"Keep going," Larkin says. "I'm fine."

"I have to get to Fen." Silas's voice is harsh, but worry paints his expression.

I nod. "I know. Go."

The wide-open sky shines around us, and even in the darkness of the night, I can see that dawn will grace us soon. We head up the hill leading us back to Silas's house, and even though we've made it from the kingdom, I fear what lies ahead.

I glance back toward the town. Screams rise from the center, like smoke filling the air. I can make out small figures as they fight. With the rebels joining, Andorwood has a great chance of emerging victorious.

Larkin flinches with every step, yet continues forward as though the pain is a distant thought. I glance up at him, suppressing the urge to ask the question I desperately want answered.

He casts a look down at me, and such sadness fills his eyes.

"My father," he says.

"What?"

"It was my father."

I stay silent, knowing my words are futile.

"I didn't even know he died," Larkin manages to get out.

"I'm so sorry." I pull him closer and encourage us to hurry up the hill. We can talk once this is behind us. We have to keep moving, even though I know his sorrows threaten to take his legs out from under him.

"You saw Barlowe like that," Larkin says.

My heart flips as I think back to my brother's face, the anger…the animal he had become.

"Yes."

"What did you do?"

"I froze," I respond. "Maines had to kill him."

He stares at me.

"I couldn't do it."

Larkin limps next to me. "I killed him. I disappointed him my entire life, and I killed him."

I take in a deep breath. "He was already gone, Larkin."

I glance up at him, and he averts his gaze, nodding.

"Bury it for now," I say, as I try to pull him back, cupping his face. "We need to focus. We can talk about this later, for as long as you need."

A tear rolls down his cheek, and he wipes it away with the back of his hand. Larkin stands taller, another burst of energy making our steps quicker as his hand wraps around mine with a gentle squeeze.

Up ahead, the wards stand strong against the chaos. I'm immediately impressed by Warrick's warding ability. If you didn't know this house was here, it would seem to vanish, save for the dim shimmer that dances in the moonlight if you look just right.

The cliff is silent, and from the chaos below, it appears as if nothing has transpired here.

Silas slows his pace as we near the grounds. He motions for us to follow his lead, and Larkin almost groans in relief from the slower pace. I release his waist, making sure he's stable, and move toward Silas.

Oak hangs back, making sure Larkin is okay, and pushes him through the ward. They quickly disappear into the house so the healer can work on his mangled arm.

Silas shoots me a glance as I stand beside him.

The moon hangs low, and an eerie silence swirls around us. The clouds move swiftly across the night sky, and the familiar sea breeze hits my face and nose. My senses flare, and I know Silas feels the same as he steps forward toward the cliff. He moves wide around the house, not wanting to draw attention to the cloaked home, and I follow his lead.

We round the house, and at the edge of the cliff stands a figure cloaked in darkness.

Silas freezes, and I narrow my eyes, trying to process who stands before us. Silas glares ahead, clenching his fists, and his shadows begin to pulse in a deafening defense.

Everything within me knows who stands before us, and I want to take a moment to pray that I'm wrong, but the time is up.

We step forward with Silas always slightly ahead of me. As we close the distance, I see him— familiar blonde hair moving in the wind—and as he turns, my heart shatters again.

He slowly turns to face us, and the moon shines off his dark eyes, like thousands of brilliant black diamonds.

Rohhit Harte, now Carobon, stands before us at the cliff's edge.

His long cloak billows in the wind, and a ringing fills my ears, causing me to flinch as Kalix screams deep within my mind.

"KILL HIM," she screams at me. *"Do it while you can. Let me forward and…"*

I block out her vicious, desperate taunts.

Silas rages and acts as if he's going to lunge for him. "Step back, Briar."

I grab his arm, preventing him from stepping forward, and he snaps his gaze to mine.

"No." I stop Silas. "Do not go near him."

A deep laugh reverberates through the air, and Carobon steps forward. The light that surrounds him is oddly dark and exudes a power that no one should ever possess.

"You know what I want," Carobon speaks, and his voice snakes into the open air like a deadly virus.

Silas laughs. "You are insane if you think you are leaving this island with her." He steps forward, and his shadows billow around him in an attempt to drown out any light—Carobon's light.

"Good thing I am insane," Carobon says with a smile, and my stomach twists.

"What do you want in return?" I step forward, and Silas reaches for me, but I slip out of his grip. "What can I give you instead?"

Carobon studies me, his gaze raking over my body. "I want nothing from you, Briar Blackbyrne. At least, not yet," he rasps.

"Name your fucking price," I bite back.

"There will come a time when you offer me this again, and I'm patient. I will wait for that moment, because what I will have…"

He pauses, and a wicked laugh leaves his throat as he shakes his head, as if trying to fight off something we can't see.

"He's strong," Carobon whispers.

I angle my head. "Who?"

The moon dips lower in the sky, and a dim light begins to fill the air with a red, eerie glow. Carobon closes his eyes and delves into his magic, as if calling something or someone forward. A change happens, and Carobon sucks in a deep breath, his shoulders caving forward before he jerks upright, sending a chill down my spine.

I remain still, and my eyes widen as I watch intently.

His hair moves gently in the wind, and my mind struggles to process this. Rohhit stands before me.

"Rohhit?" I step forward.

A heavy exhale leaves his throat, and Rohhit claws against his own temples, as if in miserable pain.

"Gods," I exclaim, and I attempt to rush forward, but Silas stops me.

"Let go." I pull from his hold. "It's him."

Rohhit slowly finds my gaze, and sheer terror sits behind his eyes.

"Briar, listen," Rohhit's voice becomes clear. "I have no idea how long I have. Don't listen to him. Don't give Carobon anything. He doesn't have the stone of Eddris. Yet."

"You are here?" Silas asks, incredulously. "How?"

"Listen to me for fucking once, Nastronde." Rohhit's voice fades in and out. "Don't give him anything."

Silas steps forward. "We aren't."

"Fight him," I begin to cry. "Don't let him forward. Where is the stone in Eddris?"

"It's…too much," Rohhit groans, fighting against himself. "I'm not strong enough."

Rohhit slumps forward, his hands pressing against his thighs as he grinds his teeth in pain.

"No," I shout. "Keep trying."

"I can't," Rohhit rasps. "The stone… it's…"

Tears fall from my eyes, and Silas keeps a tight grip on me, worried I'll rush toward Rohhit.

"Keep. Her. Safe." Rohhit's voice fades.

Fenmore.

"Tell her to…keep trying." A tear flows down Rohhit's cheek as he looks back at us. "Because I can't."

His tall frame shoots back up, his back arching in an unnatural angle. I scream, and step backward into Silas's chest. A guttural sob leaves Rohhit's mouth as he continues to fight against Carobon's pull.

The breeze pauses, and Rohhit's eyes shift back into something darker—something so sinister, I feel I'll never experience happiness again.

"He's gone," Silas whispers.

A growing presence tingles my senses, but I remain facing forward, waiting for the Great Wiitch to make his move.

Carobon rolls his head around his shoulders. "I thought he might want to say hello."

"I'm going to fucking kill you," I seethe.

The Great Wiitch stares past us and claps his hands with delight. "I thought that might do the trick."

My body tenses, and I feel a tremor move through Silas's frame.

We slowly turn away and see Fenmore standing in the shadows of the warded house. Her green eyes widen as she steps forward, noticing Rohhit for the first time. She approaches like a ghost materializing around us, and my entire body feels like it's vibrating with nerves. Fen's mouth slightly parts, and her whole body shakes with a painful urge compelling her to run toward him.

I glance back to Carobon, and for just a moment, I notice his eyes shift—as if seeing her for the first time stirs something within him—and his legs bend ever so slightly.

Rohhit.

Carobon quickly blinks away from her stare, forcing his gaze on us.

"Don't fucking move, Fen," Silas warns.

Her eyes fill with tears as she stares at Rohhit, unable to resist, even though Carobon is present at this moment.

"I… I…" she mumbles, not able to speak words.

"Fenmore," Silas's tone grows harsh.

"It's you." She blinks. "*Rohhit.*"

Carobon steps closer, brushing off his unease, extending his hand. "Do you think you can save him, Fenmore? Do you think you can pull him back from the depths of his own mind?"

She slowly nods and steps forward.

"Fenmore, fucking stop!" Silas shouts.

I rush to Fen and grab her hand. "That isn't Rohhit. I know it's hard, but you have to focus."

"I can't."

"You can't save him if you are dead," I plead.

Carobon laughs. "Gods, always so dramatic. I don't want to kill her. I just want to make sure that she can't call to him any longer. Do you know how annoying it is to always have her voice traveling through my mind?"

Fenmore barely manages to blink, never taking her eyes off the man in front of her.

"He can hear me," she whispers, her green eyes finally finding mine. "I think he's been able to hear me this whole time."

"Focus," I whisper.

She swallows hard and looks back in his direction. I look into her eyes and can see the sorrow swimming in them.

"Rohhit." Tears pool in her eyes. "Can you hear me?"

"Enough." Carobon extends his hand once more. "Now come along, or they will die."

She steps forward, as if the pull is too strong to ignore, and I tug her hand to stop.

"You will have to fucking kill me, then." Silas's shadows strike like black streaks of lightning.

I step further in front of Fen and grab an axe tightly in my hand. Silas holds his sword so tightly that I fear the jeweled hilt will snap in half.

"Just let me go," Fen says. "I can help him."

"No," Silas shouts. "Stop this shit."

"I need to help him," she whispers, a weakness seeping into her words.

From the corner of my eye, I see Warrick emerge from the shadows, like a creature of the night. His footsteps are soundless, and a rage sits behind his eyes that makes my skin crawl. His large body stalks forward, completely concealed by the night that fades with every passing second. The others don't see him.

I place my hand in my pocket and feel the pulse of the power leaking from the stone I possess. I exhale sharply, and expose the power into the open air, pointing it at Carobon.

"I'll give you this," I say, stepping away from Fenmore. "The real one."

The Great Wiitch pulls his gaze to me and tilts his head with feline grace—a smile buds on his lips, and my chest heaves.

Carobon angles his head. "Nolan possesses a fake?"

"Yes," I say, with a nod. "It was a duplicate."

Carobon studies me.

"This is the real Stone of Andorwood." I push my hand forward, bringing it into line with Silas. "I know you are after all of them. Take this one and leave."

"You clever little bitch. No wonder you and Kalix work together so harmoniously." He huffs a wicked laugh. "You are just as cunning as she is."

"Shut your fucking mouth," Silas fumes, pointing his sword forward.

"Take it," I shout.

"Tempting," Carobon says.

I step closer, uncaring of the short distance between us. "Please."

Carobon nods, and I throw the stone at him, harder than necessary.

He catches it with ease and studies the jewel sitting heavy in his hand. I know he can feel the pulses of power coming from it, just as I can. He smiles and wraps his large hand around the stone, the dark green beauty disappearing once more.

"Thank you." Carobon steps backwards.

Carobon shifts, vanishing from in front of me and Silas, and shock rattles me to my soul. We both swirl around to watch his body of light materialize behind Fenmore. His arms wrap around her body, and she screams, the sound reverberating into my mind.

Silas sprints toward his sister in a desperate attempt to stop him from disappearing with her.

Carobon's face twists with delight, and Fenmore continues to scream and kick against his grip. I lunge forward without swinging my axe, fearing that one wrong move, and I could hit Fen.

"See you all very soon," Carobon smiles.

Fenmore lifts her foot, slamming it down atop his. Carobon groans, and she spins, driving her knee into his groin. Carobon grinds his teeth and hisses from the pain, dropping the Andorwood stone onto the earth. He quickly wraps his hands around her throat, spinning her to face us once more.

"Stop," the Great Wiitch screams.

Silas's footsteps thunder, and the rage I've been seeing swarms around him like a hurricane of darkness—a storm of complete death. He tenses his jaw, and even though I was closer to Fen, he's nearing her before I can. Carobon stays focused on us, and that's when I see a figure I forgot about emerge from the darkness.

Warrick sprints toward the Great Wiitch like a streak of lightning.

A blinding glow surrounds him, and he grips a crossbow in his hands, ready to aim as soon as a spot opens. I watch in complete shock as Warrick lifts the bow, aiming for Carobon's body, and fires the arrow dripping in poison. The sharp point swirls through the air, and I watch Carobon's face change from triumph to confusion, watching our gazes look past him. As quickly as the arrow leaves the bow, it finds its mark, lower than anticipated, but lodges directly into Carobon's leg.

An inhuman scream leaves the Great Wiitch's mouth, and his arms loosen around Fen, giving her a split second to race forward, colliding with Silas in his arms. Silas immediately shifts them backward, further away from the chaos breaking out. I continue to sprint forward with the spot now open to swipe my axe across the Great Wiitch's throat. Rage fills me more profoundly than the surrounding sea, and my lungs burn, but I don't let it stop me.

Carobon slowly turns to Warrick, pulling out the arrow wedged into his leg. A thick, black blood trickles slowly down his thigh, and he wipes it with his finger, licking it slowly. He snaps the arrow in two, tossing it to the ground, as if the wound is a mere scratch. I slam my feet across the grass faster, gaining speed and closing the distance.

Carobon waves his hand in my direction, and I fly backward, landing on the hard ground. My lungs gasp for air as I work to refill them from the blow.

"You made a mistake, Lumor Wielder." Carobon glares at Warrick. "Let this be a reminder that you do not attempt to harm your Great Wiitch."

Warrick doesn't stop.

"It doesn't end well." Carobon lifts his hand into the night air, and glances at Fenmore. "This will teach her a lesson as well."

The air around us thickens, and Warrick freezes, time seeming to stand still, while his expression changes into something that will remain in my memories for a lifetime. It changes not to fear or pain, but to a profound regret—a deep regret of what could have been. His gaze slowly moves to Fenmore, and even in the darkness surrounding us, his dark eyes shine into hers. Warrick lowers the bow, dropping it to the ground with a thud, and his shoulders relax as Carobon uses his powers to restrain us all from moving toward him.

He doesn't run; he doesn't attempt to flee. Instead, he uses this time to stare right into Fen's bright green eyes. He studies Fenmore's beautiful face—every freckle and perfect imper-fections.

"Fenmore," Warrick whispers. "You are so beautiful."

"Warrick?" she pleads. "Move."

He tries to take a step forward, but his face contorts into pain as the power stops him from even blinking.

"*Don't look*, Fen," Warrick whispers, and his lip trembles. "Take your eyes off me."

She batters against Silas's hold, cutting her eyes to her brother. A tear rolls down Silas's cheek, and horror floods Fenmore's expression.

Warrick fights against the pain now coursing through his body. "*Please* don't let her watch this, Silas."

He stands tall and unafraid, looking only at her, like she is the one thing that matters to him in this miserable world.

"What? Run, Warrick, please. Shift right now," Fenmore shouts.

"I can't." Warrick smiles, sadly. "I'm sorry."

"Please," Fen weeps, thrashing against her brother's hold. "Move!"

"I'm so sorry," he whispers.

"Don't say that," she begs. "Don't act like this."

"I love you, Fenmore. I always have, and I would have forever."

Barely a whisper leaves her lips, "Warrick."

Carobon snaps his fingers, similarly to what Nolan did on the ship, and I yell, knowing what's coming next. Silas watches in horror, all of us frozen in time, and even the breeze pauses around us.

"No, oh Gods, don't," I scream, getting to my feet.

The sound of Carobon's fingers fills the air, echoing into our minds.

"Don't fucking do this," I beg.

A loud crack fills the night air, followed by a scream from Fenmore that could awaken the dead from the darkest realms. Silas holds Fen back, pulling her face into his chest as she pushes against his grip with everything she has left in her crumbling body.

"Let me go," she pleads. "Let me go to him."

"Fen, stop," Silas begs, a sob breaking from his lips. "Please."

Warrick's strong legs buckle under his weight.

Time moves in slow motion as he falls into the ground, so hard the earth dents around him. A sob fills the air that makes my blood run ice cold.

"Warrick," Fenmore weeps. "Oh, Gods. NO!"

I gaze in horror at Warrick's motionless body, his closed eyes no longer reflecting Fen's terrified gaze—his strong body crumbled to the ground, and a horrifying, unnaturally twisted neck.

CHAPTER 48

I blink in shock, horror, and devastation.

Silas continues to hold Fenmore back, even though she screams, begging to go to Warrick—to help him. I slowly turn my gaze to Silas, and even though rage floods his eyes, they well with heavy tears.

"Silas," Fen begs, sobs distorting her speech. "Help him. Please help him, brother."

A shattered cry escapes her throat, and her entire body convulses.

Carobon just watches us with a blank stare, indifferent to the life he just took—the trauma he just caused—and the loving bond he just broke between two people. With the snap of a finger, Carobon created an everlasting pain that may heal over time, but will never fade.

Silas just holds her, his fingers clutching to her arms in a frantic attempt to keep her at a good distance from Warrick, and in turn Carobon, but I think he also holds her so tightly to keep himself from crumbling.

He holds onto her in hopes that she won't have the same fate, and with each passing second that she can't go to Warrick, I know the pain in her heart only grows.

"I can't," he whispers.

"Why?" she cries.

"I…I can't help him, Fen." Tears stain his cheek. "He's gone."

With a violent turn, Fenmore rips free from Silas's grip and sprints toward Warrick's fallen body. She crashes to her knees, letting out a scream that shatters the fading ward surrounding the house. With each blood-curdling scream, Carobon staggers away from her, as if her misery seeps into him—into Rohhit. The Great Wiitch covers his ears as she continues to bawl, screaming into the air, allowing the sadness and grief to consume her completely, like the darkening shadows around her. Sorrow fills the air, along with the smoke of the burning kingdom in the distance, and tears roll down my cheeks as I watch her process her pain.

I glance at Carobon in shock as his body contorts from her pain, but it isn't Carobon that is suffering.

It's Rohhit.

He isn't gone; Rohhit's still in there, hanging on, and he's pushing with everything he has to come forward because he hears her screams. And, just like I would for Silas, he fights to get to her with all his strength.

Rohhit *needs* her.

She clutches Warrick's broken body and places his head in her lap, gently stroking his hair. Fen falls forward, wrapping herself around him, holding onto any moment she can to still feel his presence. His motionless body appears so fragile, and she clings to him, unable to let go.

Tears fall like rain from her eyes as the sobs continue unabated.

Carobon steps closer to the cliff's edge, watching Fenmore's reaction in disbelief. No longer does contentment paint his face, but instead, a gritting pain as he attempts to fight back Rohhit in his own mind. I slowly gaze toward Silas, who watches his sister sob through uncontrollable pain.

Warrick, his longtime friend—his brother, and most trusted warrior—gone as quickly as he had run toward his sister, uncaring for his own life. He is gone, and despite the recent pain, he cared more about saving her than he ever worried about himself. A single tear rolls down Silas's face as he watches one of his worst nightmares come to life.

Silas wipes the wetness from his cheeks and slowly turns toward the cliff's edge. Shadows darker than the darkest realm flicker against his back, and he lowers his gaze, his blazing green eyes glowing in the night.

A voice I've never heard before leaves his lips. "Get out of here while you still have the fucking ability to do so." His voice claps like thunder. "Because if I reach you, if my shadows touch you and I wrap my hands around your miserable throat, I will wipe you from this realm."

Silas's shadows grow even larger as the words leave his lips, and magic pours from his body, creating a threat of darkness in his wake.

"I will shatter your very fucking existence, whether the Prince of Eddris is there or not, Carobon." Silas fumes as his voice becomes deeper. "That is a promise."

Fen continues to cry behind him, and Carobon steps back one last time.

She raises her head and stares directly into Carobon's wild eyes. "Help him, Rohhit. Please, help him."

The plea is desperate and realm-shattering, and from a distance, I can see Carobon mumbling to himself, screaming at someone who isn't physically there. I know for certain that Rohhit fights. We can do this. We can pull him forward with Fen's help.

"Rohhit," she whispers, reaching for him. "Help Warrick."

Carobon gasps and takes one last look toward us before vanishing into thousands of blinding, bright lights.

Fen slowly bows her head again, aware that her pleas and begs will remain unanswered. She caresses Warrick's face with her trembling hands and rests her head against his as she rocks back and forth. Through the chaos, through the howling wind that seems to lament his death alongside us, I hear her whisper, "I love you too, and I would have always chosen you, Warrick Pierce… always."

Silas staggers backward, dropping his sword to the earth, letting the exhaustion of his outburst and emotions nearly take his strong body to the ground.

The sharp metal sticks into the soil, and I watch him. His chest heaves, and his shadows don't dim as I slowly walk to him, placing my hand on his shoulder. The darkness emanating from him seeps into my hand, but I hold still. He flinches from my touch and turns around, grabbing my wrist. Fury sits behind his glowing green eyes, which pulse between the Wielder I know and something else entirely. My jaw slackens at his twisted, unfamiliar face.

"Breathe," I say, trying to keep my voice calm. "Try to breathe."

His hand stays wrapped around my wrist, and for a moment, he looks through me, like he doesn't recognize my face through the anger, pain, and panic. His eyes shine into the darkness, and only chaos swirls behind his gaze.

"Silas," I say, reaching forward with my free hand to cup his face. "Let go of my wrist."

He blinks, coming to his senses once more, and drops my wrist. He fights back tears and collapses to his knees on the ground, weak from devastation and exhaustion. I fall alongside Silas and wrap my arms around his neck, pulling him as close to me as possible.

"He's gone." Tears fall from Silas's eyes. "Warrick. He's… dead."

My hand slides up, and I place it on the back of his head while he weeps into the crook of my neck. His desperate sobs fill the air, and my heart shatters, feeling his entire body tremble against mine.

"I'm sorry." I begin to cry with him, squeezing him tighter. "I'm so sorry, Silas."

With the ward gone, the house comes into view along with the rising sun. The screams coming from the kingdom are replaced with cheers from the Andorwood civilians. A thick smoke fills the air, and a blazing fire roars from the ship of the resurrected—they've set it on fire.

The Kingdom of Andorwood has survived this battle. We've won, and we can rebuild this kingdom, but the damage done to Silas and Fen can never be repaired.

Fen softly kisses Warrick's cheek, whispering something only she can hear, before standing, a numbness settling behind her dull eyes.

She turns, and her bloodshot eyes land on us. Fen crosses the yard and reaches for Silas's hand, pulling him to stand. He follows her lead and stands, slipping from my embrace, and turning to face the house.

Oak races out of the house and freezes when he sees Warrick's body on the ground.

He slows but makes his way toward me, his face paling.

"Fuck." Oak grabs my hand. "We need to get them inside. Larkin can't see this, not after tonight."

I nod and glance toward Fen and Silas. They stand hand in hand, staring at Warrick's lifeless body on the ground in silence. Never have I seen Silas appear so tired—so defeated—as his shoulders curl in. His head drops as his messy hair falls across his face, and his hand wraps tighter against Fenmore's. She doesn't break her forward gaze, only focused on the last few moments she has with him.

"I'm going to get something to cover him up," Oak says, and rushes back into the house, leaving me outside with Fen and Silas.

I slowly approach them.

"Let's get you two inside," I whisper, and wipe the falling tear from my eye.

Fen looks at me with a blank stare and nods, pulling Silas to follow her. The rising sun casts hues of pink, orange, and red across the sky, and I grimace. Red—always so much red—and I'm sick of the color always surrounding me. I turn, and my gaze lands on something glowing in the yard—the stone.

Carobon, so distracted by the sobs coming from Fen, left the stone. I pick it up and pocket it before I follow them into the house.

We pass Oak on the way in, and he carries a white sheet—his face frantic and filled with grief.

Silas and Fen walk down the staircase, and Oak grabs my arm, making me stop a few stairs up.

"What the fuck happened?" Oak's eyes flash concern.

"Carobon," I muster the words out. "He killed him without even touching him."

"My Gods," he responds.

"But…" I stumble over the words. "Rohhit. He's not gone, Oak. He's in there, holding on. Fen's cries shocked Carobon, like Rohhit was fighting to come forward."

Oak mumbles. "She can help us pull him back, then."

I glance down the stairs, and dread settles into my core like a brick. "I don't think she'll help us do anything regarding Carobon again."

Oak makes a pained face before rushing from the house to attend to Warrick.

I move down the stairs to find Fen curled in on herself before the roaring fire, her bright green eyes contrasting with the reddened skin around them. Her blank stare tells me she's in shock, but at least the numbness has taken over. I think back to my times of grief, and being dazed is the only reason I made it out a few times.

Rose stands in the kitchen, doing what she does best—making food. She shows her love that way, and in a few hours, every open space in this house will be covered in treats. She gives me a relieved nod and continues her work. Maines's bedroom door is shut, and I pray she's sleeping peacefully, unaware of what's happened.

I look toward the balcony, and I see two figures standing there—Silas and Larkin.

I tiptoe to the edge of the threshold, and they speak quietly. Larkin's arm is in a sling, tightly placed against his body, but it's okay and will heal.

Their whispers fill the air, and I hear Silas say, "He's gone, Larkin."

Larkin's head drops forward, and his eyes close tightly as he grips the edge of the railing to steady himself. He curses under his breath, and I watch a tear fall and soak the concrete railing of the balcony.

Their friend, after all these years, is gone. After they have always protected one another.

Silas places his hand across Larkin's back and squeezes.

"How?" Larkin's voice cracks, as a near-silent sob leaves his lips.

"Protecting her," Silas whispers. "Like he always did."

I walk to the edge of the railing and remain silent on the other side of Larkin. I hear quiet sniffles come from his lowered head, and he doesn't raise it when I join them. Instead, Larkin's hand slowly slides toward mine and wraps around it tightly. I glance on the other side of Larkin and gaze into Silas's bloodshot eyes.

Silas's face harbors such sadness, but for the moment, I'm glad the rage is gone. He needs to feel something—anything—other than fury in this moment.

The three of us stand there together, gazing at the vast world before us, hand in hand.

Together.

We have many things ahead of us—pain, suffering, and endless worries—that stack higher than the surrounding mountains. We will endure exhaustion, sadness, and maybe, just maybe, we will have a few moments of togetherness—moments where the pain seems worthwhile.

We will have our time to fight back, to reclaim what we lost, and we will have our time when peace falls over this land once more. I have no idea how we are going to get there, but I look around me and see a group of people who want the same things that I do. They desire peace, love, and a world where no suffering falls upon those who wish to thrive in a simple life.

I glance at Silas, and he looks at me intensely, our souls connecting for a moment. Neither of us speaks, hoping not to disturb Larkin in this moment of pure silence.

"We will get through this," I say in my mind.

"How can you be so sure?"

"Because we have to." I attempt to smile. *"And because we have each other."*

Silas nods, glancing back to the sea and the rising sun on the horizon.

"We can do this."

"Together," he responds.

"Together."

CHAPTER 49

A few days later.

The crisp morning air stings my face as we all move to the edge of the cliff. The sun sits low in the sky, bestowing a peaceful glow upon us that fills the world around us. The air is light, and we walk in unison toward a small area prepped by Oak and Rose for this moment—a memorial for Warrick.

A small, grassy path leads us toward the area, and I keep my gaze forward. I walk hand in hand with Silas. Larkin and Fen walk behind us, while Oak assists a limping Maines down the path. Rose stands before the small pillar, and I hold my breath, forcing myself to look.

A white sheet flutters in the wind, covering a large body—Warrick's.

I squeeze Silas's hand, letting him know that I'm here, as I fight back the tears that want to flow. The morning sky is filled with a beautiful warming light, and I can't help but think that

Warrick is here right now, using his Lumor abilities to cast us—and this moment—in such a lovely glow.

A few chairs have been placed around the area for us to sit, share a few words, and dedicate a lovely moment to Warrick, and Warrick only. Fen quietly sobs as she sits closest to him, followed by me and Silas, with Larkin on the other side.

Since the trip was far, Maines and Oak stay at a distance, so we don't exhaust her too much. The healers warned that even shifting her during this fragile state could be detrimental to her healing journey, so heading back to the mainland isn't going to be an option for a while.

We can continue our plans from here. Plus, Andorwood seems like home at this point.

Over the past few days, Oak has mentioned the darkness that seems to sit on Maines's shoulders like an ever-present shadow, but I can't feel it—it's like I've been shut out. He's so worried about her, and I can't blame him.

Seeing someone you love suffer like that changes you—always for the stronger, but never for the better.

Rose stands before us, dressed in a beautiful gown, and begins to speak in her softest voice about what it's like to love and to lose. She talks about how people cope with grief, and how, over time, everyday pain eases, but the deep wound that death leaves never disappears—like a dark stain on your soul.

Death is an invisible, deep scar that we all will share.

Everyone except Fenmore fights back tears, but we all listen together, letting the soft breeze surround us like a peaceful whisper.

The sky above us is beautiful. White clouds that look like you could sit on them fill the sky, and the sea is like a sheet of brilliant glass. A small fire burns near our chairs, and a torch sits close by.

The past few nights, I've spent time with Silas, talking into the late hours until he passes out from exhaustion—usually in my arms. Larkin has also been keeping close, while Fen prefers her own company. Oak spends most of his time with Maines, helping her recover by going on short walks and engaging in various forms of therapy. We've had no luck reading anything further in the book we retrieved from the Archives. We will have to wait until Oak's grandfather can get his hands on it to truly understand what we possess.

In the meantime, we will study, train, prepare, and rebuild Andorwood from the losses of the battle before we make our way back to the mainland.

Rose steps down from her post and is replaced by Fenmore. She stands on unsteady legs and moves toward the platform with Larkin's assistance. Her footsteps are silent on the soft grass, and her hands quiver at her sides, but she remains tall. Fen stares at the white sheet covering Warrick for a long while before facing us in the small gathering.

A tear rolls down her cheek.

"I've gone back and forth for days about what I could possibly say to you all that might help ease the pain—the wound we all feel—but I couldn't think of anything." She shakes her head. "I couldn't think of a single fucking word that would help any of us."

Silas squeezes my hand, trying to keep himself from falling into despair.

"Grief is an odd thing." Fen's voice trembles. "It ebbs and flows like the tides, building and crashing into us like the waves at random times, and it's deep—deeper I fear, than the sea that surrounds us and deeper than the love that he had for you all." She fights back tears. "Warrick wouldn't want us to be sad. In fact, he would be so annoyed that we sit here today doing this."

A hushed giggle mixed with a painful sob leaves Larkin's lips, reminiscing on his friend and how true that statement is.

"Warrick was strong, so we must be strong." Fen glances

behind her at his body. "Warrick was wise, and he was quiet, because he used every moment to soak in his surroundings, watching us as if he were always memorizing the best parts of his life." She turns her gaze, the pain of looking at him too much to bear. "I will live my life that way, now. I will be strong, wise, and quiet in my efforts to absorb the world around me, and I will always remember the good moments and cherish the hard ones for shaping me into the person I am today."

She pauses for a moment and leans down to grab the blazing torch.

Larkin and Silas rise, walking to stand alongside her as they ignite the wood with an intense flame. They move toward Warrick's covered body together.

Fen stumbles backward, as if getting too close pains her. From my chair, I see Larkin's hand go to the small of her back, and Silas takes the lit torch from her trembling hands.

Larkin steps back a few paces with her, holding her as she buries her head in his chest, letting the sobs pour from her quivering lips.

Silas stands alone at the edge of the cliff before Warrick, having a moment of silence with his friend for the last time while the lit torch roars in his unwavering hand. His hair whips in all directions, but this time he's steady, as if the task before him is sure. He releases a long exhale and takes a step forward.

Tears stream down my cheeks as I watch him slowly lower the flames, and my hand slowly covers my mouth. My heart flips, causing uneven breaths to come from my lips.

Even in the breeze, the sheet covering his body becomes engulfed in a red glow. Silas takes a moment before turning his back slowly. His eyes are red, but no tears fall onto his expressionless face. He walks back to where I sit, and in this moment, I can tell that his body is an empty shell.

We sit in silence, watching the flames devour the platform.

Given the horrors we've witnessed and with the resurrection stone still out there, there was no way we could bury Warrick—it isn't a risk we're willing to take.

I glance across the sea and watch as the sun shines brighter, casting thousands of diamonds that dance on the water. The warm breeze moves around us, and Silas takes my hand.

I place my other one on top of his.

"I'm here," I say in my mind.

He doesn't respond; instead, he tightens his grip around my hand, desperate to remain steady. He's restraining himself from crumbling.

"I'm always here," I repeat.

It's quiet except for the crackling flames, windless breeze, and crashing waves below. It's peaceful and even in this devastating moment, defeat doesn't surge through me. Hope does.

The minutes pass by as we remain as a group on the cliff.

Together.

Silas opens his mouth to speak, but pauses, a twisted look of concern etching his face. The wind changes, sending a gust of icy air swirling around us. I glance over at Silas, who furrows his brow as he looks toward the forest behind us. The puffy, white clouds begin to rush across the sky, and a leaden sky replaces them quickly, making all hope I had disappear. I slowly stand and look toward Larkin and Fen, whose faces reflect the same level of unease.

"Briar," Silas whispers. "Do you feel that?"

My shadows scream at me to run, to get up and race them all somewhere else, but I don't react—I can't—and the familiar haunting feeling I've once felt creeps into my body, soul, and mind. I'm frozen, and I'm taken back in time to when this happened twice before.

"Hello, Briar." An ancient male's voice snakes into my mind, and I go deathly still. *"Hope I'm not interrupting."*

I whip my head in all directions, and Silas notices my panic.

We all look around, each of us feeling the apparent shift from lightness to a devastating darkness.

Oak slowly stands, and his hands begin to tremble at his sides. We all shift our gaze away from Oak, unsure of what he sees in this moment.

The color drains from my face as I think of who also sits back there.

Maines.

I slowly turn, and a dread I've never felt before settles in my chest, causing me to stagger backward into Silas's body.

"No," I say.

Malachi stands behind Maines, Hux at his side, with his hand wrapped around her shoulders. Her face is horrified, and she sits still, too afraid to move and still too injured to run. Oak stands nearby, but is frozen. His head is slightly tilted, and I notice something pressing into the side of his throat—an invisible claw ready to end his life if the order is given.

Fen and Larkin slowly take a step toward us, unsure of what to do or how to help.

Malachi wears a smile of triumphant madness on his face, and Hux's face remains hard, uncaring that his once friend lies dead before him. Hux's shadows dance in the sunlight, and an evil radiates from him, mimicking Malachi's.

"What a lovely morning," Malachi's awful voice sounds toward us.

"Maines," Oak says, attempting to take another step forward. "You are okay."

"Oak," her lips quiver, understanding the severity of the moment.

"It's going to be alright." Oak attempts a reassuring smile but fails. "Just sit still, darling."

She nods, trying to remain calm, but the panic shows all over her face.

"No, it actually won't be," Malachi responds. "You shouldn't lie."

"Get the fuck out of here, Malachi," Silas's voice booms, and black shadows begin to swirl around us from the King of Darkness.

In the morning sun, you can see the shimmers of the creatures surrounding Malachi. He's not alone, even though one would think he is, besides Hux. The Travelers lurk invisibly, ready to do Malachi's bidding and strike should he give the signal.

We are completely surrounded.

He traces the side of Maines's face, and a whimper leaves her throat.

"You see, the thing is, I've grown increasingly bored since leaving, and I had a thought I couldn't shake." He angles his head and stares at Maines. "The night of Yara's unfortunate death, I said something to Briar."

I go deathly still, but my heart knocks as if it will break through my chest.

"Do you remember what I said?" he asks, staring directly at me.

No one responds, and the dark, rolling clouds begin to churn like a growing storm. The sea below us no longer resembles glass, but is a hurricane of pure chaos.

"Oh, you all are no fun," Malachi teases. "If I can't have Briar, I had an idea that drawing you to me against your will would be so much more amusing."

I step forward. "Don't you fucking dare."

"I think I will," he says, smiling maliciously.

"We will fucking kill you," Silas warns. "This is a death sentence."

Malachi leans forward, wrapping his arms around Maines's shoulders. He tilts his head, smelling the nape of her neck, and uses his tongue to trace up the side of her jaw. She winces against his touch, and I hear her spit. A wetness coats his face, and Malachi takes his finger, wiping the spit off, before sticking his finger in his mouth.

"Yes, she will be just the entertainment I'm looking for," he laughs.

I hear footsteps first as Oak races forward, faster than a bolt of lightning. He grinds his teeth and dives into his power, summoning a blinding light that rests in his palms.

"Come find me when you are ready, Briar," Malachi calls. "We will be waiting."

"Malachi," I whisper.

"Tick-tock," he smiles.

Hux vanishes before our eyes, shifting into a darkness that settles into my soul.

"Fuck!" I scream.

Malachi disappears next, and I watch Maines fade into the darkness around him.

Oak yells and refuses to let his magic escape, for fear that he will hit Maines, but he powers forward.

Tears well in my eyes as I watch a dark trail of shadows move through the forest. Oak releases his magic, and a blast of white light envelops us, knocking us all backward. My ears ring from the explosion, but I ignore the pain, propping myself on my elbow to watch the shadows retreat deeper into the forest, further away with each passing second. I stand and race forward, disregarding the pain radiating through my body.

"Briar," Silas screams after me.

No.

No.

This is my fault.

I run, shifting in small bouts to chase the shadows with Oak at my heels, but they fade faster than we can move. I watch in horror as Malachi drags Maines directly to a place I never wished to revisit, a place that haunts me—the place I died.

Yet, it's a place I'm willing to enter, even if it means dying again to save her.

My hazel eyes fade away and are replaced with unholy black as anger, rage, and desperation pile on top of each other, sending me spiraling into a blind madness.

Their shadows vanish, and my fierce heart splinters into a million pieces as Malachi drags Maines directly into the place where the shadows were formed and darkness will be destroyed.

The closest place to the darkest realm that exists.

Where I will confront my demons and enemies directly, and… Bring. Her. Back.

From Death's Opening.

CHAPTER 50

BONUS POV

Maines Madden

After the Forgotten Archives

I'm awake, yet I don't open my eyes.

A blinding pain forces my eyes shut, and I don't dare move out of fear and the burning sensation that travels through my legs and lower back. The sheets are soft, but nothing matters except the pain. I hear shuffling around me, and the scent of herbs fills my nose. I know that healers are here. The rhythmic motion of their actions and the scents immediately clue me in that they are working.

On me.

I remember the Archives, the beast that haunts the space, and the overpowering smell of smoke. So much smoke. I squeeze my eyes tighter, perhaps hoping that this time I'll wake up and this won't be real. I won't be injured, and my legs won't feel as if they are melting from my body.

Around me, I feel the warmth of the sun filling the room, yet no matter how many blankets lie upon me, I still feel cold to my very soul, as if something stains me. I move my hand over the soft sheets, still sluggish from sleep and the medicine, and I pause. Another hand rests gently on the bed. My fingers trace the large, calloused hand that lies on the sheets, and I immediately know who it belongs to.

Oak.

I hear the rustling of the sheets, as if someone is lifting their head off the mattress. I keep my eyes shut, not quite ready to see the pain I know will rest upon his handsome face. As quickly as I find his hand, Oak's fingers slowly trace mine. His skin is warm and almost burns my icy flesh. His hand travels up my arm, and he slowly pets my broken body, but doesn't speak. I can only imagine the chaos swirling in his brilliant mind.

Even with my eyes closed, I feel as though I can perceive a bright light radiating from Oak. However, no matter how much light spills into the room around me, I can't shake the feeling of something dark creeping into my mind.

It started slowly, like a dull itch I could never scratch, but every day, it seems to be growing like vines up a decaying tree. Darkness is normal to us as Shadow Wielders, but this is different. Darker and more ancient than anything I've ever experienced.

I need to inform the others, but doing so would only lead to more concern, and I'm not trying to frighten them further than I already have.

I hear Oak whisper something to one of the healers beside the bed, but I can't make out the words, as if the daze I'm in is dulling all my senses. The large wooden door creaks open and is quickly shut once more, as if she is alerting someone in the hallway to my growing consciousness.

"Maines," Oak whispers, but I keep my eyes shut. His hand travels back down to mine, and his rough fingers wrap around it like a perfect fit.

I don't respond, partly because I'm not sure if I can, but instead, I squeeze Oak's hand twice. I hear a muffled sob escape his throat as he stands, moving even closer to the bed this time.

"Maines Madden, open those beautiful eyes, darling," his calm voice calls. "Please."

I feel myself drifting back into the darkness of sleep, as if someone else is calling to me, pulling me deeper into thoughts of nothingness. I try to speak this time, but the pull drags me further down, and I can't fight the sleep knocking at my mind. But fear floods me, because my last conscious thought is, *this isn't sleep.*

Seconds, minutes, hours pass—I'm not sure which—and I feel myself resurfacing into reality again. I return to the pain and my own body, where I sense the ever-present light—Oak—surrounding me once more.

Another opening of the door catches my attention, and I hear footsteps approaching the bed. Oak lifts his head from the sheets once more to greet whoever is coming. The familiar smell of fresh florals mixed with a dark amber fills my nose, and I know who stands at the end of the bed.

Briar.

I slowly crack open my eyes, and the bright light blinds me momentarily. I squint against the contrast of the darkness I'm used to, and she comes into focus. Her beautiful black hair falls to her waist, and it's soaking wet as she wears a face of concern. I smile, unable to resist the sight of her before me.

A rat.

She looks like a soaking wet rat.

I let my lips part, and a soft smile spreads across my face. Briar moves around the bed and sits next to Oak. I slowly shift my gaze until my eyes find his. Oak's eyes are red and swollen, and a pang of hurt fills my heart, knowing I caused the worry reflected in his expression. His usually cheerful, handsome face is now clouded with anxiety and unease.

"There you are," Oak whispers. "Thank the fucking Gods."

He leans forward, kissing my forehead and nose, then moves to my lips, even as exhaustion washes over him. Oak's kiss is tender and perfect like usual, yet I can taste the desperation on his lips, as if he never believed this would happen again.

I say a silent promise to myself that I will never cause him pain again until the day I die.

"I'm… here," I respond.

Through the worry, he smiles, and I feel the pain in my legs disappear as happiness spreads through my body like wildfire. His dark eyes burn into mine, and I take a deep breath. Oak gently brushes my hair from my forehead, and I can't help but let myself beam with love for him.

I'm safe.

I'm not sure what I've done in my life to deserve Oak Hombern, but I thank the Gods every day for him. He quickly stands and helps me sit up a bit in bed to get a better look at my friends before me. I can't help but make a joke about Briar's rat-like state, and her laughter fills the air like a wonderful dream.

We engage in a conversation about the chaos I caused, and I learn all the information I missed while I've been asleep. I try to stay alert and as cheerful as I can, but the pain is nearly unbearable. Every time I wince, Oak is right there, checking in or ensuring I can shift in bed to keep me as comfortable as possible. Without him, I doubt I would be here now.

The healers approach the bed, slowly lifting the sheets to examine my legs, and I fight the urge to give them orders, as if I'm back at the House of Hedro working on my own patients.

With each question I pose to Oak and Briar, I'm met with resistance, as if the true news they possess would overwhelm me too much. Exhaustion hangs over me like an ever-present veil, and I can't shake the feeling of darkness coursing through my veins. Everything hurts, but this only amplifies my discomfort.

"You rest right now," Briar says. "I love you, Maines."

I smile and watch their faces fade as I close my eyes, only pretending that I've fallen asleep. I can hear them rustling around the room, and their voices begin to fade. Briar likely pulled Oak to a corner of the room to give me the quiet I need to rest.

Yeah, right.

I hear them begin to speak about me in hushed voices that I can barely make out. Their voices are filled with concern, and I fight the urge to open my eyes to announce that I'm not asleep and they should stop talking about me as if I'm dying. However, I guess I'll cut them some slack, because I almost did.

The door opens once more, and I hear another person enter the room. Darkness envelops the space as it always does when he enters a room, and I recognize who has crossed the threshold.

Silas Nastronde.

I remain completely still, not alerting them to the fact that I'm awake and listening to their conversations. I hear Oak and Silas drift into their usual annoying banter while Briar huffs at them to pay attention by snapping her fingers in their face. I fight back the urge to giggle.

A discussion arises about the recent events. They share their findings about the book, the ancient language, and how Oak's grandfather can likely assist with the translation once we reach the mainland again.

The longer I remain still, listening, the closer I get to falling. I fight it as hard as I can, but the nothingness that sleep offers knocks on my mind. Oak argues with Briar and Silas about when his translations will begin, and warmth spreads through my cold body when I hear Oak mention that he won't be leaving my side anytime soon.

I tell myself that it's okay for me to drift off to sleep when I hear the words leave Oak's mouth, and my entire body goes rigid, sending a wave of pain through my system.

"I have to tell you both something," he whispers to Briar and Silas. "I can't shake the feeling that there's something more. She seems to be her normal self, but there's something else—a darkness I've never felt from her."

He knows. Oh, Gods, he can feel something too.

My entire body goes rigid, causing a flash of pain to nearly make me flinch.

Briar chimes in, assuring him that it's nothing to worry about, and I relax a little bit, knowing that she doesn't feel anything out of the ordinary. Maybe it's in our heads, and the effects of the injury are making me feel off. That's all.

Oak speaks again, "I felt it before that."

Dread envelops my broken body, and I nearly jolt up at that. He's felt it longer than I have. How is this happening right now?

Sleep is near now; I can't resist it or the medicine coursing through my body.

Stay awake.

I drift further down the tunnel of my mind, unable to make out their words. I only hear mumbles and the faint movements of my friends in the room with me. Before I completely fall asleep, I feel Oak sit down beside me, and his glow shines into the darkness of my mind brighter than the sun. I'm safe with him around; the darkness can't find me with him close.

"*You are not safe,*" I hear a voice whisper into my mind as I fall asleep.

I awake in pure darkness.

I take a moment to focus on my surroundings and calm my racing heart. Pain surges through me, but by now, the persistent throbbing feels normal. The house is not quiet. I hear footsteps echoing through the hallways, and the clang of metal resonates in the living space down the hall. Hushed whispers bring me back to my senses, and I muster all the strength I can to sit up in my bed.

Oak is in the far corner putting on his clothes when he notices that I'm awake. He bounds over to me.

"I'm so sorry I woke you up," he says, cupping my face. "You should go back to sleep."

"What is going on?" I ask.

He sighs, and I watch his face harden into concern and misery. "The ships are here."

My stomach flips, and a wave of nausea almost makes me sick that very second.

"It's going to be alright, darling," Oak leans closer, his delicious scent flooding my system and calming my pounding heart. "Rose is going to stay with you. She is more than prepared."

"You can't go," I move my hand to his and tighten my grip. "Please don't go."

"I have to." Oak's hand, still cradling my face, begins to trace softly along my jawline. "I can't let them do this alone."

Silence envelops the dark room, and I grimace for several reasons. My body aches now, echoing the pain in my heart.

I lower my gaze. "You are right."

"I'm coming back, Maines." His dark eyes shine into mine. "I will always come back to you."

"If anything happens to you, Hombern." Tears begin to well in my eyes. "I'll… I'll…"

"Nothing is going to happen to me," he interrupts, noticing my increasingly frantic state.

"Oak," I whisper.

He wastes no time in crashing his lips to mine as he slips his calloused hand behind my neck, gently bringing my face even closer to his. Fragile state or not, he's using this moment to say goodbye. His tongue sweeps through my mouth, and despite the pain, I kiss him deeper.

A low guttural growl escapes from his chest that vibrates into mine, and his fingers tangle in my hair as he curls his hands into a fist.

"Maines," he whispers against my lips, and I pull him back into the kiss.

He gently pushes against my body, lying me back down against the warm mattress. He carefully moves his hands to my waist, slipping them underneath the hem of my shirt, and a thrill rushes straight to my core. His rough hands draw circles against my skin that chase away the icy feeling in my bones as they travel closer to my breasts.

I wrap my hands tighter against his neck and pull him to me as his body nearly falls onto mine. I shift under the pain that moves through me, uncaring of anything other than our connection, but he flinches.

"I hurt you," he whispers against me, pulling back slightly.

"No!" I snap. "I'm okay."

"Liar." He playfully kisses me, his hands still wrapped in my hair.

I narrow my eyes at him, still only inches away, and he playfully licks my lips, then my nose, giving it a playful nip.

I smile.

"I need to get going," Oak says, looking toward the door.

"I don't want you to leave." I feel the lump form in my throat.

"I'll return to do that again as soon as I can." Oak smiles. "I'll be safe."

"Stay by Briar," I respond. "She will keep you safe."

"That's already my plan," he winks.

"Be safe, Oakie," I call, as he bounds toward the room's threshold.

"Seriously?" He pauses, slowly turning his eyes to meet my gaze. "Please don't call me that right before I'm about to go into a literal battle. I need to be tough, Maines."

"Oh, you are so tough, Oakie." I tease.

He bounds across the room once more and presses his lips against mine, nearly making my eyes roll to the back of my head.

"You are only allowed to call me that in the bedroom."

I smile. "We are in the bedroom."

He quickly pulls away, our foreheads resting together for a second.

"Be back soon," he whispers, breaking our connection.

"You better be."

His chuckle follows him into the hall as he pulls the door closed behind him, and even though I giggle with him, my heart slowly breaks, matching my body as the distance grows between us.

I sit alone in the dark room, hearing the continuous shuffling of feet. With every passing second, the hustle becomes more frantic, and I know my friends are out there preparing to fight with everything they have. My anxiety bubbles in my chest like the rising sea, and I can't remain here. I can't just sit back and let them go into battle without at least saying something to each of them.

I rip back the covers and stare at my legs—the first time I've allowed myself to do so. My jaw drops open. My skin is healed, yes, but deep scars line my legs, and a blue discoloration paints them like bruises that will never fade. I remind myself that the healers still work on my legs daily to dull the scarring, but my stomach falls at the sight.

I dangle one leg over the bed, and a blinding pain washes over me. The air leaves my lungs, and I grind my teeth, pulling my other leg to join the dangling one. With careful ease, I touch both of my feet to the cold floor. The sensation is odd, considering I haven't stood in days, but I trust my body to know what to do as I shift my weight onto both of my legs.

My body trembles, and I curse, already feeling defeated by my own body for betraying me.

Damnit.

I hang onto the bed, gripping my fists into the sheets, knowing I don't have much time to get out there before they leave, and I'm possibly too late. I release the comfort of my stability and allow myself to stand freely on my own. Pain jolts through every inch of my body, but I ignore it and shuffle one foot closer to the door.

I reach the handle and pull the door open slightly to get a better idea of what's going on in the house. Hushed but panicked whispers fill the air, along with the rapid footsteps of the others moving to prepare for what's coming. Their shadows dance off the walls, and I know they are trying to be as quiet as possible.

For me.

I shuffle down the hallway and lay eyes on them as the room opens up. They don't notice me tucked into the last pocket of shadows in the corridor, but I watch them for a moment. Briar talks quietly with Rose as she sips her tea while Fen and Oak finish dressing in their armor, and Silas watches the balcony—as if waiting for the creatures to rush into the house at any moment. I clutch the wall nearest to me to keep it from crumbling, but I can do this. I can say goodbye to my friends.

"Briar?" I whisper, not realizing how weak my voice is.

They all pause and whip their heads in my direction as if they have seen a ghost. Briar bounds across the room in my direction, and she wraps her arms around my waist, keeping me upright. I can't help but smile, their faces registering pure shock, and I feel a sense of accomplishment that I've at least made it this far in my current state.

Oak quickly moves next to Briar.

"I'm offended you all think you could leave without saying goodbye to me," I say.

Oak chimes back, reassuring me that he did say goodbye, and I know he did. I roll my eyes. I mean the others: Briar, Silas, and Fenmore. I needed to see Briar— my best friend—before she left.

"Promise me, Briar, that you will return." My eyes fill with tears, and I can't stop my body from trembling from the pain and sadness flowing through my system like a river.

"I will come back, Maines," Briar says. "I promise."

I hear her words and register them; however, it's her tone that puts me on edge. I know she will return, that I will see her again, but she made that promise to me, not knowing in what state she would be in when she returned.

I glance at Silas; his face is as hard as usual, but he gives me a nod without speaking—our silence an understanding that we've grown to share between each other. I understand what he means at this moment. He's going to do everything in his power to return her to this house in one piece, regardless of what that means for his own life. He will protect Briar and will make every effort to do so. Silas Nastronde might be many things, but he is loyal, and I'd happily entrust Briar's life to him.

Oak places his hand on the small of my back and leads me down the hallway back to the bedroom.

"I'm going to lay her down, and then I'll shift to the pier to meet you all shortly." He calls to the others, and they nod.

Briar keeps her gaze fixated on me as I disappear down the dark hallway. My hands begin to tremble, and I feel as if my chest is caving in. Panic rises in me, and with each step I move away from my friend, the more isolated I feel and the more I feel the darkness creep inside—as if it thrives when I'm alone.

Oak opens the bedroom door, crosses the room, and assists me into bed once more. A tear rests heavily on my lower lid and drops, swiftly rolling down my cheek like rain. Oak uses his thumb to wipe away the tear before sitting next to me on the bed.

"Are you alright?" he asks.

The tears don't let up. "I think something bad is going to happen."

"I'm going to be okay, darling." Oak grabs both of my hands, pulling me to face him. "Nothing is going to happen to me, because I won't allow it."

"How do you know?"

"I told you I will never leave you, Maines Madden, and I meant it. I've done a lot of stupid things in my life, but lying to you will never be one of them. We have too much left to do in our lives for that." He cups my face tighter. "Too much to do together."

I nod, and Oak leans closer, pressing his soft lips against mine.

"If you needed another kiss," he says against me, "you should have just said so."

My tears wet his cheeks, and he pulls back, gazing into my eyes. I chuckle at his ridiculousness, and he takes the opportunity to smile at the sound.

"Maines Madden," Oak whispers, his forehead against mine. "I love you. And I needed to tell you that."

A hushed sob leaves my throat, and the darkness subsides for only a moment.

"I love you too, Hombern."

He smiles, and I know he's happy, but the weight of what's to come dulls his joy.

"I need to go," Oak says, standing and moving across the room, but not before turning back one last time to look upon me.

Even in my disheveled state, he gazes at me as if I'm the only person in this world. As if I'm the only person of importance, and despite being beaten, burned, and bruised, he makes me feel beautiful.

Oak leaves the room, and the door closes behind him, leaving me alone in the darkness with my thoughts. My chest heaves. I can't shake the unsettling feeling that looms over me like a dark storm moving in. I told him I felt that something bad was going to happen, but I didn't mention that I thought it was going to happen to me.

The moon shines through the window, and with each passing second, the shadows grow in the bedroom. Even with the others gone, I can hear hushed whispers traveling around the room. The hair on the back of my neck stands up, and although I'm chilled, a bead of sweat forms on my brow. The darkness is all-consuming, and instead of the usual comfort I feel, I'm overpowered by terror. The whispers begin to grow louder, but the words are a mix of chaotic chatter that I can't make out.

I slap my hands over my ears and carefully sink deeper into the bed. My head lies flat against the soft bedding, and I close my eyes. The exhaustion of traveling just a short distance hits me hard, and I feel myself slipping into sleep. A sudden noise jolts me awake one last time; the room is empty, but I scan it, seconds away from slumber. My eyes begin to close, and I must be dreaming, because a dark figure stands at the end of my bed with a smile on its face.

A few days later...

I move slowly behind the others. Today is a quiet day dedicated to paying our respects to Warrick. Andorwood emerged victorious in taking down the ships of the resurrected; however, the battle was brutal. My friends returned home beaten, bloodied, and wounded—both physically and emotionally.

We lost Warrick, and even though I was just beginning to get to know him, I understand that this is a significant loss for our group. Losing people changes you, and we are in no condition to have our world shaken this way. I watch Fenmore walk ahead of me. She stands tall, but each step seems to cause her pain, knowing this is her reality.

Larkin moves with her like a second skin, always close by in case she needs anything—a true friend. Briar and Silas travel hand in hand beside them, and they don't speak aloud, but I know they are talking privately—they always do, now. I see her squeeze his hand, and a sadness washes over me. Silas has also lost someone dear.

Oak looks at me, and a small smile spreads across his face. Dark circles rest under his eyes, and I know he hasn't been sleeping. Every time I wake up, no matter the hour, he's there watching me—like he thinks that I may vanish at any moment.

A stone in my path trips me, and a searing pain courses through my legs. Even though the healing is going well, the scars have faded somewhat, and I've begun a new therapy, the pain hasn't stopped. It's as if someone has an open tap pouring misery into my body at all times. I can't figure it out; by now, the pain should have subsided somewhat, but it hasn't. It's like the darkness and burns have inflicted more damage on my internal body than my external body. I feel like I'm fighting a battle that no one can see.

Oak feels my stumble and immediately catches me.

"Let's stop here, darling," Oak whispers, letting the others continue forward toward the ceremony site.

"Thank you," I respond, breathless from the trip taking a toll on me.

The ceremony begins with Rose, followed by Fen, who, against our pleas, wanted to speak for Warrick today. Her stern voice conveys themes of love and loss, filling each of our hearts with hope, sadness, and pain as we remember the hardships we will face in this life.

She pauses at the end of her speech and turns to gaze upon the white, flowing sheet that shields Warrick from our view. The wind rips her hair in all directions, but her gaze holds, taking this moment to look at him one last time.

Their relationship wasn't perfect, but it was genuine. I believe it helped us all understand how fragile life truly is, regardless of your strength or determination. Life can be taken away in the blink of an eye.

She grabs the torch, ready to set the sheet aflame, when her instincts stop her. My breath hitches as I see Silas instead take the flame and ignite the white sheet. The others remain deathly still, focused on the scene before us, and I close my eyes, already filled with such sadness that I fear that if anything additional hits me, I'll crumble.

A faint voice flows through the wind, striking my mind. *"Maines."*

I freeze, half hoping what I've heard is my own imagination, but the voice persists.

"*What did they do to you?*" The male voice fills me once more. "*You are broken and beaten.*"

Terror floods me, and I can't move, unable to respond. I try to turn my head to get Oak's attention in front of me, but I can't, realizing the others don't hear this voice.

Only I can, and I can't move.

"*I will heal you.*"

A tear rolls down my cheek, realizing that the voice I hear is Malachi.

"*I will help you.*"

I shake my head, as if he's directly in front of me.

"*You will be reborn.*" The voice becomes darker. "*I'm not giving you an option.*"

A sob escapes my throat, causing Oak to snap his attention to me after momentarily stepping closer to Silas. His eyes widen, and a look of horror distorts his expression. My heart races in my chest, and I feel the icy touch of a man's hand rest upon my trembling shoulder. The wind shifts, the sapphire sky darkens to an ashen gloom, and I feel as if I'm going to be sick.

I look forward to see the grass blades bend under the weight of something moving in the in-between.

Travelers.

"Such a smart, observant woman," Malachi whispers.

A tear falls from Oak's face, and I notice the soft skin of his neck slightly press inward. An invisible claw rests directly where one single swipe would end his life. The others notice the shift and slowly turn. I watch as their faces turn to horror, and I can't stop my body from quivering.

They speak, but I don't hear them.

They instruct me, but I can't listen.

I'm frozen in fear.

Completely *helpless,* which makes anger begin to burn in my chest like the torch in front of me.

I take a final moment to look at Oak—only him. I memorize what I can and pray that my memory won't betray me when I need it. I'll hold onto this: his handsome face and his dark eyes that, even in terror, have such love. I'll cling to his memory, because it may be the only thing that keeps me going.

"*Find me,*" I mouth to Oak, watching the color slowly drain from his face.

A final tear rolls down my cheek, and I force a smile, making sure the last thing Oak ever sees of me is just that.

"*Don't give up on me. Find. Me. Oak.*"

I feel my body turning to mist in Malachi's hand. The familiar sensation of shifting hits me, but this is darker, faster, and unlike anything I've ever experienced. It's as if I'm moving between worlds, trapped somewhere in between.

I scream, letting the raw sounds tear my throat to shreds, and I don't stop. Scream after scream, he pulls me, dragging me further away from where I am desperate to be. The darkness becomes too much to handle in my state, and my eyes begin to flutter closed.

"*You are entering my domain, Maines Madden. I need your help,*" Malachi whispers through the shift. "*Whether you want to assist or not.*"

STAY TUNED

Book 3 in the Darkness series is coming.

Acknowledgments

The challenges, struggles, and hardships that come along with this insane journey are all worth it when I sit down to write another acknowledgment. And here I am, just doing that.

First, I want to thank my family. They understand better than anyone how much love and time I dedicate to writing each of these books. They are gracious, understanding, and the most supportive people in my life. Thank you for always listening to my crazy ideas, helping me pursue my goals, and pushing me to keep going when I need the motivation to stay focused and not give up on the hard days. Each of you always reminds me of why I started, and each of you gives me a reason to keep going.

Thank you to my beta readers. I am incredibly fortunate to have a small group of people who make me laugh harder than anyone. In this world, it's hard to make connections, but I know I have made it with this group. They support me, push me, and challenge me in the best ways possible, but most importantly, they believe in me. Without this group, I wouldn't even be halfway to where I am right now, so thank you dearly for that. You all mean so much to me, and I hope you know that.

My editors! You are all amazing, and without your help, guidance, and wisdom, I would absolutely NOT be here. I also want to apologize for anything in this that doesn't meet your standards, since this was edited by yours truly.

My wonderful friends, you all deserve the biggest shoutout for always supporting me and sharing in the excitement over the stories I tell. Thank you for always being there for my late-night and early-morning texts when I have self-doubts, question every-thing, or need advice on how to move forward when I have crazy thoughts about the storylines. Thank you from the bottom of my heart. These friendships in the Darkness Series are rooted in my real-life friends, and I hope the friendships you see in these books make you realize how much you mean to me and the lengths I would go to for each of you. To the darkest realm and back, besties. There isn't anything I wouldn't do.

Emily, you deserve a whole section dedicated to you as a friend, PA, editor, and everything in between. As my PA, I can't even begin to express what you have done for me throughout this journey. Your hard work and love for these stories show every single day, but more importantly, your friendship is what keeps me going. You are willing to go above and beyond for me, on top of your own life, and I can't thank you enough for keeping me going with your kind words, your unbelievable support, and your willingness to always accept and love my crazy ideas. We are just getting started here, and I can't wait to see what the future holds for us as a team.

Lastly, there are always many bumps along the way. There are plenty of laughs, doubts, and some tears, but it's all worth it. I look forward to all of you continuing this story with me. As always, please keep reaching for your dreams, because with hard work, you can make them a reality.

Much more is coming for the Darkness crew. On to the next, and onward to book 3.

Thank you all for the support and love.

-KB

About the Author

Kathryn Breaux is the author of the Darkness Series—The Trials of Darkness and Isle of the Forgotten. This is a four-book fantasy series.

Her love of reading has ebbed and flowed throughout her life, but her love of fantasy has never faltered. She typically spends her downtime with her family, reading fantasy, romantic, or thriller books when she is not writing. But let's be honest: she's writing a lot these days.

Kathryn received a bachelor's degree in communications, which helped her pursue her dream of being an author.

She is thrilled to be reaching for her lifelong dreams, and she hopes you take a leap of faith and chase your own.

To learn more about Kathryn, upcoming projects, and her socials, please visit: www.kathrynbreauxwrites.com

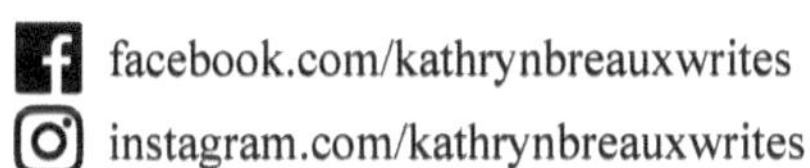

facebook.com/kathrynbreauxwrites

instagram.com/kathrynbreauxwrites

LEAVE A REVIEW

Thank you for reading Isle of the Forgotten - Book 2 in the Darkness Series. I hope you enjoyed the book.

Please consider leaving a review on your platform of choice.

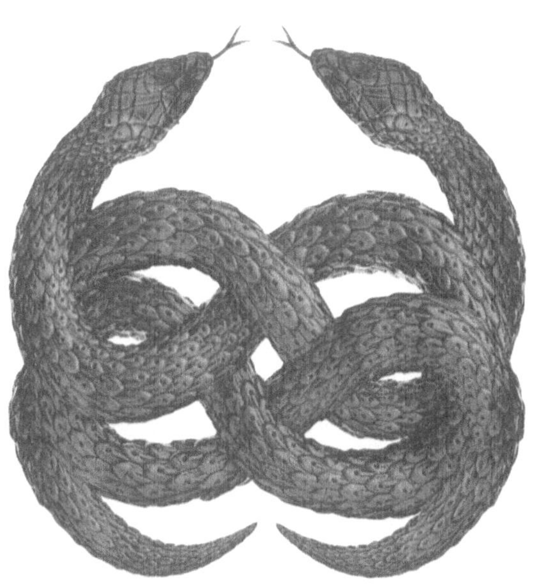